THE COWBOY'S KIDS

*Barbara and Carl Goodwin were the children of
Chalk and Wanda Goodwin.*
Both grew up living on a ranch near Bandera, Texas.

Kenneth Orr

Bloomington, IN Milton Keynes, UK

AuthorHouse™
1663 Liberty Drive, Suite 200
Bloomington, IN 47403
www.authorhouse.com
Phone: 1-800-839-8640

AuthorHouse™ UK Ltd.
500 Avebury Boulevard
Central Milton Keynes, MK9 2BE
www.authorhouse.co.uk
Phone: 08001974150

© 2008 Kenneth Orr. All rights reserved.

No part of this book may be reproduced, stored in a retrieval system, or transmitted by any means without the written permission of the author.

First published by AuthorHouse 4/8/2008

ISBN: 978-1-4343-6563-7 (sc)

Printed in the United States of America
Bloomington, Indiana

This book is printed on acid-free paper.

ACKNOWLEDGEMENTS

This book was written about times that were almost 100 years ago. Much of the content is fictional but all of the dates and events covered in this story happened. I was born in 1936 and experienced the Second World War first hand from a stateside front row seat. We lived near Wright Patterson Field in Dayton, Ohio and the sky was always full of military aircraft. My first cousin was a P-47 Thunderbolt pilot and he was in Dayton several times during the war He was an "Ace" flier and his efforts were well know to many. I acknowledge **Randy Willingham** for his stories.

My Mother worked for a company, Univis Lens that made the precision glass optics for military bombsights. She was a polishing specialist and her work was part of the total Dayton effort put forth in build Norden Bombsights. I acknowledge **Alice Orr**, my mother.

My Boy Scout scoutmaster had been a pilot in The Army Air Corp and had flown both B-17's and B-24's on bombing missions. He has a lot of connections at Wright Patterson Field and would take several of us boys into places were we probably not supposed to be, just to see airplanes. I acknowledge Francis Trick.

In my professional career I worked for Lockheed Corporation for several years. One of my close friends had been a final inspector on B-17's at the Burbank, California production plant and he passed several great stories on to me over the years. I acknowledge W. D. "Alex" Alexander.

I also want to give special thanks and acknowledgement to my wife for her help and support in this book. She has been one of my best support and proof reading people and her contributions are a vital part of this book. I acknowledge **Jewell Orr**.

I also want to thank many of my friends and relatives who have helped me finish this book. Susan Ridley was an excellent proof reader and her efforts are appreciated. I also want to recognize Mrs. Becky Brock, who lives in Tupelo, Mississippi with her husband Stanley. She works in the accounting offices of a nationally based fabric corporation. Virginia Williams was a classmate in school who married an Air Force guy. They now live in San Antonio, Texas. Richard Clemenson is also alive and well and lives in Ashby, Minnesota. All of these people have been supporters of my book writing efforts.

BOOK 1 OF 3
The Family's Beginning

CHAPTER 1-1
The Parenting Family

Chalk Goodwin was born in rural Harlan County, Kentucky. His father, Jacob, was an Englishman who had come to the area to work in the local Kentucky coal mines. His Mother, Irene, was a Cherokee Indian from the Carolinas. She had come to Kentucky to find a better life and to become separated from the traditional image that was associated with being an Indian.

Irene was proud of her Native American background, but knew that staying with the tribe would only lead her to a dead end life. Jacob saw her working in a local restaurant and somehow they found a reason to get married. Jacob built a small house located immediately west of the town area on some ground that he had been buying with his spare money. It was simple and basic and had little comfort other than keeping the outside weather away.

Chalk was born in 1863. He grew up among the local people and learned to survive on very little. When he was physically big enough he found a part time job working with the coal mine where his dad was working. His duties included tending to horses and mules and doing simple blacksmith work. Chalk learned quickly and developed a close friendship with the mine owner's son. Life was hard but the education that came from being dirt poor was a valuable experience.

Kenneth Orr

Jacob had become a part time moon-shiner and often had trouble with the local peace officers. An incident occurred in a local bar where a man was shot and killed. Jacob was held as one of the responsible individuals. He ended up in jail and was never heard from again. The local rumor was that he was given a life sentence for murder. Irene continued to live in the same house that Jacob had built and took in cleaning and small sewing work to keep Chalk and herself in clean clothes and basic food. Two years later she became deathly sick and died in the house where she and Chalk lived.

Chalk was now alone and soon made up his mind to leave Harlan County. He sold the house and everything that was of value. He gathered all of his personal belongings and went north to Lexington, Kentucky.

Finding a job was not easy but his persistent attitude led him to several racehorse farms that were nearby. He was hired as a stable keeper and soon became a respected employee. His boss had given him opportunities to learn more and to become skilled in managing high-spirited horses. The horse farm blacksmith took Chalk under his wing and taught him the skills needed to make horseshoes and to tend to the problems that were common on horse's hoofs. He also taught Chalk how to repair broken metal implement parts and how to make new parts when required.

Chalk often went to Louisville, Kentucky to deliver racehorses to people who were in the high-class horse racing business. One such trip, where he was delivering a very special horse, developed into a trip on a riverboat.

The boat captain observed Chalk's livestock handling skills and before the trip was over offered him a job working with animals that he commonly transported on the riverboat. Chalk jumped at the offer. Over the next 10 years he worked on the boat and often became associated with people who were traveling west to become settlers.

Chalk learned how to gamble and built up a large nest egg of money, mostly in gold coins. He never told anyone of his

The Cowboy's Kids

private wealth but kept it locked up in a strongbox that he kept under his bed in his small cabin. He also kept all of his earnings and other tip money in the same box. There was nowhere to spend money on the boat and his cask assets grew quickly. His early childhood lifestyle had taught him the value of money and how important it was to keep your financial situation a private matter. If somebody had money they immediately became the target for some crook.

On one riverboat trip he met a gentleman who was organizing a wagon train that was going west to Texas. The train was starting from Memphis, Tennessee. His name was Carl Harmony. Mr. Harmony had traveled up-river to Cincinnati, Ohio where he boarded Chalk's riverboat. He was going back down the river to Memphis. Along the way he would gather people together who wanted to go to Texas and set up a wagon train. Mr. Harmony had made this trip several times. He watched how Chalk worked with both livestock and people and was impressed with his skills, work ethic and attitudes. He made friends with Chalk and soon was offering him a job as his assistant on the upcoming wagon train. The wagon train was planned to travel west from Memphis, Tennessee to a destination in a small town in Texas named Bandera.

Chalk couldn't wait to take the wagon trail job offer. Ten years on the river was a long time and he wanted to do more with his life. When the boat arrived in Memphis he told the riverboat captain he was going to leave "the river" and go to Texas.

The captain was happy for Chalk and wished him well. He also gave him some "seed money" to help him if he ran into hard times. He told him if he ever wanted to come back to his old job on the riverboat, it would be available. Chalk thanked him, and they parted company.

Chalk Goodwin traveled to Texas as an "assistant wagon train boss". The wagon train boss, Carl Harmony had hired Chalk because he saw a young man with a lot of skills and potentials but was not doing something meaningful with his

Kenneth Orr

life. He saw him as a potentially desirable resident of the Bandera community.

One settler's wagon was owned and driven by a young man named Walter Anderson. He and his young wife, Wanda, had recently married in Cincinnati, Ohio where they both had been working. Wanda was a schoolteacher and Walter was a young Lawyer. Chalk had become a casual friend with both of them on the riverboat. This friendship was strengthened on the wagon train as he worked to guide their wagon, along with all of the others west to Texas. Making friends on a wagon train was part of the experience. It was also a necessary part of helping each other when problems came along.

Walter was healthy, but he was a small and frail individual. He enjoyed the wagon trip and often would share his advice on legal matters with other wagon train members. Near the end of the trip the trail headed straight south through central Texas. Travel became easier as they went further south. For no explainable reason Walter became sick and within a few hours he passed away. One of the men who had some medical training thought he had suffered a heart attack. The wagon train stopped along the trail and buried his body. Carl Harmony conducted a simple funeral over the stone marked grave. His wife Wanda was in shock and the people on the wagon train all offered to help her go forward and continue with the journey. She decided to continue on to Bandera, Texas where she would be among people that she had made friends with while traveling on the wagon train. Going back to Ohio was not an available option.

The wagon train, along with Wanda, finished the trip to Bandera where Carl Harmony's wife hired her as a sales clerk in her general store. Chalk quickly found a job working as a blacksmith. The blacksmith's shop was near the Bandera General Store and he and Wanda soon formed a mutual friendship. Chalk was still a young man and over time their relationship grew much stronger.

The Cowboy's Kids

Many of the other travelers settled in the local area and all of them were friends with both Wanda and Chalk. The bonding they had started on the trail grew stronger and became a lasting part of everyone's lives.

Carl and his wife Charlie, kept in close touch with both of these young people and soon they became members of their informal family. This relationship developed quickly and lasted for the balance of all of their lives

Chalk and Wanda continued to see each other and soon they fell in love. Carl and Charlie helped them plan their future and provided them with a large Mexican style wedding. Carl had promised Chalk a "homestead start" as a part of his payment for working on the wagon train. Carl gave Chalk a small house with a good spread of good grazing land. The land was south and east of the center of Bandera and was located on the banks of the Medina River.

Carl turned the property over to Chalk before he and Wanda were married. Soon, they had it ready to become their home. They lived on that property for the balance of their lives. Over the next couple of years, Chalk added on to the house and added a lot more land and other buildings.

Chalk set up a cattle ranch and shortly thereafter he added a large section devoted strictly to horses. At the same time, Chalk had become the county Sheriff. He earned a reputation as a tough, but fair, lawman. Their two children, Barbara and Carl, were born and raised on the ranch and learned the basics of life from the surrounding community. The kids were both basically cowboy cultured at heart. As they grew up they enjoyed the freedoms and lifestyle that comes from living on a working ranch.

The "kids" were born into a life where livestock was the only income. They both learned that the source of a ranche's income was determined by the condition and sale of livestock. This recognition made them appreciate hard work, having good friends and the need to work together to keep things within control. Chalk and Wanda were both committed to

Kenneth Orr

providing both of them a good life and strong roots in life to build upon. This attitude was the beginning of both of the kids' education. The Goodwin family regularly attended church and developed strong personal relationships with the people who where their neighbors and friends. They learned that money was not the only way to measure a person's real worth.

CHAPTER 1-2
Barbara Goodwin and Her Early Years

Barbara Goodwin, the first child, was born in the family ranch house with a mid-wife and country doctor attending the birth. She was born on December 24th, 1899. She was born on a cold and windy evening and the weather was not typical for this time of year. Daylight was scarce after about 5 PM as the shortest days of the year always come in December. The house was lit with kerosene lamps and the heat came from the living room fireplace and also from a small wood burning stove in the hall between the bedrooms. The house was comfortable and the healthy newborn little girl and her parents saw to it that she had every convenience that the local economy could provide.

The Goodwin home was large enough that Chalk hired a Mexican housekeeper. She became more like a member of the family than a servant. She was a middle-aged Spanish speaking Mexican lady who lived within a mile of the Goodwin ranch. She always made the house as comfortable for the Goodwin's as possible and had paid special attention to a small crib to hold the new little girl. Her name was Anna Marie DeLaRosa. She wanted to be called Rita. Her mother had nicknamed her after a family member, whose real name was Marguerite. It stuck with her for the rest of her life. She told Wanda "My name was probably given to me by my dad. He liked to drink tequila mixed up as a margarita. I was never sure as to who to believe".

Kenneth Orr

Christmas was almost at hand and a small cedar tree was growing just outside the front door. The strong smell from the fresh green tree filled the front of the house. Wanda often told Chalk, "I love the smell from cedar trees. They always smell so fresh and the trees are never without their green color. They always remind me of summer and they are never killed by cold weather. Cedar trees have a special smell that was most noticeable when it rains". Wanda always loved the cedar smell and said this smell was what a home needed to smell like.

Chalk had placed some Christmas decorations on the outdoor cedar tree and the bright winter sun would make the ornaments shine and sparkle. This ranch house was more than just a house; it was genuinely a very happy home.

Chalk and Wanda were very proud of Barbara. Chalk had picked out her name. He wanted to select a name that was completely new to his and Wanda's family. Barbara had to be the name! Wanda quickly agreed.

Chalk said "Barbara" was a reflection of the name of the town of Bandera. The name Barbara sounded similar to Bandera. They both dearly loved the town, which had become their adopted home.

Barbara was born with a small wave of jet-black hair and a skin that was darker than Wanda's but a lot lighter than Chalk's. Her eyes were blue. She weighed in at 9 pounds and 7 ounces, more or less. They used a kitchen scale to weigh her and it was known that the scale readings were never very accurate. Everyone was impressed with her smile and her strong lungs. She was a great baby.

Wanda soon learned that tending a crying baby was a major part of being a mother. Chalk just tolerated the crying but was frankly glad to see her go to sleep. Wanda and the housekeeper shared the diaper detail. Chalk was not up to doing this part of parenting. He said it made him sick at his stomach.

The Cowboy's Kids

Within a week Barbara was on a regular routine and life around the Goodwin home began to settle down. Chalk was gone a lot. His work was demanding. He was now the county sheriff and his firm and clear leadership was needed in town most of the time. He had given up his blacksmithing job when he got elected. The local law officers who had served prior to Chalk had all been from local roots. Chalk was a new man with a lot of friends. He was also a mixed race man who was similar to many of the current residents. His election was well received by most. Wanda became the primary "kid keeper" and was soon out and about visiting friends, and showing off her new baby.

The seemingly endless parade of local women to the ranch was also impressive. The Goodwin's had a lot of friends and their first child's arrival was a well-received local event. Everybody wanted to see Barbara and they all brought gifts and parenting stories to Wanda. There were many small dresses and quilts that the local women had made just for her.

Barbara's first year saw the first teeth come in and the crawling turn into simple walking. She had a temper and was very vocal when she was hungry or when she was not getting her way. She would scream and cry at the top of her voice until she got what she wanted or wore herself out and went to sleep. Wanda knew that over time the temper would mellow as she had seen a lot of kids in her Ohio school class who had the same start in life.

Wanda soon broke this pattern and the predictable firm hand on the rump worked extremely well. All Wanda had to do to get Barbara to come in line was to tell her she was headed for a whipping if she did not come around. This approach worked almost every time. If that did not work she had to stay in her room for a time. When she came out she was aware that there were going to be more problems if she did not behave. She would get a whipped tail and even more time in the room. It was easy to see that Barbara had a mind of her own.

Kenneth Orr

Barbara's dad was a skilled horseman. He wanted to get Barbara up on a horse as soon as she could walk and he did so by holding her in front of him on the saddle. Barbara loved to ride.

She would get close to her dad and say "horse". It was soon understood that she wanted to go riding and if she had to wait too long, she would become a typical child. Her urging and prodding always seemed to work.

Wanda would go to town or to see a friend riding in a covered, one horse drawn buggy. She would wrap Barbara in a warm blanket and put her on the seat next to her. Barbara soon learned to hold on and became an excellent passenger.

The wind in her face was a thrill and she would smile at Wanda as she rode beside her. In time she would hold the loose ends of the reins and Wanda would let her "drive" the wagon. This was a real thrill and she would smile and holler out commands just like her mom. Barbara got a real thrill in hollering, "Woooooo" and "Giddy Up".

At the age of two, Barbara was walking and running, and was soon all over the house. Chalk would try to keep up with her as a game. Barbara soon learned to move very quickly and developed her running skills. The time they spent together was always a joy for everyone and Barbara would watch out the front door to see when her daddy was coming home.

Wanda's classroom teaching job back in Ohio was ended but her ties to being a schoolteacher were never broken. Several local women wanted her to be on the school board. Occasionally, Wanda gave a special speech that she had developed, on ways to help problem students. Her experience in helping to train children who were out of control, was something new to the community. Plenty local students were from this mold. The low level of education for most of the children who lived in the area was a real

The Cowboy's Kids

problem. Schools were not mandatory and the parents often pulled the boys out of school to do ranch work.

The girls were normally able to get more education. Growing up and going to get a job was hardly ever a planned part of life for girls. They were often anxious to be home, get married at very young ages or hopefully leave home to go live in the bigger towns. It was obvious to Wanda that the level of meaningful things to do at the local school was limited and often boring. Wanda had developed several presentations that gave education a lot of credit for making children better citizens. She was a strong advocate for making both male and female children appreciate that they could go forward in life and have better lives, if they had a good educations.

Males dominated all of the skilled professions and filled almost all of the better jobs. The future for a young girl was very limited. Women were not allowed to vote and their primary roles were considered to be child bearers, homemakers, teachers, and to do simple office work. Each of these careers was even more limited in a small town when the local economy was not moving. Wanda's speech focused on each of these issues and expanded the reality that was around each.

These sessions probably did little to advance women's rights but she hoped that the local children would become inspired to go to school longer and possibly go on to higher education.

Chalk was proud of his wife and how she was putting education's issues on the table. He hoped that someday, Barbara would go to college and then follow in her mother's footsteps. He saw a need and a purpose that was very real and very worth the efforts Wanda was putting into her work.

Everywhere that Wanda went, Barbara was with her. Barbara soon had a lot of friends who were her age and the childhood years were a good time for everyone.

Kenneth Orr

Wanda would have dresses made for both Barbara and herself from the same material. They would often wear them when they went visiting. The biggest thrill for Barbara came when her daddy bought her a pair of shiny, black leather boots. They had a big "B" tooled into the upper sides. Barbara would show everybody the boots and tell them how big she was becoming.

In 1907, on the same day of the month that Barbara had been born, Wanda had a second child. The second child was a boy and he was raised in the same ranching environment. His hair was black, his eyes were blue and his skin was a little darker than Barbara's but still was considered as being a light color. He was named "Carl" after Judge Carl Harmony who had been a dear friend to both Chalk and Wanda since they arrived in Texas.

The Judge had died a few years earlier but his wife, Charlie, was still alive and lived nearby. She was impressed and very happy with a child being named after her husband. The Harmony family had two sons, Jim and John, and they had not named any of their children after their dad. Carl was a special baby for the entire community and everyone was glad to learn of his arrival.

CHAPTER 1-3
A Special Brother for Barbara

Christmas at the Goodwin ranch was now doubly special. The situation that both of the children were born on December 24th, and then Christmas being the next day, created a double reason to celebrate. Birthday and Christmas presents were often combined, and the end of December became a very special part of the year. Over the years that followed Chalk and Wanda would tell friends that they had twins, but they were born seven years apart. This was always good for a laugh and some good conversation.

Carl was a lot like Barbara but soon he was adding a lot of weight. He was almost twice as heavy as Barbara by the time he was three years old. He was not fat, just big and heavy and strong. He had a larger bone structure and a lot of big muscles. He loved to eat. His appetite never really showed any signs of slowing down. He also loved to ride on a horse with his dad, and by the time he was three years old Chalk had bought him a pony. A small saddle was just right for him to fit comfortably on the pony's back. Carl loved to ride his pony along side his dad as he rode around the ranch. Carl named the pony "Bud". He never said why he picked this name but he soon had Bud answering commands to his name.

Chalk had been drafted into the army just after Barbara was born. His efforts in support of an army base in west Texas were recognized as outstanding. Military duty had caused him to be gone from home for extended periods. The children learned to depend on Wanda for guidance more than most ranch children. Barbara was doing just fine, but Carl was missing his dad a lot. The horse ranch foreman, "Sarge", soon became his running buddy and Carl would go out to the horse barns and look him up.

Carl's big dog would always follow beside him when he rode his pony. "Gator" was a tan colored, mixed breed dog. He had short, thick hair and was built a lot like a hunting hound. Chalk had brought the dog home from Fort Clark, Texas when he was a puppy. A soldier had found the puppy roaming around the stable area, and it appeared that his mother had abandoned Gator. The soldiers had fed him and brought him up to a good level of health, and made a small box for him to sleep in. Chalk saw the puppy and knew it needed a good home. He offered to take it to his ranch in Bandera.

Sarge understood Carl's situation of being lonely for his dad, and he actually encouraged Carl to hang out with him when he had spare time. The Medina River was nearby and Sarge taught Carl how to fish and how to do a lot of outdoor things with ropes and sticks.

Carl would catch a small fish and Sarge would brag on his skills. This support gave Carl a lot of pride and he always had to tell Mom about the fish. One time Carl caught a large catfish on his line and it was so big that it was pulling the pole right out of Carl's hands. Sarge came to the rescue and they landed an angry 12-pound catfish. They put it on a stringer and headed for the ranch. Carl told everyone, "See what I caught!" Sarge never said a word; he just smiled and let Carl enjoy the moment. The fish was cleaned and became a great supper for several people.

Sarge taught him how to fish in big water lakes and ponds for big bass. He had a simple wooden boat that he would put in the back of a wagon and they would carry it to the lake. Going to the lake was normally a Saturday trip and Carl was always excited to hear Sarge say, 'Lets go fishing." Before

The Cowboy's Kids

they put the boat in the water Sarge had a small net that he would use to catch minnows. Then he and Carl would paddle out to a spot where there was deep water.

Sarge would pull a very small stick out of his pocket and tie a line to the middle of it. He would then measure out about four feet of line and attach a small hook. He would take a lively small minnow out of his bait bucket. The minnow was attached to the hook, and the stick, line and bait were put into the water. The minnow would swim and pull the stick along as it moved.

In time a big fish, normally a bass would spot the bait and take it in his mouth. The big fish would than dive and the stick would go down into the water. That would mark a spot where big fish were feeding. Sarge would paddle the boat near the spot and use the remaining minnows as bait to catch more fish.

This method worked almost every time and Carl was always able to go home with a nice string of fish for Wanda to cook. Gator would wait on the shore and stay with the horse and wagon. The dog was always anxious to see the fish when the boat returned and his tail was always in motion.

Barbara was always jealous that Carl got to go fishing a lot. She would go see Sarge and ask if she could go the next time. Sometimes she did go and her fishing skills were soon as good as Carl's. A real "tomboy" always wants to be out where the guys are having fun. Barbara was no exception.

Sometimes there were other lessons that had to be learned. South Texas was still largely the way it had been since the beginning of time. Snakes and coyotes were always easy to find. Scorpion bites were also a problem in the summer months. To make things worse, a small boy was never really looking out for any of these critters and he could get into trouble before he knew that there was any danger.

One warm July afternoon Carl was out by the horse barns playing with a small lizard that had caught his attention. The

Kenneth Orr

lizard was green when it was on a leaf but would change its color to a darker shade when it got on a tree trunk. This was fascinating and it had his full attention. Carl was poking at the lizard to keep it moving and watching the colors change. He poked the stick into a bush and to his surprise a big dark colored snake came racing out.

The snake frightened him and he immediately ran to the barn. Sarge saw Carl running and knew that something was wrong. He ran over and instantly got Carl up in his arms. He sat him down on a table in the barn. He then went back to the spot to see what had scared him. The snake was still crawling away and was soon spotted. Sarge recognized it as a monster sized copperhead.

He took out his pistol and shot it. Carl heard the shot and was scared. Sarge came back into the barn and told Carl that he had just killed a snake that could have killed him. The impression this made on Carl was both immediate and lasting. Sarge told Carl that he was lucky and suggested that he never poke a stick into a bush again. Carl understood completely.

When Carl turned 3 Barbara was ten years old. She had her own horse and was skilled for her age at riding. She was still a tomboy in every respect.

Barbara's favorite past-times were riding horses, going to see the animals at the local "sale barn" and hanging out with her school friends. Most of her friends were girls but almost all of them had brothers who were about the same age. These conditions made for some interesting situations. The young boys were aware of how pretty Barbara was becoming and some of them wanted to hang around her a lot. She never picked any favorites but just let them be boys. After all, she enjoyed all of the attention.

Carl would always want to go with Barbara when they went to the sale barn. There were two reasons for Carl's interest. First, Carl liked the company of the young girls that always were with Barbara. He was already aware that they were

The Cowboy's Kids

special and that he had a special interest in them. Second, the Goodwin Ranch normally would have a few cattle to sell. Carl would tag along with the ranch cowboys who were involved with getting them there on time. When they arrived Carl would find Barbara and stay with her.

Animals always fascinated Carl, but the most interesting part of "sale day" was watching the men selling and trading things outside the barn. There was one special oak tree where the men would gather and make deals. They would sell pocketknives, saddles, guns and anything that were appealing to another man. There was always a big crowd under the tree as soon as the bartering started. Carl would go there and hang out until the activity actually started.

Carl just listened to their talk and learned that anybody who wanted to buy or sell something would never pay the asking price. That was just not how to make a "good deal". The haggle that went with the deal was a normal part of the process. Carl loved to listen and watch this part of "sale day", and soon he was spending all of his free time under the big tree.

Barbara would keep Carl with her as much as she could. Chalk or a designated ranch hand always had both of them under close watch. Chalk attended the sale whenever he was home but most of the time it was Sarge and the ranch hands that were taking animals to town to be sold. There were always a couple of extra ranch cowboys along and they would trade off watching "the kids."

Carl saw money changing hands and soon learned that coins were valuable, especially the gold colored ones. He also had learned that before anyone would make a deal they needed to talk and haggle a long time. Haggling was an art form of sorts and some men were much better at making a good deal than most of the others. Barbara was always carrying a few pennies with her to buy some snacks or drinks. She would do all of the buying for Carl and herself. Carl had no idea as how to count money or make change.

Kenneth Orr

What fascinated him about money were the pictures on coins and the color of the shiny metal.

The simplest of their transactions were sometimes a little different. Carl would tell Barbara what kind of treat he wanted and they would find a place to buy it. When Barbara would get out her money to pay for the treats Carl always wanted to haggle and fuss with the person who was doing the selling. Carl thought this was part of the fun and enjoyed the verbal exchange. Often his "kid's way of buying" got him a free snack. Everyone always laughed at him and had a lot of fun teasing him when he was trying to haggle. His reputation soon grew into a trademark of his way of doing business.

Sarge was a lot like a second dad to both Barbara and Carl during their younger years. Chalk was away in the army and his time at home was always limited. Wanda trusted Sarge completely and she knew that the time they spent away from her with Sarge was a normal and necessary part of growing up.

Sarge had found a small cave down by the river, and he and Carl would go there often to cool off in the hot summertime. The entrance was right down on the bank of the river and when it was raining a lot, the river would rise and the entrance was underwater. This made the place really special to Carl. The entrance was well hidden by bushes, and the inside was usually dry and dark. The cave became a really special place for Carl. When he had something special to keep or hide he would take it to the cave.

Carl had shared the cave with Barbara a couple of times but he claimed it as his. Sarge knew that a young boy would always be happy with a special secret. Having a cave fit this part of growing up to a tee. Carl loved to build a small campfire outside the cave and watch the flames dance as the fire burned down.

When a fishing trip was over or a trip to town was done Wanda always thanked Sarge and made sure he knew that

The Cowboy's Kids

his efforts were appreciated. Bandera was a friendly and exciting place for everyone, especially children. The things that "the kids" were learning were going to stick with them all of their lives.

CHAPTER 1-4
A Time For Family and Friends

In 1912 World War One was going on in Europe. The United States Army was right in the middle of all the heavy action. The horse cavalry soldier was still a basic part of the army's fighting forces, but new mechanical equipment was being used to support a lot of the battlefield fighting. Chalk was getting older and saw that his efforts to support an army that fought with trained horse mounted soldiers was going to end. The new modern ways of fighting a war were shifting rapidly to mechanical approaches and away from the traditional horse mounted fighting cavalry soldiers.

Change had become a normal part of his life and Chalk accepted what was happening as a normal part of the growth if the military. Change was not always comfortable but it was reality. Chalk was not skilled in the new mechanical ways of fighting or maintaining a mechanized army. He went to his Superior Officers and requested that he be allowed to leave the army.

General Allen, who had been Major Goodwin's sponsor and his best military friend, had retired two years earlier. The General had developed serious health problems and considered himself unfit to serve. He also was ready to retire. Chalk had always been considered the next in line for promotion to the Post Commander's office at Fort Clark, Texas.

The Cowboy's Kids

When the opportunity did come, he told his superiors that he was not interested in spending the rest of his life in the military and wanted to be passed over. He had seen how much time he was losing with his family and wanted to get home before his children and wife had grown any older. He was offered a promotion to stay for a reasonable time, to allow a new man to take over. Chalk was also promoted to the rank of Lt. Colonel with a nice increase in pay. Chalk agreed, but said as soon as the new commander was on board and comfortable, hopefully at less than two years, he wanted to go home. Everyone agreed to the deal.

A younger man, from Fort Sam Houston in San Antonio had recently been assigned to Fort Clark to learn the situations on the base, and to take over some key roles before General Allen had left. His name was Lt. Colonel George Holmes. He was a West Point Graduate and was well seasoned in the army's traditions and practices. He and Chalk had become good friends quickly. After Chalk had turned down the assignment to be the Commander Colonial Holmes' name was quickly popular as the best candidate to assume command. Soon the Fort Clark command transition was under way.

Less than six months later a date for the Change of Command was set. The same date was selected for Chalk to muster out. The plan included a formal discharge and a dinner of recognition at Fort Clark.

This event would allow Chalk to say goodbye to all of his friends and troops. He did not want to become a distraction in any way for the new commander.

In addition, a special recognition ceremony was scheduled later, to be held at Fort Sam Houston in San Antonio. Chalk and his entire family were invited to attend this event.

Chalk attended the ceremony at Fort Clark and was given a traditional military exit of honor. Chalk packed his personal things and got ready to return to his home in Bandera. He was wearing civilian clothes when he left his quarters and

Kenneth Orr

had his saddlebags full of small gifts and mementos that the local troops had given him. One special gift came from a buffalo soldier that Chalk considered a close friend. He gave him a leather pouch that had an eagle feather inside. In the Indian culture an eagle feather represents a very high honor and is never taken lightly. His last look at the base commissary and horse barns were a tender and special moment. He was offered a carriage ride home but said he preferred to ride his horse. That was more of his style.

So much time during the past few years had been spent working to improve the base and providing leadership for the troops. The buildings around the parade ground perimeter were now repaired and in good condition. The quartered troops were more comfortable and were much better soldiers. There were still some problems, but the next officer to take command would be in charge of finding the answers that were required. The trip home was an equally significant event. The trails were all familiar and he thought about the many times he had made this trip as he traveled each mile.

In Uvalde, Texas, he stopped to see the sheriff and told him that he had retired from the army. They went to a local restaurant and had a quick late afternoon snack. There were also a lot of good friends in the restaurant. Everyone had a lot of old stories to exchange. One old timer named Josh had been an army sergeant for a while after the army base was reorganized. He was now working in the restaurant as a part-time cook. He was a former Buffalo Soldier and had moved to Uvalde after his discharge. He had a lot of old stories to revive and the whole crowd at the dinner table was in stitches as the old timers told about how he had chased a bandit toward Mexico and the man lost his saddle and had to ride on a slick, sweating horse. Josh said, "He had on slick, leather britches and they got so slick that the bottom of his rump was sliding around every time the horse took a stride." He never made the border. Chalk finished his meal, got on his horse and rode the rest of the way home.

The Cowboy's Kids

Three days later, a special military carriage from Fort Sam Houston arrived at the Goodwin ranch and took the entire Goodwin family back to Fort Sam Houston. Chalk, Wanda, Barbara and Carl were all quartered in the visiting officers' building and given the highest level of respect. A special evening dinner, in Chalk's honor, was served in the officers' mess hall.

Several of Chalk's old friends were in attendance. Everything was casual and relaxed. Military rank was not that obvious and was not that important for this event. What was clear to everyone was that Chalk was a respected man. Chalk was wearing his civilian clothes and his family was dressed in casual attire.

The main event was scheduled for the next morning at 10:00 AM. Chalk knew that an officer was expected to wear his best and most appropriate uniform for only formal events and the rest of the time other, less formal clothing was the accepted standard.

The next morning was the beginning of a beautiful spring day. The smell of fresh flowers and freshly cut grass was thick in the air. Chalk and his family were given a special officer's escort who led them to breakfast. After breakfast Chalk and his family were given a special base tour in an open sides coach. After the tour they were driven to the Officers Club promptly at 9:55. They were individually escorted to a center table where there was a nearby speaker's podium set up. Everyone was seated and the Brigade Commander took the podium.

Chalk was obviously the person of honor and was toasted by the Brigade Commander. He invited Chalk to join him for a formal awarding of a special army honor. Chalk stood up, walked to the Commander's side and immediately was given a standing ovation. The Base Commander quickly traced through Chalk's military career and had praise for his service to the country. The Commander outlined his work as a horse supplier and then as an army officer. The

Kenneth Orr

introduction lasted for 20 minutes and was filled with both facts and funny tales from Chalk's past.

A military aide brought a special envelope to the Commander who quickly opened it. The Commander looked at the paper he withdrew and called the entire audience to "Attention." The Commander then read a special message from the President of The United States. Chalk Goodwin was being honored with a special Presidential Citation for his distinguished military services. He was also given a permanent and immediately effective Commission as a Full Colonel in the United States Army Reserve. After the reading was completed the gathering was told to be "Gentlemen, as you were," and the crowd immediately gave Chalk a rousing applause.

His family was also recognized for the part they had played in supporting him over his career. They were all asked to join the group at the podium and everyone applauded as they went to Chalk's side.

The formal ceremony was concluded and a magnificent Mexican lunch was served to everyone. Everybody knew that Chalk loved Mexican food, especially hot chilies and melted cheese. After the lunch everyone mixed and mingled for a while.

Chalk and his family spent the night at the base in San Antonio and went home to Bandera the next morning, riding in the Base General's personal coach. Chalk was now a civilian and home to be with his family.

Barbara had finished high school level schooling and was getting ready to go to College. She planned to attend classes at the University of Texas in Austin for two years.

The educational part of her schooling was going well but the lure of the ranch lifestyle was still in her blood. Somehow, the University of Texas was too far away from this lifestyle. The classes were attended mostly by boys and were focused on subject matter she had little interest in learning. The

The Cowboy's Kids

closeness to her friends and to the smells and sounds of nature were just not there.

For her third year of college she transferred to the Agriculture and Mechanics school in College Station. They called the school the Texas A&M School. She told her mom that the people there were more her style and they understood exactly what horse manure smelled like. Her career field was in education but her heart was on the back of a good horse.

Barbara was still following in her mother's footsteps and was studying to become a teacher. The classes she had taken were much more progressive than what her mother had experienced. She was seeing a much broader world and her ambitions to teach grade school were slowly changing. Her ambitions were widening and the view for her future was still taking shape.

After graduation she applied for a job at Texas A & M to work as a student teacher. She was quickly accepted. She also wanted to continue her education while she was teaching. There was also a secondary reason to remain in College Station; she had met a young man whom she admired and enjoyed being near. He was from San Antonio and was a lot more like her father than anyone she had ever met. She told Wanda that his first name was Stanley. She called him "Stan", as it was shorter.

Carl's experience at his dad's ceremony was really a major turning point in his life. He had seen all of the Army's horse related hardware and listened to the speeches. His attention span was satisfied in a very short time. He was glad when the ceremony was over and wanted to get back to more enjoyable things to see and do. Sitting in a long meeting was just too much for his level of patience. He was far too active for this kind of stuff.

The base tour had taken everyone by the hangar area at the new army airstrip and there were several airplanes actually flying. Fort Sam Houston had become a training base for Army Air Corp Pilots. Now this was interesting.

Carl had listened to the stories between the officers at the ceremony about the new airplane fighting force and their new role in the war. The original intent was to use airplanes for Army Signal Corp work; however, that soon was expanded and guns and small hand dropped bombs were being taken into the skies.

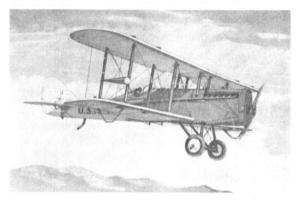

Public domain from the US Government

Fort Sam Houston's air training efforts were a major part of the new Air Corp effort. Carl also had seen several young men who were learning to fly. One older officer said that these men were daredevils and just wanted a thrill.

The airplane was still a major question mark in many people's minds as to the value of its military role but Carl tuned all of that kind of thinking out. He had found something in life that really had his full attention. He wanted to fly like a bird and spend his next few years being around airplanes.

Young men that finished the flying school and were qualified to fly were given a special badge to wear on their uniform. The badge looked like wings. He was amazed that a person could actually get into a machine and fly like a bird. This was overpowering to his young imagination.

The Cowboy's Kids

The next few days back at the ranch were really special for everyone. Chalk got back into the routine of being a rancher and the family was gradually learning what their life would be like with him being home all of the time. Happiness was a common experience for everyone, even the ranch cowboys. The boss was home and he was still the same good guy he was when he went away. He enjoyed the moment just as much, but he knew changes were going to be coming soon.

Daddy being home was a completely new experience for Carl as he was born and grew up when Chalk was in the army. Carl and Chalk were always good buddies. Carl was really glad to having him home. Being able to spend time with his dad was really a special new part of life for both of them.

Barbara had a similar sensation. Her life was now part time at home and part time at school, so her exposure to Chalk did not have the same level of impact. Wanda was beside herself. She had never seen everybody all under one roof for such a long time. Her associations with local neighbors and friends were now being altered.

Barbara had completed her first year of college student teaching at Texas A&M in late May and was not going to start teaching until the beginning of the next school year. She returned home to the ranch and was able to spend some time with her family. This was the first time that the entire Goodwin family had been together and had nothing that was going to cause any of them to leave in the near future. Wanda and Chalk were excited and together they decided to have a good family vacation.

Chalk contacted the right people in San Antonio and ordered train tickets for everyone to travel together on a train to southern California. When Chalk was in the army he had heard a lot about California and had always wanted to go see what was there. This was the perfect place to go and the right time for the trip.

Kenneth Orr

News and stories from friends and other contacts all described California as a lush and very progressive part of the country. The trip to get there would require a train ride that would take them over mountains and across hot dusty deserts. This would be a new experience for everyone, and when "the kids" were told of the plan they were excited and anxious. Chalk had been on a passenger train several times in the army but the rest of the family had never had this experience.

Sarge was informed of the plan and he was to be in charge of the ranch until the Goodwin's returned. Becky Brock was managing the business affairs and had everything under control. Chalk already had developed a plan of calling or sending telegrams to her and keeping himself aware of any ranch problems. He also had used this communication system to help her make decisions while he had been away and was serving in the army.

The train ticket notice finally arrived and the whole family began to get excited. Chalk received a confirmation of the reservations and was told that the actual tickets would be issued to him when he was ready to board the train. There was apparently a lot of change involved with passenger trains and the actual tickets were not issued too far in advance. Chalk then sat down with Sarge and Mrs. Brock to do the planning for a month or more away from the ranch. Everything was planned and finalized. Everything was finally ready.

Chalk made a special effort to get information from friends about areas to see in California and the best places to stay. The "del Coronado Hotel" on Coronado Island, just south of San Diego was highly recommended, as were several other oceanside hotels in Los Angeles.

An interesting idea came from a retired Army Major who had been living in California. He thought Chalk would like San Francisco, as it was a city that was on the ocean and had a lot of developing ties with foreign companies. However,

The Cowboy's Kids

there had been a bad earthquake there in 1906 and the town was still not fully rebuilt.

Los Angeles was ruled out when Chalk read some newspaper stories about mudslides and a lot of crooked merchants. San Diego had always been the destination of choice.

Chalk had always talked about how he would like to buy some property and watch it grow in value. The stories about the southern California area seemed to fit into this objective. He had saved a lot of money and was sure that a good investment in land would not lose value. He had watched the value of land around San Antonio grow more expensive as the years had passed. He knew the railroads taking people to the west would cause the property values to grow over time.

Chalk called the railroad ticket office in San Antonio and made sure the times to leave were correct. He was concerned about the actual time and went to a local store and bought a new gold pocket watch. He knew that the railroads were sometimes confused by the actual time when long trips were being planned. He put the watch on a gold chain and made sure that the clip to fasten it to his trousers was working well. He had paid a lot of money for the "Hamilton watch" and did not want to lose it.

CHAPTER 1-5
The Family Vacation and The Train Ride West

On June 14th the Goodwin family all went to San Antonio and got a room for the night. The train they were traveling on was scheduled to leave the next morning at 6 AM. The route on the tickets indicated that they would go to Dallas. There, they would change trains and travel on to Albuquerque, New Mexico. Then, they would board a third train and go further west passing through eastern Arizona where they would change trains again at Flagstaff, Arizona.

Another train would take them to Phoenix, Arizona. Finally, another train would go on to San Diego, California. Each change of train required a layover. Some were scheduled to be as short as an hour but the one in Phoenix, Arizona was for about 13 hours, and possibly more. This route was not the first choice but a problem in southern New Mexico with some bad track had shut down all travel in that area for a few days and could not be re-opened until the tracks were repaired.

Trains normally traveled both in the daytime and at night. Night travel was sometimes limited in areas where there were few towns and people were required to man trackside-refueling stations. Steam powered trains require coal or wood and a lot of water. Taking on water at night was sometimes dangerous as bandits could approach in the

The Cowboy's Kids

darkness and attempt to rob the passengers. The train had to make steam and that required either wood or coal. Loading fuel at night was never as safe as doing the work in the daytime. Summer days were very long and the actual time of darkness was much shorter, especially in June. This helped to make more night travel possible.

The next morning everyone was up early, dressed and off to the San Antonio train station. There was a small restaurant, of sorts, near the train depot. Breakfast was currently being served. The train was waiting in the station and everyone, along with their baggage, was soon loaded. The conductor showed them their seats and put his punch mark in their tickets. The engine had already built up a good head of steam, and when the conductor hollered out, "All aboard", the engineer sounded the whistle. The train pulled out. The train tracks were built in between the city buildings in the downtown area. The noise from the whistle and the steaming engine created a loud echo off the sides of the buildings. Within a few minutes the train rolled past the rail siding that Chalk recognized as connected to Fort Sam Houston.

Every time the engine approached a crossing, the engineer would sound his whistle. This was done to warn everyone to stay clear from the track area. Wanda was looking out the windows and talking to Barbara as fast as she could about the things she recognized.

Carl was taking it all in but just looked at Chalk and smiled. Chalk smiled back and in a low voice told Carl, "Keep a good eye out for what's out there, you might just see a pretty girl." Carl understood the message and the subtle humor from his dad and he just looked on.

New Braunfels soon came into view. On arrival at the local train station the train stopped, people got on and people got off. The people in the baggage car threw out a bag of mail and took three more from a man wearing a post office cap. The whistle sounded again and the train was quickly back

Kenneth Orr

in motion. The same pattern was repeated again at several more towns and special stops along the way.

About every 50 miles a scheduled stop was made to take on more water and more coal. These stops were short but helped keep the people on the train awake. There were four freight cars attached to the rear of the train. Whatever was inside was going to Dallas. The last car of the four was a cattle car and it was obvious. The rank odors coming from this car were very noticeable when the train was stopped. At about noon Chalk found out how to get to the dining car and everybody had some lunch.

The clock said 5:55 PM when the train finally arrived in the Dallas train depot. Travel was tiring but the fun was overpowering. Everybody seemed to have never ending sharp eyes and bodies that were able to go on forever. The layover in Dallas was only for two hours, and they took this time to find some dinner. There were several good restaurants within a block or two from the depot and they selected an Italian smelling restaurant. The smell was certainly better than the cattle car odor that had filled their area when they were eating lunch on the train. The strong aroma of garlic and cooking tomatoes was too strong to just walk by. The food was excellent and the service was very good. They ate, tipped the waiter and went right back to the train depot.

Their next train was parked on the siding next to the train they had just left, and was boarding. Chalk took his tickets out and showed them to a conductor who was standing next to a train car door.

The Conductor told them to go two cars further up front and someone would help them to their compartment. This was a great sound to everyone's ears. Compartments were private and had seats that were adjustable to become more like a bed. Chalk had told Wanda about these kinds of cars and had requested one for his family when he bought the tickets. The ticket seller told him that he would try to get one for his family but the exact makeup of a train was never finalized until the day it was being made ready to travel. Chalk felt lucky and everyone was happy.

The compartment interior had two seats that were facing each other and they were long enough to stretch out on and take a nap. There were two similar fold down berths above these seats, which could also be folded down to become bunks. This was a welcome site as everyone was wondering what it was going to be like traveling at night. Now it was becoming clear, they were going to be able to get some sleep and to still be moving west at the same time.

It was still very bright outside but the evening shadows were appearing on all of the surrounding buildings. At 7:30 the train sounded it's whistle and pulled out. The Conductor came by and told everyone that he would come by shortly and bring pillows and blankets. He told Chalk that there was a dining car and club car at the third and fourth cars back and they would be open until about 10PM. He suggested that the children might watch out the windows in about ten miles, as there had been a small herd of buffalos seen on the tracks earlier in the day. Carl and Barbara watched with an eager interest but the buffalos were never seen. They must have been feeding somewhere else.

Picture by K. Orr

Kenneth Orr

The train stopped twice at small whistle stops and picked up passengers and then went on to Ft. Worth. The depot in Ft. Worth was a maze of cattle cars, freight cars and passenger train cars. There seemed to be a constant parade of switching activity. There were two passenger trains in the station at the same time and the area next to the tracks was busy with people who were going places. Chalk's train was a so called "Express" train which was supposed to mean it would make fewer stops and was given the right of way when possible. Twenty scheduled minutes in Ft. Worth turned into 45 minutes and finally, the train pulled out.

Soon afterwards the conductor came by with nice soft pillows and fresh blankets just as he had promised. He introduced the porter who would be on duty full time on the train and told everyone to contact him if anyone needed anything.

It was almost dark outside and soon the only thing that could be seen was the small ranch house light off in the distance. The light provided by the stars and moon in the night sky saw the shapes of large trees and some distant buildings.

Chalk helped Wanda and the kids get comfortable for the night and decided to go for a short walk. Trains were often darkened when they were traveling at night so people could try to get some sleep. All of the remaining activity would shift to the club car. Only a small lantern was lit in each car to allow for anyone who was walking through the cars to see the way.

Chalk went to the club car and found a seat at a small table near the back end of the car. The door was open and the air that was moving through made this spot a lot more comfortable than tables further up front. The train's bartender came over and took his order.

Chalk informed the bartender that he liked good Kentucky whiskey. The bartender said, "The bar is very well stocked." Chalk had a bottle in his luggage, but the bar was a lot more

The Cowboy's Kids

comfortable and a lot more fun. A "Club Car Atmosphere" was a lot more fitting as a proper place to drink while you travel. He was served quickly and thanked the bartender. Chalk asked him to keep a tab and said he probably would have another.

Time was passing quickly and the day had already been an experience that Chalk would always remember. He had a second drink, paid his bill, tipped the bartender well and went back to his compartment. Wanda and the kids were sound asleep and did not hear him enter. He kicked off his boots and lay down so he could rest and get ready for the next morning. Soon he too was sound asleep.

Dawn came very early as it always does in the month of June. Five o'clock brought the first strong rays of bright light from the east. The train had traveled all through the night and was about 300 miles west of Dallas. The town of Lubbock was just coming into view and the scenery and land outside was much different from what they were traveling through when it got dark. Wanda woke up first and she shook Chalk. He was almost awake anyway. Carl was still in a deep sleep and Barbara was beginning to blink her eyes. Wanda had been to the sink where she had washed her face, combed her hair and made herself feel fresh. Chalk followed her and did the same. Barbara woke up soon after and Carl was close behind. The kids got freshened up and the first thing out of Carl's mouth was. "I am hungry." They all looked out the windows and saw the area around them was more like a desert than anything they had ever seen.

Chalk said the dining car was nearby and they all went to see if it was possible to get breakfast. Keeping time on the railroad was always a problem. The local time for every area was not always the same time that the railroads used. Breakfast time comes when the sun comes up!

Railroads had schedules and had to be on time or the results could cause train wrecks and similar problems. Chalk knew all about this problem and had asked the Conductor what his watch was set to and matched his to the same time. It

Kenneth Orr

was now 6: 10 AM and the diner was supposed to open at 6:00.

They all walked down the swaying train car aisle to the dining car and were shown to a nice table next to a big window. Fresh flowers were in a vase that was fastened to the tabletop. They were beautiful and set the mood for a good meal on the train. The waiter, who was also the same bartender from the night before, came over and Chalk recognized him. He told them that country ham and eggs were on the menu. They were being served with cooked apples, whole-wheat toast and hot coffee. This fit well with everyone except Carl. He wanted cold milk, which was also available.

The food was delicious and everyone was full from generous portions. Chalk paid the bill and tipped the waiter well. He was happy that the meal had fit his family's appetites and was all well prepared. Good food always starts the day off in a pleasing and happy direction.

The train was passing through a small Texas town called Muleshoe where it stopped and took on fuel. Everyone was laughing at the name but it was real. The conductor assured them that it was not just a nickname. From there they rolled on to the Texas and New Mexico boundary. The conductor told them when they were out of Texas and said that there was another small town and fueling station about 10 miles down the tracks. There were a lot of freight trains parked just past the border and the area was a crossing location for several smaller rail lines.

The next town was named Clovis, New Mexico. The railroad had a repair shop next to the tracks where locomotives and train cars could be repaired. The conductor told Chalk it was common to have some small problem fixed there before going further. They could service trains from both the east and the west and were a vital part of keeping the rail line open. Several track repair teams were also located there and when needed they would go to the damaged track

The Cowboy's Kids

and make sure the track was safe and ready to resume service.

The train service stop included taking on fresh drinking water and ice in the club car. When the service stop was completed the train went to the small Clovis passenger depot. Several people got off and several more got on. Carl said, " Those big green baggage wagons are really neat. They would be great to have for hauling hay back on the ranch." The wagons had big signs on each end saying "Railway Express."

Chalk was interested to see that several of the people who got on looked to be Indians. All of these people were riding in the passenger coaches and were carrying large amounts of luggage.

Picture by K. Orr

From there the train went west into an area where the ground was almost bare of any trees or thick vegetation. The land by the tracks was becoming flat and dry. Off to the north were large uplifted landmasses. Chalk told his family these were called mesas and were very important to

Kenneth Orr

the local people's traditions. He had read stories about the Indian tribes that had lived there but knew little beyond that level. The red and gray stone colors were shining brightly in the morning sun.

All of this beautiful scenery was a new experience for everyone. They were all looking to see what was next. The train soon arrived in another small town called Fort Sumner. Chalk had read a lot about the army fort that was nearby and how it had played a major role in the conflicts with local Indians and bandits. The west was still not completely settled and there were still a lot of bandits robbing small town banks and back-road stagecoaches for their money.

The army was in firm control and was working to hand all of the local policing authority to the local law officers. Chalk told Wanda that this was a special place to many people. It was one of only a few areas where there was predictable running water. The railroad had built several large water towers to keep an adequate supply on hand to fuel their locomotives.

The next portion of the trip was over a landscape that had a lot of deep wash-outs and open wind swept dry lands. There were now a lot more bridges where the train would slow down to almost a crawl, while crossing each span. The bridges were made from timbers and wooden ties that were all anchored deeply into the earth. The tops surface was all tracks and had a small center walkway located between the rails. Before crossing, an engineer would signal with his whistle that he was about to cross.

Should another train be coming from the opposite direction they would use a track switch and park on a siding until the first train passed. Building a railroad was an expensive and labor-intensive job.

The common railroad practice was to have one main line and sidings every so often to allow trains to pass. Chalk's train made several stop and wait departures and the kids

The Cowboy's Kids

would say, "Here we go again. How long are we are going to wait this time?"

The waiting sessions turned into fun events. Carl would look for wild animals and other things that he had never seen before. Barbara and Wanda were looking for flowers and sometime there were Indians who were riding horses. Chalk told them not to worry, these people were out looking for something to shoot for a meal or rounding up their sheep and goats. Cattle were really scarce. Jackrabbits were everywhere.

By nightfall they had reached the base of several tall and tree covered mountains. The conductor told Chalk that Albuquerque was on the other side of the mountains and the train would travel slower in this area. Trains were still using mechanical brakes and they were not completely dependable. The engineer would keep the train speed slow and speed was never a real concern. Going too fast could cause all sorts of problems.

The conductor also told everyone that they were ahead of schedule and their slow speed would not cause any problems with making connections to other trains. There was a big fuel stop at the foot of the first major mountain and the engineer took on a full load of water and more coal. Then the first major climb began.

The engine could be heard chugging endlessly to pull the train up several small grades, Chugging and letting off a lot steam were common when the train was climbing. When a flat area was reached the noise level would go down. The engineer was on the whistle almost constantly when the tracks were crooked and made his presence well known. His major concern was hitting a big elk or deer and derailing the train.

The engine had a large wooden "cowcatcher" built on the front to knock animals and other small objects away from the train's path but a big animal or a herd of big animals

Kenneth Orr

on the tracks in a narrow and crooked ravine could cause real trouble.

By now the conductor was a regular visitor to Chalk's compartment and he had become a hero to Carl. Chalk told him that he appreciated his visits and his good influence on Carl. Carl was an endless question machine and his energy to keep going seemed almost unstoppable.

The train pulled into the station at Albuquerque at 8:30 in the evening. A lot of people got off and an even greater number got on. They also changed the entire train crew and switched out the engine for a more powerful one that was more capable of pulling long mountain grades. The conductor that had come from Dallas brought the new conductor to meet Chalk's family and told him they were going all the way to California.

This train was going to end its trip in Arizona but the same railroad company was operating the next train. Everyone had already had supper and the new crew made sure that fresh pillows and blankets were supplied to the compartment. The entire stop took about two hours and the train was rolling westward once again.

Darkness settled over the compartment and everyone but Chalk was sleeping in a very few minutes. Chalk had his customary whiskey nightcap and joined his family for some rest.

Western New Mexico was a mixture of flat plains, small mountains and lots of places where the tracks were built along beside old drainage washes. The tracks were often next to small Indian settlements and small cooking fires could be seen from the train. The altitude here was much higher than it had been back in Texas and the night air was cooler and less humid. The warm blankets were most welcome and the windows were not open at night, like they had been during the day.

The Cowboy's Kids

Somewhere about 100 miles from Albuquerque the train had to slow down and was pulled onto a siding. The passengers thought this was a routine stop to allow other trains to pass. The conductor broke the news that there was a problem. There was a "hotbox" on one of the passenger cars and to continue without fixing it, well, it would be a mistake.

The engineer pulled the train onto a siding that was off the mainline and the train crew had set up flairs at both ends of the siding to let other trains know they was there. The hot axle bearing had to cool down and have a fresh dose of axle grease and new cotton waste material packed into the bearing housing. This repair would allow the train to continue but the car could possibly be pulled from service when it reached the next repair facility.

There was a small Navajo Indian village next to the siding and the engineer had stopped here before. The conductor knew that they were friendly and helpful people. They spoke English, of sorts, and wanted to sell their goods to the train passengers through the open train windows.

The next locomotive servicing station was further west in Arizona and was about 200 miles down the tracks. The train sat quietly on the siding and waited for the bearing to cool down. The engineer wanted to pour water on the housing to cool it faster but the brakeman told him that the bearing might seize if it cooled too fast. The wait seemed like an eternity, but they waited.

The conductor spread the word about the problem and told everybody to sit tight and they would be under way as soon as they could do the repair. He also said it was a good time to get some sleep as the train was going to be stopped for at least 3 to 4 hours.

This kind of problem happened a lot and the crew knew what to do to fix it. It was still a hard thing to sell to the passengers, that they had to just set on a siding out in the middle of nowhere and wait for a hot wheel bearing to cool down. The conductor asked everyone to stay on the train

Kenneth Orr

and not get off. There were snakes and other critters in the desert that would bite you if they got a chance. Carl looked at his dad and said he was not going to even get close to the door.

By dawn the bearing was cooled down, new grease and cotton waste were added and the engineer was ready to move the train out onto the main line track. He blew his whistle and everyone that was awake cheered. Those that were still sleeping woke up at the sudden loud whistle blast.

Several people had opened the train car windows to allow the cool night air to cool down the inside. When they awoke there were several Indian women walking along beside the cars selling beads, blankets and small pottery items. They were making deals through the open windows and a lot of the passengers were buying things.

The whistle had signaled that the train was about to leave and the buying ended with a last minute sale or two. This stop was not all bad. The tired passengers had gotten some sleep and the up-close sight of real Indians was a first time experience for many travelers.

Carl was thrilled at this adventure and never became distracted. This was an event he would never forget. He told his dad that he was going to tell all of his friends' backs in Texas that he was on a broken-down train and the Indians were all around.

Western New Mexico was a completely different looking place in the early morning. The soft light and cool mountain air seemed to add a special charm to the brown and yellowish soil that was everywhere. Small brushy plants were growing on most of the land. Jackrabbits could be seen running under the long shadows caused by the brush. It was very still and a few blooming desert flowers were adding small amounts of red, orange and yellow to the landscape. Colorful birds were darting in and out between the small

The Cowboy's Kids

plants. The evening before had shown much less color and was hot and repressive.

The train continued down the tracks for about five miles and stopped. The brakeman got off and inspected the problem bearing. The bearing was now running cooler and was no longer considered a problem. A small town was visible up ahead and the conductor told them that they would stop to take on passengers. The town was named Grants. The stop was short and the conductor went into the small depot and asked the man in charge to telegraph a message ahead that they were running about six hours late.

There was another passenger train sitting on a siding on the west side of town, waiting for this train to pass so they would have a clear track to the east. This train had obviously been there a long time and had to wait until Chalk's train passed before going any further.

The two engineers exchanged whistle blasts as they passed. A water tower was just past the siding and the engine's water tank was quickly refilled.

The train was obviously going into an area where the land was much higher above sea level that it had been back to the east. There were large pine trees and the ground was covered with a built up thick pine straw matt. The conductor told everyone that the continental divide was just ahead and the engineer would sound his whistle for two long blasts when they passed over the top.

Carl asked Chalk, "What is a continental divide?" Chalk told him that the United States was made with mountains in the middle. The rains that fell in this area would either drain to the east or west depending on which side of the divide, or the mountain, they fell. Carl said OK. But, he still had not understood the importance of such a condition. Within a couple miles the whistle gave the signal. Carl looked at Chalk and said with some confusion on his face, "Is it going to rain?" Chalk laughed and Barbara tried to explain the whole thing to Carl again.

Kenneth Orr

The tracks passed by a small Indian village that had houses built like a small fortress. They were constructed from mud and straw. The Conductor told everyone this was a pueblo dwelling and it was very old. Everyone was looking out with interest. These buildings were old and had the markings of Indian style horses and wild animals painted crudely on several sides. Snakes, birds and four legged shapes were common symbols. There were also a few tepees mixed in with the pueblo. They all showed signs of life like people were living inside. Old men and women could be seen going about their business and they always seemed to be walking with a group of small children.

The tracks were now winding through the low hills and shallow valleys with no seeming pattern. The train was obviously moving slower but was trying to make up some of the time that was lost from the hot bearing.

Soon the small town of Gallup, New Mexico came into sight. There was a small depot and the center of town was built along the south side of the train tracks. A dusty dirt road was running along the side of the tracks. The train station was a wooden building with a small platform extending out to the edge of the railroad tracks. It was full of people who all looked like Indians.

On the other side of the street a lot of people, almost all of them dressed in Indian style clothing, were congregated there watching the train pull in. They had blankets and jewelry displayed on small blankets on the ground and were looking to sell these items to tourists. Several people got on the train but nobody was getting off. The stop was quick and soon the click of the wheels on the joints in the track was making a now familiar click, click sound.

This was the last scheduled stop in New Mexico and hopefully the beginning of a better experience in Arizona. Chalk told his family that they were now about half way to San Diego. The train was now moving a little faster as the land had a lot of flat places where pulling a slight grade was not a big

The Cowboy's Kids

problem. The bigger engine had provided a lot more power and it made the mountain grades easier to climb.

Chalk had made the club car a favorite place to go when the trip became boring. He would take Wanda with him and they would enjoy a cup of hot coffee or a cool glass of water just to cool down. The southwestern deserts were hot. The wind coming in the open windows helped to make it a little cooler. The only bad thing was the smoke from the engine. The wind would sometimes blow it away and at other times make the air thick and dirty.

Eastern Arizona was becoming much different from New Mexico. There were more trees and the air was finally becoming cooler. There were even small streams flowing along beside the train tracks and the undergrowth in the woods was green. The trees and cool air were soon behind and a more barren and dry landscape was surrounding the tracks.

Picture by K. Orr

Kenneth Orr

The wind was always blowing and again, was much warmer. Tall snow topped mountains outlined the far off western horizon. Tall stately cactus plants were starting to be seen lining the small hills and wind blown tumbleweeds were blowing over the open areas of the fields.

This country was nothing like anything any of the Goodwin's had ever seen. Carl and Barbara were glued to the windows watching for what ever they could see. There were few people and even fewer places where water was present. There were fewer towns and the ones that were beside the tracks were either in despair or partially abandoned.

The train finally came to a small town called Holbrook. The railroad had built a small repair station and a big water tower along side the tracks. There were a few small houses for the workers to live in. The local Indians had also built several adobe huts and had tepees along the north side of the settlement. There were sheep and goats grazing in a big fenced field. These huts and houses were all that the local people had. They were all poorly built and appeared like they could wash away if a bad storm would hit the town.

The engineer stopped the train and had one of the repairmen look at the bearing that had heated up back up the track. The passengers never heard any of the discussions but the problem obviously was over. The train left in about 20 minutes without any additional work being done.

Chalk asked the conductor, "Where do the town people and the railroad get their water, this is a desert?" He told chalk that there was a natural spring just to the north of the town and it always provided good, clean water year round. He added, if this town did not have that natural spring, the town would not be here.

The next town was not much better. Winslow was another dusty and dirty whistle stop location. A few more businesses and houses had been built there. The predominant structure in the whole town was the water tower for trains. The conductor told Chalk that many of the people around the

The Cowboy's Kids

town were miners. Several were digging for gold in the mountains and some were digging out ore that supposedly was full of copper. There were a couple of open top freight cars on a siding and a ruddy colored material was being dumped into the top.

The area was also semi-popular for people looking for old Indian settlements. Several deserted pre-historic Indian settlements had been discovered in the nearby mountains and valleys.

The train made a quick stop on a siding and within fifteen minutes after another train passed it pulled out again. Another train that was headed to the east was on a different a siding waiting for our train to pass.

The engineers all sounded their whistles and it sounded like they were having fun seeing how loud they could make them sound. The conductor came by and told Chalk, "Engineers need to have some fun too, especially when they are near the end of a long run."

The next stop was Flagstaff, Arizona. This was a much nicer and larger town. The railroad depot was much bigger. Chalk and his family were to leave this train and board another that was going south to Phoenix. The train they had been riding was scheduled to go back to the east the next morning. Everybody was tired of riding for so long but they were still in good spirits. Barbara was busy talking to her mom about a lot of things and Carl was an endless powerhouse of activity and questions to his dad.

Carl helped Chalk gather up all of their baggage, while Wanda and Barbara combed their hair and tried to look reasonably fresh when they got off. Chalk looked up the conductor and thanked him for the way he had helped everyone enjoy the trip and ride in relative comfort. It was hot, dry and windy. Their next scheduled train was setting on another siding and was scheduled to pull out in an hour.

Kenneth Orr

Chalk and Carl took their personal luggage to the next train and the new conductor looked at their tickets. He told them to go to a car near the front and he could put his baggage in a rack over their seats. Chalk asked the man, "Will our other luggage be transferred on time?" The answer was "Yes." This train was different from the first train. This was a narrow gauge train and the passenger cars were narrower than the one they just left.

There were no compartments, just seats. Chalks family had been assigned 4 seats that were facing each other. The seats were adjustable to make the backs move up or back.

The conductor told Chalk that his things would be safe on the car, as each car had a man who was helping people board and he was a security officer. There was no dining car on this train and the conductor said they might want to get some food at a local restaurant before they left. He said there was a water cooler and a small bathroom.

Chalk and Carl found Wanda and Barbara who were inside the depot. They were hungry and there was a small restaurant within sight. They quickly went there and got some food to take with them. Chalk saw that they also had cold beer in brown glass bottles so he bought 2 big bottles to take along. Wanda got some water and the kids got iced drinks. They quickly boarded the train, got to their seats and ate their food. There was an ice cooler in the front of the car with iced water and paper cups. Soon the conductor came through the car, punched their tickets and hollered out the door, "All Aboard! We are about to leave the station."

The train pulled out slowly and headed south. Soon they were in a very narrow canyon where the walls were much higher than they had ever seen before. The train began to make sharp turns and was descending deeper into the canyon very slowly. The sound of the brakes dragging and screeching on the wheels was almost constant. The engineer driving the train was controlling the train with obvious care. There were ten passenger cars on the train and on the

The Cowboy's Kids

sharp corners; the engine was in full view from the cars in the rear. The canyon was a steep drop off on the right side of the tracks and Wanda was nervous as they made their way even deeper into the canyon. Carl was wide-awake and was having the best time of his life. Barbara was setting next to her dad and holding onto his arm like he was the only stable thing left.

Chalk tried to calm everybody by discussing how beautiful the view had become and the different sights that were constantly passing the windows. The only distraction was an occasional hot spark that was coming from the engine. The black and gray smoke was abundant and the smell was saturating their clothes.

This down grade-track section was about 15 miles long and then the canyon was giving way to several lush green mountain meadows. There were several small streams running past the tracks and there were small wooden bridges where the train tracks crossed fast running streams. The air was cooler in the meadows than it had been at Flagstaff and the area was filled with beautiful red rock formations.

Carl was still wound up and anxious to take in everything he could see. His eyes really sparkled when he saw a large bull buffalo in a clump of trees close to the tracks. This was a sightseeing treat he had not planned on.

There were several whistle stop junctions by the tracks and when the engineer would near one he sounded his whistle to let the people know the train was approaching. Sometimes he would stop and someone would get off. At other places a wagon or buggy would be parked next to the tracks and people would get off and board the train.

The mountains, all around the tracks were beautiful and the trees that were growing down by the small streams were a deep green healthy color. The odors of fresh grass and pine trees were abundant. Chalk took time to watch the scenery but he also took time to drink his beer before it got too warm. This part of the journey was beautiful and

Kenneth Orr

everyone was having a really good time just watching the scenery roll by.

Within a couple of hours, the train stopped at a place with a small sign on the station identifying the area as Montezuma's Wells.

There was a water tower and a large pile of cut wood next to the track. Some young men threw wood up into the tender and the waterspout quickly refilled the tender's tank. The whole stop took about 15 minutes and the train was back on its way.

The next stop was at a wide spot between the mountains called Black Canyon City. Additional water and wood were loaded onto the engine again and several rough-looking male passengers boarded. They were dressed like cowboys, but were wearing badly worn dirty clothes. They also had saddlebags that contained what was probably all of their belongings. Chalk speculated that they were miners.

The rest of the trip to Phoenix was pretty much a joy ride and by 9:00 PM when they finally arrived, everyone was tired of the hard unpadded seats, constant rocking of the passenger car, and the smell of smoke from the engine.

Everyone felt dirty and was anxious to arrive at they station so they could get off. It was almost dark outside and the sky was full of stars and a magnificent full moon.

The next train going to California was not scheduled to leave until the next morning. Chalk checked with the ticket agent and was told that the train to California would be about 4 to 5 hours late in leaving. Chalk confirmed that his family had a compartment reserved on this train. This train was equipped with standard sized cars and was supposed to be a mixed train. This term implied that there were freight cars and passenger cars, both being pulled by the engine.

Chalk understood all about this message but Wanda was just learning the descriptions that were being used in describing

The Cowboy's Kids

train travel. Carl was hoping that the mix did not include a cattle car with a "ripe" cargo.

Phoenix was a nice town. There were several very nice appearing hotels near the train station. Chalk got his family and luggage together and found a carriage and asked the driver to take them to a good hotel to spend the night. The driver told Chalk that there was a nice hotel nearby and it was priced reasonably. It was only a few blocks away but it was too far to walk for such tired and unfamiliar people. The driver took them to a hotel named "La Casa Grande" and it was really nice. Chalk paid the carriage driver and thanked him for his choice.

A doorman greeted them, helped them unload their baggage and showed Chalk where to check in. The rates were reasonable and Chalk got two adjoining rooms, one for he and Wanda and one for the kids. They went to their rooms and the bellman took their luggage into the rooms, showed them the bathroom and shower and asked, "Is there was anything else that I can do for you folks?"

Chalk asked where the best place to get a big steak was and the bellman gave him the name of a restaurant that was only a couple of doors down the street. He recommended the grilled t-bone dinner, as he said, "It is all you can eat and it is delicious."

Chalk tipped the doorman well. Then he asked his family to be ready to go for dinner in 20 minutes. The time passed quickly. Everyone took a quick shower, put on clean clothes and got ready to eat in a very few minutes. The smell of coal smoke was still in their dirty clothes and Wanda put them in a big bag by themselves. She did not want to stink up any of the clean clothes they had in the suitcases. Carl was hungry and he went to his parents' room and knocked on the door. Wanda answered and she was all dressed up and ready to go. Chalk was also ready but was enjoying a quick nip of good Kentucky whiskey. They went and got Barbara who was fixing her hair. They were all off to eat dinner.

Kenneth Orr

The walk to the restaurant was short, and when they arrived an older gentleman greeted them. He asked them where they would like to be seated. He strongly suggested that they eat outside, as it was cooler. They agreed and followed him to a big table under a large tree. Clean white tablecloths covered all the tables and fresh flowers were in beautiful vases on the table.

The waiter brought a menu for everyone and added, "The special for dinner is wood cooked roast beef with vegetables." He asked what everyone wanted to drink. Carl and Barbara ordered a cold fruit drink. Wanda wanted ice water and then a glass of white wine. Chalk asked for a large margarita with salt.

Everyone looked at the menu while the waiter went for the drinks. A second man brought a large dish of fresh warm corn chips and two bowls of hot salsa dips. A third man brought a dish of fresh sliced oranges and delicately decorated avocado sections. Everything looked delicious and the hunger within everyone was taking over. Everybody dug into the fruit and chips, and they hit the spot.

The waiter brought the drinks and asked if they were ready to order. Wanda had told Chalk she wanted the T-bone steak the bellman had suggested. Barbara also wanted a steak. Chalk was of a similar appetite. The waiter told everybody that the meal came with a Mexican salad loaded with chicken bits. Carl ordered a similar salad and asked for a big slice of rare cooked roast beef. A steak was just too much to eat for such a young boy.

The waiter said they were famous for great steaks and they could bring several to the table so he could pick out the one he wanted. Chalk smiled and said, "Great." The waiter went to the kitchen and brought back a cart lined with ice and a dish of fresh sliced fruit. He also brought a cart covered with lettuce. On the top of the lettuce were 6 beautiful lean red t-bone steaks. Wanda selected one and then Chalk picked the one he wanted.

The Cowboy's Kids

Chalk also picked one for Barbara, as she was shy as how to order in this restaurant. It was so fancy she wanted to not look backward. Everyone enjoyed their drinks and waited in anxious anticipation for some good FOOD served on real dishes! Train food on enameled steel plates and dingy ceramic cups were getting to everyone.

This moment was special. Wanda started the conversation by discussing the train they had just ridden. She commented that the scenery was beautiful and the mountains offered beauty at every corner they passed. She also said it was scary and thrilling all at the same time. Barbara spoke up and said she was scared at the ride and was glad it was over. Chalk smiled and said it was just part of the experience of riding a train in the mountains and it was something worth remembering. Carl just smiled and said, "Where's the food?"

The waiter soon reappeared with salads for everyone and a big dish of warm cooked and buttered yellow corn on the cob. He said it was going to be about ten more minutes and the steaks would be ready. The corn and salads were attacked, with good manners, and were almost all gone when the main course arrived. Fresh cold water was also served as was fresh hot bread and fresh sliced avocados. Chalk ordered a second margarita and asked Wanda if she want anything else. She asked for a cup of coffee. The kids spoke up and wanted more fruit drinks. The waiter went quickly to get their additional drink order. The meal was great and the timing had been perfect. Everyone had a piece of fresh "cactus jelly pie" for dessert and finished their drinks.

The cactus pie was a local dish and was a sweet, but tangy mix of freshly picked cactus pods with sugar, cinnamon and chopped pecan nuts. A thick but flaky piecrust captured the filling. Everyone liked the pie and thanked the waiter for his good services. Chalk paid the bill and left the waiter a nice tip.

Kenneth Orr

Everyone got up and left the restaurant. They walked outside where the sun had been down for about an hour. Chalk asked if anyone wanted to take a short walk. Some of the stores on the main street were still open. Everyone said "yes" and they started down the street. Wanda and Barbara saw some dresses that were beautiful in a window display. They told Chalk and Carl they were going in and that they would only be a few minutes. Chalk told Wanda to take her time and he and Carl and he would be somewhere nearby. The first vacation shopping had begun.

Chalk saw an outfitting store that had guns, ammunition and similar items that would be useful in the mountains. He pointed it out to Carl and soon they were inside. Carl saw a snappy looking leather vest that he liked. It was fur lined and had big buttons to keep it closed tightly around one's body. He told Chalk that he would like to try it on and see if it fit. The clerk helped him put his arms through the holes in the sides and then buttoned it up.

It just about fit but was a little loose on him. Carl had no concerns and told Chalk he wanted to buy it. Chalk asked the price and the clerk said three dollars. Carl looked at him and thought a few moments then he said, would you take two dollars? The clerk smiled, looked at Chalk and said, "Your son drives a hard deal. OK, for two dollars it's yours." Chalk paid the clerk and Carl kept the vest on. They looked around some more and Chalk saw several things he liked but he really did not need, so he gathered up Carl and walked back outside.

Wanda and Barbara were still not in sight. Chalk walked back to the store they had gone into and looked in. They were still there and Barbara had a dress on for trial. Chalk told Carl that they had just as well look some more, as they were not going to be ready to leave for a while. They walked up the street a little further. An Indian had opened a jewelry shop in a small cramped section of a bigger building. He had several rugs, baskets and small pots setting on small display shelves. They were all colorful and the shop was empty of people except for the Indian. Chalk and Carl walked in. The

The Cowboy's Kids

man was glad to see a potential customer. It was late in the day and he was just about ready to close.

Chalk looked around and a special necklace caught his eye. It was silver, and had a figurine the Indians called a "kokopelli" hanging from the chain. It was obviously hand made and was beautiful. Chalk asked Carl, "Do you think your mom would like that necklace?" Carl looked at it and said, "Sure, it is beautiful and simple. Mom likes things like that". Chalk asked the price. The Indian said, "Two dollars.

Chalk took out some money and paid the man before Carl could get involved with the deal. The man took the necklace from the table and put it into a leather pouch that he said would keep it shiny. Chalk thanked him and gave the pouch to Carl to give to his mom.

Carl put it in a pocket in his new vest and smiled at Chalk. Chalk also saw a beautiful jeweled pin that was priced very reasonably. Chalk told the salesman to wrap it up. He packed it in a leather pouch and gave it to Chalk. Chalk looked at Carl and said, "That one is for Becky Brock."

They went into a store next door where they were also selling Indian jewelry. Carl was looking around but none of the jewelry caught his eye. However, he took an extra long look at the lady who was selling the jewelry. Chalk noticed that Carl was impressed with the young lady's good looks and smiled to himself. It was becoming obvious that Carl was finding out about what girls were all about.

They went back outside and soon Barbara came out the store door. Chalk asked where her mom was and she said she would be out in a minute. She came out in a couple of minutes and had a big sack under her arm.

Chalk smiled and said he thought she looked like a lady having a good time. She smiled back and said in slow and calculated reply, "Yes......." She noticed Carls new vest and said how good it looked on him. Carl smiled at Barbara and

Kenneth Orr

said he really liked it. "It was going to be one of his favorite things to wear when it was cold outside back in Texas".

The day was over and all of the stores were closing. Chalk and Carl led the way and they went back to their hotel. Their rooms were on the north side of the building and the cool night breeze was coming down from the mountains. Chalk went in both rooms and opened the windows a crack.

Barbara was all smiles and asked Carl to leave for a minute while she and Wanda did something. Carl agreed and went to see his dad. Wanda took the bag her mom had been carrying and went to Barbara's room. Chalk had opened his suitcase and fixed a drink with his good Kentucky whiskey. He told Carl he could have a drink when he got older but he was still too young for a big man's drink. Carl said he understood, **"but, *he was getting older really fast.*"**

A knock came to Chalk's door and Carl opened it. Barbara was standing there in a beautiful white dress that was cut in a style reflective to the local Phoenix dress styles. Her cheeks were rosy red with some new makeup that Wanda had in her suitcase and her dark hair was brilliant as it touched the top of the dress. Barbara said, "Do you like it?" Chalk had never seen her be so happy over a dress and he loved the way she looked as she walked across the room. He complimented her and asked Carl what he thought. He said she was really neat and had better be careful not to get the dress dirty.

Carl knew that white cloth and a dusty train ride would not work. Barbara smiled and said she was going to pack it in a place where it would be safe. Chalk realized that Barbara was now a full-grown lady and her place in life as a child was over.

Chalk looked at Carl and asked him if he had anything to say to his mom? Carl thought a minute and said, "Oh yea, Mom we got you a present." He reached into his pocket and

The Cowboy's Kids

pulled out the leather pouch and handed it to Wanda. She was really surprised. She looked at the pouch and slowly opened the end with the drawstring. She reached in and the chain soon began to come out.

She pulled it and the medallion came out. She looked at Chalk and then looked at Carl. "You two are in cahoots, I can tell, and I love this necklace." Barbara looked at it and helped Wanda put it on. It just fit her neck and looked great against her brilliant white blouse.

The excitement finally slowed down and Chalk said, "We all need to get some sleep." Tomorrow will come quickly and we are going to get back on a train in the morning, so lets all go to bed.

The next morning was warm and Chalk woke up at 6 AM. The train was scheduled to leave at 9 AM. Everyone needed to get dressed, eat a good breakfast and go to the station by 8 o'clock. Chalk had the hotel clerk check and make sure he had the right schedule and it was confirmed that the timing was correct. The baggage was all packed and Chalk paid the hotel bill. They went into a small café and got a quick breakfast. Chalk hired a carriage to take them to the train depot.

The trip was short and when they arrived there was a brightly painted train setting on the tracks. Chalk got his tickets out and found the conductor. He told them to get on the next car forward and a man on board would help them get to their compartment.

The baggage was transferred to the train and the Goodwin's found their compartment. The room was much nicer than the one on the first train. This compartment had the same style seats plus there was also a small bathroom. The conductor told them this was a deluxe unit and was used for special passengers.

The passenger car had two compartments and several passenger seats toward the rear. The entire car was well

Kenneth Orr

equipped for a western railroad and was obviously insulated to block out some of the outside noise. They had moved Chalks family up to this better compartment at no additional cost, as there were no high dollar passengers on this trip. The second compartment was not occupied. Chalk thanked the conductor and told him that his wife would really appreciate this level of comfort.

The conductor told Chalk that the train would arrive in San Diego at about noon on the following day; that was, if there were no problems. He also told him that the dining car had a great chef who was great at fixing steak and cabrito. Chalk and Wanda took a walk through the train before it pulled out and got familiar with the accommodations. It was very nice and the entire train appeared to be practically new.

The train sounded the whistle and pulled out on time. The first few miles were over flat desert areas and the temperature was getting warmer quickly. By noon they had reached an area where the hot open desert took over everything. The wind was always blowing and dust devils were often seen off to the side of the tracks. The conductor told them it would be cooler to keep the windows partially closed and the smoke and dust would be less of a problem.

There were several stops at sidings near small towns where water was added and mail was exchanged. The next and last major town in Arizona was Quartzsite. There were several tall tan hills along the sides of the tracks but the tracks were never in the shade.

About an hour before they were scheduled to reach Quartzsite the train slowed down and the Conductor came through telling everyone that the heat was so high the engine needed to slow down to prevent overheating. He said this was not a serious problem but they knew too much heat would damage the engine parts. The time went by slower and the heat was already becoming much more obvious. The water in the bathroom sink tasted hot and bad, but it was wet. Everybody was drinking water and getting ice from the club car. Chalk mixed some ice and a little water he had

The Cowboy's Kids

in a small bottle with some Kentucky whiskey and made it taste better. The water on the train had a spoiled egg like taste and it smelled bad.

The train reached the small town of Quartzsite and stopped. The local depot attendant threw a track switch and the train backed onto a siding. Two freight cars were uncoupled and the train pulled back onto the mainline tracks. Several people then got off and a few more boarded. The engine tender was refilled with water and wood and the whistle sounded loudly. Everyone was surprised to hear an answer from another whistle off in the distance.

The train pulled out and about a mile out, there was another train setting on the siding. The engineer stopped the train next to the engine on the other train and went over to talk to him. The meeting was short and soon the train was back underway. About 5 miles down the tracks a small green strip of color could be seen standing out against the tan desert sands. The conductor came through and told everybody that they were looking at California. Everybody cheered. Carl spoke up and told his dad that he wanted to see the ocean. "Where is it, he asked?"

The train was still running slow but the anticipation from the passengers in the Goodwin compartment was very high. Carl was anxious and he had his nose pressed tight against the window. Barbara was equally anxious but did not let it show. Wanda just watched and Chalk sat back and had another shot of Kentucky's best in celebration of the arrival into California.

The desert changed quickly to a lush thin green strip of land that flanked the sides of a big river. Chalk told everybody that this was the famous Colorado River. He said it flowed all the way down from Colorado to the Pacific Ocean. He added that the river was the same one that flowed through the Grand Canyon. Everyone was impressed and said that they wanted to see it up close. Soon their desires were more than satisfied.

Kenneth Orr

The tracks were built into a pattern that curved to line up with a new bridge that had been built specifically for railroad traffic. The railroad tracks ran across the center. The center and both sides of the tracks were lined with timbers that would allow horse drawn wagons to also cross the bridge. Small guardrails were built along both sides to keep people and wagons from falling into the river.

Crossing this river was a serious concern to the passengers. Everyone was a little nervous about crossing over a fast running river on such a long bridge. The bridge was about 20 feet above the water and the river flow was fast and furious as it came around the pilings supporting the bridge.

The train slowed to a crawl and began to pass over the first section of the bridge. Carl was looking out the window with intense interest. Wanda looked once and then looked away. Barbara and Chalk just sat back looked at the sky and let the moment pass.

The crossing took about 5 minutes and was uneventful. The real event was the sigh of relief that went up in the passenger cars as they entered California. A mile further down the track the train pulled into a railroad depot identified by a well-weathered sign as Blythe, California.

The conductor came through the train and told everyone that the train would be stopped for about an hour. The freight cars on the rear would be removed and the engine was going to be serviced.

He added that the long run in the desert heat required the bearings in the engine to be serviced. He said this would change the arrival time but that was normal when you rode a passenger train.

Passengers would be allowed to leave the train but must take their tickets with them to reboard. Chalk got his tickets out of the luggage and told his family to follow him. He wanted to stretch his legs and was sure everyone else needed a break from the train.

The Cowboy's Kids

The town was small but looked like there was local prosperity everywhere. The water from the river was obviously the reason the town was there. The fields around the river were full of green crops. Fresh vegetables were for sale along the north side of the tracks. Date palm trees were growing next to a ditch and the farmer who was tending them had several sacks of freshly harvested dates for sale. He gave a sample date to Carl to try and it was a hit. The date was sweet and chewy and had a big seed in the middle. Carl asked Chalk to buy a bag, as he knew that Barbara and Mom would like them. Chalk bought a big bag and gave it to Carl to carry. Wanda was looking in a store to see what they had to sell. Nothing interested her. Barbara was walking with her and she was equally not interested in anything they saw.

Two new freight cars were added to the end of the train. They were dripping water, which indicated that they had cargo on board that was being cooled with ice. The club car took on several large blocks of ice and more fresh water. The sight of water, green grass and growing green crops was a stark difference from the surrounding dry and hot desert. This town was a real oasis in the desert and was something special to see.

The engine and freight cars were all reattached and the whistle sounded. Everyone immediately got back onto the train. When it was determined that everyone was back on board, the conductor sounded the "All Aboard" signal. The whistle sounded again and the train pulled out and headed toward the west.

It was getting late in the afternoon and the sun was dropping lower in the sky. The next 4 hours were hot and much like the trip before they got to California. The engine was running slow as the green cool area around Blythe soon faded away and the land by the tracks quickly turned back to a hot desert landscape. The next major train station was called Twenty Nine Palms. Several rough looking passengers got on and got off at whistle stops along the tracks. The whistle would sound and the train would be off again. These folks were obviously miners who were digging in the hills near

Kenneth Orr

the tracks. Chalk told Carl that they were probably looking for gold or silver, but he was just guessing.

Just ahead were tall mountains that had green trees and steep peaks. The train was still moving slow, but the tracks were gradually gaining altitude going up small grades and around curves and sharp corners.

The trip to the west was going slow. Time was dragging on and eventually they reached Palm Springs, California. The area along the side of the tracks was beginning to look a lot greener. At Palm Springs more passengers got on and the train started to stop more often at whistle stops. The train seemed to be moving a little faster. The next major stop was at Riverside, California.

The conductor came to Chalk's compartment and told everyone that their car was going to be uncoupled at Riverside and attached to a train that was going south to San Diego. The rest of the train was going to travel on to Los Angeles. This was news to Chalk. Chalk understood what was being done but was disappointed that the ticket agent in San Antonio had not told him what was going to happen. It was too late now to get upset as the trip was near the end. Chalk said he was going to check with the ticket people in California before they went home about the shorter and quicker southern route.

Chalk and the rest of the passengers in the car were all going to San Diego. Everyone sat tight and settled back into their seats and watched out the train's windows, as the passenger car was getting ready to be redirected.

The train pulled onto a siding at Riverside and the car switching was done quickly. The train to San Diego had been waiting for them to arrive and the engineer was anxious to get underway. The evening sun was almost down and the air was cooling. The seats were converted into bunks and everyone settled down to rest and enjoy the rest of the trip. The next part of the trip was going to be scenic but at night the area outside was not going to be available for passenger

The Cowboy's Kids

viewing. A beautiful mountain lake came into view and the sun was setting over the mountains to the west.

The engine was going faster and was burning a lot of coal. The smoke was of a much different smell that the wood-smoke from the other locomotives. Wanda's clean dress had become soiled from black smoke that was filtering into the compartment.

It was dark outside in a very short time and the conductor helped fix everyone's seats into a bunk. The comfort from having clean sheets and a warm bed were missing but the opportunity to rest was most appreciated. Riding across the desert had drained everybody and sleep was welcome. Having a small restroom area had been a big help in making this part of the trip more comfortable. Water at any temperature was most welcome.

Chalk went to the club car, which was well stocked at the last stop. He got a bucket of ice and a big bottle of fresh fruit juice. He returned to the compartment and fixed everybody a cool drink. He then got a clean glass full of ice and finished off a bottle of Kentucky's best. He had the porter order sandwiches from the diner and everybody had a quick meal. The food and drinks were soon gone and sleep overtook everyone.

The train made several stops during the night but the Goodwin's were all fast asleep and had no idea as to what was happening. The trip had been a long and exiting experience and they were tired of the constant motion and sounds that always goes with train travel.

The dawn arrived quietly and the long shadows from the early morning sun peaked over low surrounding mountains making a lot of strange shadow patterns. Wanda woke up first. The darkness in the compartment was still hiding almost everything from view. She sat up and saw that everyone else was still sound asleep. The area outside the train was a lot like a desert and the morning sun was showing a barren and harsh looking land. Wanda tried to

Kenneth Orr

remain quiet so as not to wake anyone. She looked over her family and a feeling of pride and happiness began to sink in. Wanda was growing older and between Chalk and herself they had enjoyed a good life.

They had raised two wonderful children that were making their lives complete. The train sounded the whistle and Carl sat up and looked startled. Wanda said, "Good Morning, Did you sleep well?"

Their conversation woke up Chalk and Barbara. Everyone went to the sink and washed their face and said they wanted to put on some clean clothed. Taking turns in the small bath took a few minutes. Chalk said, "Lets go get some breakfast".

They went to the dining car and the smell of fresh coffee was most welcome. Everybody but Carl ordered coffee and a glass of ice water. Carl also wanted juice. The menu was simple fried eggs and meat or pancakes and meat.

Everybody ordered eggs and the waiter had them on the table in a very short time.

Chalk asked the waiter where they were. He said they were about 25 miles north of San Diego. The train had made good time considering the several stops that it made and they should arrive at about 9 AM. Chalk asked what time it was then and he said it was just a little before 8 AM. Chalk knew that time changes on the railroad were a problem, especially out west. You needed to ask somebody who knew what the local time might be. Chalk's watch was still running on Bandera time and he was trying to keep things straight in his mind. So far he was doing a good job of keeping his time considerations straight.

The Goodwin's all went back to the compartment and made sure all of their things were packed and ready to carry off, when the train arrived. Then they started looking out the windows to see what was ahead. The train rounded a curve and off to the west was the Pacific Ocean. Everyone

The Cowboy's Kids

shouted, "Look! That's the Pacific Ocean!" A small lighthouse was visible on a point of land that was in the distance well away from the seashore.

The sky was clear and the blue water was sparkling into the morning sunlight. It was a sight they talked about for years to come. Some small buildings were built along the sides of the tracks and there were people in wagons and riding on horseback. Apparently a favorite past time for the local people was to watch and wave as the trains go by. They waved and many of the passengers waved back.

The train came down a shallow grade and pulled into a small depot that had a bright sign labeled "La Jolla". Carl asked Chalk how to say the name? Chalk thought a bit and said, "Lets ask the conductor? The did and he said the J was supposed to be pronounced like an H. They got it figured out and Wanda asked if this was typical of California names? Everybody laughed.

The stop was quick. Mail and passengers were exchanged and the train moved on. The tracks were not far from the main part of town and the area around the town was built up with nice homes and quaint business buildings. They were back in civilization again.

The train slowed and began going through a much more settled area where the building were closer to the side of the tracks. The streets were full of people and wagons. Chalk saw an automobile and pointed it out to everyone. He said he thought it was a Ford. This was the first one they had seen since seeing one in San Antonio.

The harbor area soon came into view. There were ships with tall masts, there were also large gray navy ships and small sailing vessels berthed all along the pier that was next to the street. Carl's eyes were glued to the window. Finally the train sounded a couple of whistle bleats, then slowed and stopped. They were finally in San Diego, California.

Kenneth Orr

Everybody gathered their luggage and got off the train. Chalk shook the conductor's hand and thanked him for his services. The area next to the train was full of people who were meeting travelers who were on the train. Hugging and kissing were common sights.

There were several carriages waiting by the train and Chalk spotted one that looked like it would be comfortable. He went to the driver and asked him if he knew where the del Coronado Hotel was located. He said, "Yes sir, indeed I do, it's the finest hotel in southern California".

He asked if he could take his family there. The driver said that he would suggest they go to the ferry and take it to Coronado Island. "You can get there by land but it is a long time and it is a boring ride". Chalk gathered his family, they boarded the carriage and the driver put their luggage into a compartment on the backside of the carriage. The trip to the ferry was soon underway. The ferry to Coronado Island was docked a couple of miles south of the center of town. The driver gave everyone a good city tour as they went south. He pointed out the navy base and the nearby downtown shopping area.

Up ahead there was a large sign that pointed to the ferry ramp. He told Chalk that they would need to get out of the carriage at the ramp and board the ferry. There would be carriages at the other side of the water to take them to the hotel. They arrived and everyone got out. Chalk paid the driver for his services and tipped him for being so helpful.

The ferry was loading and everyone got in line. Chalk paid the ferry's fee for everyone and they went into a big cabin where there were long wooden seats. The cabin was not full and there was plenty of room for everyone and for the luggage. The ferry pushed away from the dock and started across the water. The small engine was noisy and the exhaust smoke was black and blowing back toward the passengers. The captain tried to maneuver the ferry to make the smoke go off to one side and not bother the passengers. The smell of salt water was obviously different

The Cowboy's Kids

from the fresh water back in the Medina River back in Texas and everybody took note of the smell.

A young man was sitting in a nearby seat and Chalk thought he looked like a local citizen. He went over, introduced himself, and asked him what he knew about the hotel. He was polite and said it was a grand place and everyone that went there was always happy with the services. Chalk thanked him and went back to Wanda and told her what he had learned.

The ferry trip took about 30 minutes and was a new experience for everyone. The landing on the other side was easy to pull into and soon everyone was on dry land again. Chalk spotted a carriage with a sign that said "del Coronado Hotel" on the back. He went to the driver and was greeted like an old friend. He told Chalk that he was there to take customers to the hotel. He told Chalk, "Load you family and I will be glad to load your baggage and we will be on our way."

The streets were lined with tall trees. Many were palms and several were tropical wide leaf species. The yards were full of blooming flowers and lush green grass. The contrast between this area and the hot and barren desert was dynamic. Wanda loved the new setting and told everyone how nice it was to be here. Barbara was equally pleased at the sights of high fashion homes.

The carriage was elegant and the driver was dressed like a professional servant. His black coat and small black hat were spotless. The trip wound down streets that were full of expensive and elegant homes. The driver pointed out the main buildings and good restaurants to everyone as he drove. The carriage finally arrived at the del Coronado Hotel.

The driver pulled the carriage under a canapé and two doormen came out to meet them. Everyone got out of the carriage and Chalk started to pay the driver. He said there was no charge as the hotel provided free carriage service to

Kenneth Orr

all of their guests. Chalk tipped him anyway. The doormen put the luggage on a cart and pointed Chalk toward the lobby.

Chalk led his family into the lobby where there were several nice leather chairs and couches. He told everyone to have a seat and he would get some rooms. Three people were manning the hotel desk. Two were oriental looking ladies and one was a young white man. He approached the first clerk, the white man, and told him that he needed two rooms for his family of four. He was not sure that the women were able to speak English and he made a decision that was probably safe. The man told him they had several suites with a living room, two or three bedrooms along with a small kitchen. He said these accommodations were very nice and suggested that he consider this option rather than separate rooms. He said several suites were on poolside locations. Others had ocean views and some were inside courtyard locations.

Chalk thought a moment and asked the prices. The costs were very reasonable for such a fancy deluxe hotel. Chalk went to ask Wanda what she would like to do? She said courtside was the least expensive and she was not planning to go swimming that much.

Chalk returned to the desk and informed the clerk of their decision. The clerk asked how long they would be staying and Chalk said he was not sure as they wanted to see a lot of the area and it might be convenient to go to another city and hotel in the process.

One of the young ladies behind the desk came over, and in perfect English said that she would suggest a specific room as it had just been cleaned and was very nice. Chalk thanked her and said he would like to see the suite.

The clerk gave Chalk a form to fill out that outlined the cost structure. He filled in the information, signed it and gave the form back. The clerk looked it over and said, "Sir, I see

The Cowboy's Kids

by your signature that you are a Colonel in the U.S. Army. Is that right?" Chalk responded with a proud "Yes."

The Clerk immediately said that the room rate was automatically adjusted to a price that was 75% less. He said, "The hotel honors our military visitors and we always give them special rates". Chalk was surprised but pleased. Chalk gathered his family and a bellman led them down a hall, out into a beautiful courtyard and to a door that was the main entrance to their suite. He opened the door and led the way inside.

The bellman showed Wanda the rooms and the other facilities that were in the suite. It was elegant and Wanda was very well pleased. The bellman unloaded the luggage and Chalk gave him a nice tip.

The rooms all had tall ceilings and very nice furnishings. The floors were all carpeted and the ocean air was cool and comfortable. The bathroom was tiled and had a big shower and a nice big white tub. Everybody was well pleased.

Ten minutes later there was a knock on the door. Chalk answered the knock. One of the oriental ladies from the front desk had a basket of fresh fruit and candies.

She asked, "Are you Colonel Goodwin?" Chalk answered yes, and she handed the basket to Chalk. She added, "Compliments of the hotel for you and your family". Chalk thanked her and took the basket to a table in the living area.

Wanda had been in her bedroom, as were the kids. They did not hear the door and when they came back to the living room they were surprised at the hotel's hospitality gift. The kids got samples and soon there was a big hole in the center of the basket.

Everyone had freshened up and wanted to go see the ocean. Putting their feet in the Pacific Ocean was a much-discussed thrill that everyone had talked about for the entire trip.

Kenneth Orr

Wanda made sure everyone had on shoes that could be taken off easily. Everyone was ready and anxious to leave the room. The hotel was large and the maze of halls and doors were all going to be a new challenge. Carl found a hall that had the ocean staring at him and said, "Lets go this way." Soon the shoes were off and the sand and cool salt water was up to everyone's knees.

Wanda looked at everyone and said, "We have finally completed our trip and we are finally here in California. The next few days are going to be a lot of fun".

The evening was ending and the sun was falling into the ocean. It was time to relax and get ready for the next day of fun.

✪ CHAPTER 1-6 ✪
California and The First Evening

California was still a new and overwhelming place. The first evening was spent walking around the hotel looking at several shops that were built into the halls of the central hotel. The dinner hour approached and everyone cleaned up and went to the large dining room. Entering the dining area Wanda looked at Chalk and said, "The room ceiling is unusually tall. The room looks like something from a fine castle or an elegant mansion."

There seemingly were hundreds of tables and chairs for the customers. The lights were low and the atmosphere was formal but not too crisp. Every table had a white tablecloth and a vase of fresh flowers in the center. Everything was dripping in elegance. The waiters were all dressed in white shirts, black trousers and black vests and were wearing bow ties.

The headwaiter greeted them at the doorway and asked Chalk where they would like to sit. Chalk wanted a table on the side where they could be a little more private. The waiter selected a specific table and everyone was seated. Shortly another waiter brought ice water and menus. He asked everyone if they would like something cool to drink. Wanda had Chalk ordered a bottle of white wine with four glasses. Chalk asked the waiter to also bring some fruit juice, as the young man was not of drinking age. Carl looked

Kenneth Orr

at Chalk and smiled. He said, "Dad, I am growing up and you need to allow me have some freedoms."

Everyone was served their drinks quickly. Chalk was given the first taste of the wine and he approved. It was cool, not too sweet and delicious. The waiter told Chalk that it was from a fine California winery and was considered one of the very best.

They all sat back and relaxed and talked about how fancy things were in the hotel. Carl was hungry and was the first one to open his menu. He saw several items that had fancy names and had no idea as to what they were. Barbara was having the same problem. Chalk looked at the menu and told Wanda they needed to talk to the waiter. He was having the same problem. Chalk saw the waiter and motioned for him to come over. He came quickly. Chalk said that they were not familiar with the names of items on the menu and needed help. The waiter got a big grin on his face and said he had come to California from Kansas and had the same problem when he arrived. The names were just fancy ways to describe red meat, seafood and chicken. Chalk asked which ones were the steaks. They were pointed out and soon everyone's main course order was on the waiters pad.

The waiter told everyone that a choice of any salad came with every meal and the salad dressings were always on the side. Orders were finalized and the food order was taken to the kitchen. Chalk kept the wine glasses full and soon the bottle was dry.

The time between ordering and the food arrival was short, but the conversation was going top speed. Everybody but Chalk wanted to discuss what they were going to do in the morning. Chalk wanted to just sit back and enjoy the moment. Wanda wanted to go see the shops, Barbara wanted to go swimming and Carl wanted to take a carriage ride and see the pretty girls who were stretched out in the sun down by the beach. Chalk just listened and smiled. The waiter brought fresh hot bread, butter over a bed of ice and

The Cowboy's Kids

a dish of sliced carrots and celery to munch on until the main course arrived. Wanda sipped on her wine and told Chalk how good it tasted.

The food was served in different courses. The salad was first and ten minutes later the main course was delivered. Wanda had a steak filet of beef served in a special wine sauce. Chalk had a big t-bone steak, cooked rare served in a similar sauce. Barbara had the same as Wanda and Carl had a nice rare slice of prime rib. Every plate had white rice either as a bed for the entrée or on the side and was topped off with boiled, parsley new potatoes. Everyone dug in. The food was delicious and the waiter's promise that they would like their individual choices, proved to be true.

When the main course was completed the waiter pushed a cart up to the table that was filled with every kind of fancy cake and pie one could hope for. He said the dessert came with the meal and they could have their pick. Everyone's appetite was just about satisfied but the desserts were too pretty to pass up. Everybody took their pick and dug in again. When they finished they all took their napkins and wiped their mouth clean and placed it on the now empty desert plate.

The waiter came by and asked if there was anything more that he could bring them? Chalk smiled at him and said the check was the only missing item. He brought the check and Chalk looked at it and saw the total. The total bill was very reasonable for such a fine meal and such great service. Chalk added a nice tip, signed it and put his room number on the bottom. He had noticed that cash was not in use and all of the other customers were signing the tickets. The waiter had made their first day in California a real success.

The walk back to the rooms was slow and comfortable. Everybody was full of good food and the thought of a nice soft clean bed was a welcome thought. The passenger train was not horrible but it sure was not paradise. Night had arrived a few hours before and the sound of the ocean

Kenneth Orr

waves on the beach was soothing and welcome. A maid had been in the rooms and pulled down the sheets on everyone's bed. The temptation to get ready for a good nights rest was overpowering and soon everyone was quietly asleep.

CHAPTER 1-7
Vacation Time and California Fun

Sunrise, the next morning, came early. The time seemed a lot later than it really was due to the time difference between Texas and California. The time adjustment had started to make an impact of everyone on the train. Nobody was completely adjusted in everyone's natural daily habits. Chalk was the first one to wake up and he saw Wanda was still sleeping soundly. He put on some casual clothes and walked outside. The air was cool and fresh. He walked to a place where he could sit down in a lounge chair and look out over the ocean.

The Pacific was calm and sea gulls were flying along the shoreline picking up small bits of food from the ocean's edge. Out to sea there was a big military looking ship coming close to land. It was obviously headed for the San Diego navy piers. Chalk watched and waited as it came closer. His career in the army had never taken him to a Navy base and the sighting of a ship outfitted with large guns fascinated him.

He sat there for about ten minutes and without warning he felt a soft hand on his back. Barbara had awakened, got dressed and come out to find her missing dad. He gave her a big hug and asked her if she slept well. She said that she didn't remember, she was too tired to recall when she went to bed. Chalk pointed out the approaching navy ship and told her that he wanted to visit the navy base while they

Kenneth Orr

were in San Diego. Barbara said she knew this would be fun and she wanted to go with him.

Shortly after, Wanda and Carl came walking up. They both had woke up and put on some clean clothes and were anxious to see where Chalk and Barbara had gone. They all looked at each other and said, "We need to get some real California clothes. We all look like a bunch of Texas cowboys. Our Texas stuff is just not the style they wear out here." Everybody agreed and said right after breakfast they would go shopping. Wanda was the most excited about the decision. She loved to shop for clothes and this was a perfect time to get some really new fashions for herself and for Barbara.

Breakfast was easy. There was a small café style restaurant in the lower level of the hotel lobby and they had all kinds of good breakfast food. It was quick and it was great tasting. Then they all went back to the room and did a final scrub before leaving to go shopping.

Chalk had never met a stranger and over his life his personality skills had helped him greatly. California was no different for him. Everybody got ready to shop and Chalk said they should go to the hotel lobby and ask for some local directions. They found the lobby and Chalk and Wanda went to the front desk.

He was quickly approached by the desk clerk, an attractive Oriental lady, and he asked her where was a good place to shop for some casual clothes. She was a local native and offered up several store names for locations that were close by. Wanda listened and wrote the names and addresses down on a pad. They both thanked her and turned to go out to the street. Before they got too far the lady hailed them down and asked Wanda to come back to the desk. She told Wanda that there were a couple of smaller stores on a street about a block off the main shopping are where they carried the same clothes, but the prices were much more attractive. Wanda thanked her for the information and they were off to shop.

The Cowboy's Kids

A young man was standing by the door selling newspapers and the way he was holding them made the headline on the front-page stand out powerfully. It read. "War has Become More Deadly, Many American Troops are Missing." Chalk bought a copy and asked everyone to wait for a minute while he read the story. The story was not very complete but the message was clear. The information told a grim story that General Pershing's forces were taking heavy casualties and that the German army was not slowing down. Chalk knew that many of the men he had helped train in Texas were in Europe and were in Pershing's unit. He was pained at the thoughts but there was little he could do. He folded up the paper, stuffed it in his rear pocket and gathered his family together. They were off to shop. This paper was dated about two day ago and he knew the news was already late when it arrived in the USA.

The first store they visited was very nice and the clothing was just what they were looking for. Wanda was more conservative and when she saw the prices she reminded Chalk about the lady at the hotel desk's suggestion about better prices around the corner. Chalk agreed to look at a few more stores then go to the other stores. Carl was a little fussy but agreed. The next store had an even bigger selection and the prices were much better. Wanda was still not ready to buy. They went to two more stores and found that the further away from the hotel they went, the lower the prices.

The clothing styles were all about the same. Barbara noticed that the local people were more commonly seen in the lower priced stores. They finally found a place where the clothes were just right and the prices were about 50% of what they had been in the other stores. Everyone got some new vacation duds. Chalk noticed that the ladies swimwear was a lot more colorful, and a lot briefer than the swimsuits in Texas. Carl had also noticed! He told his Dad that he was ready to see the beach and see what was going on.

They all walked back to the hotel and put on their new clothes. Chalk said that it would be nice to hire a carriage

Kenneth Orr

and get a tour of the local sights. The day was still young and the ride would help them get a good idea of what was there to see.

Everyone walked out to the front of the hotel and several carriages were lined up and were ready to haul passengers. Chalk found one that had big seats and got a price for a good tour. The fee was reasonable and everyone got in.

The driver was a native and he knew every interesting spot to see. He drove them all around the business area and when they got on the north end of the residential area there was a big fence and a sign that identified it as the Coronado U S. Navy Base. Armed sailors were guarding the base entrance. It was obvious that there would be no unauthorized carriages permitted beyond the gate area. There was a war going on and base security was at a high level.

Chalk asked the driver to stop and he got out. He walked over to the gate and approached one of the guards. He told the guard that he was a retired army officer and wondered if there was any way he could get a base tour. The guard, who was an enlisted man, called for an officer from a small building to come over. He responded quickly and Chalk introduced himself and provided his credentials that identified him as a retired army officer. He told him that he was vacationing with his family and everyone would like to see the base if it was possible.

The officer rechecked Chalk's military identification and saw that he was a colonel. Chalk's military rank was an automatic key to get into many places. The base officer quickly contacted someone on a phone. He finished his call and came back to Chalk and asked him if he could come back at 8:30 the following morning. He said today was not a good time to have visitors and tomorrow would be much better. Chalk asked him if he could bring his family. He said yes, but they would be restricted to some of the things they would be allowed to see. The officer took down everyone's name and age and put it on a document and put it in a

The Cowboy's Kids

special envelope. Chalk understood the reason for tight security and thanked him for the appointment.

Chalk went back to the carriage and told Wanda that they had an appointment for a tour the morning and everyone had to be ready and be at the gate on time. Carl was excited. He loved seeing new things and the thrill of seeing a navy base put him in a high expectation attitude.

They rode on and saw even more fine homes, private sailing boats and a lot more good places to eat and shop. The Coronado island tour was a big success. They saw a lot of new interesting things to talk about and were comfortable with the carriage ride.

When they returned to the hotel Chalk asked the driver to be available the next morning at 7:45 AM to take them to the Navy base. The driver agreed to be waiting, and got back in the line of available carriages parked in the front of the hotel.

It was lunchtime and there was a small oriental sidewalk café on the street, just a short way from the hotel and Wanda said she wanted to try it out. Lunch was great and the outdoor table was very comfortable.

After lunch they decided to tour the hotel. It was a grand building and there were shops and special little snack shops mixed into the complex. The shops located in the hotel were extremely nice but they were priced way above what Wanda thought was reasonable. The result was they bought very little.

The swimming pool was huge and there were cabanas all around the sides where good-looking ladies of all ages were all trying to get tanned. Carl was quick to point this out to his dad. The atmosphere was geared for relaxation and fun. Stress was not an obvious visitor anywhere.

The hotel was near several seafood restaurants. Wanda had passed one that looked especially nice and the menu

Kenneth Orr

that was posted in the window, had a wide variety of fresh seafood choices. Everything was advertised as "Fresh caught that day". She had pointed it out to Chalk and said she wanted to eat there that evening. Chalk agreed and said they would enjoy the walk in the cool evening ocean air. Carl was anxious to go for the walk as he had developed a noticeable habit of watching the young girls. Barbara noticed his new interests were developing quickly and she thought it was the first signs of his coming of age.

Chalk told Wanda and the kids to do what they wanted around the hotel. He was going to try and get in touch with Becky Brock back in Bandera on the telephone. He went to the room and called the hotel telephone operator. She told him it would take a few minutes to get the connections made and told him to wait by the phone. She would call him back when she had the call connected. He waited and was sure that it would take a while. Phone calls were difficult to place, especially long distance.

While Chalk waited he took out the newspaper he had purchased and read a few of the key details of the war story carefully. The story was not detailed but it was obvious to him that the soldiers that were involved were from Texas. Chalk knew that the cavalry troops were always the hardest hit in a ground war. There were no names or numbers of dead and injured in the newspaper story. He was deeply concerned. He felt a little guilty because he was not there helping the men he had once commanded.

The phone rang and the operator asked him to hold on for a moment. Soon, Becky Brock was connected and Chalk was glad to hear her voice. He told her they were all doing well and the trip to California had been a real eye opening experience about the western United States. She was pleased to hear all was well.

He asked her how the ranch was doing and if anyone had been trying to get in touch with him. She said no, but a young man named "Stan" who said he was Barbara's friend had called. He had left a message that his older brother

The Cowboy's Kids

had been injured in the war. The young man said he was planning to join the army right away and see if he could be of any help to the war effort. He told Becky that he would send Barbara a letter as soon as he knew where he was going to be.

He had also asked Becky to tell Barbara that, "She was very special to him". Chalk understood all to well what was happening and he asked Becky to try and keep in touch with the young man if she could.

Becky said the ranch was in good order and that they had been asked to sell several horses of lesser quality to a man from Dallas. He was going to use them in a dairy business to pull small delivery wagons. Sarge had picked out eight horses and sold them for a fair price. Chalk told her that the train trip home might be quicker, as the detour they had made, was supposed to be fixed very soon. Chalk wished her well and the call was ended.

Wanda came in the room just after the phone call had ended. Chalk told her to set down and help him find the right words to tell Barbara about her friend. Barbara had not talked about him a lot. Barbara was the quiet type and her private life was always kept just that way, private. She had chosen to use the term "my friend" rather than to use Stan's name, as she was still not willing to make an open commitment of any kind about their relationship.

Wanda had talked to her about her friend and the few time his name came up Barbara would always blush and remind Wanda that he was just a good friend. Wanda's woman's intuition told her that this was just a cover up for a much deeper feeling.

Wanda told Chalk that she would handle it, and that when Barbara and Carl came back to the room, she wanted Chalk to take Carl for a long walk. The newspaper was in full view and Wanda saw the news. She put the paper away and made sure that Barbara could not see it.

Kenneth Orr

The afternoon was getting warm and soon the kids came back to the room. They were happy and had been walking the beach picking up shells. Carl had a small can full of colorful shells and a couple of rocks that looked a lot like some kind of coral. He was quick to show them to Wanda. Wanda saw them and said they were pretty. Barbara sat down and said she needed to get out of the sun. She was going to get sunburned if she stayed out any longer.

Chalk asked Carl if he wanted to go look at some fishing equipment they had seen in a nearby shop. Carl said "yes" and they soon were out the door. Wanda and Barbara were alone and the time had come to tell her about the phone message.

Wanda asked her if she had heard from Stan before they left. Barbara said, "Yes, about two weeks before we left." Wanda told her that Stan had called Becky Brock yesterday and had some bad news. Barbara became very quiet and was anxious to hear more. Wanda said that he had told Becky that Stan's older brother had been injured in the war. Barbara asked "How bad?" Wanda said she did not say.

Wanda then said there is more news. Stan told Becky that he is joining the army at once to go help the men fight the war. He left a message that he would write when he could and he had told Becky that you are very special to him. Barbara hung her head and began to cry. Wanda went to her side and they both were crying and holding on to each other like they had never done before.

Wanda said, "Lets go for a walk. It will help to make the pain go away." Barbara said she would go but when they got back she wanted to be alone. Wanda understood.

While they were gone Chalk had told Carl what he had learned and asked him to be especially kind to Barbara if she was not her normal self. Carl was young but he understood what was happening and he told Chalk that he would be as helpful as he could. He loved his sister and her pain was also his pain. They went back to the room and Wanda and

The Cowboy's Kids

Barbara were gone. Chalk fixed a stiff drink of Kentucky's best and a tall glass of ice and juice for Carl.

Chalk took a couple of small drinks from his whiskey glass and told Carl that he could have a very small sip if he wanted it. He said, "You are about to become a man and you need to learn about a few of a grown man's habits. You also need to learn that this whiskey habit can go out of control if you don't watch it."

Carl took a small sip of his dad's drink, made a sour face, smacked his lips a time or two and quickly got a big drink of juice to get his mouth back in order. He did not want to look like he was not liking the taste, but he knew his face had already told his story. He told his dad that he was not ready yet for a shot of whiskey. Chalk laughed and patted him on the back.

The door opened and Barbara and Wanda came in. Wanda looked at Chalk and blinked one eye. He knew that Barbara had been told. Carl went over to Barbara and hugged her. They both had a good cry and then they seemed to be a little more able to talk to everyone. Chalk went to a small hotel restaurant and got some food to take to the room.

Bedtime came early and they were all trying to take their minds off the bad news by discussing the natural beauty in the San Diego area. They were also talking about going to the navy base the next morning.

CHAPTER 1-8
The Navy and The Sailing Men

An early sunrise was the best signal for Chalk to get out of bed. He was up at 5:00 AM and soon he had everyone else up and getting ready. His appointment at the navy base was physically not that far away but he wanted to make sure that everyone had the time to shower, dress nicely, and have a good breakfast. Just being allowed to visit the base during a time of war was a special privilege and Chalk wanted to make sure that his family was properly dressed for the occasion. They would still need to have time to ride in the carriage to the navy base gate. Chalk was not one to be late and he was always firm about schedules with everyone, even his family.

Breakfast was quick at the local café in the hotel and everyone took one last stop in the room to make sure they were ready. Barbara's eyes were red but she was doing what she could to find her best looks and best attitude. Wanda was sticking close to her to add a supporting effort if it was needed. Not knowing what was going on was much harder than having some level of information. Wanda and Chalk both knew about this kind of fear.

Chalk walked out to the hotel lobby and the carriage driver was standing in the shade of a big tree drinking a cup of coffee. Chalk went over and made contact and said he would be back shortly with his family. Soon everyone was

The Cowboy's Kids

in the carriage and the carriage horse was clipping along toward the navy Base.

The carriage arrived right on time and there was a military coach parked just inside the base gate. Chalk walked over to the guard's station and identified himself. The guard saluted Chalk and told him the base commander's personal coach driver was waiting for him and his family. Chalk went back to the hotel coach and paid the driver. He told everyone to follow him into the base gate area. The guard waited until everyone was in the coach and gave everyone special base badges. Each person had to sign a paper to get their badge. Carl could write fairly well but filling out a form required help from dad. The gate guard said there was a war going on and security was never relaxed on an active military base, especially during times like these. Signatures were finally inscribed and the commander's carriage was boarded and started toward the north.

Thick trees bordered the road and the military installation was not visible for about a half mile. Then, just like a door opened in front of the carriage the tall masts and gray color of naval fighting ships came in full view. Everyone was impressed. Carl was looking and straining to see everything. The driver spoke up and said the base commander, an Admiral named "Hancock" wanted to meet Chalk and his family and be the first to welcome them to the facility. The Admiral's office was in a formal looking building next to a beautiful white home.

The carriage pulled up and two young seamen instantly came over to help the guests get out and to lead them into the base commander's office. They all went in and immediately inside the door there was a big American flag draped over a ship's anchor. The seamen asked to wait for a moment while they were announced. Everyone stood and looked and within a minute a tall middle aged Navy Officer dressed in a spotless white uniform came through the door. He said his name was Admiral Hancock and wanted to be the first to welcome a well-known and outstanding army officer to his base. He saluted Chalk and shook Chalks hand.

Kenneth Orr

He also gave him a simple hug. Chalk saluted back and returned his gestures of respect. It was obvious that the normal formality associated with an Officer's meeting was being forgotten and this put everyone at ease.

Wanda, Barbara and Carl were then introduced. The Admiral asked them to come into his office and make themselves comfortable. The Admiral had several pictures of navy officers and sailors on his desk and it was obvious from his decorations that he had a level of authority that was well earned. Everybody sat down and a seaman served fresh iced tea. The Admiral asked Chalk where they were staying? Chalk said at the "del". The Admiral said it was "The finest" and they always took the best of care when military personnel were guests.

He said he was very busy that day but had arranged for one of his senior Officers to show them the base and to take them to lunch at the Officers Club. Chalk thanked him and said he wanted to extend an invitation to him to come visit his ranch if he was ever in Texas. The Admiral smiled, looked At Wanda and said, "My wife is from Kilgore, Texas. I am from Houston and we always enjoyed being among fellow Texans". Chalk knew the visit was off to a great start.

Admiral Hancock said his wife would like to join them for lunch but he was going to be busy at that time. Wanda was smiling and said that would be wonderful. He then added. "I do want to see you again before you leave. He then looked at the escorting Officer and said, "You make sure the carriage is back here by 5 PM." The Senior Officer had got the message and agreed. He stood up, saluted the Commander and looking at the Goodwin family said, "Please follow me."

Everyone got into a larger coach that had more room and a chest full of ice and freshwater canteens. There was a basket of fresh fruit and individually wrapped hard candies. The driver had pulled the new carriage up in front of the office building while the visitors were in with Commander Hancock. The driver, who was a seaman, started the tour.

The Cowboy's Kids

The first route was to review the official business building and then the residence areas. The facilities were nice but Carl was still looking for the ships. The carriage turned around a corner and right there in front of the next big building was an airplane. It was the first navy airplane that anyone had seen and it was painted gray, just like the ships.

Carl's jaw dropped and he was completely interested in what was in front of him. Ships somehow had just been relegated to a lower level of interest. The carriage stopped and the host told everyone. "You can get out and look at the airplane up close, but please do not try to get inside. The next few minutes were full of wonder and amazement for everyone.

This was a **man made machine** that could fly, and two men could ride inside. Powered flying was unheard of in the history of man and Wanda and Barbara were frankly beside themselves to realize what they were seeing.

The officer said, "Follow me" and he went to a door next to the biggest building. He opened it and invited everyone to come just inside the door and stop. There were several more airplanes inside and a couple of them had boat shaped bottoms. The officer said they were developing airplanes that would be able to land and take off from the water. He had to keep everyone away from these airplanes, they were considered as a secret navy program, but he made sure that the tour gave everyone at least one good look.

They all went back to the carriage and got back on. The driver drove them a bit further and soon there were several ships docked at piers next to the road. The officer explained about how different naval ships were designed to do specific jobs. He explained some of the assignments each ship was designed to do and how each one was a special part of the navy's total strength. Chalk was taking all of this in and Barbara and Carl were starting to see what a navy ship was really all about.

Kenneth Orr

The carriage pulled up to a small pier and the officer asked everyone if they had ever been for a ride in a navy boat. Of course the answer was "NO". He said, "Follow me." They walked down a wide pier and soon they saw a navy launch boat that was obviously waiting for them.

The officer spoke up and to the crew on the launch said, "Requesting permission to board a guest party with the Admiral's request." An answer came back immediately, "Permission granted." Everyone climbed on board and the seamen issued each person a military life vest. He helped them put them on and got them all seated on cushioned seats. He them said, "Cast off the lines." The boat trip was underway.

The first part of the trip was alongside several small destroyer class ships. They were currently being manned by a small crew of men who were doing port maintenance work. Then, a big battleship was approached.

The Officer said this ship had just returned from being at sea for several weeks and was in port to refueling, having maintenance performed and to replenish supplies. There were also work ships; a ship that was painted white with a large red cross on the side and a ship that was identified as a "special project ship".

The white ship was identified as a hospital ship. Sick and injured sailors are taken on board this ship if they are injured while on duty at sea. Nothing more was said about several other ships and Chalk understood this was not the time to ask more questions. We were at war and navy business is just that, navy business. He also knew that Barbara would not want to be reminded of the casualties of war.

The launch turned across the harbor and sailed to a navy pier area near downtown San Diego. Several wooden ships with tall sails and a few smaller metal ships were docked nearby. There were merchant ships and were not associated with the navy.

The Cowboy's Kids

Many of the merchant ships were flying flags that were not from The United States. Sailors were working on the decks doing repairs and moving freight. The officer said these were freight and passenger vessels and often were in port for only a few days. "These ships were always in a hurry to deliver their freight, get new freight and get out to sea again. They are going all over the world".

The launch continued to go toward the west and soon there were strange shapes sticking up out of the water. The officer told everybody that they were submarines and they were about 90% or more under water at all times. He stated a few basic facts about the submarine fleet and than said that was all he could say right them.

The launch went back to the navy pier where they had boarded and docked. Everyone was a little rocky when they stepped off. They had not yet learned about getting "sea legs" or how to ride in a launch in water that was not completely smooth. It was a funny experience for everyone but they all managed. They went back to the carriage and the senior officer said, "Lets go have some lunch". The carriage moved briskly and soon was unloading everyone in front of the Officer's Club.

Everyone approached the front door, and just as they arrived, it opened and a well-dressed lady came out. She walked up to Wanda and said, "Welcome, You must be Colonel Goodwin's Wife."

Wanda nodded to confirm she was indeed. The lady said "I am Bonnie Hancock and would like to host you and your family for lunch". She added, "Please lets use first names as you folks are here on vacation and the military stuff is not what we want to hear over lunch". Everyone agreed and Wanda introduced Chalk, Barbara and Carl. Bonnie looked at commander Buddy Rush, the escorting senior officer and said, "Buddy, have you been showing them a good time"? He replied, "Ask them." The formal ice had been broken and the rest of the luncheon was conducted with much less stiffness.

Kenneth Orr

They went to a small but elegant dining room where important guests were obviously entertained. Bonnie told everyone that the chef always had a delicious seafood selection and signaled a waiter to come over. He asked for a drinks order and everyone had iced tea. He left everyone a menu and went for the drinks.

Bonnie told Chalk that the redfish was extra good and it was always served with a wine sauce and boiled new potatoes. He said, "That's for me." Barbara also said this was her choice and Barbara and Carl looked at Wanda and said "Me too." The waiter returned left the drinks and took the order.

Bonnie said, "You know I am a Texan too and so is Admiral Hancock." She told about growing up in Kilgore and going to Houston to attend school. Her future husband was in school there and when he graduated they got married and he went straight into the navy.

Her husband's career and being a navy wife had taken her all over the country, and for a while they were stationed in England. The Admiral was a junior officer back then and was at sea a great deal of the time. She always looked forward to him coming home. He had commanded several different ships, and had recently been involved with the war in Europe. He had only been in San Diego for less than a year and was eligible to retire the next year. Retirement she hoped, would let them go back to Texas and someday buy a small ranch. It was so obvious that she was a little bit jealous of the Goodwin's as they were already living what she considered to be the good life.

Lunch was served and everyone was well pleased with the food. When the meal was over Bonnie said she had the afternoon free and would be glad to take everyone on a tour of the downtown San Diego area. She said there was a launch on the dock that could take everyone to a navy dock in the downtown area.

The Cowboy's Kids

From there they could ride in an open carriage and see the area. She looked at Wanda and said that shopping stops were no problem and the men could see some of the stores where "men things" were for sale. She said that the Admiral wanted to see them before they went home for the night and he would be in their home awaiting their return.

Wanda smiled and said, "Lets go." Chalk helped her out of her chair and Carl tried to help Barbara. Buddy helped Bonnie get out of her chair and all six of them headed for the carriage. The same navy launch that they had been on earlier was waiting and shortly they were in downtown San Diego. Two seamen were at the dock and they were watching over the launch while everyone was shopping.

Buddy had slipped off his navy jacket and put a more casual shirt in its place. He was looking more like a civilian than an officer and he and Chalk put Carl in between themselves and went along with the city visit. Wanda saw some beach clothes and Barbara saw a fancy sun hat she liked. They told Chalk they wanted to buy them and he went to the cash register and paid the bill.

A few stores on the same street had a lot of navy style clothes. Carl wanted a sailor cap and he picked one out that had "San Diego" sewn into the edge. There were several small trinket shops in the "Old town" area and everyone was anxious to buy something to take home.

Bonnie had the carriage driver take them down by the commercial piers and ride down the main streets. Bud showed Chalk the Tattoo parlors and the local Seaman's bars. They all appeared to be doing a good business.

Several loosely dressed women were standing by several of the bar room doors. Chalk looked at Wanda, smiled and said, "Yes." The tour was over at about 4:15 and the carriage went back to the navy launch. Soon they were back on the navy base and in a carriage headed for the Admiral's home.

Kenneth Orr

The Admiral's home was near the base offices and there were big trees on both sides of the carriage path that led to the door. The carriage stopped in front of the front entrance and everyone exited. The Admiral stepped out the front door and said, "Welcome to my home, fellow Texans."

He had his uniform unbuttoned at the collar and looked a lot more relaxed. Everyone immediately knew they were welcome. He opened the door and said, "Come on in and lets all get comfortable." The Admiral was looking like a man who wanted to relax. Everyone went in and soon they were in a very nice big room that was a lot less stuffy than the military offices. The Admiral told Chalk that his first name was John and he liked to hear people call him by his first name once in a while.

Chalk understood and said "John, You are running a real busy base, you must be glad to find a few minutes to relax once in a while". John agreed and said he would like to have Chalk and Buddy join him for a good drink of some special whiskey he had brought back from England. Chalk agreed, smiled and started looking for Wanda. Bonnie had already taken her and Barbara out to the kitchen area and was showing her around the house. Chalk looked at John and said, "Women always want to show off their homes. They take every opportunity to do this that comes along." John Just smiled and winked at Chalk. Carl was sitting next to Buddy and soon they were talking about airplanes.

Chalk had been taking it all in for the whole day. He was finally in a place and with a man he could relate the thoughts that he was thinking. Chalk always had a problem talking about military things when there were women around. They were never aware of what was really being said and soon all they had were pointless questions.

John, Buddy and Chalk had a good talk about military life, about the war in Europe and the planned role for the airplane in the navy. Admiral Hancock told Chalk about several of the ships that were currently at sea supporting the war in

The Cowboy's Kids

Europe. He also talked about how the Germans had tried to sink them. Carl sat by his dad and listened intently.

The Admiral told Chalk that he had to be at a special dinner for an injured seaman who was being honored in about an hour and was sorry that he and Bonnie could not have them for dinner.

He told Chalk that his carriage would take everyone back to the hotel and that his aid had already arranged with the restaurant at the "del" to serve everyone a dinner of his or her choice, courtesy of the Admiral. He asked how long they would be in town and Chalk said they were supposed to leave for home in about a week.

The Admiral suggested that they visit the La Jolla area. He said that it was a beautiful place and there were a lot of bargains in land and new homes in that area. He said that he and Bonnie had already invested in land in the area. He said he might retire and live there or sell it and move somewhere else. He knew that he was probably going to make a good profit on their investments with either decision.

It was time to get ready for his meeting and the Admiral looked at Chalk and said, "If you get time please come back". He parted by saying, "If you run out of time and cannot come back I wish you calm seas and favorable winds on your trip home. You will always be welcome at my door." Chalk returned a similar invitation to have the Commander visit his Ranch.

The carriage pulled up to door, good by's were exchanged and the Goodwin's were on the way back to the hotel. This had been a day everyone would remember for the rest of their lives.

The del Coronado restaurant was always a welcome place to visit and everyone had a delicious dinner. The day was over and everyone was tired and soon ready to go to bed.

CHAPTER 1-9
Time in Southern California

The next morning came quicker than most everyone wanted it to happen. Sleeping in was a real blessing after such a long train ride. The day before had been so exciting and the California visit was just beginning. Chalk asked Wanda if she wanted to go back to the downtown area of San Diego. She said she would rather see more of the sights in smaller towns. The San Diego area was full of bars, sailors and rip off high prices. She was not interested in any of these and her idea of fun was seeing the sights.

Admiral Hancock's suggestion had caught her attention and she said, "Lets go see La Jolla". Carl said he also wanted to see the ocean from somewhere that was not filled up with buildings and ships. Chalk looked at Barbara and she smiled in agreement.

Chalk told everyone to pack up and get ready to travel. He went to the front desk and said they would be leaving and asked for his bill. The desk clerk said it was already settled and he owed nothing. Chalk looked puzzled and asked who paid the bill? The clerk said a navy officer had given him authorization to summarize what ever the total bill ended up being and send it to Admiral Hancock. Chalk understood. He asked for a sheet of paper and wrote John a personal thank you note and asked the clerk to attach it to the bill when he sent it. He agreed. Chalk had already invited the Admiral and his wife to come visit Bandera if they ever had the

The Cowboy's Kids

opportunity. He repeated the invitation on his note. He and Wanda both hoped that someday John and Bonnie would come to Bandera and they could repay their hospitality.

The luggage and the Goodwin's were all loaded into a hotel carriage. The driver took them to the motor launch pier and soon everyone was standing by the dock in San Diego. Chalk got directions to the local train station where he could catch a train to La Jolla. He hailed a waiting carriage and had the driver take everyone there. There was a local train going to La Jolla leaving in about 20 minutes. They were all onboard when it pulled out. The trip took a little over twenty minutes and they were standing on the street in La Jolla looking like a bunch of tourists. Chalk looked down the street to see if he could see a hotel.

A nice carriage pulled up and asked Chalk where he wanted to go. Chalk told him he wanted to find a nice hotel with an ocean view, but not too far from the main part of town. The driver said, "If everyone will get into the carriage, and we will be there in a few quick minutes."

His prediction was accurate, and they pulled up to a small hotel called "La Casa Grande." Wanda was impressed when she saw that the street side of the hotel was decorated with beautiful flowers, hanging baskets of flowers and lush shrubs. The rear side of the hotel was facing the Pacific Ocean.

The hotel was located high on a bluff and the Pacific Ocean view was spectacular. Chalk went to the front desk and inquired about getting two rooms that were adjoining. The desk clerk said he had two such combinations but suggested he consider a residence style suite. It had three bedrooms, a living area, a small eating and cooking area, and a large patio that overlooked the ocean. He asked if he could have his wife see the suite and the clerk said, "No problem." Chalk got Wanda and they went to see the rooms. Wanda was more impressed with this room than she had been at the del Coronado. She said, "This room is just right." Chalk made the arrangements and everyone moved in.

Kenneth Orr

The morning had passed quickly and everyone was hungry. The hotel had a nice restaurant but the kids wanted to see some other restaurants that were also nearby. They all spruced up a bit and set out on a "walking hunt for some lunch." The street that ran in front of the hotel had several shops and small restaurants all of which were within a few hundred yards in both directions. Barbara saw a sign that said "Oriental Station". She had been looking for some good Chinese food and this was tempting. She looked at Wanda and they agreed this was the lunch stop.

The food was delicious and the service was authentic oriental. Chopsticks were optional, rice was on every plate and the menu was full of great choices. The restaurant owner was a genuine Chinese cook and his food was very special to him. Four hungry people soon became stuffed and they all were glad they had stopped there.

They walked back to the hotel and settled in for a few minutes. Chalk walked out on the patio and found a comfortable chair. Wanda soon joined him and they sat quietly and looked out over the ocean. There were several ships coming toward the shore and they were obviously headed for the San Diego harbor. One was a high mast sailing vessel and it was flying a large set of white sails.

Chalk and Wanda knew that the kids wanted to go walking on the beach. There was a path in the back of the hotel that ended at the beach area. Chalk pointed it out to Carl and he told Barbara that the beach walk was going to be fun. They both put on some new swimsuits and were ready. They went down the path and were gone for about two hours.

Wanda and Chalk were relaxing in their chairs. They talked about the Admiral and how nice his wife had been to take them to see San Diego's shopping area. Chalk said he had been thinking about what the Admiral had said about the investment opportunities in La Jolla.

Chalk told Wanda that he had been thinking about what they could do with the great amount of money their horse

The Cowboy's Kids

ranch had accumulated. The two different subjects were seemingly more related that they thought.

Chalk thought back and told Wanda what he thought money was really worth. He remembered that as a kid he had very little money and if he wanted something, he could usually trade something he had for what he wanted. He had become good at bartering and often was able to get groceries for favors and small amounts of work in the local stores. He seldom had any real money to spend, but when he did, the things he bought were always worth more to him than the money. Wanda had always been thrifty and she fully understood how he was thinking.

Wanda commented that Carl was already learning how to watch his money. He would never want to spend money if he could work a better deal. They both thought about his bartering habit, then they laughed.

Chalk's work on the Kentucky horse farms and on the riverboat had provided him with a fair amount of money and soon he had become good at gambling. This had provided him with even more money. This money was all in the form of coins. Gold coins were heavy and he had bought a strongbox to keep them out of sight and secure. When he got to Texas he was paid more money and in addition he was provided a small home and some land to get started in the cattle business.

Chalk said, "The real value of things is not measured in the amount of money you must spend, it is in the value of the thing that you buy with money." He added, "Cattle and horses are a form of value but they will someday grow old, get sick and die. The only thing that really lasts and cannot be destroyed is land. That's why I always have looked to having good land and property over having a lot of cash money."

"Having land that is located in the right place is the best place to put your investment money. Wise investments will return good profits and supports the local economy.

Kenneth Orr

Land values will normally not go down if they are managed properly. The land's value will become more desirable to other people over time. Because of this, well located land will normally become more valuable."

He sat a bit longer and took out his money pouch and pulled out a paper $50 bill. He looked at it, showed it to Wanda and asked her what she saw. She was a little confused but looked at the money for a few moments and said, "That's paper money." Chalk said, "You are right but if I set it on fire it will soon be gone." He added, "Bank notes and checks are just another way to manage money and checks are just as weak as paper money in providing real value and long term security."

Chalk commented that "Bankers were always looking for ways to make money and they were not above using your money to help them line their own pockets. Paper money and bank paperwork are all ways to help them confuse the realities of value."

Chalk said, "The real value was safe when you could both see and touch what you own, and you know that it cannot be destroyed. Paper value, in any form, is always subject to some form of loss." Wanda agreed and started to wonder what he was trying to tell her.

Wanda said, "What are you really trying to tell me"? Chalk said, "We have a fortune setting in the bank in Texas and if the bank should burn down today, the records and the money we supposedly have could all be gone." Wanda smiled and said, "I never thought of that."

The sun was going down and the view across the water and on into the coastal mountains to the north, was beautiful.

Chalk told Wanda that he still had most of the gold and silver coins that he had earned in his younger days and they were still in the strongbox back in their Texas bedroom. Wanda said she still had all of the coin money she brought to Texas, plus a great deal of the money she had earned

The Cowboy's Kids

while she was working. They both were very thrifty and never spent money unless it was for something they really needed. The only exception that Chalk ever made, was to keep a little side money for a good poker game. Wanda never had any concerns about this part of Chalk's spending. She knew he was always looking at his purchases and all of the impacts they would have, a long time before he finally made up his mind.

He told Wanda that when they got home he was going to have Becky Brock do a complete financial summary of all the monies they had and of the properties they owned. He said he wanted to get rid of the majority of their paper dollars and put his value into land and property that would last beyond everything else. Wanda added, "We need to start thinking about the next few years and how we are going to make a fair distribution of our estate." Chalk agreed.

The evening came slowly and everyone had a nice dinner in the hotel restaurant. The sun was almost gone and the whole family was sitting on the patio as the last signs of daylight faded over the western horizon. They went inside and all sat around discussing the highlights of the day. Everybody had enjoyed a great day. Then they started to plan what they were going to do tomorrow. Chalk said he wanted to rent a carriage and take Wanda all around the area and see what the homes and surrounding hills had to offer. The kids were not interested in looking at houses. They both said they would like to stay around the hotel, go down on the beach and go to see some nearby nice places to eat and shop. Carl made a comment that he had met some really nice young girls and wanted to go back to the beach. Tomorrow had been planned.

The next morning got off to a slow start. Chalk was awake first and he was taking a shower when he realized it was 8:30. He hardly ever slept that late. Soon everyone else was up. Wanda put on some cool cotton clothes and Chalk put on some brand new casual, but nice summer shorts.

Kenneth Orr

Breakfast was eagerly eaten in the hotel restaurant and the food was really good. The sun was high in the sky by 10:00 AM and Chalk took Wanda by the hand and said, "Lets get out of here and see the town, these kids want to be away from us old folks for a while."

They went to the street and quickly found a carriage and driver who was aware of all of the local places and neighborhoods. They spent the day riding and looking and talking. It was a lot of fun and Chalk was making mental notes about the different areas and development opportunities he saw.

When they got back to the room the kids were gone and there was a note saying they had found some stores that sold *the right kind of clothes* and they both were looking around. Wanda had given each of them some pocket money and it was burning a hole in their pockets. In about an hour Barbara and Carl returned. They had bought several small tourist targeted things and they were happy.

Chalk sat down and Wanda told him how much she loved this area. Chalk was equally impressed. Chalk told Wanda that he wanted to see if some of the open land they had seen was for sale; that is, at a reasonable price. She smiled and said, "That's a great idea." They agreed that this area would be a great place to spend the winter and land in this community would certainly become a good long-term investment.

The next morning they went to a small building that had a sign advertising "Land For Sale." Chalk and Wanda went in and said they were looking to see what was available in a certain area. The lady at the desk said that the man in charge was in the back and she called him to come to the front area. He came quickly. Chalk introduced Wanda and himself and told him they were looking to see what land was available in an area just north of the town. Chalk also asked if there were any good buys in homes in that area. The man smiled and said, "I think I can help you in both areas of your interests."

The Cowboy's Kids

The salesman got out a big map and unfolded it on a big table. The map had been marked to identify plots of open land in the surrounding area. He said that some land with ocean views was still available but was going quickly. Chalk spoke of a specific plot he had seen the past day and the man said it was available. He also said that his family owned this particular land and they were anxious to find a buyer. The land had been in his family for many years but they were now looking to dispose of it.

Chalk asked what the asking price might be. The salesman told him $1,275 per acre in a 30-acre minimum plot. Chalk looked ay Wanda and said, "Oh my, "That's really a lot of money for such a small plot of land. Back home in Texas, an acre of prime land was never over $100, and sometimes it's only $10." The man just looked at them and was waiting for another response. It did not come.

The salesman thought they had been turned away by the cost and he said, "If you buy two or three plots the price will go down to $750 per acre." Immediately, Chalk knew that this was a buyer's market so he told Wanda to come outside with him.

They talked and went back into the office. Chalk had seen the land and he knew that this was an outstanding investment but he did not want to make a commitment until he had negotiated the best price. He and Wanda sat down and said, " Would you give us a better price if we bought 10 tracts?" The salesman scratched his head and said, "Let me do some quick math." He went to the back room and it seemed like he was gone forever. Then he came back and said, " This is choice ocean view land and the only reason that I have been able to cut the price is that most of the best home builders and most of the skilled labor are all in San Francisco rebuilding the city's homes. But, my family has owned this land for several years and we want to get rid of it now. If you would buy 100 acres I can let you have it for $500 per acre. We also have a new home that my brother built and is trying to sell that we can make you a great deal

Kenneth Orr

on. It is located in the largest tract area. We want $33,000 for the home, and it is elegant."

Chalk told Wanda that they needed to think this over and told the salesman that they would be back to him within a day or two. He understood and said the prices were good for 48 hours. Chalk went back to the hotel and immediately sent a telegram to Becky Brock back in Bandera.

He knew he had a lot of money in his personal account but he wanted to see if the ranch property account had enough available money to buy this property on a cash basis. He knew he had enough money on hand but did not want to become too thin financially to maintain the ranch operation. The telegram was sent but it was late in the day and the arrival would not be until the next morning. Wanda was thrilled and she knew that this was a really great deal if they could pull it off.

The next morning Becky got the telegram. She got out her books and saw that the ranch operation had a little over $1,877,000 on deposit in the local banks. She called the local Bandera bankers and verified the balance. She sent Chalk a return telegram telling him the account balance. Becky added that word had come concerning Stan's brother. She had heard late the day before that he had died in France from his injuries.

Chalk got the news at about 9:00 AM the next morning and he was careful to keep the telegram away from Barbara. He knew she would be very upset. Wanda suggested that they not tell Barbara while they were on vacation. Chalk agreed. He told Wanda the financial news and they agreed to go and try to make a deal on the land and potentially on the new home.

The salesman had identified the home that was for sale. It was the same fancy new home that they had seen when they were just looking around the day before. Wanda really liked the house; as the backside was facing the ocean. The outside of the house was all stone. The inside was well

The Cowboy's Kids

designed. It had large rooms and all the floors were tiled with beautiful colors and floor designs.

They went to the sales office and the salesman was eagerly waiting. He had placed all of the land maps on a big table and had everything in good order for Chalk and Wanda to review. Chalk went over to the table and Wanda followed. They had told the kids that they were looking to buy some land but that was all that had been said. Wanda knew that if they bought more than land, especially a house, it would surprise the kids and get them all wound up on California. They looked at the maps and asked to take a ride out to the property and see what they were about to consider buying before they said anything.

The salesman hired a nice large carriage and everybody went for a ride.

The land was indeed a choice piece of property, as the ocean was in full view from most of the land. Most of the sites were level and would be choice locations for home building. Big trees and good soil were common on the entire tract. There was undergrowth on much of the land but that could be cleared and the view would be outstanding.

Wanda and Chalk went inside the house and looked at all of the features. It was located on the best plot of land. She told Chalk that she really liked it. There were no paved roads, just dirt trails but that was not a major problem to Chalk. He knew that improvements were going to be a part of the cost if he wanted to make the property more marketable. He also knew that not having paved roads would be a good bargaining point for him to get a better price.

The carriage went back to the sales office. Chalk and Wanda were very quiet all the way back. It was near noon and Chalk said, "We need to get something to eat." The salesman took them to a nearby restaurant and recommended the Mexican menu to the Goodwin's. Food was selected and Chalk had a large chilled glass of Kentucky's best bourbon with his meal.

Kenneth Orr

Wanda had a glass of California white wine. Everyone agreed that the food was delicious. Chalk looked across the table at the salesman and said, "Your land appeals to us and I want to make you a hard and one-time offer." The salesman said, "I am listening."

Chalk said, "I understand you are asking a fair price for your land. We are looking to buy this property as an investment and we will need to have a better price to make this worth our investment and time. I am willing to pay you cash if you accept my offer." The salesman said, "That's great." Chalk said, "I will give you $48,000 for the 100 acres of land and $22,000 for the house. That is a total of $70,000. I can write you a check right now and the bank in Texas will verify the validity of the check with a telegram.

The salesman looked at them and said, "Now I need to make some considerations." He said, "Can I have a couple of hours to get with my family and to see what they think?" Chalk said his offer was good for 24 hours but he was going to be leaving for Texas in a couple of days and needed to have this deal all wrapped up prior to leaving. Chalk stressed that this was raw, undeveloped land with only dirt roads and no major utility improvements. Everyone agreed to the timetable and went their ways. When they got back to their room, Carl was sleeping on an outdoor hammock.

Wanda and Chalk got a nice chair on the patio overlooking the ocean. They talked a few minutes and then called the kids to join them. They told them, "We have made an offer for the house that everyone had liked. We should know before we go home if this deal is going to happen." Chalk took a long breath and said, "Carl, you may have to live in California some day to keep this house in shape." Carl said, "I liked it here and this is a really nice place to have a house." Barbara said that the thought of a house this far from Texas was going to be a lot of confusion and problem. She loved Texas and did not want to live this far away. Carl spoke up and said, "There were some really pretty girls walking on the beach and that was really a good reason

The Cowboy's Kids

to have this house." Wanda smiled and saw that the house would be a great purchase in Carl's way of thinking.

Dinnertime came and everyone was sweaty and hot from sitting outside in the sun. Everyone cleaned up and Chalk suggested that they get some dinner. Everybody was excited about the potential new house deal but they were also getting hungry. They all enjoyed dinner and said they would get up early the next morning and go look at the house one more time.

The next morning Chalk hired a carriage and they drove off to the north. The house was about a 10-minute ride away and the road went right by a great looking Chinese restaurant. Wanda liked the looks and said she wanted to eat there before they left the area. Chalk agreed. He always wanted to please Wanda and good food was an easy approach.

They arrived at the house and the real estate man and three other people were there. They were all glad to see Chalk and soon everyone was looking at the house and talking about the ocean view. The salesman identified and introduced the other people as his brother and two sisters. They were discussing Chalk's offer and trying to come to a final conclusion.

The salesman took Chalk aside and said that they had discussed his offer and wanted to make a counter offer. He said that if Chalk would add $4,000 to his best offer they would accept.

Chalk went to talk it over with Wanda and they both said that they had told the salesman that this was a firm offer, not a haggle point with the price offer. They were a little upset with the salesman suggesting a counter offer.

Chalk also said that they were obviously good people and this was substantially less than they originally wanted. He said, "Let's add $2,000 to our original offer and make this

Kenneth Orr

our best and final offer, take it or we are not interested." Wanda agreed.

Chalk went back to the salesman and told him of their final decision. He looked at them a minute and took out a house key and said, "Mister, this is now your house." Chalk was not surprised. He went to Wanda, showed her the key and told her the news. She called the kids over and let them know that the deal was done. Everybody was happy. Chalk signed a bill of sale covering the total final price and gave it to the salesman.

Chalk invited the salesman, his brother and sisters to have dinner with them in the Chinese restaurant. They said that there was a much better restaurant just a short way from town so everybody agreed to go there and eat. The meal was great and the people had more in common than they knew, before they sat down.

The salesman, who also was one of the property owners, said he was a former navy officer. His family was a long time native California family. They were all deeply religious Catholics and were currently involved in several local retail businesses. The salesman's brother and one sister owned a furniture store. The other sister owned several apartments where sailors with families could live while on shore duty.

Wanda liked his sister and told her that she wanted to furnish the new house in local fashions and to have it ready to live in by the next time they came to California. The meeting was beneficial as they agreed to furnish the home and to make it into a vacation place for the Goodwin's. Wanda gave her an idea as to a budget and said that she could use her judgment for the most part, but to keep her informed by mail as to what was happening. This relationship grew over the years and they all became good and trusted friends.

After dinner the Goodwin's and the real estate salesman went back to the hotel. Chalk opened a new bottle of white wine and everyone had a nice smooth drink. There was also a small glass, just for tasting, for Carl. Chalk wrote a check

The Cowboy's Kids

to be a down payment toward furniture. He also requested that the salesman have the proper documents concerning the land and the house ready to sign the next day.

Chalk said he could have the check for the land and house ready when the paperwork was in good order. He also wanted to have a lawyer review the deal and verify everything before he turned loose of any funds. Everybody agreed to the schedule and the near nighttime ocean view watching, was the next order of business.

Train travel was now becoming a concern to Chalk. He wanted to see if the return trip to Texas could be scheduled to avoid the major detour they had taken to get to California. He went to the local train station with all of his return tickets and asked the ticket agent for the current status. To Chalk's pleasure, the ticket agent announced that the most southern route was now open and he could reroute their trip. New tickets were issued and Chalk now had a scheduled departure time for 4:30 PM, three days from then. That was great, it allowed some additional time for the real estate deal to be completed. It also allows more time for Wanda to look at furniture and everyone to see some additional places around the area. Wanda wanted to go back to see some more of the stores in the better districts of San Diego; so did Barbara.

The paperwork covering the real estate transaction was completed and everyone was satisfied with the new situation that had been created. Wanda and Barbara spent an additional day in San Diego shopping.

While in the city center area, they saw a beautiful Mission building and decided to go inside. When they entered they saw several worshippers kneeling at the front altar preying. They just stood quietly in the back and looked around. Soon, a religious man dressed in a white robe came to them. He said he was Brother Benedictine and identified himself as the Mission's Priest. He welcomed them and asked if they were Christians. Wanda said that they were and that they went to a Lutheran church back home in Texas. The Priest

Kenneth Orr

thanked them for stopping and took them for a short, but very interesting tour. He told them how Spanish monks had traveled to the area from Mexico over 100 years ago and established missions all along the California coastal area. The Monks, he told them, had traveled as far north as San Francisco and had built missions at several locations as they traveled north.

The Monks had brought the Christian religion to the area and built missions in places where the local people needed to be taught about Jesus. Soon the missions were the religious centers for the local communities. The Missions were the center of the early social activities. The Missions helped keep peace in areas that were not always safe. Wanda and Barbara were interested and told the priest that they had an old Mission near their town back in Texas. She said the Mission was named "The Alamo". Wanda thanked him for his tour and turned to leave. The Priest came forward and put a hand on both Barbara and Wanda's shoulders and blessed them in the name of the Church. Wanda dropped a coin in the donations box that was sitting by the doorway.

Carl and Chalk went for a fishing trip out in the ocean. The boat was harbored at a pier near the commercial ship docks. The area around the docks was also full of bars and brothels. The whole fishing experience was tempered by an uneasy feeling when they caught the boat. The people in the area were not friendly looking and the San Diego police were visible on every corner.

The fishing boat went out to the open sea and ventured out to a reef where the captain said the fishing was sometimes very good. They never caught any fish but the trip was a real experience for both of them. They both saw first hand what life on a fishing pier was really like. They both were glad to be headed back to the hotel. The final days in California were relaxing and were a lot of fun for everyone. Carl and Barbara were very happy and the entire Goodwin family was starting to look forward to going home.

The Cowboy's Kids

The real estate paperwork was complete on the second day. Chalk had a local lawyer review everything and he found the documents all to be in good order. The final part of the transaction was for the final check to be written. The paperwork was all done and the sellers were anxious to get their money. Chalk told them to have everything ready that evening and he would write the check. The salesman had Chalk and Wanda meet him at the county clerk's office and the documents were filed and Chalk wrote the check. The transaction went smoothly and the bank in Texas quickly approved the funding.

This event was a final ending for the vacation in California. Now it was time to get ready to go back to Texas.

CHAPTER 1-10
Going Home and Counting Their Blessings

The "Go home to Texas day" arrived and everyone arrived at the train station in San Diego about an hour early. They had taken a carriage from LaJolla to the train station in San Diego just to see the local sights one more time. The night before was busy as they packed, ate at their now "favorite Mexican restaurant" and got ready to travel. They all got as much rest as they could because they knew sleeping on the train was not that easy. The train to the east was going to be hot and jolting and everyone knew what was coming. The Goodwin baggage stack was bigger and the list of vacation stories to take home seemed endless. Carl was glad to be going home but he was also sad to leave the ocean. He had made a personal connection with the area that would stay with him all of his life. He told Chalk that the girls in California were really pretty.

Barbara was quiet. She told Wanda that she was worried about Stan and his brother and wanted to get home and see if there had been any further messages. Wanda understood but still was keeping Becky Brock's news to herself.

The train was on time and everyone boarded about 30 minutes before it was scheduled to leave. They had a four-person compartment and the area was the same size as the compartment on the previous train. Carl checked out

The Cowboy's Kids

the whole train and had developed a good understanding of what accommodations were on board. The club car was real nice. Chalk went to see if the bartender was qualified to supply good Kentucky whiskey. The bartender passed the test and Chalk had a good big glass over ice before the train pulled out. Wanda just settled back with Barbara and got comfortable. The seats were upholstered in soft mohair fabrics. The compartment was comfortable and the trip was hopefully going to be less stressful than the one they had when they came to California.

The train conductor told Chalk that the train was going to travel east crossing a hot desert area in southern California. They would be crossing a bridge over the Colorado River north of Yuma, Arizona. Then the tracks would go almost directly east to Tucson, Arizona. The entire area in western Arizona was a desert and there were few towns in this area. The only stops would be at water towers where the train would quickly refuel and be off toward the east again. From Tucson, the train would go east to Benson and then Wilcox, Arizona. The next stop would be in New Mexico and then they would go thru Deming and Las Cruces. The train would cross the Rio Grande River in New Mexico and go south to El Paso, Texas.

The train they were riding, was going to Dallas, Texas. Chalk's family would need to change trains and wait in El Paso for a train to arrive from somewhere else. This was anticipated to be a five-hour layover.

The second train would leave El Paso at 7:30 in the evening and was supposed to take about eighteen hours to get to San Antonio, Texas. The trip would be about eight hours of nighttime travel and would arrive in San Antonio the following afternoon.

Chalk thanked the conductor for taking time to explain the trip so well and Wanda was equally thankful. She asked if the train would be going through any steep mountain areas? The conductor said the route was not in any major mountain area but there were some long track grades in California

Kenneth Orr

and Arizona. He said he had made this trip many times and the ride was much less stressful than going through the high mountains further up north. The conductor had traveled on most of the western routes and understood the concerns that were present. Everyone was thankful.

The time to leave arrived. All of the passengers got on board, the whistle sounded, the conductor hollered out "All Aboard," and the trip began. San Diego was soon far behind and the hot tan sand and low desert plants were everywhere. Several water stops were made in route. When the train would stop, the hot desert air would fill the car and the temperature would go up. There was plenty of ice in the coolers at the front of the car and cold drinking water was plentiful. Just as the conductor had outlined, they crossed the river at Yuma, Arizona and they were in a not–so- beautiful small border town. The train stopped and a new crew of train personnel got on board.

The Mexico international border was just south of the town and many of the buildings looked a lot like ones in south Texas. Chalk told Carl that he needed to look out the window and study the land. Where water was available, there was green vegetation and where water was not available there was a brown colored desert. Chalk pointed out several other differences. The area had some deeper areas where water would run off during rains. There were a few things growing in the bottom these areas. The Indians had built adobe houses using mud that also required water. Carl was all eyes and questions.

At Yuma the train took on mail, more water and fuel. Some new passengers got on the train. Nobody got off. The stop was quick and soon the train was traveling east again. Chalk went to the club car and ordered his regular Kentucky whiskey. He was by himself and had a small table next to a window that was cracked just enough to let some outside air circulate. The area was soon crowded with men who had similar thirst desires.

The Cowboy's Kids

A tall thin man saw that there was an empty chair at Chalk's table and asked if he could join him. Chalk said, "Sure, that chair looks like it needs a fresh butt in it." They laughed and began to talk. The man said his name was Malcolm and he was going to Tucson. Chalk introduced himself and said he was a rancher from Texas.

Malcolm said he was going to Tucson to look at a job as a reporter for the local newspaper. He had been working at a major newspaper in San Francisco but the earthquake and fires had wiped him out. He said his wife was killed from falling building parts and his son had been injured but survived. His job went away when the newspaper owner told everyone that the paper was not going to need as many people in the future, so he and his son had gone to Los Angeles to find a new life.

His entire savings were gone. The bank, where he had a bank account, had burned and all of the records and proof of his holdings were lost. He had been lucky to get a ride on a cargo ship to Los Angles. When he arrived there, he was broke. A local church had helped him and he soon had a small job in another newspaper office. Two months later his son died from injuries he had suffered in the earthquake. Malcolm was now all alone. He had given up on living in California and was going to Arizona where he had a brother. The work situation in Arizona was better, but the pay was much less. He was desperate to get a new start and this was an opportunity.

Chalk just listened and let Malcolm talk. He was obviously a man with problems and needed to have a way to let off some of his frustrations. Chalk asked him about what he thought of the efforts to rebuild San Francisco. Malcolm immediately got red faced and said that the bankers and money institutions were all out for themselves and that the working class of people were being made into slaves by unreasonable loans and crooked lawyers. Malcolm said, "Never trust a lawyer, a banker or a preacher". Chalks asked "Why?" Malcolm said, "The bankers are out to line their pockets with your money, the lawyers are not honest and

Kenneth Orr

are working the law just to make money and the preachers all tell you that they can save your soul. Well, all of that soul talk is useless when you are starving and the roof over your head was the open sky." Chalk smiled and just let him talk.

Chalk knew that there was a lot of truth in what Malcolm was reflecting and he was trying to remember everything he was saying. The key thing was that the banks were burned and the man's wealth was gone. The lost money was the real problem that was keeping Malcolm in a destitute condition, he had lost all of his assets. This was the same topic that Chalk just been thinking about while in California He had met a man that knew first hand what losing our wealth in a fire could do.

Malcolm had been a good family man and his place in society was relatively important and comfortable. Now it was all gone and he was looking to find a job and to get his life back on track. Chalk bought him a second drink, wished him well and then he went back to his compartment.

Chalk told Wanda about his conversation with Malcolm and said, "We are blessed to be where we are, with a fine family, money in the bank and good friends." He added, "We need to be sure we protect these blessings and that we are able to pass them on to others who will appreciate them when we die. That's going to become a major part of our life from here on."

The train pulled into Tucson and Chalk watched as the passengers left the train. Malcolm was one of the first people to get off. A man and woman, who were obviously glad to see him, extended a warm greeting. They all disappeared into the crowd and soon the new passengers were on board and the train pulled out heading toward the southeast. There was a fuel stop about five miles out of town and the train made a short stop for servicing.

It was now getting dark and Wanda said she was hungry. Everyone went to the dining car but there were no available

The Cowboy's Kids

tables. The porter told Chalk that they could order food from the menu and he would bring it to their compartment. This arrangement was fine with everyone. Everybody selected their dinners they wanted and went to the compartment. Soon the food arrived. It was warm and delicious and soon everyone was ready to go to sleep. The entire vacation trip had been a series of adventures and new experiences. Now, with the train chugging along, going toward home, in the cool Arizona desert nighttime, everyone could relax and not be concerned about tomorrow.

The train had passed through all of Arizona, and when the sun was coming up, the small town of Deming, New Mexico was coming into view. The porter came through the passenger car announcing that he had hot coffee and sandwiches. Wanda was awake and she shook Chalk and told him she wanted a cup of coffee. Chalk went to the porter's cart and got two cups of coffee and two small bottles of milk for the kids. The compartment had a small icebox. All of the ice had melted and the water and juice that they had put in the box the night before, was too warm to drink. The kids still liked milk and juice for breakfast, and this would hold them over until they went to the dining car. The smell of fresh hot coffee, by itself, was refreshment and it made the first taste even more satisfying.

The day went quickly and soon the train was on a steep downhill grade headed for Las Cruces, New Mexico. The local train station was right in the center of town and there was a train on the track that was headed west. The eastbound train had to pull off onto a siding until the other train finished it's local business and pulled out. The other train was almost a full hour behind schedule and the conductor was not sure as to why. Finally, they saw the westbound train pass and they pulled into the station. The stop was not long, but the railroad employees attached several freight cars onto the rear of the passenger train.

The conductor went in the office and did some railroad business and returned. He saw Chalk and said the westbound train was so slow because there had been a man die onboard

Kenneth Orr

as the train was traveling. The local undertaker had to take the body off the train and several of the passengers who were traveling with the man also left the train. This situation took a lot of time that was not planned. Chalk thanked him for the information and asked him if this delay was going to be a problem. The conductor said he was sure that there was no problem in making his connection in El Paso.

In about an hour the train crossed the state border into Texas. Soon it was at the passenger terminal in El Paso. The Goodwin's were now back in Texas and they all were happy to be getting closer to home. They collected their compartment baggage, left the train and loaded all of their baggage and personal items onto two small carts. They found out that they were going to be required to wait about three hours to board the next and final train. For convenience, they put all of their baggage in a depot luggage locker, got the key and went to find a restaurant. There were several nearby restaurants, but they were all rather dirty and were focused on feeding the workers who were working at the railroad roundhouse.

Chalk hailed a passing carriage and asked the driver to take them to a good restaurant. Soon they were standing in a fancy hotel lobby. The hotel had a really elegant restaurant overlooking the Rio Grande River. The menu said they specialized in beef and cabrito and everything was served family style. Wanda saw the menu and said it all looked good and the waiter instantly disappeared. Soon a line of waiters with platters of meat and fresh vegetables appeared. The food was delicious and the cost was way below what Chalk had anticipated. He tipped the waiter, got a carriage and they all went back to the train station. Chalk always liked to eat well and while on a vacation he made sure every meal was good and adequate for his family. Everybody was adding weight from all of the rich and delicious food.

Their next train had just pulled into the station and soon the conductor started boarding passengers. The train had come south from Albuquerque, New Mexico and was about half full of passengers. Chalk had reserved a compartment

The Cowboy's Kids

and the conductor said that the deluxe unit was available for no additional charge. Chalk gladly said he was happy to have the better accommodation and tipped the conductor for his kindness. Everyone got on board, got comfortable and started to relax again.

Carl went to all of the different cars and surveyed everything. He had already learned to make a quick trip all the way through the train so he knew what was on board. He returned to the compartment and told Chalk that the club car was nice and the bartender had a lot of bottles on the rack behind the bar. He also told Chalk that there were three pretty young girls in a car just ahead. Chalk just smiled.

The day was about over as the train left the station and soon the night sky was lit up brilliantly by a full moon. It almost seemed like a dim day outside as the shadows of trees and small plants reflected across the west Texas soil. Bedtime came quickly and the click from the wheels was working like a smooth melody to put one to sleep. It was obvious to everyone that sleep was in order. Soon the compartment was quiet, except for an occasional snore from Chalk.

The sun came up right on time, and Chalk was awake with the anticipation of getting home. The train stopped at Junction, Texas and took on water and passengers. Chalk asked the conductor if the train would be stopping at Hondo, Texas. The conductor said, "Yes, we take on water there." Chalk asked if they could get off there rather than go all the way to San Antonio.

The conductor said, "Sure, but we do not refund any money on your tickets if you get off there." Chalk said he understood and a refund was not an issue.

The Conductor told everyone to get their baggage together and be ready to get off quickly as this stop was short and the train was trying to make up some time. The conductor went to the baggage car and had all of the Goodwin's other baggage brought to their compartment. Everybody

Kenneth Orr

understood and soon the train pulled into the small water tower and station area in downtown Hondo. The Goodwin's got off and all of their baggage was with them.

The train sounded the whistle and was soon on its way to San Antonio. The Goodwin's were all standing beside the railroad tracks and smiling as they watched the train pull out of sight. They were almost home

Chalk owned a small wagon and ranch supply company that was located about five blocks from the railroad station. Chalk saw a man with a wagon passing and hailed him down. He asked if he would take them to the small store he owned and the man said he would be glad to do the favor. They all climbed on the wagon. Wanda took a seat next to the driver and everyone else found a place to sit in the back. The baggage was stacked in the middle.

The wagon went straight to the store and the store manager saw them coming and was shocked to see a wagonload of folks pulling up. He did not recognize Chalk until he went to the back of the wagon. When he saw it was Chalk and his family, he got a big wide smile on his face. Everyone got down and Chalk thanked the wagon driver and offered to pay him. He refused any money and said, "Just glad to be of service to such nice people." He drove away.

Chalk asked his manager how things were going with the business. He got a positive response. He asked Chalk if he needed a ride to Bandera. Chalk replied, "I guess that would be a lot easier than walking all of the way." Everybody smiled and soon there was a nice new wagon with two fresh horses parked in front of the store. Chalk said, "I will drive this rig home and have it back here within a week."

The manager said, "That's fine. I have got a customer interested in buying that wagon and he is not going to be back for about four weeks. I can tell him it was a demonstrator model and he will think he is getting a better deal."

The Cowboy's Kids

In about three hours the carriage pulled into the Goodwin ranch front gate. Nobody had been expecting them to be home at this time and their arrival was a surprise to everyone.

Gator, Carl's dog, was the first to greet them. His tail was going back and forth and he wanted to lick everybody. That was his standard method to welcome people that he knew.

The housekeeper heard the dog and came to the door. Everyone was getting out of the wagon and she was all smiles as she opened the door and hugged Wanda and Barbara. They all went into the living room and soon the commotion for the unannounced arrival had died down. Everybody was doing a lot of talking and drinking a lot of cold well water.

Sarge, who was working out in the barn, had heard the commotion and went up to the main house. He saw an unfamiliar wagon and went to the door to see who was there. He had not expected Chalk, and was concerned that somebody new had come to visit. He opened the door and saw Chalk sitting in his favorite chair, fortified with a glass of Kentucky's best. He went in and Chalk stood up, shook his hand and asked him to join him for a drink. Sarge gladly agreed.

Chalk and Sarge had a good conversation. The Goodwin family was exhausted from all of the travel. Chalk suggested that everyone rest a little. The vacation was over and the next few days were going to be full of free time to talk about all that they had seen and done. Carl and Barbara unloaded the baggage from the wagon and put it in the house. The wagon and horses were put in the stable and everything was in a proper place. The vacation was over.

Nighttime came quickly and the housekeeper made sure everyone went to bed with a full stomach. The day was done and tomorrow would be a good day, just because they were all safely home.

BOOK TWO OF THREE
Reality, Pain And Adjustments to Manage The Future

CHAPTER 2-1
Facing The Realities of Life

The first day back home was filled with the sounds and wetness of a summer thunderstorm. Large bolts of lightning were striking all around the ranch. Everyone was awakened early and the morning was off to a bad weather start.

Before Wanda had gone to sleep, she had a long talk with Chalk as how to let Barbara know that Stan's brother had died in France. They decided to have Wanda and Barbara go for a walk sometime in the morning and along the way Wanda would bring up the subject. Wanda was hoping that Barbara would not be upset that she was not told earlier. Wanda had already determined, that to have told her earlier, served no good or timely purpose but would spoil her vacation.

Wanda loved Barbara very much, as did Chalk, and they both wanted to be by her side if they were ever needed. This was going to be one of those times. Chalk was going to be home and said he would watch Wanda for any signal, should he be needed.

The storm had changed the timing of the planned walk but within an hour after dawn the clouds cleared and blue skies reappeared. Barbara was anxious for news from the war and as they were eating breakfast she asked Chalk to

Kenneth Orr

call Becky Brock and see if there was any new messages from Stan.

Chalk said he was getting some things together to talk about with to Mrs. Brock, and he wanted to allow her time to get the office open and the mail picked up. Barbara agreed with Chalk's schedule and went on with having her breakfast. The rain had stopped and there were several places in the horse barn where people could sit down.

As soon as Wanda was finished eating, she asked Barbara to join her for a walk out to see the horses. Wanda said that they had not seen their favorite horses since the went to California. Barbara stood up and went to the door with Wanda. As she went out she looked at Chalk and said, "Don't forget to call Becky". Chalk said, "I will remember." Barbara went on outside with Wanda.

Wanda and Barbara went out to the horse barn and there was a small bench just inside the main door. The doors were open and a clear view of the interior from outside was available. Wanda said she wanted to sit down for a minute. Barbara joined her. Wanda opened the conversation and asked Barbara how much she really cared about Stan. Barbara said, "He is a really good person and he reminds me of dad a lot. He has the spunk and the attitude that it takes to get ahead and he wants to be a doctor someday."

Wanda asked Barbara if she had become serious about Stan and how much he talked about his brother. Barbara said she was more serious about Stan than she had realized and that Stan's brother was very close to him. Wanda said, "Barbara, I am afraid I have to bring you some bad news. I love you very much and this is a hard thing to talk about." She spoke very slowly and with a trembling voice said, "We have learned that Stan's brother had died in France and that he was probably buried somewhere over there." Barbara just looked at Wanda and her face went blank. Then she grabbed Wanda and began crying and holding on to her as she wept. Chalk had been watching from the window and went to be with both of the women in his life. He knew they

The Cowboy's Kids

were both crying, and when he joined them, everyone was crying.

Carl was watching, but had no idea as to what was happening. He went to be with his family and asked Chalk what was wrong. Chalk told him about Stan's brother and explained that Barbara cared a lot for Stan and she was very much concerned.

In a few minutes everybody went into the house and Barbara went into her room and asked to be left alone for a while. Wanda knew she needed some time to get a grip on herself and get over the shock. Chalk went to the phone and called Becky Brock.

Becky was surprised to hear his voice and told him that she was looking forward to seeing him and his family. Chalk told her he would be coming into town later but wanted to know if Stan had sent any further messages. Becky said yes, one had come yesterday and it was not good. He was leaving that day on a troop ship to go somewhere in Europe and join the fighting men on the front lines. The army wanted him as he had training to be a veterinarian and they needed his talents.

Chalk thanked her for the information and told her he would see her later in the day. He then went to Wanda and told her the latest news. Wanda took Chalk by the hand and went to Barbara's door and knocked. Barbara came to the door and opened it slowly. Wanda said they had some additional news and wanted to come in and talk with her. She quickly agreed and when everybody was in the room, Chalk closed the door.

Wanda said Chalk had just talked to Becky Brock and she had a message from Stan. Chalk told her what he had learned and Barbara was obviously concerned. She also knew that it would not be possible to get in touch with him, as he was away from all communication sources.

Kenneth Orr

Chalk went out into the living area and looked at Carl. He said, "Carl, lets get our horses out and go see Becky Brock. The women need some time alone and we are in their way." Carl understood and he put on his riding boots and his new white navy cap.

They went to the stable, got their horses out in the center area, and put on the saddles. Chalk went back into the house for a minute and told Wanda that they were going to town and if she needed them, to call Becky. Wanda understood, and Chalk and Carl were off to Bandera.

Bandera was still the same town that they had grown to love, but as they rode into the business area Carl spoke up and said, "Bandera was really a small town." Chalk said, "Well son, you have seen a new part of the big world and as you get older a lot of things will become a lot more exciting and challenging. This country is growing so fast and the opportunities out there are going to become ever more interesting. As I look back I see just how much change has happened and it really has surprised me. However, the changes over your life will probably be even more dynamic and certainly a lot more challenging."

They pulled up in front of the downtown ranch office and tied the horses to the hitching rail. They went in and Becky saw them coming. She went outside and hugged them both. She told Carl that his cowboy hat had lost the rim and he was going to get his ears sunburned. Carl laughed. Chalk took out a small leather pouch and gave it to Becky. She was surprised. Chalk said, "Open it Becky, it's for you. It came from Arizona." Becky opened the pouch and saw a small turquoise studded pin. It was shaped like a horse and had a nice pin on the back to put it on her dress. She put it on her dress and looked at it for a minute. She was very happy. Then they got down to business.

Becky said she had done a complete inventory of all of Chalk's assets and she had been surprised to discover just how much profit the ranches had earned. Chalk said, "That's good, but I'm hungry and that can wait until we get some

The Cowboy's Kids

lunch." Becky was always a thrifty lady and took her lunch to work.

Chalk told her to skip her lunchbox and let's all go get some great Mexican food. They walked down the street and went into the best restaurant in town. Carl was always ready to eat and he was pleased with Chalk's decision. He had been on a scale and said he had gained about 10 pounds over the past couple of months. He was becoming a big boy!

They ordered lunch and everyone had a giant glass of iced tea. Chalk brought up the message from Stan and said that Wanda was at home with Barbara who was very upset with all of the bad news. Chalk said, "But, I have some news that you will be interested to hear." Becky said she was waiting to hear and sat back. Chalk told her about the land and house they had just bought in California.

Becky was all ears and her attention went immediately to the new house. She said, "Mr. Goodwin, are you going to move to California?" Chalk just laughed and looked at her like she was supposed to be in shock. He said, "The house is just an investment and we will probably use it as a vacation home when we want to get away from Texas. The rest of the time we will probably rent it." Becky looked relieved.

Chalk told Becky that he had made some serious financial decisions while on the trip and over the next year he was going to find some safe ways to better protect his assets. Becky just listened and was wondering what was ahead.

Lunch was over and they all went back to the ranch office. Becky's two assistants were busy and were glad to see Chalk. Carl had a big and obvious food drip from his lunch on his shirt. One of the office ladies took him into the bathroom and cleaned him up. Chalk wanted to spend some time with Becky and look at the books, sign some checks and review the financial summary she had put together for his review.

Kenneth Orr

He gave Carl a few coins and told him to go find some windows to look in. He was supposed to be back in about an hour. He understood and was off to see the pocketknife selection in the hardware store.

Becky had all of the bills ready for review and as usual all of the big dollar checks were made out and only needed Chalk's signature. The ranches were still making a reasonable profits but the rate of return was much lower with smaller orders for army horses. Cattle were still making reasonable money but the profits were also lower. Chalk noted this and asked Becky to plot the pattern over the past three years and show him what was happening as a trend. She agreed and the next subject was brought up.

Becky had made a list of all of the ranch properties that were owned, all of the other business interests that Chalk had acquired, the bank balance for the ranches and the personal accounts that Chalk and Wanda had in all of the several banks where they were doing business. The total dollar amounts were much higher than Chalk had realized.

He told Becky to set up a new category that will be called "Goodwin Investments". He told her to make sure the bank balance at his primary bank reflected the purchase price for the California properties and to add the value of the land and new house in this category. Becky called the bank, checked with them on balances, made some quick pencil adjustments and the books were verified as accurate.

He told Becky about what he was thinking about how he wanted to protect his wealth and how he also wanted to keep his valued employees financially secure for the rest of their lives.

He said he had met a man on the train who went from being well off, to being a completely broke man because of the San Francisco earthquake. He also told her that the man had never trusted bankers, lawyers, preachers and quick-tongued salesmen. They are all out to make themselves wealthy while they use other people's money. He had also

The Cowboy's Kids

discussed that printed-paper; both money and securities, can become worthless with no warning. He said. "There are only a few things that hold value and cannot be destroyed." He pointed out that good land, gold, silver and natural assets like copper ore and water rights, were much more secure. Becky understood and listened with a high level of interest.

Chalk said that one of the fastest growth areas for the country was going to be in California and in the states that were surrounded by the new hydroelectric dam being built in Nevada.

Chalk added, "The state of California is building long canals to bring water to the coastal cities and these two new assets will spark the development this area is ready to undergo. Land in the right locations will be extremely valuable in the near future." He also added, "California is also a high-risk real estate area due to earthquakes and soil that will shift easily. However, the southern part of the state seems to be more stable that the north."

Then he talked about the ranches and their futures. He said. "There were several people who had been working to support with him since the beginning and he wanted to have them become owners of part of the property. He also wanted them to have the means to live comfortable for the rest of their normal lives.

He knew the horse ranches were going to become less valuable because army horses were going to become less marketable in the near future.

Chalk asked Becky to order a local map of the areas where the two ranches were located. The county offices had a service that made such maps and sold them to property owners. He wanted to see exactly where his land lay and how it could be divided into smaller ranches making sure that each one had available water. Becky understood.

Kenneth Orr

He asked Becky if she still had a loan against her home? She said, "Yes." He asked her what it would take to pay it off? She thought for a minute and said about $2,000. Chalk told her to get in touch with the bank and get an exact amount, then write a check from the ranch account to cover the amount. He would sign it and her house would be all hers. She asked him why was he doing this. Chalk said, "You have earned it and Wanda and I want to do this for you. You are one of our informal family and we want to treat you with the same respect that you have given to us." Becky thanked him and cried a little.

She told Chalk that they had received two large government checks and they needed to be deposited. Chalk asked the amounts. Becky said together, they were over $6,000.

Chalk asked Becky not to deposit them, but to cash them for gold and silver coins. He wanted to reduce his bank accounts and convert his assets into durable money and valuable land. He told her to call him when the coins were ready and he would come pick them up himself.

Carl was back from his looking in the windows, and Chalk heard him in the outer office. He told Becky to keep everything they had discussed confidential and he then tripped the door catch and opened the door.

Carl had bought a piece of chocolate candy and it was melting on his hands. Becky saw his hands and took him to the bathroom and put soap and water to work. He was clean again and ready for the next adventure of the day.

Chalk folded his financial data sheet up and told Becky he wanted to take it home and study what it was reflecting. Becky said she had made a duplicate and it was accurate except for the one change that Chalk had just made. He told her to change it and he would get back to her. He and Carl got on their horses and rode out to the pipestone horse ranch.

The Cowboy's Kids

During the last year he had started to reduce his staff at both ranches, as there was less government business. He had put Sarge in charge of both ranches and he knew that the era for army horses was fading. He also knew that cattle were less profitable as the railroads were now able to haul either cattle or processed beef to markets much quicker and less costly than ever before. Competition was much more intense and profits were predictably much less.

When Chalk arrived back at the ranch one of the old hand cowboys came up to him and said that there were three new foals in the horse barn and Chalk ought to go see them. He smiled and went to see the newborn colts. They were all barely walking and each was marked with a white spot on their head and all of their coats were shiny brown. The cowboy said that the same stallion was the sire for all three and that all of these new horses were males. Chalk was impressed to see such fine colts and he knew that his efforts to breed quality stock were working.

Sarge walked up and smiled at Carl. Carl said he liked the new colts and thought one of them should be named "California." Sarge looked at Chalk and said, "Well, what do you think?" Chalk said, "Fine, but Carl will need to pick out the one to wear that name". Carl selected one and said the spot on his head was shaped like a snow-covered mountaintop in California that he had seen from the train. Chalk spoke up and said, "OK, the other two are to be called "Mr. Diego" and "Mr. La Jolla." The new colts now had names.

Sarge and Chalk caught up on ranch business and other routine matters. Chalk asked Sarge if he would get an accurate inventory on all of the horses on the ranch, as he wanted to know the status and quality of every animal. Sarge said he would have the information by the next morning and then they both went to see the cowboys.

Chalk always liked being with the men while they were working the ranch. He often joined in with the work and made his presence known. He loved to shoe horses and to

Kenneth Orr

ride the remote fence-lines. He said these activities were just part of taking care of what you had and was vital to remaining a successful ranch. Carl was just as involved but he had a lot fewer skills than his dad.

Everyone knew that the horse business was slowing down. Chalk and Sarge had reduced the number of cowboys twice and it was becoming obvious that there were still too many men. There was less to do and too many men to do it.

Everyone wanted to see if Chalk was making any more changes, but they were almost afraid to ask. Chalk was aware of the tension in several cowboys and he said, "Lets all go to the dining area and have a good honest talk." Soon everybody was sitting and waiting to hear what Chalk might have to say. The last two cowboy reductions had made everybody nervous and everyone was wondering what was next.

Chalk came in and went to a position at the head of the longest table. His words would be heard best if he stood there. He wanted to make some preliminary statements to help cut the tension.

He began to speak. He said, "We all know that the horse business is slower than ever and it probably will become even slower when the war in Europe is finally over. The army had a big surplus of horses when the war began and they still have more than they really need. The new motorized machines are beginning to take their place in the modern army. The designers have gotten most of them working much more dependably. All of us know, as the change continues the horse soldier will become a part of our history. If any of you want to leave the ranch and find work somewhere else, I fully understand. I will also give any of you that do want to look elsewhere a reasonable parting bonus to help you along until you find new work. You have all earned the right to this."

"Your efforts have made this ranch successful. It is my intention to make some changes but right now I am not

The Cowboy's Kids

sure as to what those changes will be. Over the next few weeks I will finalize a plan and I will let everyone know what it means to all of us. I will also do everything possible to reflect my respect for each of you."

"I do not want to answer your questions right now, as my answers might be wrong. I know each of you has a lot of good questions and they are important. Give me some time to do my homework and keep on doing your best work. You are cowboys and you are Texans; that means a lot these days."

Everybody clapped and thanked him for his honesty and went back to work. Sarge knew that the time was near when the ranch would be shut down and military horses would be history.

Carl and Chalk rode home and Wanda and Barbara were setting on the front porch. Barbara was still upset but she had regained most of her composure. Wanda was still the strong the strong "Mom" and was helping to keep the day going as well as possible. Dinnertime came and passed and everyone was soon sleeping in their own beds.

CHAPTER 2-2
Taking Care of Life's Obligations

Chalk and Wanda woke up early. They were both concerned what major changes at the ranch were going to be required. They got dressed and went for a walk. The walk was slow and was focused on talking about what each wanted to leave behind for their family. Men were normally concerned when they reached the age of 50, as it was common at this time in history, for a man's life to end soon after.

Women were expected to live a little longer, but not much. Chalk was now 51 and Wanda was 50. They said they wanted to set some priorities and discussed what they wanted to do with the ranch property.

Their first concern was their children. Barbara was now sixteen and Carl was nine. Barbara had finished her grade school education early and was involved with teaching at Texas A&M College. She was well ahead of the majority of other students and had already received her undergraduate degree. That fall she was scheduled to return to College Station and start work on an advanced degree. She was also working as a respected student teacher. Her future was beginning to take shape and her future needs were easier to plan for.

Carl was still in grade school. Like Barbara, he had been an outstanding student and was on a fast track to higher

The Cowboy's Kids

grades. His future was still taking shape and Chalk had detected a real interest in his love for aviation. There was a lot to look forward to in his life. Carl was just beginning to understand what was out there beyond ranch life. The trip to California had made a strong impression on him, and the opening up of a bigger world to Carl had made him a lot more interested in expanding his career plans.

The ranch staff had three key people who had been long-term faithful employees. Chalk wanted to do something special for them. They were Becky Brock, Sarge and The Mexican cook, Pedro, who had provided the cowboys with great food for so many years. Chalk had already paid off Becky's home loan, but she had not built up much reserve for her older years. Wanda wanted to keep her housekeeper and cook after the ranches were re-organized She also and wanted to set aside some money for themselves to make their life a little easier as she and Chalk grew old.

Chalk told Wanda that all of their wealth was more than he had ever imagined they would accumulate. Both of them wanted to leave some money to support several small activities within the community. Wanda's first wish was to set up a scholarship fund at The University of Texas for a worthy student to study and become a teacher. Chalk agreed with this idea.

Wanda also wanted to leave the local Lutheran Church some money to build a new addition for a Sunday school.

The congregation size was growing. Chalk also agreed on this. Chalk thought a few minutes and said that if they split up the ranch property into smaller sized plots he would like the cowboys who worked there to have the first chance at buying land. Chalk wanted to make land available to them for a very reasonable price. Barbara agreed and soon a simple but workable plan was created in their minds.

They walked back to the ranch house and Wanda fixed breakfast for the family. While they were eating, Chalk brought up the subject of breaking up the ranching business.

Kenneth Orr

Chalk told Barbara and Carl that they were both going to be inheriting what was rightfully theirs but before he and Wanda were too old, and possibly of lesser capable minds, they wanted to begin making some changes.

Chalk and Wanda asked both children to think about what they wanted to do in life. A direct question about ranching was asked to each. "Is ranching something you want to do as a life's work?" He told them to think about it for a day and not to discuss this conversation with anyone other than Wanda or himself. The kids ate breakfast slowly and began to take a serious look at what they were being asked to decide. Carl was a whole lot more mature about what he wanted to do than anyone thought and he said he would have some answers in a few days. Barbara was already making decisions about her future and ranching was not her real calling.

Barbara was already building a plan for her life. Carl was just beginning. After all, he was still in grade school. However, Carl had seen a lot for his age and his mind was so wound up with the things he had seen, that he had a lot of things to consider about his future. Wanda and Chalk had always required that they both do ranch work and be a part of the working ranch team. They did this for two reasons. First, they needed to appreciate the value of work and for the money that could be earned. Second, they were going to grow up and need to have a plan for their lives. Ranching might be a good choice, but it might not. There were a lot of other opportunities that lie beyond the ranches fences and the required hard work.

The time for decisions was being moved up to the front of everyone's priority and the need to start planning for what was ahead, was a really big concern to everyone. Nobody had asked for this decision time to happen. It was being brought about by the decline in the horse business and the need to keep a good control of business matters. Age was also a growing concern.

The Cowboy's Kids

Breakfast was over and everybody went about the day doing ranch business, having fun and thinking about what was happening.

The evening meal was special. Wanda had asked the housekeeper to fix a picnic lunch and told her that they were going to eat at a picnic table that was down by the Medina River. The meal was ready and Chalk got the picnic basket.

Everyone followed him to the picnic table. Wanda spread out the tablecloth and put the food out to be eaten. She had to be careful to keep the pesky ants from invading the picnic basket and spoiling the food. Everyone was hungry and soon everything gone.

Chalk looked at Carl and smiled. He did not say anything to get Carl started, but without any prompting he said, "I have been thinking a lot, I want to do something where I can fly an airplane and be a part of the new programs that are being developed in the military." Chalk asked him, "Does that mean you are not interested in being a rancher?" Carl thought a while and said. "I love this ranch but I don't want to become a rancher. My horses and dog are very special to me but that big world out there is really interesting too." Chalk said, "Son, I understand".

Barbara said she was also thinking about the future, and said that the ranch was home and she would love to have a place to come home to when there was time. She really wanted to be a teacher and someday get married and be a wife like Wanda." Chalk said he would remember what each had said and soon they were headed for the ranch house. The mosquitoes were coming out and everybody was swatting and complaining.

Soon after the next morning's breakfast, Chalk saddled up his horse and went to the horse ranch where Sarge was working. He found him and told him to get his horse, "We need to go for a ride." Sarge was a little surprised but he knew Chalk wanted to talk in private. They rode off into

Kenneth Orr

the biggest pasture and found a shady spot under a big sycamore tree.

Chalk had brought along a bottle of Kentucky's best and he invited Sarge to join him for a drink. Sarge gladly agreed and the two men sat down, leaning on a convenient log. Chalk opened the conversation by saying, "Sarge, you know things are changing and like all of the times in the past, I want to get your help in helping me make some hard decisions."

"The horse business is slow and we are not making any real money right now, we are just breaking even. We need to get out of this business soon and go on to the next adventure. We are both getting older and we must also be sure we are not cutting our ability to continue to have a good life." Sarge got very quiet and it was obvious that he understood completely and agreed.

Chalk said he wanted to cut the horse ranch into smaller plots that could be still used for ranching, but not on such a large scale. He also said he wanted Sarge to have the current Goodwin Ranch barns and the small house that had served as his home while he was working there. He told him he would sell everything in this section to him for a reasonable price. Sarge smiled. Chalk said that the cook was also a long-term good part of the ranch and he wanted to make a similar offer to him on one of the smaller plotted ranches.

He asked Sarge to take a map he had brought with him, and mark off the boundaries for plots that were reasonable for setting up small, but nice ranches. He added, "They all must all have access to water and a clear access road. A ranch will not make it without a good year-round supply of water and a good road to the main traffic roads."

Sarge said he would mark up a map, making sure that Chalk's wishes were satisfied and bring it over to Chalk's house later that week. Chalk said, "That's fine but take as long as necessary. Once the map is drawn, I do not want

The Cowboy's Kids

to make changes". He also added that he wanted every cowboy that had worked at the ranch for a year or more to have the first options to bid on the new ranch plots. If they did not buy all of the available land, then other buyers would be invited. Chalk asked him to keep this quiet until the platting were done and they had talked some more.

Sarge had done an inventory of all of the horses on the ranch and he gave it, with an explanation, to Chalk. The three new colts were special to Sarge and he wanted to buy them for himself. Chalk told him that they were already his, as he wanted to make them a gift anyway.

Chalk went back to the ranch office in Bandera and told Becky what he was doing. He asked her who was the current procurement person at Fort Sam Houston and asked her to get him on the phone. She had a phone connection in a short time. Chalk told the procurement officer, sergeant Burl Hardy, that he was going to shut down the horse operation and wanted the army to have the first choice at the remaining inventory.

Chalk reminded him that his original contract with the army had front-end money as a part of the deal. Chalk wanted to make sure he was not going to be required to repay any of these funds. Chalk said he thought he had satisfied all of the requirements that would negate any repayment. The army sergeant dug out the contract and verified that he had not only met the complete requirements it contained, he had far exceeded them.

The army officer said he would get back to him within a couple of days and they parted. Becky told Chalk that she had cashed the checks and had the gold coins in her safe. Chalk said, "Fine, I will take them home with me and put them in a safe place."

A weekend passed and everybody was busy and planning for changes. Sarge had plotted the Goodwin Two Ranch into seven smaller ranches. The Goodwin Two was about four times larger than the Goodwin One Ranch and the land was

Kenneth Orr

better for grass and other grazing plants. The Pipe Creek water supply was a year round good source of water and the ranch was on both sides of the water supply. Each plat was a nice size and all of them had good grass stands and road access. Two had a few ranch buildings.

Sarge had marked the map to show where a new small dam could be built on the creek that would assure all of the plots would have plenty of water. This dam would be easy to build and would not cost a lot of money.

Sarge brought the map to Chalk, opened it and rolled it out on the table and said, "Does this look good to you? You are a good rancher and you understand the needs and problems that must be considered to have good ranch land?"

Chalk looked it over and said, "It looks just fine. I see the main buildings and the plotted land around it are all well situated for good ranching. We could use some of the spare time the cowboys have to build that small dam."

Then Chalk looked directly at Sarge and said, "Like I told you the main plot with the house and big barn are yours if you want it. In the same spirit I want to express to every long term employee, it is yours for $1.00, cash money."

Sarge was completely surprised and said he was thankful for such a good friend. Chalk said that he would come out to the ranch soon and go over his plans with the cowboys. He wanted to personally let everyone know how and where the planning was going. Sarge was told to keep this all very quiet and to sort our any horses that he might want to keep on his ranch, they went with the land deal.

Sarge smiled and rode back home with a new outlook on life. Chalk also smiled and thought about what Sarge had done over the years to help him run his business. Chalk had the ranch cook come in and he and Sarge gave him his first choice to any of the plots at the pipestone ranch he wanted. His price was also going to be $1.00. "Pedro" thanked them and everyone went their own way.

The Cowboy's Kids

On the way back to the ranch house, Chalk went to the riverside graveyard where Carl Harmony was buried and prayed. He was there by himself, and his time in life as a rancher, was about to end. He was truly thankful for the good fortunes that had come into his life, and for the help and inspiration that Carl Harmony had been to him. He was now trying to do the same for the people who had helped him as he went through life.

He also stopped by the sheriff's office. He had not been there for a long time and the reunion with old friends was a lot of fun. Everybody had a lot of stories about the past. He took a few old friends to lunch and then went home.

CHAPTER 2- 3
Family Advice

The Goodwin ranch house was always a joy to Chalk. His family had grown up on this property and the whole story of his life was hidden in the many memories that were still alive and living there. The Goodwin ranching business that was started on the ranch house kitchen table had grown to a level nobody had ever expected. The part of life where one sees the need to get the next generation ready to carry on was at hand. Chalk was more concerned about Wanda and the kids and their future, than anything else. Family always was his first priority.

Saturday morning breakfast was always a time when everyone took the time to listen to each other and to discuss the week that just ended and the week that was approaching. This habit had been in place for several years, so the timing was just right for Chalk to bring up several things. Everyone had a good breakfast and Chalk asked everyone to listen to what he was planning to do during the next week.

He reminded Barbara and Carl that they both had indicated that they were not really interested in being ranchers. He asked them both if they still were of the same opinion. They both said they were, and then he looked at everyone and said, "It was time to plan to get out of the horse and cattle ranching business."

The Cowboy's Kids

He went over the plans he and Sarge had started to develop to get out of the horse business and how they had plotted off the Goodwin Two Ranch into smaller plots. Wanda had known all about the plan but the kids were just now hearing what was happening. He went on. "Now we need to decide what to do with the main Goodwin ranch".

Barbara spoke up and said," I sure would like to keep our home for Carl and me to have in the future and always have a place to come back to when we want to go home". Carl spoke up and agreed. Chalk said, "I am of the same opinion and your mom and I want to live out our lives here. We have too many good memories here to just leave them behind and move on. There is something special about sitting on the Medina River banks and watching the sun go down." Wanda said she wanted to do what her family wanted to do but she also knew that the cowboys who were working there also needed to be considered. Everyone agreed.

Chalk suggested that the main house, barns and several acres of land be identified as one plot, and that the same cut-up of the remaining land be done as was being planned for the horse ranch.

The total Goodwin ranching operation had grown in size over the years and there were almost 10,000 acres being either owned or rented and managed by the ranch cowboys. Cattle were still easy to sell and the longhorns were always in high demand. Keeping a small operation going on the main ranch house property would be possible and the money that they would earn would keep the taxes paid. Everyone agreed.

Chalk said that the monies that would be raised from the sale of land would be put into other hard assets, as he was still not happy with the way the American financial system was working. He repeated his attitude that land and hard money were the only stable of wealth.

He brought up the land he had bought in California and said that the entire west was full of land that was going to become much more valuable as soon as electricity and

Kenneth Orr

better roads were in place. He brought up the Texas towns of Fort Worth, Dallas and Houston. He said that they were still being developed, and the people doing the work were becoming wealthy, almost beyond anybody's dreams. He brought up the money system again and said the only real wealth was in the land, and banks were still not his favorite place to keep money.

Chalk said that he had seen several good people go broke just because they borrowed money and could not repay the bank. When this happened the banks took their land. He added that he had never bought anything on credit or borrowed money just because he saw how powerful a banker could become when a workingman had a few bad years. Chalk said that the only reason he had ever started using the bank was because the United States Government had to have a bank involved to transfer money in the horse ranch dealings.

Chalk said that he had saved a lot of money, most of it in the form of gold and silver and had kept it in his strong box. He went to say why. Chalk said, "When I was a kid we had no money and the exchange of value was almost all done in what we called trading. The bankers call this bartering. We got what we needed and we never were hungry or in debt. We also had a lot of government issued coins. Coins were worth their value not only for the worth of the metal they were made from but because they were hard evidence of value."

Chalk said, "Silver and gold are worth much more than iron and lead and everybody knew this was true. The banks have big vaults full of gold and silver coins and the bandits were always robbing them to get the valuable coins. The bandits seldom rob poor folks, they don't have any money."

Wanda brought up her memories about the reconstruction times after the Civil War. She said, "The south was very poor after the Civil War and the local banks tried to create money by printing paper notes that represented value. The only place that they had value was in the local area and

The Cowboy's Kids

nobody outside of the area would accept these paper notes for value.'

"These local money notes began to disappeared when real money became available. The caused a loss of value to anyone who was holding them. Then the banks started making loans with legal paperwork to back up the loans. These loans were secured by obligating the borrower's land. The paper for value situation is still alive in the banks. Banks are issuing documents for loans that are always written to the favor of the bank. The person who signs this paper is the one who is taking the risk. The bankers are getting rich by taking advantage of people who become unable to meet the payments and then the banks take everything."

Chalk then spoke up, "The banks also are anxious to get your money and will issue you a slip of paper that says you have so much money on deposit. They claim they are secure but a bandit can steal the money or a fire can destroy the records and you have nothing. For that reason I want to draw all of our money out of the banks and putting it in a safer place".

"A much safer place is good land, rental property and in a strongbox. Money is hard to manage. The only things that you can actually do with money are spend it or save it. If you spend it you should have something that you had a good reason to want. Land is much more secure. Land is going to be here forever. They are not making any more land and if you know how to manage land, you can become wealthy. If money is in short supply the government just issues some more and the overall value of all money becomes less. For that reason I want to form a company that is based on investments and on the value of real assets, not paper slips you put in a box."

"I predict that someday the American banking system will suffer a complete and devastating failure. This is already becoming clear as a potential future event. You can see just how a financially weak bank can become strong when they use your money like it is their own. They build big

Kenneth Orr

buildings and pay the chief banker a big salary. They enjoy having money to loan and often become less critical of how they operate. Their wasteful habits always tend to grow and become standard operating procedures. They will loan money to personal friends and to people who are not good risks. Never forget this and always put your best judgment to work before you let go of any money. A dishonest banker is a fair-weather friend. When he has your money to lend, he loves you. But, if he is not an understanding and flexible friend when you owe him money, you are in real trouble."

Wanda said that the Harmony Brothers Ranch was always looking to buy cattle and that they might want to buy the entire herd. Chalk said he knew they were always looking but he wanted to get in touch with his old friend, General Allen who now had a small ranch near Boerne, Texas. The General had always wanted some nice longhorns, and he might also want some of the other beef cattle. Wanda understood.

Chalk said one more thing and made sure that everyone was listening. He said, "I want to leave some money to a university so some under privileged kids can go to school". Barbara spoke up and said she really wanted this to be Texas A&M University. She had seen how much good they were doing to educate teachers, ranchers, and to train new engineers. Chalk said that whatever they gave to any school was to be kept private and only the immediate family was to ever be told of this gift. Everyone agreed.

Breakfast was over and everybody was aware that major changes at the Goodwin Ranch were about to happen.

Chalk had noticed that Carl was growing into manhood very quickly and especially had noticed his growing interests in young women. He was acting more grown-up and his interests in the ranch were not as deep as they were only a year ago. Chalk asked Carl to get his walking shoes on go for walk with him. Carl understood. Dad wanted to have a talk with him.

The Cowboy's Kids

Both of them walked out to the barn and saddled up a horse. They rode off to the south and spent a few minutes just riding and smelling the warm Texas air. Soon they arrived at a familiar spot on the bank of the Medina River.

They got down and found a comfortable log to sit on. The area was not new to either of them, as they had gone fishing near the same spot many times. Chalk said, "Carl, you know I am getting old and soon my worn-out body will be silent. That is not all bad. The life I have lived has been good to me and to the people who I have been allowed to come in contact with. I want you to have this same feeling some day and I am concerned that you become a good man and be happy in life as you grow older."

Carl spoke up and said, "Dad, you know I love you and you know that I have tried to be a good son. What else can I do?" Chalk said, "Carl, I know you are a good son and that you love me but there is a much bigger future in life coming to you and I just want to give you some advice on how to make the most of what ever might come your way." Carl said, "I know I am young and I missed you a lot when you were in the army, but that's in the past and we both know that part of life cannot be changed."

Chalk said, "Let me tell you something about me. When I was born my family was my mom and my drunken dad. When they were both gone, my first family was over. I will never forget them, but I will also never want to go back to that life. It was not very good. Many times I had to struggle just to keep myself fed and inside a warm house in the winter.

You have had a better beginning that me and it has been your mom and my desire to make you as well prepared to meet life as we can." "Soon, your next "family" will start to come into view. The people who you associate with and who you decide to partner up with will become your next family. That's all part of life's normal journey and you will not be able to change this. You need to make your choices as to who you call friends and what you do for a living slowly. They decisions are going to be with you for the rest of your life. You know I worked in Kentucky, worked on the Mississippi River and finally went to work for Carl Harmony. All of these decisions were part of shaping the direction and purpose of my life."

"In shaping my life I found your mother on the wagon train. We both needed to find the next step in our life. When we decided to get married, my second family provided the path to the next level of life. When Wanda and I got married, we formed our third family and you were born as a part of that family."

"Carl, you will soon need to face the next part of your life and I might not be here to help you make decisions. You need to depend on Barbara from our family to help you when you need advice. She will not tell you how to decide many issues but her opinions will be focused on your best choices. She has shown me that she is a very smart young lady and she handles her problems well. I am also concerned that you find a good partner for life.

A man's wife will be there to back you up and keep you inspired to go forward when the times get tough. You will need to choose this individual carefully as you are not going to be able to change your mind once the decision has been made. There are a lot of loose women out there who want your money and name, but when they grow tired of you, and some will do just that, they leave you and go to the next man. This lady you choose to mother your children, will always be a major part of your life and she deserves to be respected to the highest level."

Carl hugged his dad and they told each other that they loved each other. They got on their horses and rode back to the ranch house. Wanda had some fresh iced tea and the guys made short order of the whole pitcher.

CHAPTER 2-4
The Final Plans

Monday came and this entire week was going to be full of activity. Chalk got the map of the main Goodwin Ranch, and drew it into several plots. He knew every acre by experience, and he knew that any new ranch would need to be close to a good road, have water, and have pastures that would grow a lot of good grass. The ranch was large. There were eight nice sized plots that each would make a nice ranch. There was also a special plot of 50 acres that included the ranch house and adjoining buildings. A big part of the 50-acre plot was down by the Medina River. Chalk planned on keeping all of this and about 20 additional acres where a read would be a major problem for his own.

Chalk went to see Becky Brock and showed her what he was doing. She was a little surprised, but the whole plan was not really unexpected. She had excellent records that documented the land ownership, all of the livestock, and all of the cowboys who were currently working there. Chalk asked her to identify how many of the cowboys had been there for five years or more. She quickly had a list of every cowboy's name and actual years of employment.

Two cowboys were away serving in the army. They had worked at the Goodwin Ranch for less than two years before going into the army. Chalk asked her to keep all of this information quiet and he wanted to have a general meeting

Kenneth Orr

with everyone as soon as he had everything in place. Becky understood.

He then went to see the local banker and told him about his plans to breakup the ranches and to terminate his army contract. He told him that he thanked him for his services but the cash flow from his ranches was about to come to an end.

The banker was shocked. He told Chalk that his operations had the largest deposit accounts in the bank and wondered what he planned to do with his assets. Chalk just smiled and said that was still being determined. The banker was obviously concerned and started to tell Chalk about all of the things the bank could do for him. Chalk said, "Thanks for the advice but as of this moment in time, I am still not sure of my plans." He then left the bank and went to the local Lutheran church.

The preacher was in his office and he invited Chalk to come in. He was not just Chalk's minister but also a good personal friend. Chalk told him about the ranch breakup plans but did not go into any details. He wanted the minister to have the right information when the local cowboys and their wives were informed.

The church community was also one of the main social gathering places in the community. Chalk knew that everyone was going to be concerned when the news came out and that they would be wondering about the upcoming changes.

Chalk gave the minister a substantial check and told him it was not to be advertised, but he wanted to help with the new Sunday school addition that was in the planning stage. The Preacher preyed that Chalk's gift would help the church and they parted. Chalk went home.

Chalk had been home about an hour and Becky Brock called him. She told him that she had received a telegram from the army saying they would take every able saddle horse

The Cowboy's Kids

that was available. They said they would do so as soon as they were informed as to the number and final price. Chalk called Sarge and passed the information on. He asked Sarge if he had selected some good horses for himself, and he had. He wanted ten grown mares, two stallions, seven half grown mares, and the three new colts that were already his. There were seven other small colts, but they were not big enough to sell and Sarge suggested they give them to the cowboys. The remaining horses, 65 total, were all good "army grade" stock. Chalk thanked him for his work and relayed the information to Becky Brock so she could send it to the army.

Chalk had five horses in the stable at the Goodwin ranch. These were his family's personal horses. Also the cowboys owned several other horses. Carl had a horse, a small brown stallion, and Barbara's horse was a small black mare. The cowboys who lived at the horse ranch, all had personal horses and they were all stabled in the ranch horse barns.

Chalk called General Allen and they had a long talk about old times. Chalk brought up the fact that the ranches were being broken up into smaller plots and the fact that there were several good longhorn cattle available. General Allen said he wanted a small herd and said he would take ten longhorns. Chalk said they would be delivered at his convenience and the money issues were settled. Chalk almost gave them to him and General Allen knew it.

Wanda was amazed at how quickly a plan could be developed and put into action. She told Chalk she was happy that everything was going quickly and it would be a welcome relief to her, to have all of the ranching business out of the picture. She wanted more time to be with the family, travel, and just relax. Chalk agreed completely.

Tuesday morning had a stormy and wet beginning. The rivers were all flooding, the wind was blowing fiercely, and the livestock were all looking to either be in a barn or on high ground in some place of shelter. Chalk went out to the barns and saw the cowboys all making plans to protect the

Kenneth Orr

livestock. They also were going over the ranch buildings to see what damages might have occurred. Everything was being managed very well and Chalk went back into his office.

Chalk knew that the cowboys were all saving some money, but none of them had enough money to buy a section of land. He wanted to find some way to allow them to become landowners, but not need to borrow money from the bankers. He pondered for the best part of the day and then he came up with a reasonable sounding solution.

He had no debt on any of the land and the real value was all based on the use of the land to ranch. He said he could form a separate land management company where the cowboys would put a small amount of money down and pay for the balance over the next ten or less years. If they gave up as a rancher, the land would belong to the land management company. During the period where the land was in use, it would be like paying a rental fee. This would allow all land sales to happen with no other outside people involved. He would have Becky Brock set up the legal paperwork in her new job, as the new "Goodwin Investment and Management Company" manager.

Chalk passed his plan by Wanda and she was happy to see what he had created. They sat down and started looking at land values and the actual value for each plot. Soon they had evaluated every land tract and established a value that it could be sold for.

Wanda thought the plan over and said that there needed to be some rules in place to keep local speculators out of the purchase plan and assure that the land was sold only to the ranch cowboys if they wanted it.

Wanda wrote down her ideas;

- The land would be sold to only employees of the Goodwin Ranch who had worked there for five years or more and had been good employees.

The Cowboy's Kids

- The prices were to be posted for each tract and the individual who purchased the land had to put 10% of the purchase price down to start the transaction. Payments were to be made twice a year, January 2nd and July 2nd. All payments must be made on time or the purchaser would risk loss of the land.

- The actual land ownership would be kept in the Goodwin Investment and Management Company until the land was fully paid for. Then the ownership and legal title would be formally transferred to the new owner.

- Should a buyer become more than two payments behind, the buyer would void the purchase contract and the land would remain the property of the Goodwin Investment and Management Company. The land, all improvements and other investments would become the property of the Goodwin Investment and Management Company and the people who are in default would be required to vacate the land. Personal property and livestock would not be restricted from removal.

- All payments would be paid to the Goodwin Investment land Management Company office in Bandera, Texas.

Chalk looked at the plan and said he wanted to add a couple more items. Wanda gave him the paper she had written her ideas on and he added:

My plans for the ranch breakup....

- The land must not be sold to any second party during the time of pay off and must remain in the original purchaser's family until all final ownership is established. The new owner is encouraged to keep the land in the purchaser's family for generations to come and to provide legal means to assure that these objectives are achieved.

- The person who signs up to purchase any land from the Goodwin Investment and Management Company must be a legal citizen of the United States and must be a veteran or be willing to serve the country in some branch of the United States military. Should an individual serve in a military capacity the requirement for scheduled payments will be extended for the time that they serve. Should a person be killed in combat, the land will be considered fully paid for and a deed will be written to the estate of the fallen soldier.

- All outstanding money owed will be charged an annual interest rate of 2%. Overdue money will be charged a rate of 8%. Interest applications to the balance would not start until one year after the initial date of purchase.

- Should there be tracts of land that are unclaimed by Goodwin Ranch employees, they will be available to the local public but the price will be 50% higher than the price that the ranch personnel were offered.

Wanda and Chalk both were happy with the plan and they called Becky Brock and asker her to be available for a meeting the next afternoon. She agreed. Chalk already knew that all of his cowboys were veterans or had sons serving in the military. He was not creating a condition that would cause any issue for the current generation.

Wanda informed Chalk that the army procurement sergeant had called and authorized the ranch to deliver the horses at your convenience. He added, the army was happy to get them.

Everything was now in place to finalize the entire plan and announce the future to all of the Goodwin Ranch employees. Wanda and Chalk sat down with Becky and went over the entire plan. She was sad to see the ranches being broken down into smaller areas, but she knew that the horse business was going away. Becky also knew that Wanda and Chalk were getting older and the kids were not interested in continuing to be ranchers.

The Cowboy's Kids

Becky suggested that they form a legal corporation to make the whole company operational with one ownership name. Becky said she would have a trusted local lawyer draw up the necessary paperwork to legally form the new corporation and to document sell the land. Chalk and Wanda agreed with all of her suggestions.

The new private Corporation would have Chalk as the President, Wanda as the Chief Financial officer and Carl and Barbara as Vice Presidents. Becky Brock would be the only employee and would handle all of the paperwork and records. The two young ladies who worked for Becky would be kept on the payroll until all of the coming paperwork activity was over then they would be given a parting bonus and sent on their way.

Chalk asked Becky to call an all hands meeting for next week and to have it in the big building at the main "Goodwin One" cattle ranch. He also told her that the plot at the horse ranch where the main buildings were located was already sold to Sarge. Becky should collect the sale price of $1.00 and issue Sarge a clear deed. When Becky went to do the paperwork she realized that she did not know Sarge's legal name. He had always been Sarge to everyone and he had never had any reason to go further. She contacted him and told him of the problem. Sarge just chuckled. He said he never used his real name, as he never liked it. Becky said, "Sarge, you cannot avoid using your name on a deed". He said "OK, it's Arnold Shirley Abernathy." Becky wrote it down. She told him that she would keep his secret as she thought it was not the right name for such a tough ole guy like him.

Becky asked Chalk what she should do with the money that she would be collecting. He told her to hold it for now, but he did not want to put it into the local bank. He was not unhappy with the local bank, but he was hoping that the money could be re-invested quickly into other property. The locations would probably be in places other than Bandera. If Becky received checks, she should cash them and hold the money in the safe in her office. Chalk knew the banker

Kenneth Orr

would not be happy with this plan. Chalk also knew that the banker had become a very wealthy man using the cash on deposit from the Goodwin Ranches to build his own personal business network.

Chalk was always concerned with some of the questionable sweetheart deals that had been made from the bank, especially the banker's close friends and members of his own family. His family was all living very well but never seemed to be having a skill or a job. Something was just not right about the whole situation.

Becky said she would set up the meeting and everybody went on their way. Chalk and Wanda had a pleasant ride back to the ranch and somehow the road, especially by the Medina River, was just a little more beautiful.

CHAPTER 2-5
The Final Ranch Meeting

Monday came and as per the plan everyone had been notified that the meeting was to be held that day in the big dining room at the Goodwin Cattle ranch. Wanda had the cook fix plenty of iced tea, some special snacks and some fresh hot pies. Chalk had Sarge set up a front table and provide chairs for everyone to sit down and be comfortable. By 1:00 PM everything was in place and ready. Soon the crowd of cowboys would begin to show up.

About ten minutes before the hour, the ranch suddenly became crowded with a lot of anxious and well-mannered cowboys. Everyone was aware that the future was going to change things, as the demand for horses was way down and the cost to keep a big operation going was not getting any lower. Everyone went into the room. Some cowboys got a glass of tea. Everyone was seated in a chair by 1:15 PM.

The mood in the room was anxious and full of eager anticipations.

About twenty minutes after the hour, Chalk and Wanda came in. Becky Brock was also with them and she had a stack of papers in her hand. They went to the table in front of the room and everyone, except Chalk, sat down. Chalk stood quietly and looked over the crowd and everyone could tell he had something serious on his mind. He had a way of

Kenneth Orr

just standing there, looking at the men and saying nothing. His mere presence would become the overpowering center of attention. He had learned this in the military and he was a master in getting everyone's full and undivided attention. Then, he began to speak. His voice was strong, his words were spoken slowly, and his delivery went straight to the point.

"First, I want to thank all of you for coming here today. There is a wonderful feeling inside me right now as I see all of you and realize how much each of you has contributed to the success of our ranching operations. First, Let me thank you and salute each of you for all of your past efforts as members of this group."

"This will be our last group meeting. I am personally sorry that this time has come. Life unfortunately is made up of a series of endless changes and sometimes unanticipated events. This is one of those events. One of my primary concerns has always been to insure that there is always a bright tomorrow, not just for my family but also for all of you. I remain focused on this goal. There is a bright tomorrow out there for all of us if we do the right things today. That will be what I want to discuss with you today."

"As of the end of this month, August 1914, all ranching operations at the Goodwin ranches will be officially ending. That's just three weeks from now."

"The army has agreed to buy all of the "army quality" horses we currently have to sell, immediately. I have instructed Sarge to separate several other horses from the herd and to keep them for his own.

Each of you has already been supplied with a good horse from our herd and this will end our involvement with horses. Those horses you are riding today, even though they have been supplied by the ranch, are now your property."

"I have sold several longhorn cattle to General Allen and we will be delivering them within the next few days to his

The Cowboy's Kids

ranch in Bourne. The rest of the cattle will be sold to other local ranchers or sold at auction. These activities will get us out of all ranching operations. All that will remain will be out personal horses. The other, and most important issue is, what will be happening to our staff."

"I want to tell everyone that each of you will be paid for your time from now to the end of the month. We have a lot to do to move livestock and to shut down the ranch. Second, I came to Bandera looking to find a good life and build a future for myself. I know most of you men have come here searching for that same wonderful dream."

"We all know that we are never the real owners of anything; we just borrow it for a while, hopefully improve it until the time to let somebody else use it for a while arrives. I want to help some of you reach out and find that success that is waiting for you. I am confident that many of you have the skills and business abilities to become great ranchers. To do this, I have had Sarge help me slice up both or our ranch properties into smaller ranches and make sure each new ranch site has water, good grass, a road and a good chance to become a successful ranch."

"Becky Brock has the marked up maps and they will be available for your review after the meeting. I will sell them to you with some reasonable conditions. First, the long-term employees will get first choice. The rule is only one plot to each employee. The number of acres and the quality of the land has determined the selling price. There are several plots to be sold. The one central plot, which is the horse barns and surrounding land at the Goodwin Two Ranch, has already been sold to Sarge. He has been my longest-term employee and he had first choice."

"The remaining land can be bought with a low down payment and you will have ten years to pay it off. The first offering will be to the five years and longer employees and will be open for two weeks. If there are any unsold plots, then the other employees can make offers to buy. There are some rules that apply to the sale of this land. Becky Brock has a

Kenneth Orr

copy of the rules and it will be posted on the wall after the meeting. Ther are enough plots available to supply about 75% of you cowboys.

The men with the least time working here will get the last choices and when they are gone, the other men will be given a small cash separation bonus to help you get by for a few weeks."

"Wanda and I are getting older and we both recognize the time to make changes is here. Our children do not want to be ranchers, but they do want to keep the family home within the family, so the original ranch area is not in the plotted land that is for sale. My children will become the owners when we leave this life and hopefully our roots will live here a little longer."

"For those of you who are not interested in owning a part of the ranch land, that's your choice. We Goodwin's are very appreciative for your services and if we can be of any help in helping you find some other job, we will gladly be here to help. All of you are good men. We knew that when we hand picked-picked out from the cowboys who applied for jobs. None of you has been a disappointment. Thank you for you attention and I hope this plan will let all of you to go forward with something to show for your past efforts. Please give this opportunity our full attention."

Chalk slowly sat down. The whole room full of cowboys stood up and applauded him and made their feelings known. Becky Brock stood up and told the group that she would hang the maps on the wall for the rest of the day and the purchasing rules sheet would be next to it. After that, they would be in her office in Bandera. Sarge stood up, came forward and stood silently in front of the crowd for a few moments. He then began to speak. "I want to tell all of you how proud I am of you and give you my best wishes for the future. I also want to thank Chalk, Wanda and Becky for being as concerned about our future as they are of their own."

The Cowboy's Kids

Everyone clapped and the meeting was over. Ranch work for the day was obviously over. The maps were hung and the men all started looking at the plots and looked at the list of names to see where they stood, in being able to choose a plot. There were no un-happy men. Chalk helped the atmosphere remain positive with a good supply of ice-cold beer and fresh tamales.

CHAPTER 2-6
The Last Roundup

August was a busy month. Things were winding down and the winds of change were blowing everywhere. The army-bound horses were all gathered into one last herd and delivered to Fort Sam Houston in San Antonio. The longhorn cattle were sold, some to General Allen and the rest to local ranchers. Some local ranchers, who were starting a new operation near the town of Medina bought all the beef cattle.

Every plot of land was quickly spoken for and soon the new steel pins, marking land boundaries, were being put into place. The land was all located in prime locations and the new owners were anxious to have a ranch of their own.

Becky Brock and the lawyer had a busy time getting all of the land contracts written and filed in the local county courthouse. The local banker became upset that he was not involved and went to see Chalk. Chalk told him that he was making land and purchase terms available to his men at rates and prices that were well below the market value and the rates normally charged by the bank.

The banker had no reasonable counter argument. He was upset but he knew Chalk was doing the right thing with his men. The men were drawing their money out of his bank and putting it down on their land purchases. The bank was

The Cowboy's Kids

in serious trouble and the banker he knew it! The bank's asset level was drying up and the problems for the banker were serious.

At the end of August, Barbara was scheduled to return to College Station and begin her new job as a student teacher. She was also doing graduate work and was becoming a busy young lady. Carl was in his final two years of school but was so much ahead of his class that he applied to Texas A and M to go to school as a freshman. They told him if he could pass the entrance exams he would be accepted. He took the tests and passed with no problems.

By the end of the month, Chalk and Wanda were home alone and the pace of life was much slower that either could ever remember. The evenings were spent sitting on the back porch looking out over the Texas hills listening to the native birds sing and enjoying the fall colors of the local plant life.

Chalk and Wanda were glad to be able to enjoy some time with no real pressures or schedules to worry about. Wanda had been watching the area grow and one of the things that were of interest, was the growing number of motorcars on the streets.

Wanda told Chalk that they needed to look at an automobile and possibly buy one. She was not sure what to expect, as one of her friend's husband had bought one and it was a lot of trouble to keep running. There were few roads where a motorcar could be driven and a horse was still a better and more dependable way to travel in the rural areas.

Becky Brock was accumulating a large amount of money from the sale of land and the final sale of livestock. She kept Chalk aware of the fact that the company safe was becoming a prime concern for keeping the money safe. Chalk decided to make a major change in the way they were doing business. He went to San Antonio and visited several local political leaders asking them where the city was growing. He wanted to become involved in the ownership

Kenneth Orr

of land in areas where the value was going to grow quickly. All of the political leaders predicted that the best area for new growth within the next ten years was to the north and west side of the city.

Chalk knew a lot about San Antonio and he saw several areas where ranch land was being used to build new homes and businesses. The military was also buying land to set up additional army operations. He asked Wanda to help him pick out the best areas, and soon he was buying open land and watching the builders move closer to his property. As in the past, Chalk bought everything for cash and he never required any loans to buy anything.

He and Wanda were soon seen as investors, and several ranch owners were always calling to see if they could sell land to the Goodwin's. Wanda talked Chalk into buying a Ford motorcar; Chalk had a sign painter put a very small sign on each side identifying it as the property of "Goodwin Investment and Land Company". Chalk learned to drive and Wanda was always seated by his side. The Goodwin's bought several thousand acres in the Dallas area and soon were busy with managing the paper flow. There were daily calls from builders who wanted to buy smaller plots for construction. Becky Brock had become a well-known name among the investing community. She enjoyed the attention and the responsibility that went with the whole situation.

The winter and next spring saw increased growth in all of their investments. Chalk asked Wanda if she would like to go back to California, There had been a lot of communication from California builders and land developers who were looking to buy some of their California land. Wanda was excited and soon they were on the westbound train. In California they were surprised to see how much new development had happened since they were last there. The home they had purchased was Wanda's main focus. She decided to buy additional furniture and household items so they could live their part of the year.

The Cowboy's Kids

Chalk found the local police chief and asked him if he knew where Admiral John Hancock, who he had met on his first trip, was living. The police chief was quick to help. The Admiral had retired and built a new home about two miles from where Chalk had bought his house.

Chalk thanked the police officer and he and Wanda went to call on the Hancock's. The relationship they developed became one of the strongest friendships that they ever had and lasted for the rest of their lives. The Hancock's also went to Bandera several times and visited the Goodwin ranch and became good friends with the Goodwin Kids.

Chalk and Wanda stayed in California until late November and then went back to Bandera. The winters in Texas were much cooler than the weather in California and Chalk liked this. The summers in California were cooler than in Texas and Wanda liked that. For the next five years, about six months out of every year were spent in Texas and much of the winter months were spent in California.

The third trip to California was a much different adventure for Wanda and Chalk. A major business group approached Chalk and wanted to know if they could rent their home for the months that it was not being used. They wanted to use it to holding company meetings. They liked the way it was designed inside and said it was ideal for corporate executive meetings. There were nice rooms for people to hold meetings and the backside had a view that was very impressive.

They offered to add a new large structure on the north side of the property, at their cost, to be used for outdoor parties and large group meetings. Wanda was not too interested, as she loved the home and did not want to see it altered.

The company understood her side of the offer and asked if they could buy the land just to the south of the home and build the new facility and for a couple of years use the Goodwin home as their temporary meeting place? They also offered to put in a swimming pool behind the Goodwin

Kenneth Orr

home and to buy additional land for the future development into a golf course. They offered a price for the land that was far above what Chalk had paid for it. The whole deal was looking a lot sweeter and Wanda was becoming more willing. Chalk said, "Lets go slow Wanda, They are still open for more concessions and we need to use time to our advantage." Wanda agreed.

In April, the representative for the company came to see Chalk and Wanda. He had an offer to pay even more for the land and would provide security fences, a gated entrance and full-time security to all of the property. The offer was for more money than they had ever anticipated. They wanted about 90 acres of raw land for the golf course and told Chalk that he would be free to live in the house and use all of the facilities free, as long as he and Wanda were alive.

Chalk looked it over and said he would never sell the home, but the other land and parts of the offer were still open. Wanda said she agreed, that selling the open land, as this was what the land was purchased for investment growth. Chalk agreed. The deal was cut and the Goodwins went back to Texas with a suitcase full of money.

Money kept coming in from the sale of the ranch land and from the buying and selling of land in San Antonio. Chalk was concerned with the amount of paper money he had accumulated so he decided to invest in a couple of businesses. He had enjoyed driving his Ford and was impressed with the convenience provided by an automobile.

A horse had to be fed everyday, but a motorcar could sit for days and was always ready when you were ready to go somewhere. He knew this new machine was going to become a popular way to move about so he decided to set up a motorcar dealership. He decided to use his current carriage and wagon company in San Antonio as the base of operations. He bought some location prime land in San Antonio and negotiated a dealership deal with Ford Motor Company. He was selling Ford cars within six months. He also was selling cars in his Hondo wagon store.

The Cowboy's Kids

A real problem existed in using a motorcar outside of a larger town. There were few places where motor fuel could be purchased. This was changing, but not as fast as most people wanted. The standard accessory for a long trip was a spare can of gas and a couple of inflated spare tires. The dealership was soon selling a lot of Ford motorcars and his new company was doing well. The success found in San Antonio was impressive so Chalk opened a second company in a small community north of San Diego, California.

Soon Chalk had over 50 people working for him and he was becoming a wealthy and respected businessman. He told Wanda that horses were still fun to ride but he was getting to like the automobile. He even took a T-Model Ford truck home to use on the ranch in Texas.

Chalk had made the change from being a successful rancher to becoming a big city businessman. He was surprised at how easy it was to change business hats, but he was always most comfortable back in his ranch home in Bandera, Texas.

CHAPTER 2-7
The Best Years and Worst Pains

Life continued, and all of the Goodwin business ventures continued to grow. Becky Brock was growing older and she told Wanda that she was ready to retire. In 1919 she did just that. Chalk had seen this coming and had hired a young man named Jefferson, who was a skilled accountant, to step into her place. He had worked with Becky for about a year and he had impressed her and Chalk with his business approaches and money management skills. Chalk suggested that he move the business office to San Antonio as the business activity was rapidly becoming centered in that area.

The move of the business office to San Antonio was made in late 1919. Shortly after the move Becky Brock passed away. After the company moved, Jefferson decided to quit. He said the big city was just not for him, he was a country boy. Barbara said she would look after the business until they found a qualified person to take over. Chalk agreed, as he knew she was a stable and smart planner and soon all of this business was going to belong to her and Carl.

Barbara had been a student at the University of Texas and at Texas A & M. She also had taken a student teaching job at Texas A&M University in College Station. Carl was now attending college at Texas A&M. He wanted to become an engineer. Barbara was spending a lot of time at College

The Cowboy's Kids

Station and in San Antonio keeping the business going and still studying. The pace was torrid and stressful.

In 1913, Barbara's friend Stan had been injured in combat in France. He had been brought back to San Antonio to recover. He had been in and out of military hospitals for several years and in 1920 his condition became so severe that he died. He had been exposed to mustard gas and his lungs were all but destroyed. Barbara had stood by him as his closest friend. They both knew that the days of his life were in short supply. Barbara would go to the hospital on the Army base in San Antonio and visit with him whenever she found time. Shortly after one of her visits, Stan took a turn for the worst and quickly passed away.

The army tried to find a relative to tell of his passing, but it was an unsuccessful effort. Stan's father had died several years ago and his mother was in a rest home and had lost all touch with reality. The nurses remembered Barbara, but did not know her name or where she could be contacted. Stan was quietly and quickly buried with full military honors in a military cemetery located at Fort Sam Houston. Barbara was devastated when she went to visit with him and discovered he was gone.

Barbara went to a phone in San Antonio and called home. She asked if someone could come get her and bring her home to Bandera. She was too upset to travel alone and wanted to come home at once.

She was not sure she wanted to return to College Station, as there were so many memories of Stan still there. Life was becoming complicated and she was not sure of any of her future plans.

Wanda and Chalk drove to San Antonio and got Barbara. They drove her back to the ranch and tried to make her comfortable. Wanda was Barbara's best reinforcement and

Kenneth Orr

they talked a lot about what she really wanted to do in the future. Three weeks passed and Barbara finally seemed to find herself. The field of teaching had always fascinated, her but there was something missing.

Barbara was fond of children, but she had lost her interest in teaching somebody else's children. Wanda saw a big change in Barbara's life and in her attitudes and asked her what she was thinking.

Barbara asked Wanda to go with her to San Antonio and together they would visit the cemetery. She had never been there and she wanted to have some sort of closure with Stan. The next morning Chalk and his two women got up and soon were in San Antonio. They arrived at the cemetery and with the military escort's help, found Stan's grave. It was simple and was in the midst of many. The plain white cross bore his name and rank and the dates that he had lived. Barbara stood by the grave silently for a few minutes. She was holding back the tears and Wanda was at her side. Suddenly, without any comment, she looked at Wanda and said she was ready to leave.

They drove to the cemetery gate and when the reached it, Barbara asked the soldier who was manning the gate, how to get to the hospital. He gave them directions and they went directly to the hospital entrance. When they arrived Wanda was confused as to what Barbara was thinking, but she said nothing.

Wanda knew Barbara was a quiet and somewhat introverted lady and her thoughts were almost always very private. They went to the main desk in the lobby and Barbara asked if the hospital director was available. The reception soldier asked if this was official business and Barbara said, "Well, yes." He went to a small office that was nearby and returned. He said, "Follow me." Barbara and Wanda followed the young man into a room where they were seated and asked to wait just a moment. Chalk was waiting in the reception area. Soon a door at the back of the room opened and an older man wearing a white coat came in.

The Cowboy's Kids

He introduced himself as Dr. Joseph Martin and said he was the Hospital Director. He asked how he might be of service. Barbara introduced herself and Wanda and told the Doctor that her best friend had been in his hospital before he died.

Barbara said she had never thanked anyone for taking care of him and she wanted to do this before she went any further with her life. The Dr. understood. Barbara began crying and Wanda gave her a handkerchief. The tears were finally controlled.

Soon Barbara was composed and told Dr. Martin she wanted to ask him a question. He said, "Fine, what's on your mind?"

Barbara told him she was a teacher and had spent a lot time on a ranch and let him know she was skilled in the simple ways of treating sick animals. Her dad and a lot of ranch people had helped her learn these skills. She said, "Do you think I could become an Army Nurse and come work here and help to take of sick and injured soldiers."

He looked at her and smiled, much like her dad often did and she knew the answer before he said a word. He said, "We are always in need of bright young people, and serving your fellow man, in his time of need is one of life's most honorable occupations. If you want to come join us I will do whatever it takes to help you join our staff.

Serving, as a nurse will be an experience you will gain satisfaction from everyday. You can become a member of the army and we will put you through a training program to make you a first class army nurse."

He asked her to leave her name, address and how she could be contacted and he would get someone in touch with her within a couple of days. She wrote her information on a pad of paper and gave it to Dr. Martin.

Kenneth Orr

Chalk was asked to come into the room. He identified himself as a retired army soldier. This was a strong reinforcement for the doctor who said he was glad to see him with his daughter. Dr. Martin told Chalk that he had raised a fine young lady and she was going to become a wonderful army nurse. Chalk, Barbara and Wanda left the hospital.

The trip back to Bandera was a much different journey than the trip to San Antonio. Barbara was back to being more like her old self and she was actually laughing and talking about the old days of her youth. When they got home, Barbara went outside to take a walk and talk to Chalk. He told her about what it was going to be like to be in the army. Chalk was pleased with her new interest and told her he was so very proud of her. He hugged her and kissed her on the cheek.

Barbara was anxious to get started and still had to close out her current obligations. She called her supporting professor at College Station and explained what she was doing. Everything worked out well and soon she was free to start her career in the Army's Medical Corp.

Carl was planning to graduate from college but his old interests in flying had never let go. It was becoming obvious that he wanted to be around airplanes and ultimately wanted to fly. He came home on a weekend and had a long talk with Chalk. Carl was anxious to get into flying and was seeking Chalk's help in finding the answers.

Carl and Chalk drove the Ford to the army pilot training base that was located at Kelly Field in San Antonio. Chalk took him to see a Major who was in charge of pilot training. Carl and the Major had a good talk about being an army pilot. Carl asked him if he could learn to fly. The officer saw that Carl was completely dedicated to his dream.

He told Carl that he was rather young to join the army and told him to finish his current year in school and then come see him again. He said if he could pass the qualifications, he could join the Army and study to become a pilot.

The Cowboy's Kids

He and Chalk went home and discussed it with Wanda. Both parents told him that it is a dangerous job but if he wanted to fly, there was no better way to learn, than by joining the Army Air Corp.

Both Goodwin kids were now young adults. In the spring, Carl finished his school year. His grades were excellent. He told Chalk that he was ready to go back to the army base and join the Army Air Corp. Chalk drove Carl to San Antonio and soon he became an Army Cadet. Barbara had joined the army and was assigned to the army hospital at Fort Sam Houston. She was now a member of the nurse's training class. Both kids still wanted to remain a part of the family and not loose the comforts of coming home. This was a special time of life. It is a time when pride is present in everyone at having grown into an adult. But it was also a time for change. The original family atmosphere was dissolving and new futures were beginning to appear.

Barbara was required to live on the Army base. She moved all of her things there and soon she was busy tending to sick and dieing soldiers. A large part of her day was spent in classes an equally large part was spent in the hospital wards tending to the sick. Much of her duty time was at night.

Carl moved to the army air base to learn to be a soldier and to attend flight school. This training group was located at Duncan Field in San Antonio. He soon was busy learning the technical facts about airplanes and how they worked. He spent a large part of the initial training understanding the impacts of weather. He soon saw why this subject was so important in becoming a skilled flier. He was enjoying every minute of the training and was looking forward to actually going up in an airplane.

Carl's instructors said he was learning quickly and was going to be a good pilot. Carl never got in a hurry. He knew that making a poor decision while flying could get an airplane into trouble quickly.

He also saw that a lot of other students were in too much of a hurry and were probably going to have problems when they were trying to fly. His instructors were impressed with the way Carl dug into the lessons and how much he was learning.

The ground school course was not very long and was actually scaled back from a previous level that had been in place when the World War One war effort was going full force. There were several "Jennys" sitting on the airfield and Carl would walk by them and look at all of the parts and control systems on the plane. He was learning and he wanted to be sure of what he was doing before he sat in an airplane's cockpit.

Chalk and Wanda had become friends with several of the key people at Texas A&M College and were always interested in the work being done there, especially the training of young people in ranching and veterinarians' skills. The college had become involved with the training of young men to become Officers in the Army. The school had supported several technical training areas for the Army. Chalk always enjoyed going to College Station and visiting with friends who were involved with teaching.

On a routine visit to Collage Station Chalk was approached by the college president and to see if he would be interested in giving the commencement address at the next graduating class. Chalk was honored, but said he was not a famous person or a man with outstanding worldly knowledge. He said, "I did not even go to grade school as a kid, and for me to talk to college graduates and try to send them off into life sounds a little spooky to me." The Dean insisted telling Chalk that his background was well founded on the same principles that the college supported. He said Chalk was just the right kind of person to deliver this message. Chalk finally agreed. The commencement was in about two weeks and Chalk had to get his speech ready in a hurry.

The Cowboy's Kids

The day came' and Chalk got on the stage wearing a new dark suit and a new pair of black boots. He had a small American flag stuck in his lapel to reflect the honor he had for our nation.

Chalk was a little nervous. Graduation ceremony speeches were normally scheduled to be the first item on the program. The crowd gathered and the stage was set for the ceremony. The college president opened the ceremony and then introduced Chalk. He was identified as the keynote speaker. Chalk was described as a man who had served his country and as a man who had earned a special place in Texas history. With this said, he turned the stage over to Chalk. With a smile and a little hesitation Chalk got up, walked over to the speaker stand and made himself ready to speak. He looked at the audience for few moments and saw that everyone was waiting. He smiled again. Then he began to speak.

"First, let me tell you how proud I am too see so many young people sitting here ready and anxious to become involved citizens in the Texas experience. Each of you is to be congratulated." He then invited everyone in attendance to stand and clap their hands is a show of congratulations and respect for the graduating class.

Then he continued, "I will try to keep this short as what I have to say is basic and simple. My message needs to be kept short so you can understand and remember the real meaning of what I want to leave with you."

"With your permission, I would like to discuss a few things that I don't think your professors took the time to cover. Going to college is a great experience. Your education normally covers a lot of things that are written in books. Your school requires and is guided by all of the scholastic formulas, that you master specific subjects to become qualified to graduate. This part of education is mandated, and that's fine. Without meaningful substance in learning your education would be incomplete."

Kenneth Orr

Now, lets look at reality. There is a big wonderful world waiting out there and when you walk out the doors in the rear of this room you will be facing life with a whole new set of challenges. A lot of what you will face will be based on the hard realities of life, not on what was written in the books."

"A few years ago each of you started to became a part of this institution. You may not have recognized this change that was happening or known what was going on, as it was a subtle and somewhat gradual change. Your first few days on campus were full of new experiences and involved with meeting a lot of new and different people. You had become an official student at this school by signing up to come here and to seek an education. You became a part of this school in spirit, when you took on the honor of being an "Aggie" and earned the respect that is given to those who come here and are successful."

"You have now become a product of this school. You altered your personal lifestyle to reflect what you have learned, and you have learned to manage the changes, and broadened goals for your life."

"Soon this school will become a big reference part of your education. You will go forward from here and begin to live your everyday life. Your education will remain a major part of your make-up for as long as you live and hopefully it will make you a better individual to face the life ahead."

"What you basically gained here was knowledge. You have also made friendships that will go with you all of your lives. I bet any one of you could stump me on any given subject. You see, knowledge is a powerful tool. But knowledge by itself can become a dangerous and divisive thing. Using knowledge for doing positive things is admirable.

But, if you allow yourself to use your knowledge to aid negative situations, that's not good. The choice is up to you. How you use knowledge and how you become skilled to

The Cowboy's Kids

work and contribute to society with your fellow man reflects the beginning of real wisdom."

"A person who has a good basic level of knowledge and acquires experience and also has the companion wisdom to use it correctly has acquired the real tools you will need to face the everyday problems that life will bring to you. Never take the attitude that education alone is wisdom, that's not reality."

"Everyone of you has been blessed by having sponsors. Sponsors are people who believe in you and have taken serious efforts to support you as you have worked to gain an education. You will always be obligated to these people and it is your duty to hold, honor and respect these people. They have given of themselves in ways that you can never imagine, to help you reach your goals."

"There are also many other people out there who you may not even know, who hold you in a high position of honor and supported your ultimate goals. These people are your neighbors, former teachers and childhood friends. But it does not end there. The bottom line in life is respect and recognition. Everybody needs to help each other to be successful. In our world and it is a part of everybody's daily duty and responsibility to encourage and support each other in the achievement of honorable endeavors. That's the American way and the Texas tradition of building a stronger nation."

"You are now obligated to be a sponsor when you know there is a worthwhile purpose or justifiable reason. Everyone needs help to make it through life and we, as Americans, understand this better than most. Being a sponsor does not always take money. Sometimes money is the wrong way to show support. Real support takes words of encouragement, your time and well-directed recommendations to help another person to become successful. The honorable things that a person has inside of their mind, need to grow all the way from dreams into achieved reality. The family, a good job, a happy home and a strong civic duty, these areas are

Kenneth Orr

where it all begins. The one underlying force under all of these worthy objectives is your religion. If you approach life with God on your side, all these ideals and positive dreams can come true".

"Life will always bring three temptations to everyone's doorstep. The classic temptations of greed, power and lust have been around since the beginning of time. You all know what these temptations are, and I am sure that you have experienced all them often. All of us have. The Bible teaches us that the pitfalls of life are found when we stray from the narrow path of honesty and honor and allow the wicked three to become in control of some part of our lives. The sacred three are the Father, the Son and The Holy Ghost. They can help you overcome the three primary temptations of life."

"You may notice that my skin is a little darker than most people. This is because my wonderful mother was a Cherokee Indian. She was a wonderful and brilliant lady, and her teachings to me as a youngster were some of the most important parts of my life's education. I have never cursed in my life. You might ask why. Well, I never learned how. The Cherokee language does not have curse words in its structure."

"This was a first and vital lesson to learning about God. God loves all of us and has given each of us the opportunity of life. We need to do our best to please him. Not cursing is just one example of how we can show Him respect. I believe that there is one Great Spirit that oversees all of us. Most of us are Christians. However, there are many different denominations and divisions within the basics of all religions. All of them are working to help people be better individuals and to live together in peace, and with mutual respect. We must follow one of these paths and not allow religious differences to become problems. If we falter, we are destined to have wars and lose our lives at the hands of some enemy."

The Cowboy's Kids

"We all have seen that in times of need, we all must come together as one and meet our needs. This was most clearly demonstrated in the horrible war that has just ended. There have been Christians, Jews and many others fighting side by side. White men and black men were sharing the same pains and the toll on life took no measure of a persons skin color. There were women in the hospital tents tending to the sick and dying. It has been reported that injured enemy soldiers were also rendered medical aid. The attention and care for those in need was equal for all."

"I am discussing these things to let you understand what I have seen in life first hand. Just because we have differences, does not make us weaker. It always makes us stronger. We need to work as teams and help each other every time we can. The differences between us, will give the team a better understanding and a much more positive direction. A team that always pulls together will go farther. Different approaches in conflict with each other as to how to proceed will slow you down. Common "society based strength" is the right way to build a strong and lasting nation. This is the wisdom and character we need to take with us as we leave this room. Life will judge all of us when judgment comes, on what we each gave back during our life time, not on what we took."

"In my life I have served our nation in the army, raised cattle and horses and worked on a riverboat. I also was a partner in a wagon train. That's how I came to Texas. In Bandera I served as the sheriff and worked to achieve peace and equality among all of our people. There is not much about life that I have not experienced or have not come close to. The one thing I never had the opportunity to do was to go to college. I know there are many others out there just like me. However, you now have had the experience of a good education."

"I also know that many other people are looking to you with pride. Education comes from many places, and everyday of our lives can teach us something if we will allow our minds to stay open."

Kenneth Orr

"I will admit, I take a drink of good whiskey on occasion to medicate my ills and pains and to enjoy a moment of relaxation. The people who say things are all wrong when you drink a little whiskey, have probably never had a joint ache or a problem with getting things clear in their mind. I always have been a normal human and suffer the normal pains and aches like the rest of you. I also have many of your same weaknesses. Yet, life has been good to me and I am proud and honored to be your commencement speaker."

"I have always enjoyed having good friends, having fun when I do something, and never getting so serious, that the real joy from living gets lost. One of my greatest joys is seeing young people like you become responsible and amount to something. If it had not been for other people helping me along the way, the life I have lived would have been much less meaningful and a whole lot less fun. Share your joys and prosperity when you can and never forget what your roots may have been. And remember, have fun along the way, that's the best part of daily life."

"My wife and my children are the most wonderful part of my life and it gives me great pleasure to see them enjoy life. They have all worked along side me and have earned as much of what we have, as have I. This is what some people describe as the "so called" good life. If they are correct, than I have achieved the ultimate goal. We are a happy and prosperous family living in peace and honoring the Great Spirit that is in charge of all of us. I wish the same for each of you."

"Let me close with one more thought. When you walk out that door in the back of this room, I want you to seek out the people who have been your sponsors, your parents, your professors and your friends, and thank them for helping you get to this level of education."

"There is no higher gift from one person to another than to hear a sincere THANK YOU from someone who has been

The Cowboy's Kids

helped. Thank you for your attention and I wish each of you a great life ahead."

As Chalk walked away from the speaker's podium the crowd stood and cheered him. He was pleased.

The college president went to the podium and asked Chalk to remain with him there. Chalk smiled and walked over by the president and stood at a position similar to a military attention. The president reached out and took his hand and shook it and thanked him for the words he had just spoken, and then a young lady brought a small package on the stage. The president took it and opened it. He began to read what was written on the paper inside.

"To Colonel Chalk Goodwin, Your contributions to life, to the great state of Texas, to the National Defense efforts and to the many people of our community are hereby recognized. You are hereby being awarded the Degree of Doctor of Humanities from Texas A&M University."

A second lady brought out a black robe which the president helped Chalk put over his suit. Chalk was quiet. He had tears in his eyes and he had a hard time saying "Thank You Sir". The speaking ceremony was then concluded.

The next event on the program was the awarding of degrees to the graduates from their specific colleges.

Chalk was busy with his business deals and was in San Antonio a lot of the time. He was having problems with his health. This was a new and strange experience for him. He was hardly ever ill and his body had never let him down. Now he was short of breath and often had to sit for a while after just a short walk.

Chalk went to see a doctor and was told he had a heart condition that was getting worse. He was told to slow down,

Kenneth Orr

and to do so immediately. Chalk went home and told Wanda what the doctor had told him. They were both concerned, and Wanda said she would do more to watch over some of the local business affairs. She wanted Chalk to stay home and rest.

Wanda and Chalk had both come to Texas with strongboxes to protect their valuables. They both had kept the boxes in a safe place in the back of the closet in their bedroom. They were full of gold and silver coins and also had the important papers to identify their properties.

Wanda asked Chalk to give her the keys and she went through both boxes and identified all of the contents. She also counted the money and put equal amounts in each box.

After Wanda was finished, she asked Chalk to come to the room and explained what she had done. Each box had the same amount of money, and all of the property legal papers were in a smaller box next to the two larger boxes. She said the two children would be treated equally in their wills and that the properties were to be settled with the children present. Chalk agreed and he knew that his time to spend on earth was growing short.

The next weekend the kids came home and Chalk asked Wanda to explain what she had done. She opened the boxes and showed each child the contents. There was well over $150,000 in each box. All of it was in coins, mostly gold.

The paperwork as to how to dispose of the remaining ranch property was spread out and there were duplicate documents that outlined the details. The two kids both understood the estate planning that had been done and both agreed.

The first was that the ranch would be left to both of them as equal owners. Should one die, the other would automatically gain full ownership. If either child was married, the split in

The Cowboy's Kids

value would be determined and the settlement of ownership was to be equitable to both.

The second point was the Goodwin Investment and Land Company. The land values were growing rapidly and both kids were going to become very wealthy. They were both agreeable to forming a new legal corporation with each as equal partners. Several smaller holdings were going to be sold or given to some worthy cause.

The nature of these was not finalized. Barbara was designated as the executor of the entire estate and she was ultimately responsible to make any decisions should there be any unresolved issues. Wanda locked both strong boxes and gave each child a key. A document signed by all of the family members was completed and given to Barbara to hold.

The Goodwin estate was now settled and everybody was happy with the result. Chalk had always said he did not want some slippery lawyer taking away from the estate and had little trust in the outcome, should a situation like that ever get started.

Chalk cautioned both kids that paper in the banks was risky and advised them to keep investing the money that was coming from the land company in more land and in hard tangible property. He was fearful that the banking system and the stock market system were running way to loose to be a safe place for investments. Barbara was most attentive but she saw that Carl was also listening to every word. They both hugged Wanda and Chalk and said such wonderful parents blessed them and they knew it.

Chalk gradually grew weaker and he was less able to be active. He was taking afternoon naps and sleeping more, just to keep a manageable level of strength. The winter of 1922 and early 1923 was cold and Chalk was sick a lot with colds and similar cold weather aches and pains. His body was obviously slowing down.

Kenneth Orr

In the spring he seemed to be getting stronger, but after a wet week, he found out that he had pneumonia. Wanda was also sick with colds and was not able to keep up with her normal life. In March, Chalk got sick and was very weak. On a Monday evening he got ready for bed. Before he lay down he had a special request for Wanda. He wanted a stiff drink of Kentucky's finest over ice before he went to sleep. His breathing was difficult and said it would help him sleep better.

Wanda had the housekeeper fix his drink, and they had a few words before he went to bed. His last words were "I love you Wanda." During the night he passed away in his sleep. He died in his own bed at his beloved home just outside of Bandera, Texas.

Chalk had asked that his funeral be just for the family and only the closest personal friends. He did not like big funerals. He had also requested that he have a simple military funeral ceremony and be buried in a simple wood military coffin.

Wanda had talked with the Harmony family and told them that Chalk would like to be buried in the same plot as their parents were buried. Carl Harmony and Charlie Harmony had been Chalk and Wanda's best friends in life and they would consider being buried next to them as an honor.

The arrangements were made and the funeral was held. The retired General Allen led a military honor guard to the graveyard and the local Lutheran minister said his final words over the simple Army wooden casket. The day was cool and a low cloudbank kept the sky and sunshine hidden. After the funeral Wanda, and the kids went to the ranch and spent a few days together. When the Kids left to go back to their respective careers Wanda was now alone.

Wanda had never been so alone in her life as she now was. Her house was full of old memories. The big chair where Chalk always sat and enjoyed his cold whiskey over ice was quiet and empty. She knew he would never return and that

The Cowboy's Kids

the only thing left was memories and the things he had left behind.

Wanda lost her appetite and often went without eating. She would go out to the barn and walk around, just to see that things were well, and when she was tired she would go back into the house and go to sleep. She was losing weight and soon her health was suffering. In August she went to sleep in a chair in the living room and never woke up.

The housekeeper found Wanda just sitting there and called a doctor. He pronounced her dead and told the housekeeper that she had died from natural causes. Barbara and Carl were contacted and came home at once.

Wanda's funeral was also very private. She was laid to rest next to Chalk and the graves were both covered with native Texas limestone and surrounded by local wildflowers. Carl and Barbara were both shaken by Wanda's passing. But they were both thankful for their parents who had been so wonderful to them.

Carl asked Barbara if she wanted to keep the ranch home open and the answer was a most certain "Yes." She wanted to keep it available, as it was somewhere to go when she wanted to go home.

Carl made arrangements with the housekeeper to maintain the place and he would send her pay in the mail. Barbara was happy to see that Carl was growing to be more like his dad and she saw a little of Wanda in herself. Life had now gone full circle and the new generation of Goodwin's was about to become of age.

CHAPTER 2-8
Life After The Loss

Barbara was now 25 years old and well on her way to becoming a first class army nurse. Carl was 18 and attending flight-training classes at the army air base in San Antonio. He was still considered a little young to become a pilot but he was working to learn everything he could about flying.

Back in Bandera the old home place was quiet except for the simple chores of a housekeeper maintaining the place. Several of the neighbors had contacted Barbara wanting to rent the pastures and run cattle in the pastures. The grass was always green and the fields were all well fenced. Barbara had contacted Sarge and asked him to consider the different offers and to select the one that he thought Chalk would have selected. Sarge took care of the matter and soon there were cattle and a few horses in the fields and in the barn.

One neighbor who was a skilled blacksmith used the old blacksmiths shop on occasion. He was trying to start a small business and his own shop was very limited. Sarge rented him the shop with the understanding it was only a month-to-month deal. He wanted to have the shop available for his needs when needed.

The automobile dealerships were selling a few cars, but the factory back in Michigan was not supplying enough

The Cowboy's Kids

inventories to meet the new demands. Barbara had hired a young man to manage all of the automobile dealerships and he was busy trying to get cars, sell cars and help the current car owners keep the ones he had sold running. The reliability of the first Model-T Fords was not great and the first cars were broke down about as much as they were running.

There was a lot of business activity in Houston concerned with the booming oil industry. The Houston area had developed several large refining companies and most of them were well financed. These companies had real estate agents buy a large plot of land in west Texas near Odessa and in north Texas near Tyler. It was extremely important to make sure that the underground mineral ownership was also included with each sale. Some of this land was near useless for raising cattle, but the potential oil under the ground was worth a whole lot of money.

Barbara knew that the oil under the ground was going to make a lot of people rich and she wanted to get in on the action. The Houston refineries were all producing petroleum products as fast as they could from Texas crude oil. There were several large available sections of poor land just to the north of the town of Odessa. A local land agent thought, would be a prime target to buy. Other surrounding land had been sold to oil companies and they were hitting oil on most of them.

Barbara took stock of all the cash paper money and available bank account balances she had in the Management Company and saw a total of about $1,400,000. She was surprised that there was so much money in the bank.

Barbara told the real estate agent to offer the owners $75 per acre for several available tracts and see what happened. The offer had to be documented to include all mineral and oil rights to any such deposits on or under the property. The several people who owned the land were cautious but they sold her all but one tract at that price. There was one tract hold out in the package. The owner wanted $80 per

Kenneth Orr

acre for his tract. The ground was near to a railroad siding and the owner said it would be more valuable because of the location. It was only 400 acres so Barbara agreed to the counter-offer.

The land was not being used for anything other than local hunters looking for wildlife. There was little water and the sun was so hot in the summer months that the little town of Odessa had to bring in drinking water. A few Russian families had settled in the area and were working for the railroad. The town had a railroad engine repair shop and many of the local men were skilled in railroad maintenance work. Nobody was getting rich but the local economy was becoming stable and growing.

Barbara had just about finished her Nurse's training when she was asked if she wanted to move to an army hospital in Washington D. C. Her skills in nursing and her obvious head for managing a business had come to the attention of several people. She was one of the better students and her grades and nursing skills were outstanding.

Barbara was impressed by the offer but said she wanted to stay in Texas until Carl was at least 21 years old and completely responsible to live on his own. She was concerned that some young lady might infatuate Carl and get his life all mixed up. He had a weakness for a pretty young lady and female sweet talk. Her response was understood and accepted.

The army was transferring major portions of their health support operations to Fort Sam Houston from other army locations. The army hospital at San Antonio had grown quickly. Local hospitals were also growing rapidly and San Antonio was becoming a major player in both active military and retired military personnel health care. World War One had produced many more injured soldiers that ever before and the government was doing what it could to provide adequate medical care.

Hospital at Fort Sam Houston, San Antonio, Texas

Carl had done well as a cadet in flight ground school and was anxious to get in the air. In 1925 he was allowed to enter the senior flight training class. He had mastered the current ground school flight programs and had waited for the chance to actually become a certified pilot.

He was patient and used the time to keep his schooling active in advanced flight support subjects. He had become one of the best students in the weather training classes and he actually helped instruct some of the classes.

The thrills of being in the cockpit were far beyond his wildest dream and he took to the sky like he was somehow born to fly. His first flight was with an instructor and it was a landmark event in his life. He had planned what to expect, but when the airplane was at about 200 feet above the ground he looked down and let out with a loud and happy, "Damn, this is fun." His instructors became impressed with his skills from his beginning flights and he was requesting that he be allowed to fly his first solo flight.

The instructor who trained Carl, told him to be patient as he had just begun to learn how to control an airplane and he wanted him to become much more confident in the cockpit before he was out there all alone. Carl had no choice but to agree. He knew that his future was always in jeopardy if he had a major accident and the thoughts of being injured were always a concern. Several pilots in training had been hurt or killed in crashes.

Kenneth Orr

Carl soon saw the value of waiting. One of the new cadets and his instructor were flying in a trainer when they hit a large bird. The bird tore a hole in the wing and the cadet went into a near panic status. The instructor brought the plane around and landed safely. The cadet soon "washed out" of the program. That student was not comfortable with even simple problems, and it had became obvious that he was not going to be a good pilot.

Barbara was always aware of Carl's status and she almost became like his second mother. Her advice and words of wisdom had always been soft and well intended and Carl knew that she was really as concerned about his future as he was. Whatever Barbara suggested was obviously for his good, and he always listened to her and respected her intentions. However, he did not always do what she suggested. He often would party too much and not get enough sleep.

Barbara went to see one of Carl's flight lessons and she was impressed with the way he was able to control the airplane. She also knew that the instructor was also in the plane and any problem was not going to cause a problem so bad that they could not recover.

She was standing on the grass next to the hangar when the airplane landed. The instructor praised Carl for his ability. The instructor took Barbara aside and told her that Carl was going to be allowed to solo during the next week but he was still not aware. The instructor told her when the flight was scheduled and asked her to be there and help him celebrate when he landed.

The instructor said Carl was well ahead of his class in flying skills and he had earned the right to solo. He had held him back so that he would learn a few more safety skills and now he was ready. Like Barbara had always known, he was anxious and sometimes got in too big of a hurry.

Barbara understood and agreed to make plans to be at the airfield and see him fly alone for the first time. She told her

The Cowboy's Kids

supervisor at the hospital about the event and there was no problem with being away.

The next week came and on Monday the instructor told Carl he was now qualified to fly solo and would be allowed to do his first flight on Wednesday at 10:00 o'clock in the morning. Carl was happy and proud to be considered for flying on his own. The time came and the instructor gave Carl a list of maneuvers that he was to perform while in the air. He told him that he would be flying in a second plane close to him and that both the instructor and another seasoned pilot would observe his abilities from the air. Carl read the list, folded it up and put it into his shirt pocket and got ready to fly. He got in the plane and soon the engine was running.

The old Jenny was not fast and the controls were simple. Carl had mastered the plane and soon he was doing all of the required maneuvers with what seemed like effortless ease.

Carl pulled out of his last maneuver and the instructor's plane flew up to his side. A big "thumbs up" signal was given to Carl followed by a finger point down to the runway. Carl knew he had passed the test and was on his way to make his first solo landing. Barbara greeted him after he landed and put a big hug around her brother.

Barbara was gradually turning loose of her self-imposed care for her brother. She had promised her dad that she would help Carl grow up the right way and she had tried to do what she could to advise him when he needed to have some advice. After all, he was now an army pilot and was a grown young man. Barbara had assumed the leadership of the financial side of the family and had done very well in keeping the investments and property selections profitable. Her nurse's job was still her primary interest. She had devoted her life to being a nurse and to helping others. Her other interests, especially running a land investment company, were not as strong.

Kenneth Orr

Carl was now available for assignment within the Army Air Corp but the numbers of openings were few. The army was having a hard time selling the national leaders, that the airplane was really much more than a circus experience. He was offered a job to train other pilots but this was really not what he wanted to do.

Carl had made friends with several pilots who were working as sub-contractors for the U.S. Mail Service. They were looking for good pilots and Carl was listening. A job in the mail service would mean a lot of flying time and Carl was looking for this type of work. The army was not expanding but they were stable and he did not need to leave.

The Army was not going to hold him on active military status if he wanted to leave so he signed up to fly mail planes. Carl was anxious to fly and a mail plane job sounded great. His first assignment was to learn a route from Dallas to Oklahoma City.

The contract Mail Service had purchased several surplus World War One airplanes and converted them to carry additional fuel and about 200 pounds of mail. There was a lot to learn about different airplanes. Foreign companies had manufactured several mail plane aircraft. They were similar to a Jenny but had a lot of different control and flying characteristics.

This was much different from being an army pilot as the whole purpose of the trip was to deliver mail. The return trip would also carry mail and often a few small packages. He went to work and soon was flying several trips a week. This job was not like work, it was pure fun for Carl. He was seeing the country and flying. What a job, flying and making money all rolled up into one!

The summer flights were always much easier and more fun than cold weather flying. The air up at flying altitude was relatively warm and the airplane cockpit was relatively comfortable. The winter trips were another story. Open cockpit airplanes were always very cold and the constant

The Cowboy's Kids

danger of having ice build up on the wings and propeller should never be overlooked. For winter flying Carl wore extra warm clothes but they were poor approaches to keeping warm. The airplane industry was working on closed cockpit airplanes but they were limited in availability on the mail routes.

Barbara was now living alone in a rented house in San Antonio. She kept herself busy with her hospital job. Nurses were given a lot of latitude as to working hours but they were on call as required. Keeping her hands on the investment businesses took all of her spare time.

Her life was never dull and she had grown into a beautiful young lady. There were several men calling on her every week to go out but she was just not interested.

She had never gotten over the loss of Stan and her interests toward another man were just not there. She bought a nice home in San Antonio in a very nice part of town and soon had everything decorated to fit her desires.

Barbara had a small one room building added on one side of her property where she planned to set up an office to oversee the land and investment business. The room was large and a small private bathroom was built into the rear of the structure.

Barbara knew she would need to have help to set this office up and to manage the daily affairs. Her dad had taught her that you can only do so much and do it well and when you were too busy to do more, you get professional quality help.

Becky Brock was not alive, but her lessons in financial management still were clear to Barbara. The current size of the business was obviously too much work for Barbara to manage as a part time effort. Her primary responsibility was still the Army Hospital. Becky Brock, she assumed, would have told her to find a good accountant that she trusted and let them do a few simple tasks for a few days.

Kenneth Orr

The first few days could be a try-out period to see if the person was qualified and dedicated to do a good job. During this period the simple tasks and responsibilities could be evaluated, and if they pass, you go further.

If the person fails, you find a new candidate and start over. Chalk had taught both Becky and Barbara to keep the real worth of everything in business a private matter. Barbara would need to make some of the business information be revealed to enable a good business manager but the balance sheet data needed to be kept private. This approach to business management was going to become a big challenge.

Barbara called an old professor at The University of Texas and inquired if there was someone special near graduation that would be a good business manager. The professor said he had one young man in mind, but wanted to think about several more before he gave Barbara any names. She understood and said she would wait for his phone call.

The next week the professor called Barbara and said he was recommending a young man who was getting his degree in accounting at the next graduation. He said this man is a good candidate. He gave Barbara his name, Billy Schmidt, and other contact information. Barbara had a lot of questions and soon was on the phone to talk with Billy. The phone call lasted a long time.

The young man was a veteran of the First World War and he had served in France before going to school. He also had been raised on a ranch near Kilgore, Texas and was from a family that was working class people.

He had claimed that he impressed the professor with his drive and abilities. The professor claimed he was never anything but a gentleman. Barbara was interested.

The need to talk to Billy in person was urgent as Barbara was very busy working as an Army nurse. She wanted to get somebody watching the business quickly as her nursing

The Cowboy's Kids

job was taking an increasing amount of her time. Barbara called Billy and had a second nice chat. She asked him to come visit her in San Antonio and to bring a record of his school grades. The following Monday, Billy caught a train and came to San Antonio for the job interview.

Barbara met Billy at the San Antonio train station and was surprised to see how big and muscular a man he was. He was over six feet tall, weighed 225 pounds, and had sandy blond hair. He was dressed well and his first impression was very positive. Barbara introduced herself and he was surprised to see a beautiful young lady meeting him. He had anticipated meeting an older and more regimented looking lady. The professor had not seen Barbara after she grew up and had never discussed her age or looks with Billy.

Barbara had driven her Ford and they went to a small quiet restaurant where Barbara had made a reservation. The dining room was small and the number of customers was small. Conversation was easy to hear and Barbara opened the discussion. Barbara asked Billy to show her his school records. He said he forgot them and was sorry. The conversation was off to the wrong start, but Barbara was still interested in finding out more about Billy.

Billy was one of six children and had been raised as a Lutheran. He was an Army veteran and his three other brothers were also veterans. He had two sisters who were married and moved away to Little Rock, Arkansas. They were several years older and they had started families. His brothers were all younger and they were all married and still working on the family ranch. Billy wanted to become an accountant but he said he wanted to become involved with some small Texas company. He had a girlfriend at school and they were planning to get married soon after he found a job. His voice was quiet and soft spoken. It was almost like Barbara had to pull any answer from him. The answers to her questions were not complete and his composure fell apart the longer they talked.

Kenneth Orr

Barbara then switched the conversation to running the financial business. Billy opened up a little and the conversation was much easier. He had been in the Army Quartermasters office and claimed he had been deeply involved with supplying the soldiers in the field with their needs. He was very detailed about his work and he had a good strong voice to express himself. Barbara asked him what he wanted to do with his career.

Billy thought for about ten seconds and said, "I want to be somebody who has both responsibility and respect. An accountant must be honest and must always look honest to his customers. Responsibility is a powerful thing and a person who has responsibility must be respected."

Barbara smiled and went on to tell him a little about her background and how her parents had built up a small fortune in land and other assets. She said she needed help to manage the business. Her primary interests in life were in the medical field. She wanted to continue to be an Army nurse. She told him that her brother Carl owned 50% of the business and he needed to be aware that there were two people in the company. He would need to work with both of them that he would need to work with.

The balance of the interview went reasonably well and Barbara drove Billy to the new office where Billy could potentially be working. She asked him to give her his comments on the office and asked him what else he might need to do a good job. He looked the office over and said he liked it but it needed to have more privacy. He said people work best when there are few distractions and the single large room was too open to allow much privacy. Barbara understood his suggestion.

The day was getting late and Barbara took Billy back to the train station. He caught the last train going north and went home. Barbara went home, changed her clothes, and went to work at the hospital.

The Cowboy's Kids

The hospital shift ended at 6 AM the next morning, and Barbara went home and got some much needed sleep. She got up after noon and had a late breakfast.

The interview the day before was still on her mind and somehow it was not as good as she had hoped. Billy's school grades were still unknown and he was almost too private when discussing his personal plans. His understandings about accounting approaches were not very professional and it seemed like he had been coached before he came to town.

Barbara had several friends in Austin and she called one of them to see if they knew anything about Billy. She hit pay dirt. Her friend, Nancy, said she knew a lot about Billy. He had been on the football team and was suspended recently for poor grades. He was going with a girl whose father was a professor and when Nancy checked, it was the same professor that had recommended him. Billy was also in trouble with the local law officers as he had been caught stealing in a local store. His dishonesty was an immediate issue to Barbara.

Barbara thanked Nancy for her help and never wasted any more time following up on Billy. He immediately became history to her. She started to look elsewhere and got Carl involved with the search.

Carl was never too busy to stop from going to see Barbara when she called. He went to San Antonio and got a good look at the new office building and looked over the latest numbers concerning the land company. Carl saw that the money balance was growing rapidly, as rent and related incomes were accumulating income. He saw how busy Barbara had become just working with the mail and keeping the bills and other business matters covered. He immediately became concerned and said he would help her find an answer.

Carl remembered stories that his dad had told him and how many times he had heard his dad say that "there is really

Kenneth Orr

no substitute for experience and common sense." Becky Brock had been solid proof of this theory.

The next obvious step was to find someone who had the right talents, a sincere interest in the business and who was available for a long-term job. Carl and Barbara discussed the situation and all of a sudden they both stumbled onto a reasonable answer.

They had never forgotten General Allen and they both remembered that his oldest son had gone to school and become a successful businessman in Boerne. He was buying and selling cattle and was doing well. His name was Arthur Allen.

Carl got a carriage and drove to Boerne to see "Art" as he was commonly called. Art quickly recognized Carl and was glad to see him. Carl asked him about his dad and he learned that the General was in poor health and had just recently been taken to live in a rest home. He had lost much of his memory and was near the end of his life.

Carl expressed his sympathy. Art's sister, Martha, was still single and was running the ranch but her interests in ranching were not all that strong. Their mother had passed away a year before and the ranch was in a state of flux. The ranch had been doing reasonably well but the demands on a small ranch to keep up with bigger ranches were rapidly increasing.

Ranching profits were declining and the new mechanical farm machinery was starting to take over some duties. The days of horse and mule powered equipment were about over. This new equipment was obviously becoming better designed and built, but it was expensive. You also needed skilled men to run the equipment. That was not possible with the increasing cost of good labor and a really poor cash flow.

Carl told Art that he was looking for someone to help run his and Barbara's land and investment business and wondered

The Cowboy's Kids

if he Art had any interests. Art was surprised but he had never before had an opportunity to consider a position like this. He sat back and just like his dad, he said, "Lets talk this over some more." Carl saw that he was interested but did not want to pressure Art. Carl also knew that Art was happy in his current job.

Art spoke up and said he would like to come to San Antonio and see Barbara and take a good look at what the business needed. Carl agreed and a date was set. Art said he wanted to bring Martha along so she could see the city and perhaps be of some help to him in making any decision he might want to consider. Carl agreed to the plan and the visit was over.

Carl went back to Barbara's home and they discussed the situation. Barbara was comfortable with what was happening and told Carl to make sure that he was in town when they came. Barbara said she would take some time off from the hospital to make sure the visit was well handled.

The following week Art and Martha came to San Antonio. Carl had purchased a surplus Jenny airplane and flown it to San Antonio for the meeting. Barbara had scheduled two days off. They all met at Barbara's home and went to dinner. The meal was great and the tone was very positive for everyone. Art and Martha stayed in a hotel and the next morning they went back to Barbara's home.

Barbara gave everyone a quick overview of the business went over the basic details of how she had set up the several approaches to value management. She kept the actual cash balances and land values private but it was obvious to Art that there was a lot of money involved with the business. The automobile dealerships were doing well financially and the number of people involved was growing. However, the maintaining the dealership stores had become a problem. There was a lot more competition and the sales management for a car company was becoming a lot more challenging.

Kenneth Orr

Art saw several of the current problems almost immediately and he started to ask very intelligent and meaningful questions. Martha was sitting in on the meeting and she was adding a lot of great suggestions. It was obvious to Barbara and Carl that they had found the right people and that this relationship could be productive.

After everything had been discussed and everyone understood the overall business situation, Carl spoke up and said, "Art, are you interested in joining up with us?" Art thought for a moment and said he was very interested but he wanted to have Martha included in the operation of the business. She was surprised at Art's comment but happy to hear his suggestion. Martha was also a skilled money manager and she was looking to get away from ranching.

Barbara looked at Carl and said, "Well, we are a brother and sister team and so are Art and Martha. It works for us and I think it can work for them". An agreement was reached and the starting wages were set. Art agreed to sell his business in Bourne and Martha said she would sell off the ranch as soon as she could. Then they would move to San Antonio and join the Goodwin's company. The path for a new relationship was established and the future looked better than ever for everyone.

The scheduled start date for Art was January first, 1929, and that was only a couple of weeks away. Barbara got a map of Texas and hung it in the business office. There were pins in every location where the Goodwin's had investments and the kind of investment was coded by the color of the pin. She told Carl she wanted to keep a good perspective on what was happening as the business moved ahead.

Barbara outlined the various areas where the business had financial interest. When Art came to work he was going to be handling a lot more responsibility than he had in managing a small business company. Martha was equally qualified and Barbara and Carl were pleased with their selection.

CHAPTER 2-8
Finding the Future

Carl was fully occupied as an airmail pilot. Barbara was working as an Army nurse and Art Allen, and his sister, were managing the business. Art had set up the business office so that the property management side of the business was his responsibility and watching over the car dealerships and other local retail store businesses were primarily Martha's responsibility. Everything was working well and the new arrangement was working smoothly. The bank account was growing and Barbara kept a close watch over the bottom line balances. Barbara kept pressuring Art to not build bank balances but to look for opportunities to invest in good assets. He understood her motive and took actions to keep the majority of the incoming money invested wisely.

Women were not normally regarded as responsible and strong business people. The men had always been the business leader and women were relegated to lesser and lower responsible jobs. Barbara was a whole lot different from normal anticipations. She was very observant and had become a little feisty when things would get too far away from where she wanted them to be.

Art and Martha understood Barbara and never let her get under their skins. That would have been easy to do if they had not gained such a strong respect for her financial skills. They would answer her concerns with facts and projections of what was happening and Barbara would always seem to

Kenneth Orr

understand. The relationship was good and the results were financially positive.

Carl was equally independent and never hesitated to show up in San Antonio and have Art go over the books with him. From the outside, Barbara and Carl both appeared to be struggling young people trying to make a good living but under the cover of the development company they were actually becoming very wealthy.

Carl had also bought a Ford to drive around town when he was in San Antonio. He had his old Jenny to make longer trips. Barbara had bought a new Ford four door coach and she drove it back and forth from her home to the hospital. Chalk's old car had been put in the barn back in Bandera and was used only when they were in town. Everyone had become comfortable with automobiles and was becoming fewer dependants on horses for transportation.

The old home in Bandera was sitting idle except for an occasional trip on the weekends. Barbara and Carl both were too fond of the old place to sell it but they saw that it was not being maintained the way it had been when their parents were alive.

Sarge, who was watching over the ranch, was getting older and he was slowing down on a lot of things. He tried to watch out for problems, but he was never as good at watching for things as Wanda and Chalk had been.

A local neighbor contacted Barbara when she was home and asked if they could rent the house. Barbara said that she would need to discuss it with Carl before any answer was available. They understood and left it up to Barbara to get back to them. Barbara saw Carl often and she told him about the offer to rent the old home. The family was young and wanted to do some cattle ranching on a small scale. Their family had a good reputation in the community.

Carl thought about the offer for a while and told Barbara that the house needed repairs and that Sarge was not using

The Cowboy's Kids

most of the barns. He suggested that they rent it on an annual basis.

This would mean that they would need to clear out all of their personal things and all of the old family furniture. Barbara was not anxious to make this change, but she agreed to Carl's idea.

Barbara hired a moving company from San Antonio to go to Bandera and load all of the furniture onto wagons and move it to a storage building she had rented in San Antonio. Barbara took all of the family's personal things and put them in her car and took them home with her. Chalk's old car was sold to a good friend. Several months prior, Barbara and Carl had loaded up the two strongboxes and taken them to a safe place in San Antonio. Nobody knew what they had inside or where they were stored, except Barbara and Carl.

The rent deal was made and the new residents were happy to move in. They both had known Chalk and Wanda and they had a lot of respect for the fact that they were being allowed to rent the place. The rent price was low with the provision that they would do all of the required maintenance and keep the buildings in good repair. Everybody was happy.

The new family had three young boys and they were perhaps the happiest of all. The first thing they did, was get some dogs and a pony for the kids. They were excited that the Medina River was next to the property and the fishing hole was a great sport for the boys.

Carl had been living in a small apartment in Dallas for the time he was flying airmail. He had no desire to own a house and considered his life style to be a lot less restrictive. He had several good friends who were also fliers and they would spend time together when they were in town. The social atmosphere among the group was always happy. Carl had met several lady friends but none of them ever were headed toward serious relationships.

Kenneth Orr

The country was undergoing a lot of change and Carl was anxious to be a part of the action. He had learned to drink a little whiskey like his dad and he had personal habits a lot like Chalk. There were several new mail routes opening up and he was often being sent to places where he had only heard about before. He loved the travel and flying was his second love.

He was not as happy with flying in the cold winter months. The airplane arrival schedules were never predictable in the winter as ice, snow and equipment failures were always threats on every trip. He always wore special warm clothing in the winter, but it was still bitter cold flying.

1925 was an eventful year. Carl had been flying for a large mail subcontractor and all of the pilots thought the pay was a lot less than it should be. He was not as worried about the money, but he thought it was wrong for the people in the front office to make the big money and he and his fellow fliers take all of the risks of flying. The airplanes were not being maintained properly, and safety when flying was a major issue.

Several other pilots had recognized this situation and they had already gone on to other flying jobs. Several had started a thrill show where they would fly airplanes at county fairs and do all kinds of aerial stunts. They invited Carl to come join them but he refused. He thought they were a little crazy to do these daredevil stunts and wanted no part of it. Several of his friends were injured or killed when things went wrong. The danger in stunt flying and barnstorming was too much for Carl to handle.

One airmail flier, who was one of Carl's best friends, had gone to work for an airplane manufacturer in California and he had been prodding Carl to come work with him. The company was named Ryan Aviation and was located in San Diego, California. Carl already loved the area. The company was working on several new enclosed cockpit airplane designs. The owner had a whole lot of good ideas as to how to make airplanes safer and more practical.

The Cowboy's Kids

This opportunity was right up Carl's alley. He went to San Antonio and told Barbara about his situation and impressed Barbara with how much he wanted to do this kind of work. He also went over to the Army Air Corp base and made sure his Army reserve status was not a problem. He records showed him as a "Reserve Captain" and he had no other current military obligations. He hooked up with an old friend, Malone, and had a good conversation about flying airmail. Malone was also a captain and he was one of Carl's best friends.

Carl then decided to take the job in California and told Barbara he was going to make the change. She was happy for him and said they still needed to keep in touch.

Carl went to see Art and Martha and had them go over the business books with him. The books were in great shape and the value of everything appeared to still be growing at a good rate. The remaining land in California had become very valuable and there were inquires every few days from wealthy people wanting to buy land parcels to build new homes. Art had discussed these offers with Barbara and so far only two had been sold. The profits were huge.

Carl said he was going to be in California and wanted to live in the house that Chalk and Wanda had purchased a few years before. Art said it was rented, but the lease renewal was coming up in about a month. The current tenant had no rights to a renewed lease and really was not living in the house full time. Carl said that was fine. Art said he would inform the tenants and make the impact as easy as he could. Carl agreed to this arrangement.

The automobile dealerships were all selling cars, but they were barely making any money. The market for new cars was strong, but there were so many new brands out now that it was a real zoo just to keep enough sales to pay the staff and all of the bills. The west coast communities had a lot of wealthy folks living there and they wanted elegant cars like Packard's, Stutz's, Cadillac's and such. Ford automobiles were selling but at much lower profit levels.

Kenneth Orr

Carl told Barbara he thought they needed to sell these business ventures and put the money into more land. Carl was afraid that the automobile market was going to become even more cut throat and he had no intention to be a part of that kind of business. Barbara agreed.

Barbara had the same concerns but had not acted to do anything, as she was just too busy. Martha was soon looking for some new buyers for the automobile sales companies and within six months they were all sold. Martha then went to work helping Art with property management issues.

Barbara's nursing career was growing steadily and she was now on the management staff for the base hospital. The Army had located an even larger medical training school at Fort Sam Houston and her job was becoming less in patient care and more in management. She liked the added responsibility she was being given but still wanted to have personal contact with the soldiers.

Another issue had come up in her life. She had become very fond of a young doctor who was working in the hospital. He was a couple of years older than Barbara and was also single. His name was Paul Wilson.

Paul was a well-educated doctor. He had specialized in internal medicine and had become a skilled surgeon. He had also served in the Army during the last year of World War One and had spent time overseas. He had seen death's face often and was dedicated to his profession with an obvious passion.

Barbara saw a wonderful spirit of caring within him and remembered how her friend Stan had been injured and died from injuries suffered in the war. The whole memory of Stan was a nightmare to her, but seeing someone who was working to heal injured soldiers was a pleasant feeling.

They talked about a lot of things that happened in the war. The troops that were recovering in the hospital were proof of the human losses a war can cause. Between them, they

The Cowboy's Kids

had developed a friendship that was more than professional. Their relationship was becoming deeply personal. Barbara was proud of her dad's military history and his name came up often. Paul's family was never in the military but he had seen the pain and suffering in many of his personal friends who had served.

Barbara was still not completely willing to let a man into her life. She was too busy with her career and with managing Art's business activities and the growth of the family business. Carl was now living in California and he was not in Texas very often to help her make decisions. Barbara missed him, but she was more than capable of looking problems in the eye and solving them. Time for a romance and for a serious relationship would need to wait a little longer.

CHAPTER 2-9
Carl's Career Takes Off

California was an exciting and comfortable place to live. California was also a place where everything was alive with new ideas. There were a lot of new progressive airplane and consumer goods manufacturing companies. Most of them were building businesses based on the new technologies that had come from the war effort and from the new availability of adequate water and cheap electrical power. Congress had approved the construction of several major dams that would make ample electricity available all over California. These new conditions were adding even more incentives for growth. The business growth expectations in the larger west coast cities had gone wild.

The aircraft industry was positioned right in the middle of everything. A lot of Army Generals and Congressmen still had a poor opinion about the use of airplanes in a war effort. They referred to airplanes as a carnival machine just a little fancier than a hot air balloon and did little to nothing to advance the Army military objectives. There were also Generals who were taking just the complete opposite approach to the use of airplanes in war efforts. It was a hot political fight and the Army Generals and navy Admirals with flying experience were determined to win this one.

Billy Mitchell was one of these people. He was a pilot, an Army General and a strong supporting force for airplane

The Cowboy's Kids

based warfare. He predicted that wars in the future would be fought from the sky. He was also convinced that airplanes would someday become useful for many other purposes. There were several congressmen on his side and they all were sticking together.

The Army was not alone in being interested in airplanes. The Navy had developed several airplanes that were capable to land and take off from calm water. Glen Curtiss, a New York motorcycle racer, had invested much of his own money into airplane development efforts and was perfecting several new designs from San Diego's Navy air base. They were also developing ships that would serve as a floating base for airplanes.

The strongest supporters of combat aircraft in World War One were from Germany, France and England. They had actually built large quantities of airplanes, and their introduction into the war became a meaningful and undeniable part of the total war effort. The United States was involved with military airplane development, but never to the level of the European countries.

Names like Messerschmitt, Spad, Foch-Wolfe and DeHaviland were common references when identifying airplanes. Carl had studied all of the information he could get his hands on that told about these airplanes.

Carl knew every major airplane by sight and how much speed and distance they were capable of flying. His knowledge level had grown far beyond what he had learned back at Butler field as a pilot cadet. His military training had served him well as he understood the background on most of the different new airplane design features.

The colleges and universities were all anxious to get courses in a new field that was being called "Aeronautical Engineering." Everybody was anxious to learn but there was very little available and proven information from which to teach. After all, the first airplane was built using bicycle parts, wood structures, sewn cloth and wires. The information that was

Kenneth Orr

available was basic and for the most part a good place from which to start.

Airplane engines were heavy and flight controls were crude. Flying was an "art form" of sort and many of the original airplanes were very hard to fly. Every airplane was hand built with a constant stream of modifications being implemented during construction. These new and mandatory changes continued to be added even after the airplanes were in service. Many lives were lost in the development of early airplane technology.

Carl had gone to California to work for a small airplane company that was trying to design a new all metal-skinned monoplane. The company hopefully could sell the airplane in volume to some military customer. They hoped the design would also have some sort of commercial market interests.

Carl was thrust into the middle of the design effort as a man who knew how to fly and knew a lot about airplanes. His background was as strong as any of the other designers. There were several good mechanical engineers in his department, but they had little knowledge about airplanes. Even worse, they lacked knowledge about how the physics of flight worked. Most had never even flown in an airplane.

Carl had flown his Jenny to San Diego from Dallas and had it parked in a small hangar at one end of the San Diego airfield. He would fly it when he had time, just to keep his skills sharp but often he would also take a fellow worker up with him. He loved to teach about basic flight and demonstrate some idea or problems associated with a design. This was not what he had planned to do in his new job but his attitude and skills at communication about technical things were valuable to everyone.

Carl's senior boss saw what was happening. He saw that Carl had become an informal and positive leader for the design group. He often asked Carl to take him up and perform some maneuvers associated with development

The Cowboy's Kids

problems. Carl jumped at every chance and soon he and his boss were close friends and professional associates.

Carl stressed the problems he had recognized about specific areas of flying that he knew were of interest to his boss. Carl always learned something from these flights and his education in the design of airplanes grew rapidly.

The old Jenny was very air-worthy, as Carl had added several improvements to the airframe to make it stronger and to make it easier to fly. The engine had been customized and the plane was fast for a Jenny.

On one demonstration flight the Boss wanted to learn more about "drag." Carl knew a little about the subject and demonstrated how any "air stream" resistance to forward motion, resulted in additional drag.

He even made a small control plate and mounted it on the area just outside of the fuselage just in front of the cockpit. Carl made it move up and down and had a small spring attached to keep it out of line with the passing air. When he manually moved it, the spring took more tension and the effect on the airflow was obvious. He had mounted a small spring-loaded gauge on the plate's rotating shaft with a dial to measure the force. Changing the angle would increase the number on the gauge and the effect was measurable. Carl's boss saw a lot of merit to the "drag gauge" as Carl called it and complimented him on his work.

When they landed the boss asked Carl to meet him in his office in 15 minutes. Carl was not sure if he had just laid the groundwork to get fired or no telling what. He let the boss climb out of the airplane and taxied the Jenny down to where he normally kept it.

The boss was named Clifford Alexander and everybody called him "Cliff". He was a good mechanical engineer and had been trained as a pilot at a private school in Seattle, Washington. The school had been basic on controls but lacked a lot of the other instruction that Carl had received

Kenneth Orr

in the Army pilot training school. Cliff had grown up in Tulsa, Oklahoma and was the son of an Army Captain.

Carl went to Cliff's office and entered. Cliff welcomed Carl as he entered and asked him to sit down on the other side of his desk. Cliff opened a drawer and pulled out a pad of paper and a new pencil and gave them to Carl.

He looked at Carl and let him just sit there holding the pencil for what seemed like forever. Cliff then spoke up and said, "I have been thinking about how to say what I am thinking, and if I screw it up, please forgive me."

"The flight you just took me on was more like flying with a bird than flying in an old Jenny. You, young man, are one hell of a good pilot." He added. "The other men in the design group all have told me that you have a whole different set of approach's as to how an airplane should be designed. They said you work on a plan based on what an airplane needs to do while in the air. Frankly, they are admiring your ideas but are afraid to try some of them."

"What you are telling them is just too far away from what they think is practically possible. On the other hand, what you are saying and what you have shown me while in the air makes sense to me. So, I want to listen to all of the good ideas out there and still keep my mind open."

"Now, I understand what they are talking about. You have done things with an old trainer that most pilots have never experienced. You just showed me that a lot of difficult maneuvers are possible and safe if they are planned and done properly."

Cliff asked Carl to draw him a chart that could be used to organize the design team so that his ideas you are promoting could be explored and developed to a usable level. He said he would not expect the chart to be done in ten minutes. Carl could have an hour to give it his best thought.

The Cowboy's Kids

Cliff asked Carl to keep their conversation private as he knew the men were all aware that Carl had taken him for several flights and the rumor mill was already working hard as to what was going to happen next. Cliff stood up, told Carl to set tight and work on the chart and he would be back in an hour.

Carl was relieved that he did not get fired but he was really not sure as to what to put down on the paper. He looked back in his life and tried to imagine what his dad would do in such a situation? The answer came quickly. Carl took the pencil and laid the pad of paper down with the sheet facing longwise on the desk. The first thing he drew was a simple picture of an airplane.

Under the picture he drew a box and labeled it Chief Designer. He knew that Cliff was in that position and Carl certainly did not want to make an enemy so he put his name under the title. He respected Cliff and he knew that Cliff would listen to almost anything that he suggested. He had always been a friend and a loyal supporter in the workplace. Carl also knew that there were several good engineers on the design team. All they needed was some concrete direction and some firm dates to work toward.

Then he started from the left side of the paper and added a new lower layer. There were 4 boxes in this layer and they were titled,

- Airframe design

- Engine and power

- Performance and Endurance

- Quality and safety

Carl drew a line from the airplane picture to each box and made sure the proper attachment point was somewhere near the design area where he wanted the box to apply.

Kenneth Orr

Carl did not put any names in these positions but he already knew that several of the designers only had skills in one area. The current organization was so loose that everyone was working on almost everything. The results were not turning out very good.

What was worse yet was the fact that the company's owner had no practical schedule in mind. He just wanted to get a new design completed and ready to build. Cliff had a real challenge on his plate. He also knew that Cliff would be taking this information to the company owner. He also saw a potential meeting for him with the company owner.

Carl then put a vertical line down from each box sub-title and began to list subjects.

*Under Airframe design he added: materials, weight and balance, controls systems, instrumentation, and maintenance concerns.

*Under Engine and Power he added: Air Cooled, Water-cooled power plant, Horsepower, fuel allowances, mounting configuration and availability.

*Under Performance he added: Distance, Altitude, Weather conditions and speed. He thought for a minute and added pilot controls, testing and problem identification.

*Under Quality and safety he added: production quality, materials selections, workmanship, service periods and then he wrote a big long series of words that he absolutely believed in. "Safe to fly, means the airplane can go into the sky, do what it was intended to do, and everything and everyone survive for a safe and fully controlled landing."

When he had completed the writing he realized that he was just getting started. Cliff had given him an opportunity to show what he could contribute in the areas of airplane

The Cowboy's Kids

design, flying experience, and potentially in the design management area. At the bottom of the chart Carl had drawn a second small picture of an airplane. He wondered what was coming next. His sketch looked a lot like his Jenny

Carl sat at the desk and thought a long time about what was really going to be required. He started to relate to the names of the current engineers. He penciled their names next to boxes where they had talent.

There were several boxes where nobody was really an expert and there were serious concerns about people who were supposed to be qualified in a specific area. He also thought that Cliff might think he was too brash by making the engineering effort he was running look like it was not being run well.

Whatever, it was too late to let these issues get in the way. His chart was drawn and he had no way to back out of this situation now. The hour was about up.

Just then the door opened and Cliff came back in. He had been to a store and bought some sandwiches. They both saw each other and smiled. Cliff handed Carl a sandwich and told him to relax. He told him that he looked way too serious and he needed to unwind a little.

Cliff opened a second bag and took out two cold beers. He opened them and gave one to Carl. As they ate, Cliff asked Carl if he had gotten any work done on the chart.

Carl laid down his sandwich and put the tablet in the center of the desk. Cliff took a quick look and said he wanted to understand what was written on the paper, but, he wanted to eat before the sandwich got cold. Cliff was a small, but deliberate man and when he was mad, he got red faced. When he was pleased it was common to see him smile. Carl was watching to see which reaction Cliff was going to have. Cliff just sat there, eating his lunch and looking at the chart. It seemed like an eternity to Carl. He just waited and bit

Kenneth Orr

his tongue, so he did not interrupt Cliff's silent review. Carl dug into his sandwich and soon it was gone. The cold beer hit the spot and the cleanup from eating went quickly, as soon as the food was gone.

Carl wanted to say something, but he did not know what. He knew if he said the wrong thing it would not be wise. Finally Cliff laid the tablet down and looked Carl straight in the eye and said, "Damn good job, son. You have seen where we are failing and it is my intention to let you be a major part of the solution." Cliff then got a big wide smile on his face and handed the tablet to Carl. Carl then knew he was in fine shape with Cliff.

Cliff then went into a short discussion about what he had seen in the aircraft industry. He said that many pilots had learned how to control an airplane from the cockpit but they were not at all aware what was going on in the airplane when they followed the normal instructions.

He said most pilots were still a lot like circus daredevils. They wanted to fly just for the thrill. They had very little knowledge about what was really happening to the airplane to back it up. He was frankly surprised that more of them had not been killed.

Cliff told Carl he had advanced far beyond this level and had a lot of knowledge that needed to be put to good use to make good design decisions. Then he said, "Carl, you still need to learn more. The aircraft industry is closely aligned with the Army."

"The ultimate goal for an aircraft company in today's economy is to design airplanes that the government would buy. There is also a growing interest in commercial applications and special purpose aircraft. I think you are one of the people who see this vision better than most."

Cliff told Carl that there was an advanced development effort going on at McCook Field in Dayton, Ohio. The Army and a group of private businessmen were heading up the

The Cowboy's Kids

effort. They would be glad to have Carl become one of their students. Cliff wanted Carl to go there and spend some time working with people who had a better appreciation for the problems that were related to flying. Cliff had friends in the right places to make this happen and he told him that he needed to spend at least three or four months there. Then he should come back to California and be a better-qualified member of the design team.

Carl was all ears. He was being given the opportunity to do what he really loved and become even more qualified to design airplanes. This was like a dream come true.

Cliff told him that his chart was going to be used to realign the efforts at Ryan's design office and he wanted to use some additional ideas to improve it more.

Cliff told Carl to catch a train the next morning and to make the arrangements for someone look over his house for a while. He told Carl that when he returned he would have a lot more responsibility and he would also be the pilot to test and make sure that a new airplane they were developing, was ready to be sold.

Carl went to the phone and called Barbara. She was always interested in what he was doing and wanted to continue being a part of his life for as long as she could. Carl respected her and knew that she would be equally excited for him.

When Barbara answered the phone she was glad to hear his voice. He told her about his new assignment and she was thrilled. After a few minutes of talk, some of it about the business and some about Barbara, she broke the normal thought process and said, "I have something to tell you Carl." Carl was stopped short as Barbara never had kept any secrets from him.

Barbara said that her Doctor friend, Paul, had asked her to marry him and she had said **yes**. Carl was happy for her, but he was also sad, as now she would not have as much time to spend with him. Paul and Barbara had agreed to

Kenneth Orr

wait until the next spring to get married and there were a lot of things that had to be set into their rightful places before they reached next May.

Barbara also said that she and Carl needed to get some additional legal paper on file, to protect both of them with their investments. Carl was happy to see Barbara start to build a family and he actually was relieved to hear that she would have someone to share her life.

CHAPTER 2-10
Going Separate Paths

The Goodwin kids were now grown adults and were fully capable of going forward as independent individuals. Barbara was going to be married soon and Carl was becoming an airplane designer and test pilot. Both had careers, but both were still co-owners of a large land investment company. The company had grown much stronger financially since their parents started to build wealth. Their holdings were located all over Texas and in California and most recently in Oklahoma.

Every three months, Art, the business manager, would take most of the available cash and find some ideal land to invest it in. Barbara would approve all transactions before they were actually made. Art was well instructed by Barbara that money was only paper and the real value of something was more certain when you could see or touch it. Barbara had watched the stock market grow and she was adamant than no money was to ever be invested in any type of stock or bond holdings. There was no regulation as to many of the stock market sales and the hungry crooks were everywhere.

The entire country was undergoing a complete readjustment to the new inventions and machines of all kinds that were rapidly becoming available. The automobile was a whole new concept for personal travel. There were few good roads and the push to develop paved routes between cities was

Kenneth Orr

underway. The plan was that these roads had to be good enough to be used by cars. The supporting businesses of selling car parts and doing repair work and teaching people to drive, were growing rapidly.

The automobile fuel industry was also booming. Oil was becoming a powerful business force. The minerals under the earth, such as oil and coal were commonly being sold separately from the soil on top of the minerals.

Coal was already a hot industry. Heat for homes and businesses were always a major concern. Fuel for the railroad locomotives, and for other steam powered industry was in high demand. Electrical utility companies were using coal to generate steam and the demand was growing everywhere. The industrial north was adding new factories to build all of these new products and the pressure to make vast sums of money had never been greater. The federal government was taking note and had authorized several additional new hydroelectric producing dams on major waterways.

The aircraft industry was also making a big impact. This impact was a little later than that of the automobile, but it was just as dynamic. One major impact was the need to be able to forecast and make timely reports on weather.

The railroads had forced the development of standard time zones all across the country and the airplane was forcing the development of weather stations and better rapid communication systems. Telephones were more common and long distance calling was getting much quicker. Many smaller communities had limited service available and the phone customers usually had to use party line hookups. This was an inconvenience and other parties on the same line could listen in on each other's phone calls.

The government was watching the countries industrial growth and trying to keep pace. The largest industrial tycoons were well rooted and were creating conditions with little regards for the pain and hardship that they were placing on the working classes of people. Their actions led to the

The Cowboy's Kids

enactment of child labor laws and the first federal safety regulations. Labor unions were also growing in strength. The battle lines between management and labor began to become clearly defines.

There were growing concerns that people have proper training to drive an automobile. People were being killed in automobile wrecks at an increasing rate. The government finally stepped in. The told the individual states to test drivers and issue drivers licenses. Those who could not pass the tests were not allowed to drive.

The big eastern city based large banks controlled much of the nations business activity. San Francisco, Dallas, Denver, St Louis and Chicago held the financial reins on many of the western states. San Antonio was still a small town but was slowly becoming a bigger city. The pace of life was still slower and still family oriented. The big money in Texas and most of the major business activity was in Dallas and in Houston. Austin was the capital and all of the political activity was focused on the state congressional activities. The New York stock market was running wild and the values of stock were not realistic.

Barbara and Carl saw all of the growing confusion from every area and wanted to protect their holdings. They both knew that the entire value of their holdings could be lost should they take some unwise chance as to the way they safeguarded everything. They both were concerned that either of them getting married would add another opinion to the way things were managed. This could become even worse should a divorce happen. Then there could be all kinds of problems. They pondered the situation and decided to do two things.

They had made up their minds that all of the money in banks over a $1,000 balance was to all be withdrawn and put in a safe place. In effect this would minimize the opportunity to lose the majority of any cash they had if a problem came up. They were more interested in security than in any interest they could make on money. They were making their

Kenneth Orr

largest profits on the values of investments and on holdings for underground oil and minerals.

When rent and payment money would come in to a bank, it would be withdrawn every Thursday as soon as the banks opened. This approach put tight controls on all of their bank accounts. The bankers were not happy with these arrangements but they had no choice if they wanted to keep the Goodwin accounts.

Carl told Art, "Bankers have few friends when they are not able to make money from handling their money at a profit." Art understood completely and was handling his own personal funds following the same financial approaches.

The on-hand cash money and all important legal papers would be held in a large safe that was in San Antonio, Texas. Barbara had enough room to put such a safe in her home and it would not be obvious. This safe was to be unknown to anyone other than Carl, Barbara and Art. The ownership of the company was to remain 50% in each other's name.

They drew up a strict legal contract that any spouse, to either Barbara or Carl, would be required to sign a document that waived any and all rights to any ownership in the company. They also included a clause that said should either of them die the other would inherit the other's 50% of ownership. All assets owned by the Goodwin Investment Company at the time that either Carl or Barbara got married, were to be included within this contract. Barbara and Carl both knew this approach would keep the company from being diluted and was in line with the wishes of their parents.

Barbara and Carl were to receive a quarterly salary of $500 for the rest of their lives. Should either want to change this contract they must have a signed declaration of agreement from the other as to what changes were to be made or the change was not going to be allowed to happen.

When both Barbara and Carl died the full balance of the account and ownership would be given to a university to

The Cowboy's Kids

invest in higher education. They both knew this is what Chalk and Wanda would like to see happen. They both liked the agreement, so they had a corporate lawyer friend put it into a legal form, signed it in ink and put it in a safe place. They also filed a copy with the Public Records registry in San Antonio.

Both children were well off financially and this agreement was not going to change anything in their life. They had good jobs and were glad and anxious to follow their careers. Work was keeping their minds busy and their life style was not going to change. Having money had never made either of them change. They were still the same simple people they had always wanted to be. They were both full of energy and ambition to lead a normal and productive life.

Barbara had never introduced her potential new husband to Carl, so a meeting was scheduled for the event. The meeting was also going to be when Barbara told Paul about the holding company and the conditions of the contract.

Paul was a neat, good looking young man who had been raised in northern Minnesota. He had an accent, and the way he said his words were always fun to hear. His birth family was from Norway and had been farming in Minnesota for several years. Paul had gone to college and medical school in St. Paul.

After finishing his training, he worked as an intern in Rochester, Minnesota at the Mayo Clinic. Paul's parents had both died and he was an only child.

The First World War put a serious drain on the medical profession and he had volunteered to become an Army Doctor. He had seen combat in France and was just as dedicated to helping the injured recover as was Barbara.

The evening for the meeting arrived and Carl met Barbara and Paul at a nice first class Italian restaurant in San Antonio. Everyone loved good garlic flavored food and this restaurant had the very best. You could smell garlic a block

Kenneth Orr

away. Carl was wearing his casual western attire and was more comfortable with his dress style, than in a suit like the eastern businessmen wore.

Paul was wearing a suit, but with a tie. When he saw Carl he asked Barbara if Carl would have any problems seeing him in more formal clothes. He was obviously more comfortable in casual clothes and he noted what Carl was wearing. Soon everyone was in an open shirt, no tie and was a lot more comfortable. The clothes really had made no difference.

Everyone hit it off very well. Paul was really a "common people" type, country guy at heart. Barbara was well aware of his real inner attitudes. They had a great meal and after the last plate was removed from the table, Barbara opened up a new part of the conversation and said, "Paul, Carl and I have something to discuss with you."

She began, "You know I love you and want to get married. We have every reason to look forward to a long and happy life together. However, Carl and I have been building a company our parents both started for us when they were alive. We have some serious, but honest feelings about how this matter would be handled when either of us get married." Paul said he understood and agreed with approaching everything now. This would prevent something of this magnitude from becoming a problem later.

Barbara went on, " Our Company has grown to be very valuable and we want to follow the same path that our parents took to protect it from any kind of negative situation in the future."

"We both know that the value is only protected when it is real and when it is not all bound up with a bunch of legal or confusing issues. We have drawn up a special contract that will allow it to remain safe and to ultimately allow it to be used for higher education."

Paul was a little set back by all of this news and he asked why they were including him in the conversation at this

The Cowboy's Kids

point. Barbara said she wanted him to know all about the company and appreciate what it had become to both her and to Carl. It was also something she wanted to make sure he understood fully before they were married.

She added, "We all need to sign a document that would allow the company to go forward with no changes in the event we were to ever get a divorce or either of us should die. She explained the situation and made sure Paul was not left out on any of the details.

Paul asked Barbara what the company was worth. She said. "There was no real way to tell. Everything is in the form of a land investments and land is only as valuable as the current market demands. However, we know that the summary value is well above one million dollars."

Carl told Paul about the home in California and how he wanted to continue living there when he got done with his training in Ohio. He also told Paul that he and Barbara would be able to draw a salary from the income being generated and that this was a very comfortable sum of money. Paul just sat and looked at Barbara and Carl. He was obviously very surprised and impressed by all that he had just learned.

Carl ordered a bottle of white wine and had the waiter pour everyone a glass. Paul was smiling but he had the inner wheels of his mind going full speed. Any doctor normally does this when there is some unexpected situation with which to deal.

Barbara looked at Paul, straight in the eye, and said, "You know I love you and I want to marry you very much, but I do not want you to ever feel this situation is something that I will use to make you or me unhappy. I hope you understand this." Carl spoke up and said that he had always wanted to see Barbara happy and Paul was obviously the man with the power to do this for her. Carl said he was extremely glad to know Paul was going to become a member of the family.

Kenneth Orr

Paul smiled and finally had something to say. He said, "I have never known anyone like you, Barbara, and I want her to be my wife and me to become your husband very much. The good news that you also have some money from another part of your life, well, it's thrilling. You know that I will be glad to agree to anything that protects this for you and to sign an agreement to that effect."

Prior to leaving town, Carl looked at Barbara and said, "Barbara Wilson. Hummm, I will need to get used to saying you name that way, I guess...

He added. "Carl, you are one hell of a young man and I look forward to us becoming the best of friends." They finished the wine and said, lets go for a ride in a horse drawn carriage to celebrate and to just talk.

The ride was planned to be an enjoyable event, a time of relaxation for everyone. Carl had the waiter ice down another bottle of white wine and furnished them with some glasses to take along in the carriage.

Carl left San Antonio the next morning for Dayton, Ohio. He was going there to get involved with the emerging aircraft development effort at McCook Field. Carl was excited that Barbara was going to get married and that her immediate world was becoming much happier for her. He liked Paul and it was good to know that he was a good and respected doctor.

CHAPTER 2-11
The Time to Always Remember

Time was moving quickly. Barbara had set a wedding date several times but because of heavy work schedules and demands from the Army she had to keep moving things forward. A military nurse's life was never going to be easy. The demands were not only to support sick soldiers but the constant pressure to report current patients conditions, keep administrative paperwork in good order, and help train new candidates was almost too much for anyone.

In December of 1929 a financial shock wave hit the entire country. The American public had lost confidence in the stock market and there wan an immediate was a run on the banks. The New York stock market had crashed.

The impact in every financial organization was instant and enormous. Barbara went to see Art when she heard about the problem and wanted to know what cash they had on deposit in any banks. Art had already gone to the local bank in San Antonio and tried to get in. The doors were locked and the crowd outside was furious. The investment company had a little over $1,200 on deposit and could not withdraw it. The bank had failed. This was the only bank they had deposits in and they were thankful for the policies they had followed that had safeguard their assets.

Kenneth Orr

Barbara and Carl had learned to be cautious from their parents and always had zero debt. They did have a lot of prime valued land and a couple of small businesses but the impact to their company was minimal as compared to others who had large bank accounts, outstanding debt, and a lot of now worthless stock certificates.

The assets they owned were safe from any take over but their real value was obviously going to be a lot less. Paul looked at Barbara and said, "It may be worth less now but someday it will come back. We still own everything and we are no worse off than anyone else, in fact, we are probably a lot better off." Barbara called Carl in Ohio and they were both concerned. But, they both knew that they had been doing the right things in the past to protect their wealth.

All of the Goodwin assets were debt-free and the deeds and ownership documents were all locked in a strong safe in their San Antonio office. The common man on the street was suffering the most. He had little to no income and buying the necessities of life was not going to be easy.

The retail consumer's world had begun to enjoy a lot of new and very desirable products. The stock market had raised capital to support these new products and to allow volume production to continue. Most of this wealth was based on the sale stock certificates and bonds.

The problem surfaced when the stock buying public lost confidence in the value represented by these documents. Most stock issues were selling for values that were far above their actual values. The banks had loaned out money using a formula called margins. This practice allowed them to loan money and only back it up with 10% of the actual cash on deposit. All of these practices were very risky.

Financial practices that add large levels of risk were dangerous. All they could show for the advertised value of something was a fancy piece of printed-paper. The public soon saw this weakness and the banks, which still had available money on deposit, were soon being drained.

The Cowboy's Kids

There were no laws to regulate this activity and most banks were too far over extended to remain solvent. They were paying low interest to the account holders and charging very high interest to the borrowers. Their greed and overwhelming rush to make more money had driven the whole system into a point of predictable disaster. Large borrowers were given better interest rates. The process of money lending and selling stock made the real and perceived value of investment paper go to almost nothing.

1929 was a cold Christmas as there was no money flowing in the economy. The depression was hardest on the poor people. Many large companies had gone broke, shut down, and the majority of the working class people were out on the street without jobs. The impact was greatest in the big northern industrial areas and the larger cities all across the country, but it affected everyone. The only people whose lifestyles were unaffected were the very wealthy.

A few individuals, who were working for government agencies, were able to keep some level of employment and make some money. These people were hurting, but still had food on the table and had something to do to generate a reduced level of income.

Carl, Art and Barbara had been ultra conservative and had a lot of cash money in hand. They were also aware that there were laws coming to go off the gold standard and use the federal government to back up the value of paper money. Only Carl and Barbara knew about the huge amount of gold money they had in their old strongboxes. They quickly developed a plan to safeguard it and to make sure the federal banks did not know about their gold money. They were concerned that they might be required to turn it in and exchange it for paper money. They absolutely did not want this to happen.

In the early winter of 1931 Carl developed a plan to hide the strongboxes. As a child, Carl and Sarge had done a lot of fishing on the lower Medina River. On one of these trips

Kenneth Orr

Sarge discovered a small cave that was about ten feet away from the river's bank.

It was well hidden by several large limestone blocks that were wedged into the front of the opening. Sarge and Carl squeezed thru the large stone opening and found a large room with several smaller side rooms. They went several hundred feet back into the hillside and the cave floor was sloped so that any drainage was flowing to the front.

There were two side rooms, and they were even higher and dry. They had once found some old Indian pots and a lot of arrowheads in one of the smaller rooms. The cave was located on a small tract of land that they still owned. This situation made them feel more secure with the plan.

The entrance to the smaller rooms, inside the cave was also hard to find. The inside of the cave was dark, dry and cool. There had been some snakes and other critters living inside at some time as old bones and shedded snakeskins were a common sight. However, Carl had never encountered any aggressive snakes.

Carl told Barbara that they should put the strongboxes in that cave and then make sure the big stones on the front were sealed. The property was part of the original Goodwin ranch. Both Barbara and Carl agreed to the plan.

In the spring, 1932 at Easter time, Carl and Barbara loaded the two strongboxes into Barbara's Ford. The boxes took up most of the back seat area. They then drove to the old home place. The renters were informed that they were on the property and that they were going to go fishing like they had when they were younger. Carl was able to drive the car to an area about 200 feet from the cave entrance. He parked the car in a position so that nobody could see what they were going to be doing.

Barbara got out a fishing pole and went down to the edge of the river and put her line into the pool of water. Her

The Cowboy's Kids

hook was empty as she was not too serious about catching a fish.

Carl took all of the contents out of the first strongbox and carried it into the cave. He had to squeeze the box through the opening but it finally went inside. Then he took it into the small room where the bones had been discovered. His light was limited as he had a small carbide coalminer's lamp on his head. Carl selected a small corner where he placed the box. Then, in several trips, he took all of the coins and the leather pouches where they were placed into the strongbox in the cave. Finally, he had the first box fully inside. He then repeated the same process and put the second strongbox into the same area. The whole process took about three hours and Carl was tired. He had taken his time and made sure that it was going to be very hard for anyone to ever find these boxes without very good instructions.

Carl went down to the river and saw that Barbara was still fishing. She was anxious to see what had happened to the strongboxes and Carl took her up the side of the riverbank and took her inside. She saw what Carl had done and was relieved that this place was a great spot to hide their strongboxes. The locks were reinstalled and Carl and Barbara placed large stones on top of both boxes so that they were completely hidden. When they left the cave they placed several large rocks in the passageway to make the entrance even harder to find.

They knew that time and bushes would fully cover the opening. There were no public entrances to the area and the cave was only known to a very few people. Most of them, other than Barbara and Carl, were very old or had already passed away.

Carl then took out a second fishing pole and a can of bait and he and Barbara went back down to the river. Soon they both had fish on their lines and several in the bucket. As darkness approached, they packed up and drove into Bandera where they got a hotel room and spent the night.

Finally, in the late spring of 1932 Barbara and Paul got married. They went to a local Lutheran Church in San Antonio and had the minister perform the ceremony on a Friday afternoon after they both got off work. They were just tired of waiting. Their lives were so busy and they were dedicated to their work. Getting married was an event that was not life threatening. It seemed like their real priorities belonged to treating patients who were fighting for their life in the emergency ward.

They were both very happy, but they both had grown into demanding career responsibilities. They decided to take a later date honeymoon trip and went back to work the next morning after the wedding.

The local San Antonio economy was in such bad shape that taking time to be happy was difficult. It would make one feel guilty when you saw the masses of hungry people lined up in food lines and looking for jobs of any kind.

They were living in the same house Barbara had bought several years before and the business office had been relocated into a bigger building on the north side of San Antonio's downtown section. Their home was filled with happiness, but the work schedule for both of the newlyweds was difficult. It was common for Paul to get home, eat a quick meal, and try to get some rest and then have a phone call to come tend to a sick and ailing soldier. His life was difficult.

Barbara was equally busy. She was working as a charge nurse in the hospital's operating rooms and had several other nurses working with her. She was never able to separate herself from the hospital very long and the pressure was never ending.

Carl had attended training at the McCook Field operation in Dayton, Ohio. He had made a lot of good friends and professional contacts. He learned a lot about airplane designing and became exposed to a lot of new ideas. Everything was focused on building better and more dependable military airplanes.

Army Aircraft Development Facility, McCook Field, 1925

Carl got to meet Orville Wright and to learn a lot about how to develop a successful project from a man named Charles Kettering. He was called "Boss Kett" by his associates and was a man who seemed to never run out of good ideas or energy. Boss Kett had started a company he called "Dayton Electric Company" where he was designing and building electrical parts for automobiles. He was credited with the invention of the electric starting motor for automobile engines. His company was later renamed to just one word, Delco.

Prior to Kettering's invention an automobile engine had to be started with a hand crank. The engine would sometimes backfire and the cranking person's arm or shoulder would be injured. Kettering's wonderful invention soon became

Kenneth Orr

a standard part on all automobiles. Boss Kett also was working on airplane engine designs.

He was deeply involved with the new systems that the Army was developing for building all metal military airplanes. His ideas were much different than what Carl had been exposed to before and they made a lot of sense.

Another key part of his education was meeting Glenn Curtiss. Mr. Curtiss was from a small town near Buffalo, New York. He was a successful motorcycle racer and manufacturer. He developed a whole series of powerful gasoline engines that were better than many of the others on the market. His designs were both air-cooled and water-cooled.

His preference was the air-cooled versions as they had fewer parts and were not prone to as many problems in winter weather. He had also branched out into building airplanes and his most famous airplane was the Jenny. Carl was impressed with Glenn and spent several hours in discussion about how he had rebuilt his personal Jenny. Mr. Curtiss had done a lot of work with the Navy and was working on airplanes that could land and take off from the water. The Navy was also developing ships with small landing fields on the top.

Carl was surprised to learn that Mr. Curtiss and the Wright Brothers were not good friends. They both were looking to build airplanes and make money. The Wright brothers had accused Mr. Curtiss of stealing several of their ideas and not paying them any royalty. The whole situation was a mess. Even the government patent office was involved.

Henry Ford had also become involved in the development of aircraft and was working to build an all-metal new passenger transport. Aluminum was becoming available in sufficient quantity to be used to build a limited number of airplanes. This material became available because of a new electric power plant at Niagara Falls, New York. Making aluminum from bauxite ore required a lot of electricity. The new electric generating plant made this process practical.

The Cowboy's Kids

Aluminum is only about one third the weight of steel and in some conditions it is nearly as strong. It is much stronger than any other lightweight metal and is easier to work into complex shapes than steel.

The Ford motor company joined into the airplane market and built a three-engine passenger plane that was revolutionary. Henry Ford's "Tri-Motor" airplane fabrication plant was located in the Detroit, Michigan area.

The metal working industry had to develop a complete new approach to forming aluminum. Steel, used to make cars has a very different set of properties than aluminum and the tools had to be less stressful when sheets were being formed into the desired shapes.

The Ford Tri-Motor airplane was a stable airplane in flight and had established a good safety record. Three radial engines were standard and the plane could take off and land on a short, mowed grassy field.

Carl got an opportunity to learn how to fly a Tri-Motor Ford and soon developed a love for this airplane. It was relatively easy to fly and having three engines gave it much more power and improved the controllability. The extra power from having three engines made it a safer plane in all kinds of weather.

Carl's interests and involvements were so many that he stayed in Dayton for almost a year. He personally saw several major developments in aviation happen around him. Henry Ford had built a paved airstrip in Detroit, Michigan and was beginning to build airplanes in quantity. The newer airplanes had enclosed cockpits and the cold winter flying was going to be much warmer. Carl soon had a new appreciation for airplane design and how the design could be build in production quantities.

Charles Lindbergh had recently flown solo across the Atlantic Ocean. He had used an airplane made exclusively for him by Ryan Aviation back in San Diego, California. Aviation had

Kenneth Orr

become a growing industry and everybody in the business was looking for new business. However, the poor economy had shut down most new commercial interest in airplanes. The only remaining strong interest was still happening in the Army and Navy.

Carl went home to Texas in late March of 1933. He wanted to stay for a few days and just relax. He was so glad to get back to a warmer climate and get out of the cold Ohio winter. He was now ready to go back to work at Ryan in California and develop better airplanes built with much better flight systems. His old Jenny was still a lot of fun to fly but it was never as much fun to fly as a hot mono-wing speedster or a Ford Tri-Motor.

The entire airplane industry had suffered from the bad economic times, but it had survived. There were a lot of the smaller less financially capable airplane companies going out of business and the aircraft industry was in turmoil.

The aviation industry was always racing to develop a new and better design. People with a deep worthwhile knowledge about designing airplanes were always being charmed to come to another company. The pay scales were finally getting better.

Carl saw a lot of people being bought but the additional money they were being offered did not interest him. He was not interested in moving to another company just to get a bigger paycheck.

When Carl got back to San Diego, Cliff called him in, and in a confidential conversation, told him that a company up in Long Beach, California was begging him to gather his best design engineers and come join them. It was not just a money deal to Cliff, they were going to design and build an all-metal twin-engine passenger plane that they had been doing research on a new design for several months.

Carl was one of Cliff's special people and he wanted him to go with him. Cliff told Carl that this was a very special

The Cowboy's Kids

project he wanted Carl to be involved with a lot of the design work.

In August of 1934 the President of Germany, Hindenburg passed away. By the end of August, Adolph Hitler had taken over as the Fuhrur. He immediately began to alter the German government and military to fit his personal plans to become a world dominant country.

One of his strongest desires was to dominate all of Europe, then invade and take over Great Britain. It soon became apparent that peace and the old agreements from the First World War treaties were at serious risk.

The United States government was aware of all of this activity and upon the request of The English government, had begun to supply small amounts of military equipment to Great Britain.

The Boeing Company in Seattle, Washington had independently designed and built a new bomber airplane that was considered the world leader in this type of aircraft. The British government had ordered several of these airplanes and by 1937 they were being built and stockpiled to improve the capability of the Royal British Air Force. It was called the B-17.

Passenger and freight transporting type airplanes were in high demand in the United States. Practical and dependable designs were still being developed. The new Douglas airplane was being built to target this market. Cliff's new job was with a company headed up by a young man who's last name was Douglas. He called his company The Douglas Airplane Company.

Mr. Douglas had been a pilot for a long time and he had organized a lot of investors who had put up a lot of money to help him. He was a good pilot and a wise businessman. He also had the government's backing to move forward with this project.

The Ryan Company in San Diego was not developing any large airplane projects. Carl thought about the job offer and told Cliff if he would go with him to join the Douglas Airplane Company.

The Federal Government was pushing hard for the completion of the big Hoover electric power dam on the Colorado River. The power generating capability from this new dam was about to come on line. The power lines to distribute power to southern California were quickly being installed.

The result was of great interest to aircraft companies to grow in southern California. More electrical power would mean more aluminum could be produced and airplanes made from this material were in demand.

The United States military was keeping abreast of the events in Germany and in all of Europe. The American people were strongly against any American involvement in a war. World War One was still fresh in their memory and nobody wanted to see history repeat itself.

This potential war situation was growing complex and the United States War Department began an increased level of preparation work on an undercover basis. Carl was in the right place at the right time.

The availabity of adequate electrical power was only one of the benefits. The massive water reserves being created behind the dam would allow the west coast cities to have sufficient water year-round. The economy in California was about to take off.

Barbara and Paul had both decided to leave the Army and form a private medical clinic in San Antonio. They both were given separation papers that kept them in the inactive reserve forces with their current ranks.

The Cowboy's Kids

In 1935 they made the move and set up an office on the west side of town. The office was small, but it was adequate to see about 10 to 15 patients a day. The majority of their patients were former military and many were old friends from the "Fort Sam" hospital. Paul bought a new Ford and used it to do house calls for people who were too sick to come to the office. Barbara ran the office and was Paul's nurse and business assistant when he needed her.

Soon, Paul's skills and reputation as a surgeon were requiring him to be at the local hospital more than in his office. Barbara was always at his side assisting in the operating room and doing a lot of the tasks that Paul needed to be done.

The Army had never wanted either Paul or Barbara to leave. They were offered several better assignments and had always said they were not looking to be on the administration side of the hospital staff. They were much happier doing what they could to assist sick and injured soldiers and did not want administrative jobs.

The working situation in San Antonio for a private medical practice was very similar to being in the Army. There were many retired soldiers living in the community. Large numbers of local poor people used the Santa Rosa hospital for health care. Paul often treated patients who had no money or who were so poor, that paying for a doctor's services would have made them penniless. The chief administrator in the Army hospital knew about Paul and Barbara's reputation in the community and he had kept in close touch.

The situation in Germany was becoming more complicated. The Versailles treaty that ended World War One had specifically halted Germany from using conscription to muster a large military force.

On March 16th, 1935, Hitler issued his orders in direct violation of the Versailles agreement and immediately began a large military buildup. Further complicating issues, on September

Kenneth Orr

15[th,] Hitler issued orders stripping Jewish citizens of all legal rights.

Hitler was taking complete control. He created his own political police force called The Gestapo. In February of 1936, Hitler ordered placing this organization above all laws and control other than that of the Fuhrer.

CHAPTER 2-12
The Years of Challenge

The Goodwin kids were well settled into their lives with one exception. Carl was never in one place long enough to find a long-term relationship with a young lady or find a wife. He had met several nice young ladies, but the relationships would slip away when he was traveling. Carl was never one to get too close to a lady, but as he grew older and saw how happy Barbara and Paul were, he started to rethink about his future and about finding a wife.

Carl's job at The Douglas Airplane Company had put him in a situation where a lot of people his age were working in the same area. Several attractive young ladies were in this group. Most of them were married but a few were still single. His job was never a day-to-day routine plan. He was involved with the design of several new airplane systems and he would often test his new designs for function on a prototype airplane. These test flights would require several days and his schedule was never firm. There were two attractive young women working in his design group and they were both single.

Several of Carl's assignments required weekend work. On one weekend when the development schedule was running behind, he had to work late on Saturday. One of the young women was assigned to assist him. When they got the day's work done, Carl suggested they go get something to eat. "Debbie" gladly agreed. They went to a nice Italian restaurant

Kenneth Orr

and after eating they had a few drinks. The moment was comfortable for both of them. This same situation happened several times and soon they were seeing each other on a regular basis.

It was springtime and the Mexican holiday of Cinco De Mayo was approaching. Carl invited Debbie to go to his favorite Mexican restaurant over the weekend and join in the celebration with him. He remembered how much fun it was back in San Antonio and he was full of anticipation about the day. Debbie was eager to go with Carl. It was becoming obvious that these two people were more than just friends.

Within a month, Debbie was asking Carl if he wanted to go meet her parents. He was agreeable but he sensed that there was something more to her invitation. Carl was slow to warm up to her request. He was feeling like he was being pushed into something and that was an uncomfortable and strange way to feel. Debbie kept pushing him and finally he agreed to go see her family.

The visit to see a girl's family was something he was dreading and he tried to put it off and move it out into the future as far as he could. Finally, there were no good ways to stall it off any longer so Carl loaded Debbie in his Ford and they drove about 40 miles east into the California countryside. The roads were really bad. The Ford had to cross ruts and gullies several times and the roads were more like dirt paths. They finally arrived at the home. The house was a small wooden shack that looked like it had been tied together with ropes and a few nails. Debbie told Carl that her family was poor and had put this house together from scrap materials and rocks that were in the area. Carl had never been given any description of Debbie's home and this place shocked him.

Debbie got out of the car and walked up the dirt path toward the house. As she got near the front entrance, a small girl came out to meet her. Carl was just getting out of the car and Debbie brought the child to meet him. She said, "This

The Cowboy's Kids

is Jessica. She is my three year old daughter." Carl was shocked. He did not know that Debbie had a child. He knew immediately that she had not told him a lot about her past. Carl was not comfortable with the situation as he was being placed in a very uncomfortable position and he was not sure as to what to say.

Carl told Debbie that they needed to go have a private talk immediately and he was not ready to go any further with their relationship until he was being told the whole truth about Debbie's past. Debbie took Jessica back to the house and took her in. She was inside about five minutes and then came back out. An older lady came with her and walked her to the car. Debbie told Carl that this was her mother and she wanted to say hello. Carl was a gentleman and exchanged kind words with the lady. Debbie said good-by to her mom and got back in the car. Carl drove about a mile and found a big tree to park under.

There was a large log on the ground that was a good place to sit. He got out and told Debbie to come sit on the log and talk with him.

Debbie got out of the car and came over. She stood in front of Carl and was starting to cry. Carl said he was sorry she was crying but he had to know what she was thinking by not telling him about her child before now. Debbie sat down and got very quiet and grabbed Carl's hand. She then began to talk. She said that she had lived in San Diego as a young girl and her mother was very poor. Her mother had been a prostitute in the bar district and Debbie never knew who her father might be. Her mother had lived in a house where a lot of women who were in the same business, lived and Debbie was never sure what was going on.

When Debbie was about twelve, her mother was forcing her to do the same thing for men. The whole situation was bad but when she was sixteen she ran away and found a man who was good to her.

245

Kenneth Orr

They lived together for about three years and when they discovered that Debbie was going to have a baby he dumped her on a street corner to fend for herself.

Debbie knew where her mother had moved, so she went to her for help. Debbie's mother and Debbie had built the shack on the hillside to live in. Debbie left the baby there with her mother. She went to Long Beach to find a job. She got a clerical job at the airplane company. She said her goal was to get a better life and then go get her daughter. Debbie said she was afraid to tell Carl, or anyone else about her past, as she knew she would not be accepted. She had hoped that Carl might feel sorry for her when he saw what her life had been, so she tricked him into coming to the shack.

Carl just sat and listened and looked off to the west. He had allowed himself to be been taken in by a girl who was an obvious fake and a person loaded with all kinds of problems. He did not know what to think or say just then and he wanted some time to understand and reflect on what he had just found out. Carl stood up and went walking down the road just to get some distance and time to think about everything. Finally, after about twenty minutes he came back to the car and told Debbie to get in the car, they were going back to town.

The trip to town was completely silent except for the noise of the Ford automobile and the wind blowing in the open windows. Carl knew he was finished with Debbie, as she had not been honest with him. He drove her to her apartment and told her that he was sorry she had lived such a hard life, but she did not need to trick people to make them like her. He said he did not want to see her anymore and asked her to not try to contact him at home or at work.

Carl told Debbie that her secrets were her's to keep and that he would not spread any stories about her at work. He added that, "As long as we work in the same work area I would appreciate it if you would keep your distance." Debbie never said a word. She opened the car door and got out.

The Cowboy's Kids

Carl drove away and told himself that he was embarrassed that such a person had taken him in.

The next day was Sunday. Carl went to church, went to a good restaurant for lunch and then went to the beach to relax. He had a lot to forget and a lot to remember. He remembered the last time he had seen Barbara and how happy she and Paul were as a married couple. He also remembered the idea that he wanted to be as happy and how much a family had been a major part of his past. His upbringing had always taught him to respect a lady as a lady, that is, until they were found to be otherwise. Then the respect goes away and something else which is less desirable takes its place.

The forgetting was easy. He soon had washed away the memories of Debbie. He was aided by some of the same brand of Kentucky whiskey that his father had used to relax.

CHAPTER 2-13
Adjusting and Corrections

The next few weeks were extremely busy at work. The new airplane was taking shape and the work pace was full of anticipations and building pressures. Carl was one of the few people who had piloted a multi engine airplane before and he was named as one of the test pilots for the new aircraft. There were several new approaches incorporated into the new airplane. Some of them were:

- An all aluminum airframe structure

- Wheels that could be retracted in flight

- Two enclosed powerful new designed engines mounted on the wings

- A built in entry and exit ladder for the fuselage

- Wings that had a back sweep on the leading edge to reduce drag

- Control surfaces on both the wings and tail section

- Electric engine starting systems

- Two pilot control stations with heated flying quarters.

The Cowboy's Kids

- On board oxygen systems for crewmembers when flying at altitude.

Each of these new features was undergoing a seemingly endless series of design modifications. Every new level of development seemed to open the door for some other new and better ideas and improvements. The program was working but the personal dedication to the design by the design staff was super human. Carl was always able to see the end vision and keep the real target in his sights.

This new airplane called the DC-1 was supposed to be the airplane to get the commercial aviation industry going. The world was just sitting out there waiting to see the new airplane fly.

In 1935 a first model, identified as the DC-1, was rolled out of the hangar.

Everybody was impressed with the new look and the shiny aluminum skin. The design team, the company officials and the newspapers were all there to see if this "new bird" would fly. The chief test pilot crawled into the left seat and Carl, acting as the co-pilot, sat down beside him. Everyone cleared the area and the airplane's two engines were cranked by the new electric starters. Smoke came out of the exhausts and soon a roar could be heard from both engines. The airplane was ready for the first test flight.

The pilots applied power and released the wheel brakes. The thrust from the engines and a small tail wheel could be used to maneuver the plane on the ground. The pilot rolled the plane to the end of the runway and set the wheel brakes. He then took time to run up the engine speed on each engine independently and as they were running he checked the various gauges that were supporting the engine.

Both engines were operating fine. He then did a control surface check and everything was working properly. Then they reported to the control booth that everything was working properly. The moment of truth was at hand.

Kenneth Orr

Both engines were brought to full power and the sound was music to every designer's ears. The wheel brakes were released and the plane moved forward. It gained speed rapidly and soon the tail section lifted and became level with the front of the aircraft. More speed was being gained and as the plane passed the reviewing stand it lifted into the air. It was flying!

The plane lifted and climbed to about 2,000 feet above the ground. A small pursuit plane was also in the air and was monitoring the new aircraft to assure that there were no fires in the engines or that parts were not falling away as the plane made it's first flight. Again, all was working well.

The pilot then activated the system that retracted the wheels. The two main wheels were folded into the cavity just behind the engines and a set of doors folded over them to reduce drag. The rear wheel was locked in place and the plane was ready to test some of its flight parameters.

The plane climbed to several thousand feet and it was soon obvious that the controls were very responsive and the ride inside the plane was comfortable. The flight lasted less than an hour and was never out of the sight of the runway. When the basic tests were complete, the plane came down to a lower altitude where the landing gear was redeployed to the open and locked position. The people on the ground verified that both wheels were down and it was safe to proceed with the landing.

The landing was without incident, but both of the pilots were a little nervous. The rear wheel was not on the runway as soon as he had expected so he had to cut power sooner than he had planned, to get the tail of the airplane to come down.

When he taxied up to the hangar, the people who had witnessed the flight were elated. The plane was an obvious winner and the crowd of design engineers was soon all over the airplane taking pictures and bragging about what they had done individually to make this event possible.

Carl just sat in his chair and watched. He knew his turn to fly in the pilot's seat was coming up soon and he was enjoying the moment. The biggest thrill for him was yet to come.

The original aircraft was soon over-loaded with test schedules and new hopefully better hardware designs. The design group knew that each of these new designs would improve performance and would make the airplane more desirable. The result was that the Douglas Company built a small number of newer aircraft that were incorporating many of the better approaches. These aircraft were designated as DC-2 airplanes.

Public domain from the US Government

This airplane was a revolution to the commercial air travel business and several companies were eager to order these airplanes. The production lines were set up, and soon the first sellable aircraft were rolling off the line. Carl had a key part in this product development and was a primary test pilot evaluating several product improvements.

A second part of the program was the interest from the Army Air Corp. The military had recognized the need for an aircraft of this quality and soon had placed orders for

Kenneth Orr

substantial quantities. The Army had several applications in mind that would be critical should the United States get involved with the war that was brewing in Europe.

Several Army Generals from Dayton, Ohio came to the Douglas Company and asked them to consider incorporating several simple modifications that would enhance the aircraft.

One modification was to add stronger engines and an increased fuel load. These improvements would allow the airplane to haul heavy cargo and to use shorter grassy fields for runways. They also wanted the fuselage to be modified to include a large cargo door and add more strength in the aircraft floor. These modifications were all incorporated into the aircraft and the new level of airplane was designated as the DC-3. The Army created a special military identification and called it the C-47. A popular nickname was also added by the people who flew it as "The Gooney Bird."

Carl had the opportunity to meet with Army officers several times and rekindled some old relationships. He was assigned to support much of the work that was being done to meet the Army's special requirements.

The Army was obviously becoming very concerned about the German aggression in Europe, and the C-47 was being planned into many potential military mission roles. Airplanes had now been accepted as a good way to fight a war.

There were several other large airplane manufactures in the United States but none of them currently had an airplane to market that would do a better job for certain applications than this aircraft.

Boeing, Consolidated Aircraft and Lockheed were all working to develop improved heavy lift bomber aircraft. Several other airplane manufacturers were developing fighters and special purpose aircraft. One of the most advanced fighter aircraft companies was the Curtiss Airplane Company.

The Cowboy's Kids

The commercial airline business was struggling to get off the ground but was hampered by several problems. The American economy was still in a poor condition.

The price of an airplane ticket was beyond most people's means. There were few cities with airports and even fewer with adequate ground facilities to service an airplane. The most restrictive reason was the potential of a major war. In a war, all of the nation's production capacity would need to be focused on supporting the military's requirements. Commercial airlines were at a turning point. There was a shortage of qualified pilots. Those that were available would certainly be drawn into the war effort by the military. The DC-3 was ready to fly but the world was not financially or politically able to take advantage of any growth opportunities.

The Douglas Company never slowed down in building DC-3 aircraft. The military market was extremely strong. Soon every branch of the armed forces had open orders on the books. Most of the airplanes being sold to the Army were painted olive drab. They all had special radio racks that fit military radio equipment. A large number were set up to carry troops and to serve as paratroop drop aircraft.

DC-3 aircraft were not designed to be armed with cannons or other weapons. At the Army's request some had added provisions for side-mounted cannons. These cannons were to be manually aimed and fired.

Transport aircraft normally depended on fighter aircraft for support to protect themselves from enemy attacks. Several aircraft were painted white with large Red Cross markings on both sides. They were destined to be aerial ambulances.

The war in Europe was becoming more than just a German territory expansion. Hitler wanted to control all of Europe and then go on to other continents.

Kenneth Orr

The United States had taken note and was not sitting on their hands. The United States War Department was in constant contact with the British leaders. They feared the war was about to spread into Great Britain. The British had requested help of any type and they were in a desperate situation. Winston Churchill was emerging as the driving force to defend England and the British people were supporting him.

On August 31st, 1939 the British military activated the entire English military force. The civilian population of London was told to evacuate. Germany had been using fighter-bomber aircraft to wage war on European countries and they were capable of delivering the same attacks on London and other large industrial cities in Great Britain. The English knew what was coming. They just did not know when.

The British had discovered that the German Navy had marshaled large numbers of ships and barges in ports and protected inlets along their coast and in the several ports in Holland. They were planning to use this armada to invade England. The RAF was made aware.

They immediately began to bomb the German fleet. Their efforts stopped a potential invasion but the threat of German terror was just beginning. On September 5th, 1939 The United States Government declared neutrality in the war. President Roosevelt was defying all pressures to join in the fight as the American people had stood behind him as a non-war President.

President Roosevelt had served two full terms in which he had seen the country sink into a deep depression and then under his leadership there was a healthy recovery.

President Roosevelt and the United States Congress altered the constitutional structure to allow him to seek a third term in office. The American people were counting on him to keep them out of the European war. Now, the situation was expanding rapidly and the future was looking more live a war that was going to draw in the Americans regardless

The Cowboy's Kids

of diplomatic efforts. On November 5th, 1940, President Roosevelt was elected to his third term.

The international diplomatic war was also extremely active. In Late, August of 1939, England and Poland signed a mutual support treaty with the hope to slow down the Nazi War effort.

Within 48 hours Germany invaded Poland and moved quickly to capture Warsaw. The British enlisted the aid of several allied countries and within two days Britain, France, Australia and New Zealand had declared war on Germany. The term, "Allied Forces" was created to identify this collective military force.

The war has now become much more intensified and it was clear to the rest of the world that Hitler would stop at nothing to spread his influence.

American aircraft companies were already building fighter and bomber airplanes. The military was working feverishly to get ready and be capable at some level of support if war should come.

The federal government began building large manufacturing plants in several cities that were internal from the American coastlines. The B-17 was in production at several locations. A new larger bomber, the B-24 aircraft, was about to go into production in several locations including Tulsa, Oklahoma.

The Army had invested heavily at Randolph Field in San Antonio. This facility was key in the training of first class military pilots. A similar effort was also just getting started at Montgomery, Alabama. Several pilots had already finished basic flight training and had moved on to more advanced aircraft. Many had been assigned to other assignments and the entire military was learning how to wage a war using airpower.

This was a new tool for the soldier and there was little history from which to learn. Some of the young men, who

Kenneth Orr

had washed out as pilots became navigators, radio men, and served as members of flight crews. The Army was developing an air based fighting force and was doing it as rapidly as people could be trained and aircraft be made available.

Other government bodies were also complicating the rapid military build-up. There were still a few old school congressmen who had little support for fighting a war. An air war was not yet understood. They always had their foot in the aisle on new spending for the military. Aircraft, new airfields and more training bases were all expensive and the nation was just coming out of a devastating financial depression.

President Roosevelt had enacted several work programs to work the nation out the depression and to get Americans back to work. Congress had added new legal protections for banks and put strict regulations on how the stock market would be operated. Most of these programs were starting to work, but they were still barely enough to keep food on most American's tables. Adding more taxes and building a wartime military program were going to stretch all of the nation's funding capabilities.

Back home in San Antonio, Barbara and Paul were also being affected by the unrest in Europe. There were many more new recruits going into the Army and many of them were coming to San Antonio for training. The hospital at the Army base was overwhelmed with business and some of the less serious medical issues were being subcontracted to local clinics.

Paul had never lost touch with his professional ties to the Army base and his name was a common recommendation for doing outpatient medical work.

Barbara was equally well known and her skills were recognized as the supporting force behind "Doctor Paul."

The Cowboy's Kids

Fort Sam Houston had become a training base for battlefield medical staff and the entire San Antonio area was becoming a high quality medical center. It was also becoming a major training center for Army battlefield medics.

October was a beautiful month as the weather had cooled. The fall rains had begun to revive the green color in pastures and fields. After the fourth of July, Texas would normally get hot, dry and the fields would turn brown. Water was always a problem in keeping the crops green and the land productive. The first of October was especially stormy and there were violent thunderstorms almost every day. On November 4th Barbara received an urgent phone call from a close friend in Bandera. The message was not good.

The old family ranch house had been struck by lightning, had caught fire and burned to the ground. All that was left was the stone fireplace and a single stone wall on the front of the house. Nothing had been saved and the people who were renting the house had lost almost everything. The only good part of the news was no one killed or injured in the fire.

Barbara was very upset and was almost in a state of shock. She quickly got on the phone and tried to call Carl. The phone on the other end of the line did not answer, even after two days of trying. She knew Carl would be very upset and wanted him to know what was happening so he could help plan for what to do next.

Barbara told Paul that she wanted to go see the old home for herself, and on Saturday morning she got the Ford out of the garage and they went to Bandera. The roads were muddy from all of the rain and there were three low-water crossings running over the road, but they got through without problems.

Kenneth Orr

Upon arrival they saw the old house was gone and the site where it had stood was full of charred wood and twisted metal roofing materials. The whole building was gone and the chimney was all that had survived. All of the bushes and shrubs that once surrounded the house were either burned away or were so blackened that they would certainly die.

Barbara turned to walk away and get in the car. A neighbor had seen them come to the house and was coming down the driveway. He had seen the fire and had helped the people who were renting the house, get a few things out of the house before it got too hot to do any more. His name was Wilbur Green. His home was nearby. He had only lived there for a year. Barbara had never met him but she appreciated the way he was concerned about the loss.

Wilbur said the renters were now living with some friends in town and told Barbara how to get in touch with them. She took the information and thanked Wilbur for helping everyone. Paul said, "Let's go to town and look up the renters." Barbara agreed. They got in the car and started to Bandera.

Bandera was a welcome site to Barbara as she always loved to come home and go see the downtown area. She had so many good memories from growing up there and every time she went back she almost wanted to say that she was going to come back and stay. Paul was from the north and the month of November in Minnesota was always a time when winter was getting a serious start. Bandera was much warmer and he loved the Texas winter weather.

Barbara found the house and address where she had been told the renters were staying. It was a small but well kept house and there were two Fords in the front yard. She went up to the front door and knocked. An older lady answered the door and greeted Barbara. She invited her to come in and asked her what was her business? Barbara asked about the renting family and the lady said they had just left that morning and were moving to San Antonio. They had found a nice place there to buy and the man of the family had

The Cowboy's Kids

also found a better job. Barbara told the lady that she lived in San Antonio and wanted to look them up and express her sorrow about the fire. An address was furnished and Barbara thanked her for her help. She went back to the car where Paul was wondering what was happening inside.

Barbara told him the new situation and he was pleased that the renters were doing well in spite of the fire and he was a little less concerned. Barbara suggested that they go see a friend who was a builder and see if he would tear down the damaged old house and build a new but much smaller one on the same plot of earth. Paul said that was a good plan and he was sure that Carl would also want this to be done. Barbara found Andy Anderson who she had known for a long time and asked for his support in the project. Andy and Barbara had gone to school together and the trust between them was never a problem. A plan was agreed to and Andy said he would try to get the work completed by late spring. Barbara gave Andy a large check as a down payment and they all went to lunch.

Andy was a life-long native in Bandera and lunch was spent filling Barbara in on the hot topics in the community. One of his favorite subjects was the lake that was located just south of town on the Medina River. The Corp. of Engineers had originally built a small dam downstream that caused it to form a large area just upstream. Last year they raised the height of the damn and this would cause the water to become deeper. They wanted to have a larger reserve of water for the city of San Antonio and this was an easy way to reach their objective.

Andy said the fishing in the deeper lake was supposed to be great. The recent rains had filled it full for the first time and the supply of water for the people who lived on the shores and downstream, was going to be better. It had been completely full for almost three months. Everyone wanted to keep the lake this full as it was a good solution to supplying a lot of rancher's water all year.

Kenneth Orr

Barbara knew that her property was on the river and was wondering how much the water level there had changed. Barbara got real interested in the exact location of the dam and how deep the water was along the banks. She never got too specific, but she said that she and Carl, when they were younger, liked to go fishing in the river.

Paul was curious as to what was bothering Barbara so much about the new lake, but he let it pass for the time. It was not the right time to go any further with her concern. Everybody finished lunch and then went their way.

Barbara took Paul outside and said she had to go see where the new lake had flooded as she had reasons. Paul took a road that always went to the place where Barbara described, but about a mile from the spot to where the old fishing spot was located, the road was flooded. A small sign said "Boat ramp on the right." Barbara's worst fears had been confirmed. The old spot where she said was Carl and her favorite fishing spot, was now under water. Barbara told Paul that Carl and she had found a small cave at the location and had put some keepsakes in there for safe keeping. That was all that was said. Barbara wanted to discuss everything with Carl before she said anything more to Paul.

They drove around Bandera a little. Barbara wanted to buy some home canned peaches from a local food store. She found her fruit and bought three jars. Then they drove back to San Antonio. It was dark when they arrived and Barbara was still upset over all of the events over the past few days. She really wanted to talk to Carl and let him know what had happened.

The evening was black as more dark clouds covered the entire sky. The only light came from the lamps and headlights on cars. Stan told Barbara that the evening matched the day and surely there would be a better day tomorrow.

Carl was normally not home a lot. He was all tied up with his work and often he would work late into the night. Barbara knew that his schedule was never predictable, but he was

The Cowboy's Kids

always home by midnight. Midnight in California was 2 AM in Texas. Barbara set her alarm clock and got up at 1:30 AM. She got on the telephone and had the operator try to get a phone line to Carl's home.

The telephone switchboard system was never manned very well that time of the night, so making a connection to a phone that far away was sometimes a challenge. Finally, the phone in Carl's house started to ring.

Carl answered the phone and was surprised to be receiving a phone call this late at night. He said Hello and Barbara answered his greeting. She was concerned as to how Carl was doing. They discussed his work briefly but Carl knew this call was more than a routine call. Midnight was not a good time to call and talk about the local news. Barbara told him she had bad news and went into the details.

First, she discussed the fire and how everything at the old home was gone. She told Carl that she had already started to remove the old building remains and to build a new but smaller house on the site. Carl was in full agreement with her plan and asked if he needed to come home and help with anything.

Barbara told him he was always welcome to come home if he wanted but he probably would enjoy the trip more when the new house was going up. He agreed and said that he was glad Barbara had called him.

Barbara paused and said, "Carl, there is more bad news." Carl was surprised to hear this statement. He asked, "What else is wrong?" Barbara told him about the lake water being over the old cave.

She told him that she and Paul had gone to the lake and looked for any landmarks that might identify where the old cave was located. She added that some of the big cypress trees along the river had been cut down and the edge of the water was a long way from where she remembered the old riverbed to be located. Carl was upset with the

Kenneth Orr

news but he knew that the water would keep the old cave hidden. Barbara said she wanted to tell Paul about the two strongboxes but had not done so. She wanted Carl to agree to this disclosure before she did anything. Carl agreed that Paul needed to know but he wanted to have him sworn to secrecy if he was told. Barbara understood. Should any information about the strongboxes ever get out to the public the fortune hunters would be diving all over the lake. He and Barbara did not want this to happen.

Carl told Barbara that he had become involved with a new project at The Douglas Company. He also was working as a test pilot for new models of the DC-3 airplane. The next week he was going to fly a special new model over the California mountains to test some new engines and to test a special de-icing system for the wings. The Army was monitoring the test, as they wanted to upgrade all of the future aircraft if these new improvements worked. Barbara told him to be careful and to call her when he got home from the trip.

Carl had never told Barbara about his fling with Debbie and he filled her in on the major details. Barbara told Carl that his life was still before him and he deserved to find a good lady to be his wife, not someone who was not telling the truth or wanted to be so divisive. Barbara suggested that Carl come home when he got some time so that they spend some quality time in Bandera. Carl agreed it was a good idea and the phone call was ended.

CHAPTER 2-14
Refocus and New Plans

Barbara and Carl were both shaken by all of the bad news. Work and the everyday routine were still important but the loss of the old home was a sad and very personal blow. The new lake was also bad news but the impact was not so severe. Barbara had taken the lead in the replacement of the old house as she was nearby. She knew that Carl was going to have a lot of thoughts about all of the losses, but she also knew he was a strong person and that time would help heal his pain.

Carl was so deeply involved with his work that he had little time to think about his problems. The Douglas Company was beginning to develop a new larger airplane that would have four large wing-mounted engines. The airplane was going to be designed to haul either passengers or cargo. The plane was going to be called the DC-6. All of the good features from the DC-3 were being incorporated into the new airplane plus, a lot of new improvements. The intent was to have it fly further and carry more payloads. The basic airplane could carry freight, or with a special interior, it could become a fancy passenger airliner.

Carl's test flight on a modified DC-3 was going to be a long trip. The airplane was going to fly high over the Sierra Mountains and purposely fly into winter weather conditions that would normally cause ice to form on the leading edge of the wings. The propellers were also a problem in ice.

Kenneth Orr

Ice would grip the leading edge of the propeller blades and cause them to change shape. This would reduce their capability to move air and the result could be a disaster. Ice was an additional concern as it added unwanted weight. More weight would cause the plane to drop to lower altitude and the airspeed would slow drastically. If the condition continued to get worse, the airplane might crash.

The leading edges of both the wings and the rear control surface assemblies would have a rubber boot placed over the surface. A heated fluid would be circulated into the space between the metal wing and the rubber boot. The addition of heat and a small shape change would cause the ice to break away and fall off. The propellers would have a heated boot over the leading edge of each blade. This modification would allow an airplane to fly in weather where ice was a potential problem and still have a higher degree of safety.

Carl was skilled in flying the DC-3 and he had flown into ice several times. The normal recovery procedure on an airplane with no ice protection system would need to descend rapidly to an altitude where the air was warm enough to melt the ice. Icing was always a real danger when flying in colder months and crossing high altitude mountains.

If a pilot waits too long to descend, the amount of ice buildup would probably cause a crash. Early airplane engines were limited as to how high they could fly. The thinner air at higher altitudes would not support engine air requirements.

Early model aircraft piston engines would lose power as they climbed and had no effective means to gather additional air in the thinner air. The original DC-3 airplanes had this problem. The newer engines were set up to use superchargers to drive more air into the engine at altitude and hopefully overcome most of this problem.

The day for the test arrived and it was windy and rain was falling. Carl and his co-pilot did a full aircraft checkout and made sure that the gauges were all operating properly. The

The Cowboy's Kids

new ice control systems were also checked out and they appeared to be working. Carl ran up the engines and made sure they were working within nominal limits. He then took off and headed to the area where the mountains were 8,000 feet tall and taller.

Flying in cold air with high moisture content soon started to cause ice to appear. Carl had a recovery plan in place should the new system fail as he had located several large grassy mountain meadows that could serve as emergency landing fields. The ice was getting more pronounced and the airspeed had begun to drop. Carl turned on the new systems and within a short time small, flakes of ice film were seen flying away from the wings. The propellers worked equally well and the air speed began to recover. The new system was working well and Carl went up to a higher altitude to try to get ice to form with the new system turned on. To everyone's pleasure, no new ice was forming. This part of the test was complete and Carl went to the second test objective.

The plan was to fly at least 500 miles at an altitude of 10,000 feet and measure the fuel being used for that distance. The new engines were supposed to add more power and were equipped with a more efficient carburetion system. Wind direction and speed, temperature and air water vapor levels were also being measured. A standard measure of fuel burn rates per hour was also being reviewed. His flight route was almost all over central California and over the lower mountain levels.

The test went well and the new engines were using approximately 12% less fuel per hour. The airplane landed in Sacramento and refueled. They parked the airplane in a safe location and found a ride to town. Everyone had a good meal and got a good night's sleep. Carl called Cliff back at the base and told him how everything had gone. They were all very happy. The next event was to return to the Douglas airfield at Long Beach, California repeating several of the testing procedures in route.

Kenneth Orr

As soon as the airport runway was in sight Carl radioed the home base control tower and told them that he was going to cut off one engine and fly the rest of the trip on one engine. The test director said that was fine and he wanted Carl to watch the readings on the one engine to see what was happening.

Everyone wanted all of the data they could get as the Army was awaiting the test results. Carl agreed and flew the rest of the flight with only the right engine running. This engine was capable of holding the airplane at the same level altitude and did not appear to be overheating. No other problems were noted and the flight was a success.

The Army was obviously concerned about the development of new flight systems as the war in Europe was become a bigger concern every day. Hitler had made such a mark on the various countries on the mainland that England and Churchill were certain that Great Britain was the next target. The United States was being called to help bolster the British military and the pace was at panic speed.

Carl filled out his test mission report and went home. He got a good dinner and good night's sleep. The next morning he called Barbara and told her about the flight. She was proud for him and told him he was a special person. His work in California was doing what he loved to do.

The recent bad news from Texas had awakened the cowboy spirit that was still alive within him. Carl was homesick for the life he had known as a youngster. He started to think about at a trip back to San Antonio and a visit to Bandera, as something he needed to do soon.

✪ CHAPTER 2-16 ✪
Old Roots and New Beginnings

The year of 1939 had not been a great year for Barbara or for Carl. The losses they had experienced and the growing pressures from work were becoming an obviously heavy load. Paul's clinic and medical practice was growing in size but Paul was happy with his involvement with so many people. Paul had noticed that his hands were not as stable as they once were and he knew that something was wrong with his health. He kept this to himself. He did not want to concern others and he hoped that this condition was just a temporary passing problem. Barbara was stressed out and Paul recognized that they both needed to make some changes.

Paul took a good look at his clinic and asked himself if this was the way he wanted to spend the rest of his life. He was certain that the clinic was now established as a solid part of the San Antonio medical effort.

Paul continued to have health problems and was also growing more concerned. He had been feeling sick to his stomach a lot and was occasionally coughing up blood. He was not his normal self.

He knew something was wrong and being a doctor, he went to a friend who was also a Doctor and they ran some tests.

Kenneth Orr

He decided to keep all of this from Barbara until he had some accurate information about what was happening.

Paul realized that the clinic's business was increasing. The facility needed to be larger and new growth would require a much larger staff. His first thoughts were to hire more people and take a smaller role in working with the patients. After he thought this over he realized that there would be a lot more administrative work. Paul was not looking forward to increased responsibilities. With everything being considered he opened his mind to the possibility of selling the entire operation. He had decided that taking on a bigger workload and putting more stress on both Barbara and himself was the wrong way to go. He saw what the long days and high stress of practicing medicine were doing to Barbara and himself and wanted a different kind of future.

Paul took Barbara out to dinner and asked her to plan on being up late. She knew he had something to talk about. This approach was how he always did things when making major decisions. They went to a small back street Italian restaurant and had a delicious dinner. After dinner they went to the clinic office. Paul said he wanted to ask Barbara about some new ideas he had developed. Barbara was anxious to hear what he had in mind, but said nothing. She was never one to ask questions until she knew what to ask.

Paul had drawn up a chart that outlined the growth of the past two years and projected the possible growth during the next three years. It was apparent that the clinic was going to grow quickly and that the business was going to become very profitable.

He asked Barbara what she thought they should do, grow the business or find someone else to run the business? She just looked at the data, looked at the calculations and said nothing for almost five minutes. Barbara asked Paul what he wanted to do. Paul had already planned several options and Barbara knew this kind of discussion was his way of including her in his decisions. Paul never made a

The Cowboy's Kids

hard decision concerning the clinic unless Barbara agreed. She respected him for this consideration.

Paul said, "We both are worn out every night when we go home and I know we can sell this clinic to a group of local doctors. Then we can get away from this life style for a while." Barbara sat back and just looked at him. She had no idea he was thinking about selling out and getting away from the pressure. She was shocked, but somehow she was also relieved.

Then Paul looked at her and took a deep breath. He took her by the hand and very softly said, "I also have some really bad news to tell you and I think this will help us make this decision. I have just gotten the results back from some tests that I have taken and I have something wrong with my lungs. You may have noticed how tired I have been lately, and at first I thought it was just being tired. Then I was coughing a lot and soon some blood was coming up. The doctors who evaluated me think it is lung cancer." Barbara was devastated and went to his side and put her arms around Paul.

Barbara was immediately in agreement that they should sell the clinic and said, "How soon can we make this happen?" Paul said he had already talked to three young doctors who were looking to set up a clinic and they had expressed an interest. He added that they were willing to pay a good price for the business, the building and all of the equipment. They had good financial backing and money did not look like it was a problem. They had agreed to buy the clinic if Paul and Barbara would stay with them for a few weeks to help transition the work, and work with transferring the current patients. After the conversation, they went home went to bed, and laid awake much of the night talking. It had been a very bad day.

The next morning Carl called from California and said he had requested a couple of weeks off at work and wanted to come home to Texas. He was tired from so much overtime work, and from a seemingly never-ending pressure to move

Kenneth Orr

faster in everything that he was doing. The old ranch home burning, and the new water level situation on the Medina River, had all concerned him and he wanted to get away from work for a few days, come home to Texas and see everything in person. Barbara was not only agreeable, she was very happy to hear he was coming home for a while. Carl was another shoulder to lean on and right now she needed his support.

He asked Barbara if he could stay with her and Paul and they could just enjoy being together as the family they had always wanted to be. Barbara agreed wholeheartedly and was visually happy that Carl was coming home. Carl had recently bought a new two-seat airplane that had a fully enclosed cockpit.

He had sold his Jenny and got a good price for the "ole bird." The new airplane could develop a lot more speed and could fly further between fuel stops than his old Jenny. In addition, it had an enclosed cabin and a lot warmer and more comfortable to ride in.

Carl left California early on a Monday morning. He stopped in Tucson, Arizona and refueled. By late in the day he was in El Paso, Texas. He landed there and refueled the plane so he would be ready to fly in the morning. Then he found a room for the night. The next morning he took off early and by early afternoon he was near San Antonio.

Carl got on his radio and requested permission to land at a newly built military runway at Randolph Airfield, which is located a few miles north of downtown San Antonio.

Carl's radio was a valuable tool in cross-country flying. He always called ahead to check weather and to get the proper clearances before he landed. Someone who was in the Randolph Airfield control tower recognized his name, gave him permission to land and asked that he stop by the base operations office after landing. The ground voice said that an old friend who was stationed there wanted to say hello.

The Cowboy's Kids

The "friend" did not identify himself but said he had been at the air training school with Carl and wanted to say hello.

Carl parked his plane on the runway's apron and immediately an Army staff car pulled up by the airplane. The driver said he had been sent to transport him to the Base Operations office building. The driver was a young Army recruit who was just learning the ropes of flying. He was anxious to talk to Carl about new airplanes that were on the design board. His conversation never slowed down all the way to the operations terminal. Carl got out of the car and walked over to the operations office. He walked in and was instantly greeted by a man his age who said Captain Malone wanted to see him. He knew immediately it was his old buddy Fred Malone. "Malone." as everybody always called him, had been a student pilot in a group just behind Carl's group and they had been good friends for years.

Malone came around the corner, walked up to Carl and gave him a big hug. He was glad to see him and wanted to have a good long talk with him and catch up on what life had been doing to him. Carl was equally glad to see Malone. Malone told him he had stayed in the Army and was now working in the Army Air Corp's training command's Senior Officers group.

World War One had made an unprecedented impact on the military and the United States was redesigning many of its military training strategies to revolve around airplanes.

Randolph Air Field had been established to become the Army's primary training base for new pilots. The Army had made a very expensive investment in the facility and everything had been built to the latest level of technology. The air base was busy training additional new pilots to increase the total number of qualified pilots who were trained to serve in military duty. The size of the facility and the staff was growing rapidly.

Malone's training staff was busy training qualified young men how to fly and how to think like military pilots. He

Kenneth Orr

stressed that a lot of old barnstorming ideas were just not acceptable in the Army. He was strict and made it clear that he expected his students to always practice safe flying and any intentional infractions were adequate reason for being kicked out of the Army.

Malone told Carl that the Navy was doing the same thing but they were also developing aircraft carriers that could be taken anywhere in the world. These were exciting times to be a military pilot.

Carl told him that he was busy at the Douglas Company working on new aircraft designs. He commented that he appreciated how much he had learned from the great basic training that the Army had provided to him. Malone asked Carl to come to the base for lunch sometime soon and told him that he really was glad to see him. Carl agreed to Malone's invitation and then said that he needed a ride to his sister's home. Malone told him that his airplane would be safe at the airfield and that the new pilots would enjoy looking at a sleek new two-seat airplane.

Malone got a military driver to take him to Barbara's home. They used a new military vehicle, a Ford pickup truck that was painted olive drab. The trip was a lot of fun for Carl as he was seeing the changes that were underway in San Antonio.

Carl went up to Barbara's front door and the housekeeper answered. She recognized Carl as Barbara's brother and invited him in. She showed him where to put his baggage. Paul and Barbara were still at work and she told Carl they would be home soon. Carl got a glass of iced tea and sat down in a big easy chair. He drank the tea and soon he was sleeping. The long trip from California had taken the edge off of his endurance and he was soon snoring loudly. The housekeeper saw him all stretched out in the chair and heard his snoring so she closed the door to the room and made sure that Carl was not going to be disturbed.

The Cowboy's Kids

About 8;00 PM Paul and Barbara came home. They went to the rear door, which was near the garage and went in. The housekeeper had made a luscious meal for them and they were both hungry. They sat down to eat and the housekeeper asked them if they wanted to invite their "guest." They both looked at each other and wondered what she was talking about.

Barbara asked her to explain. She said that Carl was sleeping in the chair in   the living room. Paul looked at everybody with surprise. He got up from his chair and went over to Barbara and said, "Lets go see if he is hungry." Paul went to the closed door and slowly opened it. Carl was still asleep, but he had quit snoring. Barbara went to the door and looked in. She said, "Let me handle this, He needs to eat and then get into a bed. He looks worn out."

Barbara went over to Carl and put her hand on his shoulder and started to move him a little. Carl awoke immediately and saw everybody standing around him. He was embarrassed, but very happy to see his family. He stood up and hugged Barbara and Paul and said, "I smell some good food".

Carl joined everybody at the dinner table and soon the family was back together and all was well with everybody.

The next morning was a Wednesday. Paul had several office appointments to see patients and Barbara was going to be needed at her job most of the day. Paul told Carl about their plan to sell their business and take a while away from the medical practice. He said the new owners were scheduled to start taking over within a month and then, in a few more weeks he and Barbara would be officially away from the medical business. Carl was not surprised, as he had detected the stress level in several of Barbara's phone calls and letters.

Carl said he would get a car and go see some of the new facilities out at Randolph Field. Paul said he had a new car, a 1938 Packard Coupe with two spare tires mounted over

Kenneth Orr

the front two fenders and a big rumble seat in the back. He wanted Carl to drive his car.

Paul had bought it to take long trips and it only had about 2,000 miles on the odometer. Paul was proud of his new car and said it was built like an Army tank and should be running for a long time.

Carl agreed to drive the Packard and said he would take good care not to scratch the shiny black paint. Barbara said they would all go to Bandera on Saturday and the Packard was going to be the transportation.

Carl went off to Randolph Air Field, and Paul and Barbara took the old Ford to the medical office. This day was one that would never be forgotten. The new clinic owners were going to be visiting the clinic and the final plans for the change in ownership were beginning to take shape.

Carl arrived at the air base and asked to see Captain Malone. The gate guard said he would see if he was available and got Carl's name. Soon he returned and said, "The Captain would like to see you soon and would wait for him at the first training building just inside the airfield entrance." Carl drove the Packard to the building, parked in the designated space, and went inside. The entire base was typical military and the formality of a military training facility was everywhere.

The guard at the front door said the Captain was expecting him and took him to his office. Malone stood up and welcomed Carl warmly. Malone asked Carl if he would like to take a tour and see some of the new airplanes they were using to train pilots. Carl was more than anxious.

The Captain got into his personal military vehicle and they headed for the flight line. The ride was short and soon they were in between rows of new shiny "T-3" training aircraft. Carl's airplane had been towed into a small hangar and was not mixed in with the military aircraft. Carl was taking everything in just like a kid in a toy store. Malone was a master salesman and he knew that Carl would fall back in

The Cowboy's Kids

love with the world of military flying when he saw all of this new equipment. Captain Malone told Carl that additional new airplanes were arriving every week and the size of the school was going to be much larger.

The flight line was busy. Several new cadets were seated in the new training planes and the trainer pilot was sitting in the rear seat. They were practicing touch and go landings and the runway was very busy. There were two parallel active runways; one for taking off and a second one for landings. Both were very busy. After the tour Captain Malone told Carl he wanted to talk with him in private when he had some free time and asked him if he could come back on Friday morning. Carl thought a moment and agreed. They went back to the office and Carl went home.

CHAPTER 2-17
Making Decisions That
Had to Be Made

Time for the next couple of days was passing quickly for Barbara, Paul and for Carl. They were all involved with activities that completely occupied their minds. The clinic was busy with patients and Paul was introducing the new doctors to everyone. Barbara was equally busy as she had two staff nurses who were getting involved with the transition and they were not sure of what to expect. By the end of the second day everything was working out smoothly. Paul was feeling comfortable with the way the transfer of ownership and patients was progressing. Barbara was equally confident.

Carl had visited the Army airfield several times and seen first hand how the new Army training base was operating. Malone had made sure Carl was well soaked in Army activities and information to set him up for a "special offer."

Friday came quickly. Carl met captain Malone and they had a nice lunch at the officer's club. After lunch Malone said, "Carl, let's go over to my office and have a good talk." Carl agreed and they soon were sitting in some comfortable leather chairs looking at each other. Malone opened the conversation. He said, "Carl, the Army needs qualified pilot trainers and you could be one of the best, I have no doubts. However, the Army is having problems with advanced

The Cowboy's Kids

training for flight crews. Seasoned pilots with multi-engine aircraft experience are scarce. You, my good friend, are one of those scarce people."

Carl looked him in the eye, smiled and said, "Malone, you are setting me up and I smell your motive all over your face". Malone looked back, smiled at Carl and said, "Well you are a prime candidate to come back into the Army on active status and we really need people like you. You should not be surprised at my interests. I know about your skills and the Army could be a very good career opportunity for you if you want to come back and be a part of our group."

Carl sat back, took a deep breath and said, "Malone, you know me pretty well and you ole bastard, you know that this life of flying has always been my longest dream. Let me have a couple of days to think this over and then we can talk some more, OK?" Malone agreed and Carl excused himself. He went out and got in the shiny Packard and started to go back to Barbara's house.

On the way he drove by Fort Sam Houston and looked over the old buildings he remembered from the times when his dad had taken him there. These were very fond memories. He then went on to Barbara's home and found some good cold beer to drink. Shortly thereafter Paul and Barbara came home and everybody was glad the day was about over.

The next day was Saturday and per the plan, they all got up early and drove to Bandera. The day was hot and dry and the dusty road left a coating of brown dust all over the sparkling chrome and black paint on the Packard. They kept the windows open a little to let in some cool air, but they were not too far as the road dust would come in. Most of the countryside was green as it had been a wet spring and the rivers and creeks were all running strong. The smell of new cut hay was in the air and the trip was a joy in itself.

Paul decided that he needed to tell Carl about his health problem so as they rode down the road, he broke the news

Kenneth Orr

to Carl. Carl was very concerned and wondered what all of this would mean. Paul was not sure as what to say, but said he had been considering a trip to Rochester, Minnesota to go see a specialist at the Mayo Clinic. Paul had friends there who were medical specialists and they were considered the very best in treating serious health problems.

Barbara spoke up and said she would be glad to see him make this trip and would go with him to be there if he needed her. They planned to set a date for the trip as soon as the clinic was well into the hands of the new owners.

Carl was not sure as to what to say or do but after a few moments he thought he might create a better mood if he told them about the offer to come back into the Army.

He began by telling them about all of the new training facilities that the Army had built at Randolph field. He went on and talked about the new training aircraft and how the basic flight education was so much more complete that what he had ever experienced.

Then he brought up Captain Malone. Carl said, "He is a really brilliant pilot and he has made me an offer to come back into the Army and become a pilot instructor. They need people with multi-engine aircraft experience and they are really short in that area of training."

Both bits of news were in everyone's head and somehow all of Carl's information seemed to take everyone's mind away from Paul's problems. Carl had outlined a new opportunity for his life.

Paul was very positive that he could get medical help from his friends at the mayo Clinic and Barbara shared his good attitude. They also knew that lung cancer was not something that pills and rest could cure. There might be more serious treatment required.

Carl was obviously looking to change his career and the Army had made him an offer he was very serious about

The Cowboy's Kids

accepting. Everybody needed to get their thoughts together and then go on to the next step, whatever they chose it to be.

They arrived in Bandera and went by the old downtown ranch business office. The old building was in fine shape but the new occupants were selling clothes, saddles and boots. The streets were paved in some areas and the local jail had been rebuilt to include more offices and cells. The sheriff had a new Ford car parked out front and the streets had a lot more cars than ever. There were still a few horses and wagons out by the old sale barn but the whole character of the town was changing. There was a new tall water tower with the town's name, Bandera, painted on the side. Things had changed a lot in a very short time. Carl said, "This ole town is just not what it was when we were growing up Barbara. It has changed a lot and I wonder what has happen to all of our old friends." Barbara just smiled, as she knew he was right. She had lost touch with many of the old group of kids they once knew and this was sad. They had been such close friends.

Paul turned the Packard onto the road that led out to the old Goodwin Ranch. About 100 feet from town, the pavement stopped and a dirt road was straight ahead. Carl made a lot of comments about the old neighbors who had once lived there as they passed several old houses. Barbara was also very talkative as they had found so much from the past to discuss. This was good for everyone and Paul was busy taking it all in. He knew a lot about Barbara's past, but this trip was opening up a lot of new memories that were obviously very important to both her and to Carl.

Paul would ask Barbara a question and Paul would listen to her reply. Barbara and Carl knew everything about what they were discussing but Paul was often lost. He had no idea as to what they were involved with in their discussion. He knew he would only confuse thing if he asked questions so he just listened.

Kenneth Orr

The last turn in the road brought the front gate of the old ranch into view. The old chuck wagon that the ranch hands once used was sitting up near the entrance. It was showing the wear and deterioration that time and use had placed on it and the seat had begun to fall apart. The carpenters who were building the new house had done some repairs to the sideboards but the wheels and metal parts were looking really bad. Carl brought up a trip they had made in the wagon when he was very small and how rough it was to ride in. He still remembered the bruises on his bottom from hitting so many holes in the road.

The old whiskey barrel flower boxes by the driveway were still there, but they too were falling apart. The roses that Wanda had planted in them were still growing and the blooms were as beautiful as ever. Paul was never aware of how much work had gone into building the ranch until Carl discussed the many times when the ranch hands were busy for a month at a time building a new barn or repairing some building. Paul was impressed. He told Barbara that now he knew where she had developed such a dedicated work ethic. She never had known any other approach toward life.

The new house was straight ahead. The whole front side was constructed from new white limestone. The windows were painted a light green color that matched the trim around the edge of the roof. The new metal roof was shining like a new silver coin in the sunshine, as it had not yet dulled from being outside for a long time. The front door had a big stone porch in front of it and the windows on either side of the door went from the top of the doorframe clear down to the floor. It was beautiful.

Paul got out of the car and opened the door for Barbara. She got out then Carl folded the seat forward and got out. They walked up to the porch and they went up two stone steps and were standing right in front of the door. Carl looked in the side windows and saw that the old stone fireplace was still a part of the house. He commented to Barbara that he was anxious to go inside. Barbara went looking for a key. It

The Cowboy's Kids

was hidden under a rock off to the side of the porch. She found it and soon the door was open.

The first room was almost the same size as the original big room. The floor was made of inlaid limestone and each stone was carefully placed into a pattern that made the entire floor look like a natural bottom to a dry riverbed.

The old fireplace was weathered from use, but a good cleaning had done wonders to make it look good. The house fire had deposited some black soot on some of the stones that had not come off. There was an open area behind the fireplace and the old kitchen and dining room were still in the same location. The kitchen had a new built-in stove and new kitchen cabinets. There was no furniture in the house anywhere and the rooms made an echo when people were talking. Carl noticed the new sound and soon they were all making a lot of jokes about the different sounds in each room.

The bedrooms and bathrooms were still in the same location but there was one less bedroom in the rear. Barbara saw no reason to build back with so many bedrooms as they were empty most of the time when she was living there. The smell of fresh paint and new brown carpet in the bedrooms made the place feel comfortable. Paul was impressed and said that this was a nice home. He said he would like to have one just like it in San Antonio.

Carl went out the back door and walked back to the old horse barn. Barbara and Paul followed him but they were not as interested as Carl. Carl had always had his private stuff hidden in a spot out in the barn and he went straight to the old hiding place. He had to climb up into the loft to get there and soon he was bringing out an old fishing pole that he had used when he was a boy. He was happy to find it and the moment was just as special to him as anything that happened the whole day. He brought it down and showed it to everyone. The old black cloth fishing line was rotten but the reel still turned and the pole was as good as ever. It was just dirty from being in the barn. Barbara said he should

Kenneth Orr

take it along and get some new line. He agreed and it was by his side until they went to the car to go back to town.

After about an hour of looking and refreshing memories they thought it was time to start back to Bandera. Paul suggested that they get some food at a restaurant they had passed earlier in the day. Barbara said that was fine but she wanted to stop by the Andy Anderson's home, who had rebuilt the house and give him his final payment in person. They got to town, ate a good steak in Barbara's favorite restaurant and went looking for the builder.

They got to Andy's home and he was gone. Barbara asked his wife if she had a final cost total for the home building work. His wife was also the business manager. She did and she presented it to Barbara. Barbara was surprised that the total she owed was so small. She thought it was going to be several thousand dollars more.

They went over the cost profile and the numbers were all correct.

The biggest savings had been in rockwork and materials and the carpenter's fees were just what she had been quoted. Barbara wrote out a check and added a nice bonus to the total. She told the lady that the work was so well done; she wanted to make sure her appreciation was recognized.

They got in the car and Carl said he wanted to drive out by the river on the way back home. He wanted to see where the waterline was standing and make some judgments about what had happened to the old cave. Paul took Carl's directions and soon they were at a dead end on a country road. The county had built a wooden barrier on the road and put up a sign saying, "Road closed beyond this point." Carl got out and walked around for several minutes and soon he was back in the car. He knew it was a long way down the road to where the cave was located and it appeared that the water was certainly over the entrance and was probably several feet deep. He told Barbara, "Someday I am going to go diving and see if I can find the cave."

The Cowboy's Kids

Paul started the car and they drove back to San Antonio. It had been a long and most enjoyable day for everyone.

The trip back was a lot more active with discussion and ideas as how to furnish the new house. Barbara had a lot of the old furniture from the original house at her house or in storage. Everyone agreed that this would be the core of the furnishings and some new things would be added to finish the total furnishing. Carl spoke up and said that he had some things in California that he wanted to put there, as they were their mom and dad's things. They had gathered them when they spent winters in the west coast house. He said he could have them shipped on the railroad to San Antonio and then they could be delivered to Bandera.

Paul had little to offer, but he said that if they were not going to rent the house, he would like to put his old office desk in one of the rooms so he felt like it was a part of his efforts to bring the old place back to life. Everyone agreed.

Carl had something that was bothering him and Barbara picked up on his mood. She asked, "Carl, what's wrong? You were happy about a lot of things, but there is something wrong and I can tell you have something that is really bothering you."

Carl looked at her and said, "I am so much in love with my old home in Texas and I wish we could all be here as a family but I am being torn between coming back from a great job in California to be an instructor in the Army Air Corp. I just am having a hard time getting my plans in place."

Paul spoke up and said, "Carl, you need to sleep on it a couple of days and somehow the right answer will come to you." Carl agreed and he was feeling much better.

The next morning was a typical Monday. Paul and Barbara needed to go to the clinic three more days and then the transition to the new owners would be completed. Carl had some free time and he wanted to fly out over the Bandera area and see a lot of the old ranch from the air. Everybody

Kenneth Orr

got ready to go their way for the day. Barbara tossed the keys to her Ford to Carl and said that Paul had a good car wash shop very near the clinic and he wanted to get the Packard cleaned up. The trip to Bandera had really put a lot of dirt and dust all over the car. Carl took the Ford keys and the left for the day. Paul and Barbara were looking forward to this week being the last week of clinic work for them and the mood in their voices was great.

Carl went out to the air base and parked his car in the visitor's parking lot. He went through the gate with a special pass that Malone had provided to him and walked to the area where his plane was tied down. He got the plane ready to fly and he noticed that the Army ramp people had filled his fuel tank to the top.

Carl knew he was low on fuel when he landed and would need to refuel. The full tank was a pleasant surprise. He thought that Malone was just adding more icing on the offer to come back into the Army. His plane had an electric starter and he fired the engine and completed the normal checkout procedure. The runway was active but the traffic was light. He pulled up to the run-up pad and did the normal engine test and he was ready to take off. The control tower issued him take-off clearance and soon he was up in the sky over north San Antonio.

The weather was clear and cool. He climbed to about 5,000 feet and headed west. Soon he saw the open hill country in front of him and the several small towns that were in the area were passing under his wings. Dead ahead was the water tower in Bandera. He knew he was about to pass over the old hometown and he descended to 3,000 feet.

The courthouse and new jail were just east of the water tower and the main street was alive with traffic.

He headed the airplane to the southeast, circled back to the south and soon the Medina River led him to the old home location. He made a couple of lower passes and then headed toward Medina Lake. The lake was not far and the new

The Cowboy's Kids

higher water level had changed many of thee old landmarks that he was looking for.

He made several loops and thought he was over the area where the cave was located. The whole area was under water and the shore was several hundred yards away. His thoughts were racing and he knew that the cave was now even safer as there were no records or reasons for people to go looking, as this was now just a great fishing hole.

He then headed out to the west and flew to the Brackettville, Texas area. Fort Clark was just to the south side of the town and it was still an active Army base. He flew over the parade grounds and saw a few soldiers going about routine Army business. They waved and he flew over a second pass and saw that the flags were blowing briskly from the east. After that last look he headed back toward Bandera. He had also wanted to fly over the old Pipestone Ranch and see it from the air. He started to thing about Sarge. The last time he had any word on him he was still alive but not in good health.

Carl found the old Pipestone ranch and the old house was still looking good. Several of the barns had activity going on outside and the place looked alive. Carl knew that Sarge was not able to do much and wondered what was going on. Time had passed quickly and Carl decided to head back to the airbase. He got into the area, got radio clearance to land and parked his plane back on the visiting aircraft apron.

Carl went inside and told the people at the control center he was going to be leaving town on Friday and if his plane was any problem, he gave them Barbara's home phone number.

He had wanted to stop by and see Malone but he did not just want to pop in unannounced. Showing up without first making your visit known in advance was not a good military practice. He headed for his car and as h was walking he was hailed by a familiar voice.

Kenneth Orr

It was Captain Malone. He had seen Carl's plane land and he was anxious to talk to him. Carl stopped and went over to Malone and they greeted each other warmly.

Malone asked Carl if he had had lunch. It was obvious that he had not. They agreed to go to a local off-base restaurant and have some great Chinese food. Carl drove the Ford and Malone said "He was buying, no back talk, please!"

They found the restaurant and went in. The food was buffet style and they both stuffed themselves. Ice tea was a common Texas drink and both men did a good job on keeping their glasses empty.

Malone asked Carl about what he had been considering of another Army career. Carl replied, "Malone, You know me pretty well and I think you know that I love to fly. I also love Texas and the way that things are done here. I also have a great job in California and if I leave to come here I want to make sure I can do so with a good exiting reputation. Do you know what I am saying?"

Malone looked at him and said. "I have been doing some checking and your military records indicate that when you left before you were not fully discharged but you were put into the in-active reserve. That means all of the time from then until now can still be considered as time in the service. This means you can still wear the rank of a Captain if you come back. Yes, I do know what you are saying and I respect the fact that a commitment by you has meaning. I also know that you are someone I trust and I need your help with the job we are trying to do."

Carl looked at Malone and got tears in his eyes. Malone said, "Carl, what's wrong? Have I said something to upset you?" Carl said, "No, I just get emotional, I guess when I am at a crossroad that has so many decisions to be made. I know my dad would love to see me in an Army uniform and I know my family would love to see me here I Texas. But, having someone like you asking me from his heart to come join him, well there is no good reason to say no." Malone hugged him across the table and said, "Captain Goodwin, You are most welcome to take your time and get your life in the proper order and then report for duty. Welcome to the Army Air Corp."

After lunch they drove back to the airbase and Malone went back into his office. Carl drove back to Barbara's and parked the Ford in the driveway. He was surprised to see the Packard was there and immediately had a concern.

Carl went into the house and Barbara was setting on the couch. He asked her," What's wrong?" Barbara said, "Paul was at work and he got sick. They knew something was wrong when he was about to faint so we all decided to bring him home and let him get some rest.

He is asleep in the bedroom." She was concerned that he get up to Minnesota and sees a lung specialist at the Mayo Clinic as soon as possible. Carl understood and he went to the phone and called Captain Malone.

Public domain from the US Government

Carl got Malone on the line and told him about Paul's health. He also told Malone that both Paul and his sister were former military medical professionals and that he needed to ask a big favor. Malone asked what he needed? Carl asked if there was a four-place military airplane available that I can use to take Paul, Barbara and himself to Rochester, Minnesota? Malone never hesitated, He said, "We have a brand new, twin engine, A-10 Beechcraft setting on the

Kenneth Orr

ramp that I am sure you can handle. If you want to pilot it, fine, if not I will fly you there." Carl said, "I will call you back shortly." Malone added, "This is one of the first new A-10 airplanes we have received and it will become one of the newest training planes as soon as we get our training plan finalized. You can use this flight as a shake-down for the plane and for yourself, the basic airplane is really a strong flying machine and it is very easy to fly."

Carl went to Barbara and told her about the airplane. He said that he could fly the airplane, as it was similar to the DC-3 aircraft he was currently flying and it was a safe and very airworthy aircraft. Barbara said. "When can we leave? I know Paul can get ready to go when he wakes up. He had mentioned that he wanted go there on the way home". Carl said, "We can leave in an hour if Paul is able? Do you want to wake him and see what he thinks." Barbara went into the bedroom and after about ten minutes she came out. She said, "Paul is getting dressed and we will be ready to leave in about fifteen minutes." Carl called Captain Malone and told him of the plan. Malone said the airplane would be fueled and on the ramp by the time they arrived.

Carl thanked him and Malone said he had no problem with helping military personnel when he could. He added, "Fill the flight log out when you return as a training flight. That will keep everything straight on the log book records."

Paul, Barbara and Carl got into the Packard and drove to the airfield. When they arrived at the gate, the guard had their name and told them to follow a special car that would lead them to the aircraft.

When they arrived, Malone was standing by the plane and asked Carl to come inside the aircraft's cabin so he could brief him on some unique features of the aircraft. Paul and Barbara waited outside standing next to the car.

In about five minutes, Carl and Malone came out and said they were ready to load the passengers. Everyone got on-board and soon the engines were running. Malone drove

The Cowboy's Kids

the Packard into a hangar where it would be safe until they returned.

Paul was sitting in the co-pilot's seat and Barbara was seated just behind them in a passenger's chair. Everybody was furnished with a parachute, which was a requirement in Army flying regulations. There were also several "barf-bags" in the plane. Air sickness was common, should they run into bad weather and military airplanes were not immune from this flying hazard.

Prior to leaving the cockpit, Malone had given Carl a weather report for a flight plan that had been filed with the control tower. The route would go over Austin, Waco, and Dallas and there would be a fuel stop in Tulsa. Then the flight plan was to fly over Kansas City and DeMoines, Iowa. From there they would go straight to Rochester, Minnesota.

There would be bad weather off to the east but it was not expected to be any problem as the winds were primarily blowing from the west.

Carl gave Paul a set of flight charts that had the travel route covered. Carl had flown several flights to Minneapolis, Minnesota in his mail flying days. This part of the country was going to be an easy flight for him. There were no mountains and the long days of late summer were normally easy flying. Everybody made sure they had their seat belts fastened and Carl took off.

Barbara and Paul had ever been up in an airplane before. The sensation of flying was a completely new experience for both of them. They trusted Carl as a pilot and they wondered how long the flight would take.

Carl told them that they should be in Minnesota by 9:30 PM and it would just be getting dark. After a few minutes, the constant drone of the two engines had made Barbara go to sleep. Paul was looking over all of the instruments and controls on the airplane's panel and discussing them with Carl.

Kenneth Orr

Soon they were passing over Dallas and Paul woke up Barbara to make sure she got to see the city from the sky. She was impressed and said it all looked so tiny from up that high. They were at about 6,000 feet elevation and the sky had a few low broken clouds. The inside of the airplane was comfortable, but rather cool. In about 30 minutes Carl got on the radio and contacted the Tulsa control tower. Carl identified the aircraft using a military designation. This always seemed to provide a quicker control tower response and Carl knew all of the tricks to getting cleared to land quickly. They gave him the vectors to use in landing and he started his descent.

Soon they were on the ground and Carl told everyone that they should go see the "monkey in the restrooms," as they would not be able to see him again until they got to Minnesota. They all laughed and got out. A fueling truck pulled up to the airplane and topped off the tanks. They gave a ticket to Carl to sign and said that the fuel was being charged to the Army. The airplane had Army identifications on its fuselage and they had an account set up for all military aircraft.

Everyone got back on the airplane. Carl went through his pre-flight checkout just like he had done in Texas. Soon they were sailing down the runway and going up into the sky again.

This take off was less tense for both Paul and Barbara. This time they knew what to expect and were ready to go flying. The clouds were getting lower and denser and soon a good view of the ground was lost. Paul said, "This kind of flying, where you use your compass and radio system to navigate, was a lot like doing a surgical procedure. You go from one known condition to the next and what you discover in between the points lets you manage the conditions until you arrive at the next one. Then, whatever you need to do to get everything back in good order, you do. There is no completely standard surgical procedure. Every operation is similar, but still it always has some differences. That's true for every procedure we perform."

The Cowboy's Kids

At 8:25 PM Carl made contact with the Rochester control tower. He told them he was over northern Iowa and was about 20 minutes out.

The control tower gave him a local weather conditions report and vectors to follow to land. He had Paul write the information down and proceeded to start his decent. At 8:35 the airplane entered the cloud cover and soon they broke out below the clouds, flying in dull and vanishing daylight about 2,000 feet over the green farmland. Carl called the control tower and told them he was about ten miles out and on the vectors he had been given and had the runway in sight. He was cleared to land. Soon the runway lights were in close sight and the tires made a squealing sound as they touched down. They taxied over to the visiting aircraft ramp and pulled into a tie-down stall that was open. Carl cut off the engines and did a good post flight shut down check. Everything was in order. He got out of the pilot's seat, opened the door and everyone got out.

Paul was back in Minnesota and he knew the procedure for getting to town. The airport was about ten miles south of town and there were always several taxicabs waiting to haul passengers. Carl arranged for the airplane to be taken care of and everybody got the few pieces of baggage they had brought and called the taxi stand.

It was now nearing night's darkness and the trip to town saw the last rays of the sun fade away. Paul had worked in the Mayo clinic and he knew the hotels in the downtown area well. He instructed the driver as to where to go and soon the cab fair was paid and everyone was soon in a nice room.

Paul and Barbara's room was overlooking the west and there were several big churches off to the south. The clinic was a nice building located about a block away and there was a big statue of Christ in front of a nearby building.

Paul, Barbara and Carl were hungry and they had a taxi take them to Wong's Chinese restaurant. Paul had eaten

Kenneth Orr

there often and was bragging about the great egg rolls they made. They all had a good meal and went back to the hotel and settled in for the night. Paul was still not feeling well, but he was in a much better mood, being he was in a place where his illness was going to be evaluated.

The next morning everybody got up, put on clean clothes and went to the hotel's dining room for breakfast. Paul's meal was simple. He was not sure what testing the clinic might do and eating too much was not a good idea. Carl had a bigger meal and Barbara had coffee and a fruit plate. When they were done, they walked over to the clinic and Paul asked the front desk clerk if Dr. Richard Clemenson was available.

Paul had called him a few days earlier and told him he would probably be coming to visit. He knew the doctor well and respected his opinions. He was a specialist on internal medicine and had a good reputation for helping patients with lung cancer survive.

The desk clerk made a call and said that he was with a patient but would see him as soon as he was finished. Everybody sat down and waited. Time seemed to drag, but in about 30 minutes Paul's name was called and he went to the desk. The lady told Paul that the doctor would see him now and started to give him directions to his office.

Paul broke in and said he knew the way, he had worked here before and he knew the halls just about as well as anyone. She smiled. Paul looked over at Barbara and Carl and signaled, "come along" with a hand gesture. They went down the hall and up a small flight of stairs and soon were at the Doctor's office door.

Paul opened the door and helped everyone into the small waiting area just inside. The door on the backside of the room opened and there stood Doctor Clemenson. He recognized Paul Immediately and came over and gave him a big handshake and hug. Paul introduced Barbara and Carl and told him they were all living in San Antonio.

The Cowboy's Kids

The Doctor was glad to see Paul but he picked up a concern as soon as Paul said, "Doc, I have some problems and I need your help". The Doctor who said, "Remember Paul, call me Clem. That's still my name to my best friends."

Paul told him about his problems. The medical names of several conditions left Carl in the dark. Barbara was able to keep up and soon the Doctor said, "Paul I am going to check you into the hospital and we will be doing some tests later this morning.

Until we know exactly what we are dealing with we are not going to know what to do. You know the procedure I am sure and we all need to just stay relaxed until we know where we are going." Barbara said, "Carl and I will stay in the hotel room until you tests are over and we will be here waiting for you to come up with some answers."

A few more words about the old times were exchanged and Paul led the group over to the Methodist Hospital. He told the nurse at the admissions desk that he was Dr. Clemenson's patient and she had already received a call. The hospital was ready for him. Paul went with a nurse and Barbara and Carl went walking on the streets of Rochester. They had been told that they could come back at 7:00 PM for visitation and that Paul would have a room number assigned by then. If they were needed prior to then, the hospital would leave a message at the hotel.

Time was dragging on and Barbara and Carl were both concerned about Paul. His problem was not just a lack of rest and everybody knew this. The blood and sudden weakness attacks were more common than Paul had let anybody know and he was still remembering his fellow doctors telling him that they thought he has lung cancer. Barbara wanted to let the time pass quietly and just keep her thoughts to herself. Carl knew this was not good as she was a serious type lady and he needed to get her talking about something else. Any topic was just fine to him, if he could just get her to unwind a little.

Kenneth Orr

He found the answer when he started to talk about his lunch conversation with Malone. He started telling her about how he had flown over Bandera and how nice the new house looked from the sky. He then brought up Sarge. Barbara had lost touch with Sarge. Everyone knew he was growing old and his body was failing. She said that when they got home they had to look him up and pay a visit. He was much like a third parent to both of them and they loved him much like a member of the family.

Carl then went into how Malone had flagged him down in the parking lot and the lunch conversation they had shared. Carl said he had made up his mind to leave California and come back to Texas and re-join the Army as an instructor pilot.

Barbara was surprised and soon she put her arms around her brother and said she was so happy at his decision. The surprise and pleasure from this news had taken her mind away from Paul's problems for a moment and Barbara was actually smiling.

Carl told Barbara that he had to do a lot of new planning about his ties in California but they were not going to be immediate concerns. He said he had made a lot of friends there and he was not happy to be leaving, but he knew where his heart was in Texas. Barbara said that Paul would be glad to hear the news and he had made a lot of comments about how much he was impressed with Carl's attitudes and abilities.

At 5:00 PM they found a good restaurant and had a light dinner. At 7:00 PM they were at the hospital waiting to see Paul. They got the room number and hurried to see Paul. When they went in Paul was sitting on the side of the bed in a hospital gown and reading a local newspaper. He was glad to see them and soon everybody was talking about Paul's examinations. He had not been told much, but he knew that tomorrow he was going to be run through a series of tests that would require he be put to sleep for a while. He was very positive and had one major complaint.

The Cowboy's Kids

He was hungry and they would only allow him to sip small amounts of water.

The tests were going to be extensive and Doctor Clemenson would get back with him as soon as he had looked at the results. There were no firm timetables but Paul was told he probably could have supper tomorrow. About then, Dr. Clem popped in and said he was looking forward to seeing what Paul looked like on the inside. He added, "It had to be better than some of the people he had seen recently. Most of them were over 60 and their insides were in bad shape from smoking too much." Paul told the doctor that he had never smoked and he always had done a lot of physical conditioning. The Doctor told everyone he would be back tomorrow night at 7:00 PM and give them a report on what had been found.

This was good information and everyone was looking forward to getting some meaningful idea as to what was wrong. Paul was the most excited. The Doctor excused himself and left the room.

Barbara went over to Paul and gave him a big hug. She said she and Carl had some good news and they thought Paul would be happy to hear it. Paul looked at both of them and was wondering what was happening.

Barbara said, "Carl, you tell Paul what you told me." Carl smiled and looked at Paul. He said, "I am going to leave my job in California and come home to Texas. I have accepted an invitation from Captain Malone to come back into the Army as a Captain and help train pilots." Paul got a wide smile on his face and got up and went to Carl and gave him a big hug. "You are such a good guy and I am looking forward to having you near Barbara has always told me a lot about you and from what I have seen for myself, she has a lot of good reasons to be proud of you. All I want to know now, is when?"

Carl said, " I am not sure right now, but it will be soon. I still need to get my cards lined up in California. I have a lot

Kenneth Orr

of good friends there and my job is not that easy to walk away from. I really want to leave there the right way. The people there have been very good to me. I am going to call them tomorrow and tell them I will be a few days late in getting back. It is important to me that you and Barbara are taken care of the right way on this trip on this trip. I do not want to make them wonder where I am and they need to keep my job's schedule covered." Paul was feeling better having learned all of the new news and tomorrow was not going to be as difficult to face. The visitation horn in the hospital sounded. This was the signal for all visitors to leave. Visitation was now over. Carl walked out into the hall, shaking Paul's hand on his way. Barbara stayed behind for a few moments and had a small private time with Paul. When she came out, they went to the hotel.

Barbara went to her room and Carl stayed in the lobby. He checked with the front desk about making a long distance call to California. He got all of the right information, wrote it down and decided to go to the bar for a nightcap. He walked in, got a seat at a small table in the corner and ordered a stiff Kentucky whiskey drink. When the drink came he stirred it with the swizzle stick just to pass time. The cherry that was floating on top soon was gone and a couple more gentle sips made the day slow down a little. The first drink was so good that he ordered a second.

Somehow just being alone and having a while to think about all that was happening around him, was a good thing. He was resting his mind. There were a lot of people in the bar and many of them were obviously not in a good mood. Rochester was a place, where people with their last hopes for life would come hoping to try to find a cure. Their families and friends also came. Facing the end of life is always a hard task, even when it is an obvious and unstoppable rendezvous.

Carl wanted to go to his room and just go to bed, but he was concerned about Paul and Barbara. He just wanted to sit by himself and think about a lot of things for a few minutes. They were both so much a central part of his life and they

The Cowboy's Kids

were hurting. Carl paid his bill, got up and walked out into the night. He walked and thought to himself for about an hour. His body was growing tired and he recognized that he needed to go to bed. When he finally went to bed he was sound asleep in a very quick time.

CHAPTER 2-18
Adjustments and New Directions

On Wednesday morning Barbara and Carl got up early and met each other for breakfast. The sky was cloudy and the threat of rain was all around the area. Barbara wanted to go over to the hospital and sit in the lobby just to be nearer to Paul. Carl was aware of her concerns but needed to call his office in California. He told her she could go over there and he would come over as soon as he got his call completed.

There was a two-hour time difference between Minnesota and California time and Carl wanted to wait until about 9:00 AM in California to make the call. Barbara put on comfortable clothes and left for the hospital. Carl went to his room and waited to make his call. Finally the time passed and Carl got the hotel operator to place the call. It took about ten minutes to get all of the lines connected properly and finally the operator called Carl's room and said she had his party on the line.

Carl got on the phone and his boss, a man who was new to Carl, was anxious to see why Carl was calling. Carl told him about the family emergency and how the Army people at Randolph Field had provided him an airplane to take everyone to Minnesota. His former boss had been replaced and the current boss was an older sounding fellow named Ralph Hensley. He was new to the company and had little knowledge about all of the individual projects in the design group. He was more of an administrative person

The Cowboy's Kids

than a technical contributor and he said he would pass the information on to the right person. Carl asked if a certain co-worker was available and Ralph was told he was no longer with the company. Carl did not know what was going on but he knew it was not good. The guy he had asked for was a sharp engineer and he was never one to just up and quit. The call was ended and Carl left the conversation with a big concern about the company's core personnel.

Carl walked over to the hospital and found Barbara in the coffee shop. She was drinking her third cup of coffee and the waiting was getting to her. Carl told her about the call and how he had concerns about the way the conversation had gone. Barbara said that he needed to be glad he had something else to go to and he did not need to worry about the situation. After all, it was not going to be his problem.

Carl said he thought that he needed to go to the airport and make sure that the airplane was being taken care of properly. The weather report had forecast high winds and large hail for the afternoon.

An airplane needs to be in a hangar when these conditions are in the area. He asked Barbara if she wanted to go with him." Barbara declined his invitation and said she wanted to stay in the hospital's lobby. Carl hailed a taxi and soon was at the airport. The flight line personnel had pulled several airplanes, including the military airplane into a hanger and they were as safe as the available facility could make them. The door was closed to keep wind gusts out and the various planes were crammed into spaces so tight that walking upright was almost impossible. Carl thanked the people for their efforts and told them that his departure was uncertain, but hopefully it would be within a couple of days. Most of the men were from local farms and worked at the airport to make some extra money. He had witnessed some excellent efforts from a very small group of dedicated people. Minnesota had made a great and positive impression on Carl and he never forgot this experience.

Kenneth Orr

The taxi took Carl back to the hotel where he called Captain Malone back in San Antonio. The call went quickly and the connection was much clearer than the one to California. Carl told Malone about the situation and assured him the airplane was safe inside a good strong hangar. Malone assured Carl that the trip did not need to be paced by getting the airplane home. He should stay as long as he needed, to get the medical results and plan for Paul's future. Carl thanked him and told him he had been in touch with his employer in California. That was about all that was said and the called was ended. Captain Malone was in the middle of a meeting. Carl washed his face, combed his hair and went over to the hospital.

Barbara was still sitting on a big leather chair near the front desk. She has found a magazine and was reading it when Carl walked up. The lunchroom was still open and Carl said, "Come on, and lets get a sandwich or some good soup." Barbara got up and went with Carl.

They found a small table in the corner and the waitress came over with a menu. Carl ordered a sandwich, some soup and a glass of fresh milk. Barbara looked at the menu and asked if she could get a meatloaf plate with mashed potatoes. Soon they were eating and making small talk.

Doctor Clemenson walked in. He did not see Barbara or Carl and took a seat about two tables away. Barbara was glad to see him and she knew that the medical procedures being done on Paul were over.

Carl told Barbara, "Sit tight, I am going to invite him to eat with us."

Carl went over and the Doctor recognized him immediately. He smiles and said, "Have a seat." Carl said, "Why don't you join Barbara and me, we already have our food and you are most welcome."

They went over to where Barbara was seated and sat down. The Doctor knew that everyone's tension over Paul's

The Cowboy's Kids

condition was high and he was going to be asked about the latest news. When he sat down he gave Barbara a hug and said that the day had been very busy. He then said that they had done some tissue removal on both of Paul's lungs and they had done a lot of related blood work. He said the lab work would be back by late afternoon and then they could plan for Paul's future. He added, "Paul is doing fine and he will be back in his room in about two hours. When I get back to my office, I will give permission for you both to visit with him as soon as he is awake and stable." The Doctor's food arrived and everybody ate everything on their plates. After lunch, Carl and Barbara went back to the waiting room.

Barbara was watching the clock and waiting for the charge nurse to notify the front desk that she and Carl could come to Paul's room. While they were waiting Carl asked Barbara how long it had been since she went over the books for the development company. Barbara said it had been about a month. They were so busy in San Antonio with the sale of the clinic and with Paul being ill the other interests in life had not been a concern. Carl asked how the company was doing. Barbara said it was not losing money but the profits were not impressive. Carl said if he sold the California home and all of the land they had acquired he thought they could get a good price for everything. The growth in the area was really going strong and the best properties were bringing premium prices.

Barbara said, "I think we need to consolidate a lot of things, but first we need to get over Paul's health issues. We both are wealthy on paper and we need to plan for our futures with all of the changes we are experiencing right now behind us." Carl agreed.

Finally, the desk clerk smiled at Barbara and she knew that it was OK to go to Paul's room. Carl led the way and the walked in to find a nurse taking his temperature. He saw both of them and a big smile came over his face. Barbara went over and gave him a kiss and a gentle hug.

Kenneth Orr

Carl shook Paul's hand gently and said, "How you doing, Doctor?" Paul just smiled some more and said, "Sit down and just let me look at both of you". He was drifting in and out of sleep from the medication that had put him to sleep for his tests. He was not really awake yet.

In about an hour he had awakened enough to hold a reasonable conversation. Barbara told him they had sat with the Doctor for lunch and he told them he was awaiting some lab reports. The news was not any surprise to Paul as he did the same think in his work often. The time was passing fast and a young nurse came in and took his blood pressure. Paul's chart was hanging on the foot of the bed but the information on it was so minimal that Barbara said it was not of any value. Carl told Paul that the weather was bad outside and they had flown into town ahead of a big weather front. The airplane was now in a hanger and was safe from wind and hail damage. Paul was interested in the airplane and he and Carl talked a lot about the control systems used to maneuver the plane in flight.

Paul said he wanted to learn to fly. It was a lot of fun and life was so much easier when you wanted to go somewhere quickly.

The clock was nearing 5:00 PM and a nurse brought in a tray with a covered dish of food. There was a small glass of orange juice and a few crackers on the side of the tray. Paul sat up a little higher and a tray holder was placed over the bed in front of him. The food tray was placed in front of him and the dish cover was removed. Under it was a bowl of watery looking soup. Paul looked up and said, "Damn, I am hungry and all I am offered is broth and crackers. This has got to be the first course and the good stuff is still on the stove." Barbara smiled and just looked at the ceiling.

About then Doctor Clemenson came into the room. He saw Paul's face then he looked at the food plate. He immediately went back out into the hall and hailed a nearby nurse. He said. "This was supposed to be a noon meal, that is if he could eat then. He needs some meat and potatoes and a

The Cowboy's Kids

big glass of fresh milk." Paul looked at the Doctor and said, "Thank You Sir, I was getting a little upset over not having anything to eat." The nurse took the first tray away and said she would be back soon.

The Doctor said, "I know all of you are awaiting the news so I will not keep you waiting. I wish I had better news, but we have found cancer cells in several tissue samples. It appears to have spread into several areas. I wish I had better news, but I always am right up front with my patients and Paul, being my friend, is not making this any easier. The next step is what to do about it. I will also be up front about that. The medical profession has developed some radiation procedures to stop cancers but they don't fit your condition. It is too far spread to contain using this approach."

There are also some medications and they are sometimes effective. I must warn all of you, Paul has a condition that is probably going to be terminal. I am sorry to tell you this, but you need to know."

Barbara began to sob and Carl went to her side. Paul just looked up and lost any hunger he had. Barbara was by his side and soon everyone was crying.

Doctor Clemenson called Carl out into the hall and they had a good down-to-earth talk about Paul and what needed to be done right now. The Doctor told Carl that Paul would do just as well with doctors at home. He said that the hospitals in San Antonio were as good at providing care as any that was near the Mayo Clinic. The Doctor said that he would contact a cancer specialized doctor he knew in San Antonio and forward all of his findings to him.

The Doctor added, "Paul needs to go home soon as his strength is going to become less in the very near future and he will be a bed patient from that point, until he expires". He added, I am going to give Barbara some pain medication for Paul and with her nursing experience she can administer it as Paul needs it." He suggested that Paul spend the coming

Kenneth Orr

night in the hospital and that he stay under observation. He wanted to be sure he was able to travel.

Carl asked Barbara to come out into the hall. The Doctor went over the same information for her and he assured her that the best thing they could do for Paul was keep him comfortable. He told Barbara he might be able to function normally for a couple more weeks but by the coming month he would be too weak to do much more than sit up. Barbara was a nurse and they discussed a lot of things that medical people know about. Soon she was back in the room with Paul.

Carl had gone to the phone and called the airport. He wanted a weather check for tomorrow and a suggested flight plan to get around the big storm that currently was over the area. He did not know what time they could get Paul released from the hospital the next morning but he wanted to be ready to fly as soon as he was cleared and able.

Barbara went to Paul's bed and in a low and gentle voice said, "We are going home to Texas tomorrow if the weather is fit. Then we can plan for the next few weeks when we get there". Paul looked at her and said, "Good, I want to spend my final days at home and with people I know and love." Doctor Clemenson made another stop by the room just to see how things were going.

He had a good talk with Paul and told him that he was sorry about his condition but the best way to keep a positive attitude was to trust in his faith in the Lord. The Doctor knew he was going home to die and he told him he had been doing God's work by caring for the sick and injured people of the world. This had been a big part of his life that he needed to remember and take pride. He parted company and told Barbara that his services were not going to be billed. Paul had more than paid for his charges by the kind of life he had lived.

The Cowboy's Kids

The Doctor saw Carl in the hall and Carl asked him what time that Paul could be discharged? The Doctor said he could leave any time after 6:00 AM tomorrow. You can have a car waiting at the discharge door. Carl thanked him for his honesty and gave him a big handshake.

The "visitation is over buzzer" sounded at 8:00 PM and a nurse came by the room and told everyone they would need to leave. The hospital was getting ready for the night. Paul gave everyone a big hug and kissed Barbara good night. Barbara and Carl walked out of the hospital and over to the hotel. There was a light rain falling and nobody seemed to mind. The coolness of the water and the night air seemed to put a calming effect over Barbara and Carl and they had little to say. When they reached the hotel, Carl told Barbara about the discharge time. She said she would be read by 5:00 AM with baggage packed waiting in the hotel lobby. Carl said he would be ready by the same time. He said he was going to call the airport and have the Beechcraft fueled and ready for flight. They agreed and somehow they did not want to go separate ways right then. They both needed somebody to lean on for a while and Barbara was holding back the tears as she walked.

Carl said he would take Barbara to her room and stay with her as long as she wanted. She agreed, and soon they were setting in her room. Barbara said she wanted to take a shower before she went to bed and she spent about 15 minutes in the water. Carl sat down on a couch and soon his head was bobbing up and down. He was tired and knew that tomorrow he needed to be read to fly. When Barbara came out of the bathroom, she had on her night clothing.

Carl said he would stay until she was asleep but she insisted he go to his room and get some rest. She knew he was going to have a full day tomorrow and he needed to be rested. Flying is not something you do when you are sleepy.

Carl called the airport and he caught a man who was working late. He said that the airplanes had all been pulled out of the hangar as soon as the weather problems had passed. The

Kenneth Orr

Beechcraft was tied down in the same location where it was originally parked. He said he would fuel the plane and check the engine oil before he went home and he would leave the bill on the pilot's seat. Carl said he would pay the bill before he left, if the office was open, or just put some money in an envelope and put it under the office door. Agreement was reached and Carl went to bed for the night.

The next morning came quickly and the long days of summer were longer in the north than they were in Texas. At 5:00 AM the sun was coming up quickly and the sky was crystal clear. It was going to be a great day for flying. Carl went to the lobby and got the hotel bill for both rooms, paid it and then he saw Barbara coming down the hall. He suggested they get a quick breakfast in the hotel restaurant. The restaurant was open all night and the early eaters were already ordering bacon and eggs. The smell of cooking bacon travels a long way. Barbara and Carl both ordered the "Sunrise Breakfast" which was eggs, bacon and a fruit plate. All of the coffee you could drink was standard and for those that wanted it, orange juice was available.

After eating they thought for a minute and wondered if Paul would have been served breakfast before he was discharged. Just in case, they ordered a big sweet roll and a container of milk to go. He could eat this in the taxicab to the airport or take it on the plane. Carl had a bottle of water in his luggage sack and he always had some cookies and candy bars when he was flying.

Carl walked outside the hotel and found a taxi. He told the driver they had to pick up a passenger at the hospital and then go to the airport. He put their luggage in the trunk said they would walk to the hospital. It was only about 500 feet away from the taxi stand. The taxi driver understood and said, "I do this kind of fare often. Rochester is a place where a lot of unusual things happen and nothing surprises me," The cab pulled up to the discharge door at the hospital and waited outside. Barbara and Carl went in and the front desk lady said she had been alerted that Paul was going to be discharged early.

The Cowboy's Kids

She called the nurse on Paul's ward and told her that his Wife was waiting in the discharge area. Carl asked the lady at the desk if she thought Paul would have had his breakfast yet. She called back to the ward and was told he had been given an early meal and they had made him a "travel bag" with several pieces of fruit and some bottled juice inside. Paul was finally going home.

The nurse pushed Paul down to the discharge area and he started to get up out of the wheelchair. The nurse said she needed to push him all the way to the waiting taxicab, as this was a strict hospital rule.

He understood. Barbara was given a package of papers with a short note from the Doctor saying he was sending the medical records with her. Her status as a nurse allowed him to do this as he knew she was a safe person to get the information to San Antonio. The drive to the airport was uneventful and when they pulled into the parking lot, Carl told the driver he wanted him to drive over to the aircraft-parking apron. The driver understood.

When they reached the airplane, Carl got out of the cab and opened the door on the airplane. He went inside and sure enough, the gas bill was on the seat. He came back out, went to the taxi and told Paul and Barbara that they could get on the airplane. He then paid the taxi driver and gave him a good tip for the great service he had afforded to everyone. Barbara and Paul got out and walked to the airplane's door. Paul looked around the airport one last time and then boarded the airplane. The taxi driver brought all of the baggage to the door and he and Barbara loaded it onto a seat near the back of the airplane's interior.

Carl went to the operations office and they were just opening. He paid his bill and thanked them for taking good care of the airplane. He got the latest weather reports for his trip and filed the flight plan for his anticipated route. He then went back to the airplane and the taxi driver was still there. He said he wanted to be sure they were ok to leave before he left. He said sometimes there have been

Kenneth Orr

last minute problems and the sick person needs to go back to the clinic.

Carl got in the plane and Paul was seated in the co-pilots seat. Carl said, "You really like this flying stuff don't you?" Paul looked up and said. " Well, it's a whole lot better than fighting a dirt road and a problem-prone car." Barbara saw that Paul was in a better mood today and he was trying to get the most out of this experience even thought it had really been a bad-news trip.

Carl started the engines and did his routine pre-flight checkouts. Soon they were in the air, flying south and headed for Texas. The route was almost the same as they had taken when they went north. This time the clouds were gone and the open farmlands and small cities were much easier to see. Paul used the flight charts to keep track of the flight's progress and within a couple of hours they were getting closer to Tulsa. They landed at Tulsa, took on fuel and got some needed refreshments.

The restroom was a most welcome experience for everyone. Carl was hungry and his snack bag of cookies was just not good enough to satisfy his hunger. There was a small café in the flight office and they had some huge hamburgers cooking when they walked in. Paul ordered one Carl ordered two and Barbara got an order of French-fried potatoes and a cold soda. After a second bathroom stop they all got back into the airplane and took off.

The trip to San Antonio was an easy ride. The weather was great and they had a good tailwind. The city of Austin came up under the wings and Carl radioed ahead to Randolph Field that he was requesting landing instructions. Most of the student activity for the day was over and he was granted landing clearance with no problem. Carl descended and soon the airplane was on the apron just about where it had been parked before the trip. Carl shut everything down and soon an Army staff car pulled alongside. The driver told everyone welcome home and told Carl that all of the new

The Cowboy's Kids

recruits loved his personal airplane. Carl knew they were back among friends.

The staff car took everyone to the hangar where the Packard had been parked. The keys were in the front seat and there was a note from Malone saying he had driven the car to lunch one day and loved the way it handled. Paul said he was happy it was used a little and he noticed that it had been washed and waxed to a brilliant shine. Carl's personal plane was in the same hangar and Paul said he wanted to go flying in it soon. Carl agreed to take him up soon and they all started for home.

Paul had been feeling well throughout the entire flight, but now that he was in the car, he began to feel tired and a little ill. Carl was driving and Paul was in the front passenger's seat. By the time they reached home he was starting to cough and it was obvious to Barbara he was having problems breathing. When they got home, Carl helped Paul into the side door and he immediately went to the bedroom and lay on the bed.

Barbara was concerned about his immediate health and called the clinic to see if anyone was in. Luckily a Doctor answered the phone. Paul had never had a specific personal Doctor to look over his health, as he never was concerned that he needed one, after all he was a Doctor himself. Barbara told the Doctor what was happening and related to the tests that had just been completed at the Mayo Clinic. The voice on the other end said he would come right over and see what he could do.

The Doctor was one of the men buying the clinic and had spent enough time around Paul to be somewhat familiar with his general health. His name was Abner Zimmerman. Paul simply called him "Zim."

Barbara told Carl a Doctor was coming over and that he was going to examine Paul. Carl was as concerned as was Barbara and soon the doorbell was ringing.

Kenneth Orr

Doctor Zimmerman came in and Barbara greeted him with a big thank you for coming so quickly. He went directly to Paul's room and started to examine him. Barbara gave him the documents from Minnesota and the Doctor reviewed them quickly.

He saw that Paul was tired and he knew his lungs were working harder just to keep him going because of the trip. He took some vital sign readings and went to Barbara. He said to get him some warm soup, give him some pills he had in his black bag that would make him sleep and call him in the morning. Barbara understood and thanked the Doctor again for coming.

The Doctor said that the transition of the clinic was going better than any of the partners had expected. He thought it was because they had kept such good records on patients and the patients had such strong trust in the services they had been given.

He said that Paul's health was now a serious concern and that he would personally take care of him if Barbara were agreeable. Barbara was pleased and the Doctor told her that he had also been in the Army but not as a Doctor. He was a medic and had served in France.

When he came home he finished his medical training in Houston, Texas and had specialized in internal medicine. He said goodbye and left.

The next morning was filled with sunlight and the sound of doves cooing their favorite songs. Carl loved to hear the birds and went out on the back porch with a cup of coffee and just listened. Barbara joined him in a few minutes and said that Paul was still sleeping. They talked about the trip and what they had learned concerning Paul's condition. Barbara was very concerned, but she was keeping a strong attitude and not letting her deepest concerns show. Carl knew that was her way of overcoming problems, to become strong from the inside and stand up for what was right. This

The Cowboy's Kids

was one of those times, and Barbara was giving it her very best effort.

When her cup was empty she went in and checked on Paul. He was starting to wake up and wanted to get up and go out on the porch with Carl. Paul put on a bathrobe and some slippers and Barbara fixed him a cup of coffee. Everyone was now on the porch and the day was starting out well. Barbara asked Paul how he slept and he said he was well rested. He said the trip had really taken a lot of his energy but he was starting to feel better now that he was sleeping in his own bed.

His mind was as strong as ever and he was talking to Carl about when he was going to be able to take him flying in his airplane.

The housekeeper arrived and she was soon helping Barbara unpack dirty clothes and such from the trip. Carl suggested that he go over to the airfield and thank Captain Malone personally for the use of the airplane for the trip. Paul asked if he could go along so he could also thank him in person.

Carl agreed and soon they were in the Packard. When they arrived at the gate, Carl asked to guard if he could see Captain Malone? He said, "No problem but he is now Major Malone, that happened just last week." The guards had seen the shiny black Packard so often, that they already knew it was Carl. He had made casual friendships with several of the guards and they admired his car. Carl was becoming a part of the cloth they called "local Army fabric."

Carl went to the usual parking spot and he and Paul got out. They walked into the office building and asked if they could see the Major. In a very short time they were ushered into his office and Malone's normal big smile greeted them.

He said, "I see you all got back in one piece and the trip went smoothly. Have a seat and let's have a cup of coffee."

Kenneth Orr

Carl introduced Paul, and before he sat down he went to Major Malone and grabbed his hand and thanked him for the use of the airplane. Malone understood the gratitude and said, "I hope all went well for you and we are always here to help our fellow Army personnel in times of need." Paul's simple response was, "Thank You, Sir."

Paul sat down and Carl opened the conversation. He said, "I have been in touch with my people in California and told them that I am going to be late in getting back. They are not yet aware that I will be leaving, but as soon as I get back my first duty will be to let them know that I am rejoining the Army. I just wanted to keep you informed. Then I plan to shut down my home, sell a few things and then come back to San Antonio."

"I expect to be here by the end of August. Is that acceptable, Sir?" Malone looked at him and said, "Carl, that fits a plan I have been working on. I want you to start a training program with a group of new cadets and see how we do our flight training these days."

"The Army has a structured plan where young men are instructed, tested and given several opportunities to learn to fly. If they pass, they are in. If they fail we send them to other army duties or send them home. Once you see what I am describing you will see the value of this system, it works and we are constantly working to improve it." Carl understood. Paul just listened, he knew he was setting in on a very important conversation for Carl.

Carl promised to call Major Malone as soon as he had a firm date to report. Paul, Carl and Major Malone all stood up, shook hands and the conversation was over.

The walk to the automobile was not very long and about half way through to the car Paul asked Carl if they could go look at his new airplane? Carl was glowing with pride and the detour happened at once. He loved his airplane and showing it off to Paul was a special joy for him.

The Cowboy's Kids

The plane, a Luscombe, Model 8, was still as bright and shiny as the day it was built. This airplane had impressed Carl as it incorporated a new design for airplanes. The fuselage was carrying the stress of the wings and control surfaces, rather that an internal set of fuselage structures. This reduced the total aircraft weight and made the manufacturing process a lot less costly. Carl asked Paul if he wanted to go for a spin? The answer was an immediate and overwhelming, YES!

Paul had to have some help but he climbed into climbed into the right side seat. Carl did an outside walk around and then reached into the control panel and turned some knobs. He then walked around to the front of the airplane and began to spin the propeller. In about three good pulls the engine started and Carl ran around to the side of the cockpit and climbed in. He made some adjustments on the dash panel and told Paul everything was working fine. The plane was on the runway apron and had wheel chocks on both main landing gear wheels. A young cadet was nearby and Carl had asked him if he would pull the chocks away when he was ready to taxi. The cadet agreed and was anxious to help.

Carl signaled the cadet he was ready to taxi out to a run-up area. The chocks were pulled and Carl increased the engine speed and the plane moved forward. Paul was just smiling and watching. He was enjoying the thrill of this flight more than he had the trip to Minnesota and it was obvious he was going to be a good passenger.

Carl did his preflight check, radioed the tower and got permission to take off. Soon the plane was gaining speed and it lifted into the clear Texas sky.

Carl said, "Let's look at downtown San Antonio." Paul said, "Great, can we fly over my old Clinic and see what it looks like from the air." Carl knew the area well and soon they were right over the clinic. Carl said, "Let's take a quick trip out to Bandera, is that something you would like to do?" Paul just smiled. It was obvious that he was glad to go

Kenneth Orr

anywhere just as long as the pilot was flying, he was not sure of what to do if there was an emergency.

Paul was asking Carl a lot about the airplane. Carl told him that it could fly about 100 miles per hour and the engine developed about 50 horsepower. The wings were fabric covered and the rest of the airplane was all aluminum.

They finished the trip, landed back at Randolph Field and went home to see how Barbara was doing. Paul was tired but he was happy. He knew he would love to become a pilot but he also knew that he was not physically up to the task of making that happen. Carl told Barbara all about the meeting with Major Malone and the flight over all of the local sights. Barbara was happy for him. Paul could not hold himself from butting in and telling her about flying over the San Antonio area and the way he felt like a bird while they were in the air.

The day ended quietly. Everyone was glad to go to bed in a comfortable bed and to get an uninterrupted night's sleep.

One thing was certain, everybody loved being home in Texas and The joy of the moment was appreciated. Everyone knew it would pass very soon.

CHAPTER 2-19
Facing The Future and Making New Plans

Carl flew back to California and went to work a week later than he had originally planned. He went to his desk and there was a note on his chair to come see a new man who was now his boss. Cliff Hensley who Carl had thought was his boss was gone. Carl was surprised, but not overly concerned. Whatever news he was about to receive would matter very little, as he had some news to give them of his own.

The new man's name was Roger King. Carl went to the office area and found Mr. King. He was a short round fellow who was dressed in a sloppy blue suit that was too small for his stomach. The coat would not button in the front and he had a soiled spot on his shirt. Carl introduced himself. Mr. King said, "Come in and close the door." Carl responded accordingly.

Mr. King sat across the desk from Carl and said, "We have reorganized the engineering department while you were gone and a lot of the men have been assigned to some important, high priority military aircraft projects. Your old program is still moving forward, but is now under a new manager. Management had decided to assign you to me to be my assistant in the scheduling of several hot programs and we are already way behind." He went on, "I want to get

Kenneth Orr

you involved with a new bomber project. Our schedule is tight and will need to push the engineers to get something going as soon as possible. You can be as tough on the men as you want; that's OK with me. I am not here to make friends. I have a project to get done." Carl just sat back and let it all soak in for a minute.

Then Carl spoke up, "Mr. King, with all respect for you and your new assignment, I am not sure what I could do to make an engineering program go any faster by getting tough on people. This is just not my idea as how to handle skilled people. And by the way, while I was home in San Antonio, I had an opportunity to visit some old friends at Randolph Field. They offered me a good job with an Officer's Commission to become an Army flight instructor. I have accepted their offer."

Mr. King looked at Carl and glared in his face. He said, "Young man, you have done what?" Carl said, "I have gone back into the Army and I will be leaving my assignment with you as soon as I can transition my work to someone else." Mr. King was upset and he had just about lost his temper.

Then, with a voice that was as cold and harsh as Carl had ever heard, he said, "Your transition is over as of right now. Lets go down to the paymaster and draw your final pay. You are free to go home right now." Carl said, "That's just fine with me."

Carl drew his pay and went by his desk to get his personal things. He saw some friends who were nearby and they were wondering what was happening. Carl said, "I will buy the beer at the local pub after you get off tonight, then we can talk." They understood.

Carl went to a local store and bought some gifts for Paul and Barbara. He wanted to go home with something for each of them. He loved to see the smiles on their faces when they were happily surprised. He found just the right thing for each of them. Paul's gift was a model airplane that was scaled after a DC-3. He had been interested in the

The Cowboy's Kids

new airplanes' design but had never seen anything except a picture of one. Barbara's gift was a gold-framed painting of the ocean and beach area near La Jolla. She had been there several times and this particular painting was well done. He knew she would like it. At 4:00 PM the shift was over and his close friends all showed up at "Clyde's Cabin," the local group's hangout.

One of the fellows named Ramos was always the most talkative. He told Carl that two days after he had left, they called everybody into a big meeting and said they had to make some immediate changes. The Army Air Corp had a lot of problems and needed some special new airplanes. The Army wanted bigger bombers and cargo haulers and they wanted them as soon as possible. The design group was split up with little or no logic as to a man's experience. Everyone was upset with the new managers that were put in charge. Several of the better men had no respect for these new managers. The new managers were all front office political friends of one of the big bosses. The old managers all banned together and walked out. The rest of them still are here but not sure of what was going to happen. If they had another job, they would be gone tomorrow.

Carl told them that he had just resigned and he was going back into the Army as a flight instructor. He planned on being stationed in Texas and he was looking forward to the assignment.

He told everyone how Mr. King had been so cold and hard about what he wanted to get done. Carl said, "I was upset, too. In fact I almost said a curse word." Everyone knew that Carl never cursed and that he really had to work hard to control himself in that room. Carl told everyone, "Just let things settle. Nothing lasts forever and in time a new and better wind will blow for each of you." He said he would like to have everyone's address and if anything that came his way, that might be right for any of them he would be in touch. Everyone wrote their addresses down, drank all of the cold beer on the table, and left to go home.

Kenneth Orr

Carl went to his small apartment in Long Beach, cleaned it out and loaded everything in his Ford. He drove to his home in La Jolla and unloaded the car and went out for dinner.

The next morning he drove his Ford over to a moving company and arranged to move some furniture he wanted to keep, to Texas. He wanted them to move the rest to a local auction house. He called Barbara on the telephone and told her he wanted to sell the house as there was no need for it now, and he did not want to rent it. The upkeep just to let it set empty, was going to be high. Barbara agreed.

There were several people anxious to buy the property and Carl put a big sheet of white paper on the front gate saying,

FOR SALE

Write your best offer and

Contact information below.

This auction sale will end

At noon on August 10,

Sale will be to the highest Bidder,

Cash Only

Thank You For Your Offer.

It did not take long for the word to get around that the property was for sale. Several real estate people came by and wanted to list the home. Carl told them if they wanted to buy it, make an offer, if not, thanks for the interest and good-bye.

By the end of the day he had several offers and each was posted in clear view. Any additional offers had to be larger

The Cowboy's Kids

than the last or they would not be considered. The offers were all bigger than he had expected and when the time ran out, there were six people standing on the front yard waiting to see what happened.

Carl looked at the clock and said, "This auction is closed." "The highest offer is from, Mr. Roy Cooper, is he present?" A tall well-dressed man stepped forward and introduced himself. He said, "I am Mr. Cooper's banker and he has authorized me to give you his check for the price we have written down. Is this acceptable?" Carl looked at the final price amount and it was twice what he had originally anticipated. He said, "Let's go to the bank and cash that check and if it is as good as you say, this property is sold."

Carl got out his Ford and followed the buyer's banker to the bank he represented. The check cleared and Carl told him he would have his lawyer help close out the paperwork as soon as he could contact him.

Carl then went to a big local real estate office and said he would like to sell the three remaining plots of land that he and Barbara still owned. Before Carl could get out of the office an agent made a phone call and got a firm offer. The offer was over four times what Carl had anticipated, and he told the agent, "Get that man's money before he decides to change his mind."

Carl gave them the information on where in Texas to send the funds and complete all of the paperwork and went out and drove to a hotel. He got a room and said he would be there for a couple of days, and then he was going to Texas.

Now all that Carl had left in California was his Ford. He loved that old car, but he knew it would be too costly to have it shipped to Texas. He drove by the Ford dealership where he had bought it and they said they would buy it and still let him use it until he left town.

Kenneth Orr

The next two days were spent seeing old friends and enjoying his favorite ocean views. Finally, he was ready to go home. He drove by the Ford dealership, got his payment for the car and paid a driver to take him to the airport in his Ford. He put his baggage in the airplane, made sure that the airplane's fuel tank, oil levels and tire pressures were all in good shape and took one last look at his old Ford.

The driver got in the Ford, started it up and waived good-bye as he left. Carl got the engine running and got in the pilot's seat and closed the door. A ground service man pulled the chocks and Carl started his trip home.

The first day he flew as far as El Paso, Texas. He spent the night and made sure he got a good night's sleep. The next day was cloudy but flying was not a big problem. Carl decided to land at San Antonio's commercial airport, as he did not want to look like he was taking advantage of any status he had at Randolph Field. After landing, Carl arranged for a hangar to keep his plane in out of the weather. Texas was under a storm watch and small airplanes were not safe when they are left outside in this kind of weather. He then got a taxicab and went to Barbara's home.

When he arrived Barbara was gone. She had gone grocery shopping and Paul was in bed sleeping. The housekeeper said Paul had been sick for two days and that Barbara had Doctor Zimmerman coming over later in the day. Carl said he would put his things in the spare bedroom and not wake Paul. In about ten minutes Barbara came home.

Barbara told Carl how glad she was that he was home. Then she said, "I am concerned about Paul. He has lost so much strength that he has to have help just to get out of bed." Carl saw her concerns as she was looking tired and in need of sleep.

Barbara asked Carl about all of the transactions that he had made concerning the land and the California house. He filled in the details and told her that they now had over $3 million dollars, in cash, coming from all of the properties.

The Cowboy's Kids

Barbara was pleased. She said that they needed to get out of the investment business and donate what they planned, to some school. The work was just too much for either of them and they were not interested in the rat race that went with all of the deals.

The business office in Dallas was not doing well as the economy around the properties they owned was very slow. Barbara said that they needed to donate the land where oil was potentially located to the University of Texas and give a similar value in money to Texas A&M. They also agreed to give Art Allen a nice cash bonus, as he had been an excellent manager. Martha was also included in the package. Carl agreed. Barbara said, "We need to cut out a nice cash amount for ourselves and then dissolve the company."

The House in Bandera was modern and much nicer than it had been when they were growing up. Barbara said that someday she wanted to sell out in San Antonio and move back to live in the Bandera neighborhood. The whole experience of living in San Antonio had become too much associated with illness and endless work. I just want to get away and get some rest.

Carl thought about everything Barbara had suggested and said, "That's a good plan, lets plan to do it as soon as we see what we need to do to help Paul recover". Barbara added, "I know Paul would like this plan but I don't know how to discuss it with him right now. I don't know how long he will be with us."

Doctor Zimmerman knocked on the front door and the housekeeper announced his arrival. Barbara told him that Paul was sleeping but he was having a very hard time breathing and swallowing. The Doctor said he would look at him and see what he thought needed to be done. He knew that lung problems are difficult to live with and he could tell from Barbara's description, that he was suffering from a lack of air. Paul's bed was in a very quiet room and the sound of his breathing was so strained that the Doctor knew he needed to go to the hospital. He told Barbara that

Kenneth Orr

he needed to be in an oxygen tent and needed to have it soon. The Doctor asked to use the telephone. He called Santa Rosa Hospital and asked that they get a room ready and send an ambulance to pick up Paul. Barbara was sad, but she knew that it was the right thing to do.

Barbara woke Paul and he saw that the doctor was in the room. The Doctor told Paul that he was going to admit him into the hospital and there was an ambulance on the way to pick him up. Paul understood. The Doctor and Carl looked at each other and they both knew that Barbara wanted to be alone for a minute or two with Paul, and they left the room and closed the door behind them. Carl told the Doctor that they were very close and this was going to be a real challenge for both of them. Doctor Zimmerman looked at Carl and said, "Paul will not be coming home. I have seen how quickly he is slipping away and he will do well to live out the week. His lungs are giving up and all we can do is make him as comfortable as we can. When the lungs give up, the end is always near. That's all that can be done." Carl understood what was happening. He hung his head and began to cry.

About ten minutes later the ambulance arrived. The Doctor went to Paul's bedroom door and knocked. Barbara said, "Come in." The door was opened and Paul was setting up on the side of the bed. He had on a robe and had his arm around Barbara.

The Doctor said it was time to go and Paul stood up and walked to the living room. The ambulance attendants asked him to come with them and he walked outside and got in the back of the ambulance on a small stretcher. Barbara went with him. Carl said he would meet them at the hospital and Barbara said, "That's fine".

The Doctor got into his car and left. Carl talked to the housekeeper about what was happening and said that she needed to be ready for bad news soon. The time for Paul was going to be limited. She just looked at him with a long

The Cowboy's Kids

face and said nothing. Carl left and drove Barbara's Ford to the hospital.

Paul had been admitted and put in a private room. There was a big oxygen tent over his bed and the material was transparent so he could see out. Oxygen was obviously being administered into the air inside the tent. The whole room looked strange to Carl. Barbara was sitting in a chair near the bed and she looked strained. Carl went to the bed and said hello to Paul. Paul smiled back as best he could but it appeared that he was under a sedative. Carl looked at Barbara and she had tears welling up in her eyes. Carl took her hand and said, "Lets go for a walk, you need to have some coffee." Barbara looked at Paul and he was almost asleep so she stood up and went with Carl.

Barbara told Carl the Doctor had told her to have Paul get his will completed and notarized and to be ready to face his departure. It was not going to be long. Carl said he was sorry, but more than, that he had grown to love Paul as a part of the family and his passing was going to be a real loss for everyone.

About 10:00 PM Carl asked Barbara if she was ready to go home for the night. She said she wanted to stay with Paul but he should go get some rest. They had a pillow on the chair for her and she wanted to be near Paul for as long as she could.

She did not want him to be alone. Carl understood and hugged her. He went back to the home and went to sleep in the guest bedroom.

The night was cool and the breeze was from the southwest. The smell of coal smoke from a passing train was coming through the window when Carl woke up. It confused him, as he was not sure what he smelled. In a few moments he came to himself and realized that there was no fire emergency and he sat up in bed. It was 8:00 AM and he started to get ready to go back to the hospital.

Kenneth Orr

He took a shower, put on fresh clothes and was getting ready to leave. The housekeeper asked him if he was hungry. He said, "A little." She had fresh coffee, fresh pastries and a big bowl of cut up fruit on the table. Carl ate a big breakfast and left for the hospital.

Upon arrival Carl went to Paul's room. Barbara was sleeping in the chair and it appeared that Paul was still under the sedative. He sat down in a chair and just looked around. He was thinking of how much a life could mean and how much the relationship of a husband and wife, could add meaning to each of their lives.

In about ten minutes, a tall man dressed in a military uniform came in. He was wearing a small cross on his shirt that indicated he was a Chaplin. He said hello and told Carl he was from the Hospital at Fort Sam Houston. He informed Carl that he knew both Barbara and Paul from when they served there. Their conversation, while low, was enough to awaken Barbara. She looked up and said, "Reverend Olson. It is so good to see you and I know that Paul will be glad you came". She obviously knew the Chaplin very well and he went to her side. Barbara told him about Paul's problems and said that it was so hard to see him so helpless. The Chaplin went to the side of Paul's bed and said a prayer. Barbara went with him and it was becoming clear that Barbara was trying to make herself ready for what was coming.

The Chaplin was of the Lutheran faith as were Paul and Barbara. He said that he would help with the final arrangements and if Barbara wanted Paul to be buried at the Army Cemetery at Fort Sam Houston he would make all of the arrangements. Barbara was pleased at his offer and said she would let him know. He gave everyone some final words of faith and left the room. Barbara was glad to see Carl had returned and she went to him and cried on his shoulder.

The current day passed painfully, and then another. In three days it was obvious that Barbara needed some bed rest. She found a bed in a nearby room and went to sleep. The

The Cowboy's Kids

Doctors all were concerned for both Paul and her, and she was given a sedative to make her sleep for several hours.

Carl was sitting with Paul and Doctor Zimmerman was there twice a day. On the fourth day Paul went into a coma and lost all contact with those around him. Barbara and Carl were sitting by his bed when he suddenly quit breathing. They called the floor nurse who got two Doctors there quickly. They examined Paul and said he was gone. Barbara and Carl were sad but somewhat relieved. Paul was not suffering any longer.

Carl asked Barbara if she had considered the Chaplin's offer for a military burial? Barbara said, "Call him and tell him that Paul has expired. Also tell him that we want to have a service here in San Antonio then we want to take Paul's body to Bandera to be buried.

He will be able to go from there." Carl went to a phone and made the call. Then he told Barbara, "We need to go home. There is nothing more that we can do at the Hospital." They both looked at Paul's lifeless body one last time, turned and left the room. Carl drove home and helped Barbara into the house. The day had been hard on everyone.

The Chaplin took care of all of the arrangements and a formal military funeral was planned. Barbara wanted the funeral to be soon. The pain of his passing was lingering and having a quick closure would help make life easier on everyone. Funeral services in San Antonio were planned as a private ceremony for the family. Paul was going to be buried in the family cemetery in Bandera. A military ambulance carried Paul's casket from the Fort Sam Houston base chapel to the family cemetery located near Bandera. The flag on Paul's casket was folded and presented to Barbara and the burial proceedings were completed. Flowers from friends, former patients and fellow doctors were everywhere.

Carl drove Barbara home and they both were wondering what the next few days and weeks would bring. In about two weeks, Barbara went out to look at Paul's grave. There

Kenneth Orr

was a small military headstone on the site that simply said, "Paul Wilson, Captain, U.S. Army". The dates of his birth and death were in smaller numbers just below his name. Barbara was pleased. She was surprised to see how soon this headstone had been engraved and brought to the grave. She told Carl, "The Army has been good to us and we are proud to have served our country. Paul has done his part."

BOOK THREE
A World That Needs Strong People

CHAPTER 3-1
Facing The Future

The next few weeks were very busy. Carl went to see Major Malone, informed him about Paul's passing, and said he was ready to report for duty. Carl took his oath to confirm his status in the Army and became a full time soldier. He was assigned living quarters on the base. He knew Barbara was going to be lonely but he also knew that he had to go on with his life. Barbara needed to have time to find herself and then build a new life for herself. These were hard realities but they had to be faced.

Carl was assigned to go through the newest pilot training program as a new cadet so he would appreciate what the Army had done since he was last involved. He was given a rushed course schedule so he could get this done quickly. Major Malone had plans for him in a new role with multi engine aircraft. The course lasted about 30 days. After the introduction course was completed "Major Malone", as he now had to be addressed, called Carl in and said he wanted him to go to Dayton, Ohio and review several new airplane designs that the Army was about to add to the flying forces.

All procurement for Army Air Corp "Materials Requirements" was being handled from Dayton. The procurement offices were all at facilities located at Wright Field. The old flight development facilities at McCook Field were all gone. Wright Field had inherited all of these offices and much more

Kenneth Orr

responsibility. The size of the Army Air Corp was growing rapidly.

Carl went to see Barbara and told her that he was going to be away for a while and she needed to know where he was going to be. She told him she had made all of the arrangements to shut down the Land Company and that she had put $500,000 in two accounts for each of them to have and use as they saw fit. The balance, land and money and other holdings, were all going to be donated to deserving Texas schools. Carl signed the papers she had prepared and this was the formal end of their land management company. Barbara said the lawyers would take care of doing the actual disbursements.

She also told him she had arranged to sell her house in San Antonio and to move back to Bandera. She had an offer that was reasonable and was planning to sell, move and start over all within the next 60 days.

Carl was pleased, as she was getting some purpose and direction back into her life. Barbara's future was still unclear but it was a beginning for her recovery. The new paths in life for each of them were only beginning to take shape. They knew that their lives were going to be different and were ready to face the changes, whatever they might be.

The following week Carl went to Ohio. He flew an Army A-10 airplane from San Antonio to Dayton. For the first time he was dressed like a modern day Army pilot. Upon his arrival he was ushered into several offices where he met several key people. They were working on plans with several multi-engine airplane manufacturers for some new big bomber type airplanes.

He also was introduced to some special people who were working to develop machine guns for airplanes, bombing systems and special ordinance systems. All of this was new to him. He loved it, as it was a world of ideas and actions all whipped into an engineering frenzy. The most obvious situation, in every area, was the speed that the

The Cowboy's Kids

Army wanted everything to be completed. They were all concerned about the war that was currently going on in Europe and the growing fear that our Army would be drawn into the action soon.

The American people were growing more concerned every day that the war Hitler was waging in Europe, was going to draw the United States into the conflict. Newspaper headlines were full of news reflecting Hitler's expanding conquests and how much of Europe had fallen to his Nazi Army. World War One had been a terrible experience and the American soldiers had suffered horrible losses. Nobody wanted to see another war of similar experiences.

After World War One, "The League of Nations" had been formed to prevent any such future wars. The idea was great but it was failing. Germany had joined into the agreements, but Hitler displayed no intentions of honoring any of the treaty restrictions. His goal was to take over all of Europe. Germany was expelled from the organization in December of 1939.

Both Europe and the United States had suffered from the First World War and were still economically weak. The opportunity for Hitler and his ideas and power to grow were obvious. He had initially promoted causes that were popular with the common people.

After Hitler had gained control he made villains and killers out of those who were in control. He envisioned a country of super human people, blond hair, blue eyes and strong bodies. His hatred for Jewish people everywhere was one of his strongest passions.

Hitler was quick to make every Jew appear to be an enemy of his state. He sat up concentration camps and started a program to exterminate every Jew he could find. Terror was everywhere and the streets and cities of Germany were turned into zones of fear. Hitler went even further and in October of 1939 he started killing off the sick, elderly and disabled citizens who were not going to be able to fight in his

Kenneth Orr

Army. The common man on the street in Germany quickly saw what was happening and for pure self-preservation they were quick to join in Hitler's efforts.

England was now becoming the next German target. The German air force and navy were equipped with large powerful fleets of war machines. The bombing of England started early in 1940 and was quickly expanded into all of Great Britain. Bomb raid were happening on a regular basis and Winston Churchill was doing what he could, just to hold off an impending German invasion. In July of 1940 German battleships and submarines started sinking British and American supply ships. American merchant marine ships were not armed and were easy prey for a submarine.

Winston Churchill was now desperate for help and went to President Roosevelt through diplomatic channels, and asked to borrow any military assets that were available in the United States. America's response was quick, but the level of support was being tempered politically by the fear of any war involvement on American soil.

American war material manufacturers were being bolstered by the United States Government to build materials in support of the British effort. The German offensive forces were so strong that the American support was still not enough to keep them from bombing Great Britain.

The Boeing Company in Seattle was building B-17 bombers for the British. Trained pilots and ground support personnel were in short supply in England. The entire European land mass was in a state of war and the Germans were obviously winning. They had invaded and taken control over most of the smaller countries in Europe and their strength had grown from every country they occupied.

The war came to the shores of the United States when German submarines started attacking American flagged merchant marine ships as they sailed out of America's ports. They also had stepped up their attacks in the Atlantic

The Cowboy's Kids

shipping lanes. The fear in major United States cities located along the eastern seacoast was growing.

It was not only obvious; it was mandatory that the United States take quick and deeply involved measures to protect itself from a possible invasion.

Carl had filled out large numbers of government security forms related to his past life. The government got as much information about him as they could. He was evaluated in several areas and soon was granted a high-level security clearance. This clearance allowed him to view and learn about several new military programs that were going on behind locked doors, all of which involved new, state-of-the-art military equipment.

A well-positioned Colonel who was stationed at Wright field had been in contact with Major Malone back in Texas. The Wright Field Army Generals wanted to set up a training facility in Texas to teach young men how to use a newly developed bombing instrument.

Major Malone told the General that Carl would be coming to Dayton to get involved with this program. He added. "He has not been briefed on this assignment, I am leaving that up to you."

The new bombing device was a precision optical bombsight that had been developed by a Scandinavian man whose last name was Norden. The new device would allow a bomber to fly over a target at a high altitude and drop bombs with amazing accuracy. Most of the new planned bomber aircraft were going to be equipped with these new devices.

Dayton, Ohio was a beehive of military activity all of which was centered on new war-focused equipment to supply the Army Air Corp. Major Malone wanted Carl to become aware of all of the new bomber types and become an expert in the use of the new bombsight. Randolph Field was an Army Training Command Base. The Army was developing

Kenneth Orr

a program to train new bombardiers. They were given six weeks to get the planning done and approved.

Back in Texas the Army was looking for a location to set up a bomber crew-training base. When a new base was established, Carl was already earmarked to go there and train bomber personnel on how to use the new bombsight. He was not yet aware of his planned future role.

The Army already had a small inventory of B-17 Bombers and had trained several crews on using earlier bombsight designs. The new models were planned to replace the current bombsights that were now installed. The men who were currently using bombsight available equipment would be some of the first people trained.

Some of these men could then become trainers to help add more men to their ranks. Their experience in using the current systems would help Carl become better qualified as an instructor.

The B-17 was a traditional airplane design and was set up using a tail wheel type fuselage. The Boeing Company in Washington State had developed the airplane on their own and had already sold several hundred to the Army Air Corp. The airplane had several advantages over other bombers in the Air Corp. It had lots of power and could carry a bomb load approaching 4,000 pounds.

The basic airplane design was constantly undergoing improvements. These improvements were commonly referred to as "aircraft modifications." The Boeing Company had designed and built the first airplane in only one year, and when the first model, airship number 299, took to the air in 1935 it already had several upgrades waiting to be installed. This was the best bomber aircraft of the current designs and it was reasonably dependable.

Boeing had advertised this airplane as a "Flying Fortress." The airplane could fly higher than any other available bomber. It had manually operated small cannons on the front, rear,

The Cowboy's Kids

both sides, top and bottom surfaces. The cannons were intended as a defense against enemy fighter aircraft. They advertised the airplane as a safer way to penetrate enemy lines and drop bombs, then return home and fly again. The British had bought several B-17s, as they were desperate for help. This airplane had sounded like a perfect way to fight the Germans.

The British Royal Air Force had put B-17s into combat roles in 1941. The "Flying Fortress" was the test bed for a lot of upgrades, and design improvements for other newer bomber type airplanes.

Everyone recognized that this airplane had been rushed into production. Many improvements needed to be installed to improve the original design. The airplane had a very large vertical tail member that was credited with keeping the airplane stable at higher altitudes and made it more accurate for high altitude bombing. The four engines were each developing approximately 1,200 horsepower. "Wright engines" were equipped with turbochargers that allowed the airplane to reach higher altitudes. Flying at 35,000 feet altitudes would give the airplane better protection from ground-based guns.

The crew was 2 pilots, the bombardier, the radio operator and five gunners. The gunners were trained to fight in every gun location. Small panels of built in armor materials at each gun location would provide some protection from enemy fighter airplane fire. High altitude flying required that crewmembers be supplied with oxygen. Bombers were cold inside, temperatures were always down to sub-zero levels, and warm clothing was mandatory for everyone.

The airplane had a range of approximately 3,700 miles, but this level of performance actually depended on the weather and other flight plan requirements. There were several serious flaws in the basic design. The original design required that the underside gunner had to get into his blister from outside the airplane. There was no way for this individual to get into the interior of the airplane. In a crash landing situation this crewmember was seldom a survivor. The wings were being used to carry fuel and bullet hole from enemy fire would cause the tanks to leak. There were several similar problems and work to correct all of them was underway.

Prior to 1941 there had been several major improvements to the airplane. The "C" models had more powerful engines; self-sealing fuel tanks and more bombs load capacity. The airplane was slow and an enemy fighter would maneuver to get behind the bomber and the tail gunner was practically useless to defend this kind of attack.

Carl observed all of the engineering activity that was still ongoing and he knew at once that he was going to become completely involved with this program.

Public domain from the US Government

In spite of the known problems the B-17 remained in high demand and the escalating war in Europe made it even more demanding.

Longer missions from bases in England required accurate navigation. Original flight crews were structured to leave navigation as a Pilot's responsibility.

The Cowboy's Kids

Wartime missions proved that this was too much responsibility to add to a man that was dodging the enemy and often had little time to think about anything else. A full time flight position and station for a navigator was added to the standard flight crew. The demand for aircraft was overwhelming and the Army and Boeing were working to expand production quickly. Additional manufacturing locations were being set up at a Douglas plant in Long Beach and the Lockheed plant in Burbank.

Carl was given a ride in a B-17 where he sat in the "Co-Pilots" seat. He saw first hand how the controls functioned and how the airplane handled in flight. He took control for a while and the Pilot told him he was a "natural." While in flight he went to the bombardier's station and observed all of the elements of the area. Special attention was paid to the area where the current model bombsite was normally mounted. He knew his new assignment would require a complete understanding of the forward position in the bombers nose and operational capability of this area.

Carl was then told about several other airplanes with which he needed to become familiar. They were the B-25, the B-26, the B-24 and the British Lancaster Bomber. Information on all of these airplanes was available at Wright Field.

The original B-25 Mitchell Bomber was a two engine airplane with similar flight characteristics to the B-17. However, there were only two engines and the entire airplane was smaller. It could not fly as far on a load of fuel and it carried a smaller bomb load. The flight crew was also smaller. The two pilots, a radio operator, bombardier and one to three gunners were the normal planned crew. The two pilots shared the navigation duties. The gunners were located in a blister on top of the airplane and in side mounted cannon positions. The radio operator sat directly behind the pilots. Like all of the other bombers, there were constant modifications being developed for this airplane. Guns and more flying range were always undergoing design changes.

Kenneth Orr

North American Aviation was the sole aircraft manufacturer for B-25's but they, like all of the other airplane manufacturers, were using hundreds of smaller companies to provide components and airplane sub-systems. No one company could build any airplane completely by itself.

There was one common characteristic about both of these bombers. The bombardier's position was located in the nose of the airplane.

The bombardier and the bombsight, when doing the final approach on a bomb drop procedure, was actually controlling the airplane's flight path. He had to remain in constant internal radio contact with the pilot as when the bombs were dropped the pilot had to fly the plane away from the drop zone and back to the air base. The same procedure was going to be incorporated into using any new bomb targeting system.

The next American bomber scheduled for Carl's review was the B-24 Liberator. This was the Army's largest new bomber airplane and it was capable of carrying larger bomb loads. This airplane was easy to identify by its four, wing mounted, engines and large twin tail rudder system. This airplane was being designed and manufactured by Consolidated Aviation in southern California. There were other airplane features on the B-24 that made it easy to recognize. The larger number of gunner positions and the tricycle style landing gear made it stand apart from all other large bombers. Carl was impressed with the engineering information but he was not able to actually get into an airplane as they were still being developed.

The B-26 was also coming into service. It was similar to the B-25 but the tail was only one vertical rudder.

All of the new bombers were trying to use the same engines and other internal components where ever they could. This would help keep the production problems less complicated and spare parts would be much more interchangeable.

The Cowboy's Kids

The British had discovered that the German fighter planes were a more serious threat than they had anticipated. B-17's could not defend themselves adequately and more gun stations were added. The B-24 was still under final design and additional gun positions were being included.

The bombardier's position was still located in the nose of all of these airplanes and the same basic bomb dropping procedures would work in any of these bombers.

The B-24's large double rudder assembly was supposed to make it more stable at higher altitudes. This feature contributed to allowing the bomb load to be dropped more accurately.

The flight crew was similar to the other bombers. Continuing airplane improvement programs kept changing many of the fighting features built into this airplane. The results were several variations to the original aircraft design.

B-24' airplanes were planned to be the workhorse of the Army Air Corp and everybody knew it. The flying range, the bomb load and the massive force a group of these bombers could deliver, were impressive. The ability to fly high served to protect the airplane from much of the ground cannon fire that could destroy a lower flying airplane. Bombing was a strategic war element and the Army Air Corp was developing as much capability as it could to achieve this advantage.

Consolidated Aviation was not going to be capable of build all of the airplanes that the Army would require. The people at Wright Field had set up plans for additional airplane facilities to build more planes. Consolidator's main plant was in San Diego, California. Additional production was being constructed at the Consolidator's Fort Worth, Texas plant.

Kenneth Orr

Douglas Aviation was preparing to manufacture the "Model D" B-24s in Tulsa, Oklahoma. Ford Motor Company was setting up facilities at the Willow Run Airport and North American Aviation was planning to start production in Dallas, Texas. It was obvious to Carl, "This is as serious as a country can get about getting ready for a war."

A "British Lancaster" bomber was located in Toronto, Canada. Carl decided to fly up to Canada to inspect the aircraft. Carl's military airplane made the trip from Dayton in a little over four hours.

An English flight crew greeted him warmly when he identified himself. The Lancaster airplane was in Canada for some modifications that would make the landing gear more dependable. The original design had a weak support point in the wings and the Canadians were working to help correct the conditions.

The Lancaster was a four-engine airplane and it lacked many of the current improvements that were appearing on the new American airplanes. However, it was the current primary airplane in service in England and they had no choice but to use what was available.

As British Pilot told Carl, "Thank God we have even this as the bloody Germans are after our skirts, and we are determined as hell they will not get them."

They did not have any bombsight equipment on the airplane and frankly they were not aware that some of the current devices even existed. They were highly classified and few people knew they were in existence. Carl kept quiet and looked the interior of the airplane over and saw that a bombsight could be mounted in the nose just like the ones in American bombers. British engineering did not impress Carl. It was not crisp and snappy like Carl had been accustomed to.

Carl, and the British crew went down to Young Street in Toronto, had a good meal, downed a few pints of good

The Cowboy's Kids

"Canadian Ale" and then went back to the airport for a good night's rest. The next morning Carl flew back to Dayton.

Dayton, Ohio was a very busy industrial city and the numbers of small manufacturing plants scattered all over the area made it an ideal location for building precision military equipment.

There was a small group of precision manufacturing plants built next to the old McCook Field location. One of them was a precision glass lens factory.

It was named "Univis Lens." Within a two mile distance there was also a precision instrument manufacturer. This company was named "Leland". Both facilities were relatively small but they both had excellent records for building quality products. Between the two companies they were secretly setting up facilities to manufacture bombsights at a rapid rate. Several other Dayton machine shops were being set up to make precision parts and the whole project was being done under the tightest of security procedures.

All shipments into the plants and away from the buildings were carried in non descript trucks and the people who worked inside were not allowed to discuss what they were doing. The work had been compartmentalized as much as possible to keep the actual product identification away from the public. Only the customer and the top company personnel were aware of what was being built. All involved personnel who had any contact with the identifiable product were being constantly screened and each was given special security clearances. There were armed security people at both locations. They were not wearing military uniforms but they had the authority, the ability and the firepower to stop anyone who was considered a threat or security risk.

Carl was escorted to the final assembly plant dressed in civilian's clothes and passed into the area as a new parts supplier. Once inside a secured area he was given a full explanation as to how the bombsight worked, how to calibrate and to use it to locate and zero in on a target.

Kenneth Orr

This oversimplified information course lasted for about six hours. When Carl was done he was given some classified manuals to take with him and they were in a locked briefcase for protection. An armed security guard, in civilian's clothes was always with Carl when he had any information about the bombsight with him and he knew that they were always being monitored.

The day was over and Carl went back to Wright Field where he delivered the briefcase to a security agent who put it in a special secure and guarded safe.

That evening Carl wanted some good Italian food. One of the local security officers suggested that he go to Annarino's Italian Restaurant. He told him how to get there and made sure Carl had the right directions. Carl got a motor-pool car from the base pool and drove down Springfield Street to the intersection of Leo Street.

He turned right and drove west, passing Kiser High School, until he saw US 25, or, as the local people knew it, The Dixie Highway. He turned north, drove until he crossed the Miami River and there, on the right side of the highway was the restaurant. He parked his car and went in. The waiter was soon offering wine and a great menu. Carl ordered his dinner and sat back sipping his wine.

As he sat there he saw the same man who had been instructing him that same day on the bombsight come into the restaurant. The man saw Carl. They both knew the rules.

They blinked once at each other and never spoke or looked toward each other again as they ate their meal. If a spy had been in the restaurant and had seen any exchange between these two it might have been a security leak. That just was not going to happen. After dinner, Carl paid his bill and left quickly. The meal and the service had been great!

The Cowboy's Kids

The next week was spent in additional information gathering and with making contacts that were going to help him do a better job in his upcoming assignment.

The pace was torrid and the level of pressure was never relenting. Carl loved it but he knew he was getting ready to do the hardest job he had ever imagined in his life.

CHAPTER 3-2
Back Home in Texas

Six weeks to the day from when Carl had arrived in Dayton, Carl got a call from Major Malone. He asked him how things were going. They had kept in touch weekly, so the update was not difficult. All of their conversation was in code sensitive language. Carl said he was somewhat familiar with the efforts to date and was probably just about as full of information as he could get without overloading. Major Malone said, "Carl. Pack up everything and come on home. We need you here and the next step in your assignment has been taking shape rapidly." Carl agreed and said he would be taking off in about two days to fly back to San Antonio.

The whole experience in Dayton had been eye opening to just how serious the upcoming war effort was going to become. The last step before leaving Dayton was to pass through the people he had worked with, align himself with them for future potential contact and express his gratitude for their help.

Carl took care of his business and got his things together for his flight. The last night in town was special, as he knew he probably was not coming back soon. He asked an attractive young lady, whom he had often worked with in the office, to accompany him for dinner. She was thin and tall and always carried herself as a perfect lady. Her name was Virginia Williams. Carl was lonely and the idea of having a good- looking and intelligent lady with him that

344

The Cowboy's Kids

evening was refreshing. He had been so busy that any side activities away from his military assignment were out of the question.

Virginia knew a lot about Dayton and was glad to be invited out for dinner. Carl drove to downtown Dayton. They had dinner in the Biltmore Hotel's restaurant. The meal was delicious and the conversation was mostly about personal things. After dinner they walked north on Main Street and ended up sitting on a bench near the south bank of the Miami River. As they talked, they watched the sun go down. There was a tall war memorial monument located in the middle of Main Street, just south of the Main street bridge. There were ample streetlights to allow the names engraved on the base to be visible and they went over and looked it over in detail.

Veterans from the prior wars were being honored with this monument. The street that ran east and west from this intersection was properly named "Monument Avenue."

Carl and Virginia found a seat back on the park bench and began to talk. There was an old fire department building on the same corner and Carl was quick to discuss the large polished brass ball mounted on the front area of the truck's pumping system. Fire trucks and polished brass were one of Carl's favorite things. They always impressed him with the way people took good care of things.

Carl told Virginia about Texas and growing up on a horse ranch. Virginia told Carl she had been born in Nashville, Tennessee. The more they talked the more they wanted to talk. Virginia told Carl she had a lot of responsibility in her job, as she was involved in the security force that watched over a lot of the classified information. Carl knew she was involved with the documentation covering his assignment, but, he never said one word as to what he was working on. Virginia's college training was in mathematics. A lot of the work she was doing was with internal military communication codes. She intentionally stopped short of saying more, as she knew the rules.

Kenneth Orr

They were both very honest about everything they had experienced in their civilian lives and it was soon obvious that they had a lot of things in common. Virginia said she would like to keep in touch.

Carl liked her and agreed to send her a letter and call when he got home. The longer they talked the more they were not willing to let the moment pass away. It was early the next morning when Carl finally took Virginia home. They were both sorry they had to part each other's company. Virginia became somewhat forward and took Carl by the neck and placed a big kiss on his lips. Then she began to cry and quickly went inside the door and closed it. Carl was also in tears and had not wanted to see her go, but he had to get some rest. Tomorrow was a flight day. Virginia was very pleased with the way that Carl had respected and treated her.

The next morning, which was only about four hours away from his last good-bye to Virginia, Carl checked his airplane out, got a full tank of fuel, loaded his things, and was ready to take off for Texas. He had stopped by the operation's hangar and filled a thermos bottle full of black coffee. He knew he might need a shot of caffeine to stay wide-awake.

His classified documents and a prototype bombsite instrument model were brought to the airplane in a special Army car just as he was about to finish his take-off loading.

There were armed military policemen riding in the car. The classified cargo was loaded and Carl went through his normal pre-flight checklist.

Then he took off. He would not need to stop but one time for fuel until he got to Randolph if the weather held as anticipated. That stop would be in western Louisiana.

As he flew, his mind was about as busy as he had ever been. First, he was making sure he had the plane operating right, as he knew the cargo he had on board was special and he had to deliver it safely. Second, he had Virginia on his mind.

The Cowboy's Kids

She had really gotten under his skin and he was already missing her more than he had anticipated he could ever miss a lady. And third, he kept recalling the conversation he had with his dad about family and life's values just a short time before he had died.

The subject of the importance of family kept coming to his mind. Barbara's experience with Paul had made a heavy impression on him as he saw her happier than she had ever been when she had Paul with her. Then he saw her suffer the worst pain of her life when Paul died. He wondered if he could find that kind of happiness with Virginia. The coffee was still hot and his small sips were making it last.

When he arrived in San Antonio he parked the airplane in a special spot on the apron and a staff car with two military police cars in escort, came immediately to pick him up. The classified documents and the packaged bombsite model were delivered to a security facility and properly checked in. Then Carl went to his quarters.

When he got his things in the room and got a cold beer from the refrigerator, he sat down and tried to relax. His mind was still running wild and the top issue had become Virginia. He knew she was due to be home from work by now, so he called her on the phone. Phone calls were not always easy to make from the Army base and a long distance operator would take the number you wanted to call and tell you to standby until she could get an open line.

She would call you back as soon as she had the other party on the phone. Carl hung up and waited. The time seemed like it was never going to end but finally the phone rang. Virginia was on the line and Carl was thrilled just to hear her voice.

They talked for several minutes and finally Carl knew he had to go see Major Malone so he had to end the call. Virginia was obviously just as happy to hear Carl's voice and they agreed to call often and to write letters. The call ended.

Kenneth Orr

Carl washed his face and spruced up a little and went to the Operations office. Major Malone was still there and was glad to see Carl. He told him that he had seen his plane land and was looking forward to seeing him before he shut down for the day.

Carl gave him a quick status on the information he had gathered in Dayton. Major Malone told him that the General at Randolph was moving along rapidly with plans for the bombardier school. Carl was going to become a key member of the training team. He looked at Carl and said, "Young man you need to get some sleep and come see me in the morning." Carl agreed, shook Major Malone's hand, thanked him for his support and friendship, saluted, and left the office.

Carl stopped by the Officer's Club and got some dinner. He also ordered a stiff drink of Kentucky's finest whiskey and sipped it slowly. He remembered how his dad had enjoyed the taste of sipping whiskey when he was tired and wanted to relax. He thought, "I hope my dad would be proud of me right now."

When he got to his quarters he called Barbara and let her know he was back in San Antonio. She was glad to hear his voice and to know he was safe. She said she had been taking long walks around the ranch and was slowly getting a new grip on her life. She added, "I got a small puppy dog that a neighbor had and she is a lot of company. It's a lot of company to have a pet and spend time just being with her." They talked for several minutes and Carl told Barbara he had found a really-nice lady up in Ohio that might someday be his wife.

Barbara was thrilled for him and asked a lot of questions. Carl was eager to talk and to let Barbara know how important he was taking this part of his life. Barbara was glad to see he was ready to settle down and to become a family man. She had looked forward to a better life for him. The phone call ended and Carl went to bed. He was really tired.

The Cowboy's Kids

The next morning Carl walked over to see Major Malone. He was glad to see Carl and gave him a big salute and handshake when he entered. Carl filled in the missing details of the trip. Carl then brought up the obvious topic, what is the next step?

Major Malone said that the General in charge from Randolph had been looking for the best sight to set up a bombing range. The purpose would be to instruct bombardiers, navigators and bomber pilots on how to properly use the new bombsight. Carl was listening intently.

The General had made plans to convert a small airfield in Midland, Texas to build a special training base. The plan was to locate qualified Army personnel at the new base and have them train bombardiers using the new classified piece of bombing targeting equipment.

The school would support the Army's immediate need for trained personnel, as well as helping the British and other allied forces military operations train some of their personnel. Major Malone looked at Carl and said, "I guess you might be wondering why I assigned the same AT-10 to you that you flew to Minnesota." Carl looked at him and obviously he had not questioned Major Malone's assignment.

Carl said, "I have never thought about it and obviously I am finding out that you had a reason." Major Malone said, "That airplane is one of the trainers that you will be using at Midland to instruct your students. I wanted you to get absolutely as familiar with how it flies and reacts to weather." Carl looked back and said, "You got me Major, I had not even thought about that." Major Malone noted that the nose on the A-10 Carl was flying had been modified to have a special window. He said these modifications make it an A-11, but that's not a problem, that's just a number.

Midland, Texas was not near any major populated areas. Several remote bomb target sites were already designated. Plans to get started soon were in place. The local area had been evaluated and 15 remote sites had been selected to

Kenneth Orr

be bomb target zones. A zone would have a large cleared area with a clearly marked target in the center. The bombs would be sacks of sand and flour.

Prior to doing any target drops, a student would be instructed in a classroom and given a complete understanding of how the new system worked. The first class of trainees would be current men who were assigned to bomb squadrons.

These men would be screened to select some of them as instructors and to add to the capability of the school. Carl was going to be involved with all phases of candidate training. Flight personnel would be trained how to use the bombsite and how to be a backup in the aircrew as a member of a bomber crew. Major Malone told Carl that he had the skill and the energy to do an outstanding job. He referred to Carl's demonstrated piloting skills and airplane designing experience, as key skills in building the right kind of training program. The current problem was time. The Army was anxious to go forward as soon as possible and the activity was beginning to pick up very quickly.

Major Malone told Carl that he would need to move to Midland, Texas and set up his residence. He was going to be required there soon so he should get his affairs in San Antonio in order quickly. Carl understood. The Army had announced the Air Training School on June 13th and ground was going to be broken in July.

Carl would have a place to live on base as soon as it could be built. The current effort was to identify the personnel who were going to be located there and have them get into one location and start building a team. In the time before on-base quarters were complete he was going to be quartered in a nearby hotel.

Major Malone reinforced the blanket of secrecy that was to be maintained about the bombsite. The only people to know what was being used to fix bomb targets were the instructors and the selected trainees, no exceptions. Those that did know were going to be sworn to protect

The Cowboy's Kids

this information and the equipment with their life. Carl understood fully. Carl asked as to when he should schedule his move and was told, "Can you move tomorrow?"

Carl knew it was Friday and he asked if he could have until next Wednesday. The Major agreed, smiled and got up from his chair and went to his cabinet. He got a small flask of whiskey and poured a small glass for each man. He took one to Carl and gave it to him with a big smile. He said, "You are an outstanding man Carl. I have the greatest respect for you and your ability. I wish you the best of everything in this assignment and I have every reason to believe you will be an outstanding soldier in this mission." He told Carl to be available to move at 0:800 on Wednesday morning.

He also said Carl's personal airplane would be safe at Randolph until Carl could come and get it. He was told there were several commercial hangars on the civilian side of the airfield and he would be able to hangar it there.

Carl had a special relationship with Major Malone as they were long time friends. He decided to tell him he had met a young lady in Ohio and he thought he was in love. Major Malone looked at him and smiled. He said, "Carl you are a good Christian man and every good man needs a good lady by his side. I hope it works out, but, don't forget, you are in the Army."

Carl went to his quarters and called Virginia. He told her was being reassigned in location and that he was moving next week. Virginia was glad to know he was moving, but not happy that he might be less able to come to Dayton often. He assured her that whatever happened, he was going to keep in touch.

His promise was obviously very important to Virginia. After the first call, Carl called Barbara and said he was coming to Bandera in a couple of hours and he wanted to tell her a lot about what was happening.

CHAPTER 3-3
Making plans for the near future

Friday night was always a time for soldiers to relax and let their week's problems go away. It was a good time to party with friends. The Army bases in San Antonio had a long tradition of having Friday night, after work, set aside for parties and good times.

Carl had always taken part in this activity. He used this time to keep in touch with several of his close friends and to catch up with all of the local gossip. This week was different. Carl went by one of his close friend's quarters and told him not to count on seeing him for a while. He was being transferred to a new location and would be gone very soon. The time he had left in south Texas was short and he wanted to spend it with his sister in Bandera.

Carl borrowed a car from Major Malone and drove to Bandera. When he arrived he went straight to the family ranch house and found Barbara waiting for him. She was glad to see him and had some good Mexican food waiting. She also had a bottle of Kentucky's finest sitting on the table next to a big easy chair. Carl took his baggage to his usual bedroom and then sat down to spend time with Barbara. First, he wanted to tell her about Virginia. He described her as a very pretty lady with a real appreciation for life's best values. The verbal description he painted made her look and sound like a perfect lady. Barbara asked a lot of questions and every question was answered with a positive response.

The Cowboy's Kids

It was obvious to Barbara that Carl was falling in love and she hoped that Virginia was really all that Carl had described. She had seen him disappointed before and it had not been easy on him. Carl suggested that Barbara invite her to come to Texas and see for herself. Barbara was understanding, but was still not so sure that Carl was really on the right path. She said, "Carl, let's sit on that invitation for a few days and then we can see what we want to do." Carl understood her approach and agreed.

Then Carl spoke up and said, "Oh by the way, I am being transferred to a new Army base in Midland, Texas. I will be traveling there on Wednesday of next week". Barbara was surprised, as she had anticipated that Carl would be staying in San Antonio for a long time. She said, "Why are you being transferred?"

Carl replied, "I am going to be an instructor at a new training base they are setting up in Midland, Texas." "They want me to go out there to help with the start-up planning". Carl added, "Barbara, I cannot say any more than that, you know how the Army keeps things secret and this assignment falls into that area."

Barbara said, "Let's go fishing tomorrow. We both need some down time and when we go fishing we both always come away from the water with a good and refreshed attitude." Carl agreed but added, "We need to be home by dark, I want to call Virginia and she will be home tomorrow evening." Barbara understood. The next day came and it was raining. Carl said he was still fine with the fishing trip and he and Barbara both put on rain gear and headed for the river. Fishing was good and by 2:00 PM they had a bucket full of good eating size fish. Before they left the water, Carl motored the boat over the spot where he thought the old cave was located. The water was too muddy to see anything that was below the boat so they went home. Carl cleaned the fish and Barbara pan-fried a big meal of bass and catfish. They ate everything they wanted and soon were sitting in the living room relaxing. Carl went to sleep and

Kenneth Orr

Barbara just watched him slump into the big easy chair. She knew he was tired and needed the sleep.

At 6 PM Barbara woke him up. He had said he needed to make a phone call. Carl got the local operator on the phone and soon she had Virginia on the other end of the line. Carl told her he was in Bandera and that he had told Barbara about their relationship. Virginia was happy to hear his voice and both were talking like people who were in love. Carl asked Barbara if she wanted to say hello. She was happy to take the phone and soon the two ladies were talking like long time friends. Carl was standing close to Barbara, just covered with smiles and listening to the women talk.

The call lasted about 15 minutes and Carl ended the conversation with a quiet "I love you" to Virginia. She obviously returned the same words as he hung up the phone with a big smile on his face. Barbara told Carl she was impressed with Virginia and told Carl to go slow. If this was going to be the right girl for him, he would know in a few weeks.

Carl told Barbara that he had to be back in San Antonio on Sunday night as he was going to need some time there to get his things in order so he could travel.

He told Barbara that he was eventually going to fly his personal airplane out to Midland soon. He would come to Bandera to see her when he could. Barbara was glad to hear this and she was happy for Carl. On Sunday evening Carl drove back to Randolph Field.

Monday morning came quickly and Carl was up early. He went to the dining hall, ate a big meal and then went to the base headquarters to meet with key Army personnel who were involved with the new training base planning. The General in charge of planning was conducting the meeting. He was anxious to meet with Carl. The room had been made secure and the military police were instructed to bring in the classified bombsite model that Carl had brought back from Ohio. Carl removed the device from the box and explained

The Cowboy's Kids

the basic functional and operating requirements. He had been trying to develop an estimate as to how long it would take to train someone to use the device and gain enough confidence to be qualified to go into an active bombing squadron. He outlined his thoughts for everyone. Then he added, "A bombardier must have several bomb drop missions under his belt where he actually used the device to drop bombs. This is the only sure way to develop his skills and confidence. Ground school is basic but flying was equally, if not more important."

The bombsight was to be mounted in a special nest in the nose position of a bomber. The pilot and the navigator had to keep the aircraft on a planned flight course until it reached the perimeter of the target zone. Then the bombardier had to make several critical settings. The bombardier and the information from the bombsight readings would assist the pilot to fly exactly where the bombs were to be released. The device compensated for wind speeds, altitude, airplane speed and the drop angle for the bombs. When the device indicated the bomber was properly located near the target, the device and the bombardier would control the airplane until it was over the target. When that exact moment arrived, the bombardier would release the airplanes bomb load. Aircraft controls would then be given back to the pilot.

Carl added, "The current design of our active flying bombers will accept this device with minimal modification. I know this information is accurate as I have reviewed all of the current inventory of active bombers personally and I am of the opinion that the time to make these modifications will not be excessive."

Everyone was happy to hear Carl's report. They all wanted to know what Carl thought an effective training program would require. The topics of time, training equipment and candidate selection criteria, were all discussed. Carl had not developed any answers to these questions, as he had not been asked to do so but he agreed to work with the teams to provide realistic answers.

Kenneth Orr

He said, "With some help from all of you now seated in this room, we can work these issues out if we address them both today and tomorrow." Carl's attitude was applauded and the General instructed everyone to hold the necessary meetings in his secure private meeting room.

A Colonel named Gordowitz was put in charge and he wanted to get started right away. He told everyone to call him "Gordo" for short and cut out with the formal crap. They had work to do!"

Two days passed and soon the answers were taking shape. They needed a fleet of A-10 aircraft with nose mounts for bombsights. This modification would be like the A-11 design that was already designed. All of these airplanes would require ground support equipment and qualified personnel to keep this fleet flying. They would also require secure hangar space for housing aircraft while bombsights were installed.

The school would need classrooms with secure walls and windows. They needed a set of instruction flight charts to use for bombing run planning and every trainee would need to have navigational skills. The Midland airfield would require a second runway that was capable of operating both day and night. Training was going to require night operations and some bomb-training missions needed to be carried out in night and other darkness conditions.

Candidate personnel must pass eye tests, physicals and attitude assessment that indicate they have the equalizations to be flight crew capable. This reinforced the need for a high quality medical unit on the base. Food service, laundry and base supply functions were also going to be key parts of the new facility.

The Colonel said, "When we graduate a bombardier, he will be assigned to a bomber training school. These schools are where bomber crews are brought together and become an assigned team. There are several training operations for

The Cowboy's Kids

bomber training now being formed and we will be supplying bombardiers and navigator personnel."

"Bomber aircraft crews are going to be trained at other airfields and when the entire crew is certified as capable they will to be sent to bomber crew operations bases. From there they will be assigned to active fighting squadrons. The best men would be rushed through the training and some would become additional training personnel. The program we have outlined is projected to take 12 weeks."

"Bombardier training would involve extensive classroom training and aerial bombing practice. Every bombardier must be skilled in trouble shooting his equipment. They should also be skilled in field level maintenance procedures. They are responsible for keeping device accurate and fully operational. Practice training missions will use sandbags and flower sacks, not bombs, to determine the students target recognition and bombing accuracy."

Every trained bombardier would then be assigned to an active bomber group just as soon as he is finished with his training. The war buildup effort was on a crash course and time was as important as skills.

Carl was looking forward to his assignment and he knew the training process had to be quick, intense and effective. The entire mission of a bomber is focused on one thing. That objective is to get the bomber's payload accurately dropped on the enemy's target. Equally important were the objectives of survival and living to fight again.

The sky had become a dangerous place in a war. The Army needs to plan today to be ready for tomorrow. The Army Air Corp, and our training Command operation have become as important to national security as ground troops had been in the past. This is a new military territory. It will over will extend over uncharted waters and require a lot of new types of planning. The whole experience is going to be exciting, demanding, and we all know, potentially deadly.

Kenneth Orr

Carl moved to Midland and was assigned a room at the selected local hotel. The airfield was located about half way between the towns of Odessa and Midland and was easy to get to on the two-lane highway that went by the front gate.

Several local oil drilling companies had private airplanes at the same airport. The civilian aircraft had been moved to one side of the current runway and the Army was already building facilities on the other side. The new Army facilities included aircrew training rooms, a hospital, a mess hall, a new larger water tower and a much bigger flight line area.

There was also a new service hangar and quarters for all of the personnel who were to be stationed there. The Army had a standard design for many of the buildings that they were using in several areas where military build-ups were taking place. They were all called "temporary buildings." These buildings were not intended to last for many years, but were substantial enough to meet short-term requirements. Building these types of structure was quick and required less complex construction requirements.

Texas is a big state. This part of Texas is at a higher altitude than the flat lands further to the east. The weather gets torrid hot in the summer and bitterly cold in the winter. This is much like the weather in Europe and the military had determined they had to do training under any weather conditions that were present. The real world was going to be similar so the training was also planned to mimic this weather range.

Virginia had a phone number where she could call Carl. His schedule was never predictable, but she would call when she thought he might be available. Carl would also call her often. The phone lines in Midland were largely party lines and getting a connection was often difficult. The phone lines were also subject to other people listening in on your call and the conversation had to be very guarded to prevent any leakage of information that was supposed to be kept secret.

The Cowboy's Kids

Virginia wanted to see Carl and he wanted to see her. After a month of calling, Carl asked Virginia if she could get off long enough to ride a train to San Antonio. He said he would make sure he was in San Antonio if she could, and they could go to Bandera and stay at the ranch. Carl's commanding officer, Captain Alexander, recognized that Carl was in love. He and Carl had become good friends and Carl told him he sure wanted to see Virginia soon. Captain Alexander looked at the training schedule and the operations calendar and told Carl to pick a date that he could be at Randolph for a program review. He told Carl he could take some liberty time while there. He suggested two dates and both were about two weeks away.

Carl called Virginia and Barbara and discussed the plan. A date, agreeable to everyone, was selected, October 10th, and plans were quickly put into place. Barbara called Virginia and spent time with her on the phone and told her that she was welcome to be her guest at the ranch, but she also knew that she and Carl were going to need some private time. The stage was set for a Texas meeting.

CHAPTER 3-4
Families in Transition

The war in Europe was getting much more intense and the German army had occupied most of the countries in the area. Hitler's next targets were to invade England and at the same time stage a strong offensive in North Africa. It was becoming obvious that he was not going to stop there and that he was looking to expand his influence to any area where he saw opportunity. The United States had aggressively been helping Churchill fight his war. Without the American's help it was certain that Great Britain was going to be invaded.

The whole world was involved in an attitude of tension and fear. The probability of a war in the Pacific was becoming a real concern. The United States Navy had a large fleet of battleships and aircraft carriers stationed in Honolulu and this force represented a high percentage of the nation's Naval strength. Some political leaders thought this level of naval strength would potentially discourage any aggressive force from attacking.

Tensions between Japan and The United States were tight and growing tighter ever day. 1941 was a time when the United States economy was beginning to recover from the major problems endured during the depression years of the 1930's. War was not a good thought, either in Europe or in the Pacific. Life in the United States was becoming more comfortable and the thought of any upsetting events was

The Cowboy's Kids

not on anyone's mind. President Roosevelt had been well accepted and his leadership was not being questioned.

President Roosevelt had reorganized the dangers of the European war and he requested the congress to pass an amendment to the constitution to allow him to run for a 3rd term as president. His objective was to maintain political stability and hopefully not become involved with Hitler's war. The United States Constitution was changed and President Roosevelt was re-elected for an additional term. Fear was a growing motivation as the Germans were not slowing down and they were in a strong position to keep expanding their influence.

Virginia had arranged to be away from work for about two weeks. She got a ticket on a train that eventually would put her in San Antonio, Texas. She had to go to St. Louis, Little Rock and Dallas before getting on the train that went to San Antonio. The trip, with layovers, would take about 36 hours.

When she arrived in San Antonio it was dark and the train station was busy with military personnel and a lot of ordinary people who were traveling. She stepped off the train and anxiously looked for Carl. Carl was not able to be there, so he had told Barbara what Virginia looked like. Barbara recognized her at once. Carl had been detained at Randolph Field in a meeting and had to stay there until it was over.

Barbara introduced herself and the chemistry between the two women was an immediate and positive fit. Both knew what the military was all about and the fact that Carl was not there was completely understood. Barbara helped Virginia get her baggage and they got into her Packard. Barbara only drove this car on special occasions. This was certainly a trip to make the most of everything. Barbara drove toward the north side of San Antonio and made sure to point out the sights along the way. They talked as they rode and got to know a lot more about each other. Virginia had two brothers and no sisters. They had all grown up living in Nashville, Tennessee. Their father was a businessman and

Kenneth Orr

was of average means. Both of her brothers had gone to school and become lawyers. They were both older than Virginia but still under 40 years old. Barbara asked Virginia what she did at the Army base in Dayton. Carl had never told her.

Virginia said she worked in a government security office and was in charge of several classified areas. Barbara asked her if she was in the military or working as a civilian? Virginia said she had started out as a civilian employee but was being inducted into the Army later this month. She wanted to expand her role as a member of the military. This would allow her to hold a more responsible job and her skills were considered as special. Barbara understood.

Barbara told Virginia that she was an Army Nurse and that she was currently on a reserve force's status. Virginia just chuckled and said, "The whole bunch of us are in the military, and all of us have gotten here in much different ways." Barbara saw that Virginia was referring to Carl like they were already a family. Those words and the way she said them made Barbara feel good. She somehow knew Virginia was just what Carl had needed for a very long time.

Barbara pulled into the parking lot at Randolph Field and told Virginia she would be right back. She went to the guard's station to see if there was any word from Carl. There was a note saying he would be out about 9:30 PM and then they could go eat somewhere. Virginia was starving and Barbara was almost in the same condition. Then, without any notice, Carl came running down the sidewalk. He had seen the Packard and his superiors had told him to leave as soon as he saw Barbara drive up.

Virginia jumped out of the car and hugged Carl. The night air was getting cold as a wind was blowing in from the north but the temperature in the parking lot was just right. Virginia was crying and so was Carl. These were tears of joy and soon Barbara joined in. They all got into the car and drove to a nice Mexican restaurant on the near north side

The Cowboy's Kids

of San Antonio. At dinner Carl informed everyone that he had five of liberty. He asked Virginia if she was up to the ride to Bandera. Virginia said she was just glad to be out of that darn old train. She said, "The thick cigarette smoke and smelly people and the constant motions were just about too much to take." Everybody laughed and finished dinner.

After dinner, Carl and Virginia sat in the front seat with Carl driving. Barbara sat in the back and soon she was sleeping. She had been up all day and her body was ready to shut down. Carl got a giant shot of energy from just seeing Virginia and every mile on the road was full of things to talk about. The darkness of night was all around and Virginia could not see the things he was describing but that was not a problem. She just listened to him talk. She just wanted to be with him. The road was black and the headlights would occasionally fall on a critter of some type making a crossing. Deer and armadillos were common sights. The town of Bandera came into view and Carl knew a short cut to go directly to the ranch.

Texas nights in the early fall are full of night sounds. The bugs and coyotes were singing a loud and familiar night song as Carl parked the Packard. Barbara woke up and said, "We are all tired, so let's go inside and get some rest." Everyone agreed. Barbara opened the door and the housekeeper had left a few lights turned on so everybody could see. Carl took Virginia's baggage into the living area and Virginia followed him. Barbara showed Virginia her room and Carl took the baggage to the room. Then everybody sat down in the living room and relaxed a few moments. Barbara was quick to go to bed and she knew Virginia and Carl needed some private time.

The next morning everyone, except Virginia, was up early. Carl had put his ranch clothes on and he was glad to be back home. His uniform was given to the housekeeper to have it cleaned.

This was home and would always be the place where he loved to come. Virginia was still asleep. Barbara had been

Kenneth Orr

up about 20 minutes. About 8:00 AM Virginia came out of her room wearing a housecoat. Carl had walked outside and was in the horse barn. Barbara's housekeeper had come over and was fixing a big breakfast of Mexican style eggs and beans. Virginia smelled the cooking as she walked in and said she was hungry.

Virginia was a tall thin lady. She had fair skin and brunet hair. Her eyes were deep blue and she always carried herself like a perfect lady. Her karma was always positive and Barbara was impressed with her in many ways.

Coffee was being brewed on the stove and the aroma was strong. Nothing could have smelled better to Barbara. She loved her coffee. Carl came in and Virginia greeted him with a big hug. She smiled and asked Carl to sit down with her for breakfast. Virginia sat down on the other side of the table and breakfast was served. The all dug in and soon the food was all but gone. Carl spoke up and said, "Barbara, Virginia and I talked last night after you went to bed and we both want to get married. "Barbara just smiled. She said, "This news was expected. All I was wondering was when. I know you both will be happy and lets all pray that you both have long and happy lives."

Virginia asked Barbara if she knew the local officials and the legal paperwork that would be required so they could get married right away. Barbara said she knew all of the right people and they could go to town and get the legal paperwork going. Carl just looked on.

Virginia was showing just how much she wanted to get married by her attitude and Carl was glad to see he was going to get a "high spirited lady" to be his wife.

Barbara knew that both Carl and Virginia would need to get a blood test. They would need to take the paperwork from these tests to the courthouse to get a marriage license. Barbara drove them over to Doctor Bluholtz's office and explained what Carl and Virginia wanted to do. Barbara

The Cowboy's Kids

explained that both of them were actively working within the Army and they were on a tight schedule.

The Doctor poked their arms with a needle, drew some blood and went into his back room. In about ten minutes he came out with two blood test certificates saying they were fine to get married. Carl paid the Doctor and they went to the courthouse.

The county clerk, Mrs. Kinser, was in her office and she was glad to see Carl. She had worked for Becky Brock back when the Goodwin ranch was selling livestock to the Army.

Before she got married her last name was Gonzales and Carl had not known about her marriage. She was growing older and her words were slow and well spoken. She told Virginia that she had known Carl when he was a small boy and he was a fine young man. They left the courthouse with a marriage license.

Carl asked Barbara if the Lutheran Church was still as friendly as it was when he was a kid. He wanted to get married there and have a simple but meaningful wedding. Virginia wanted to get married as soon as they could, as she was aware the time in Texas was going to be cut short when Carl had to leave by the coming Wednesday.

Barbara drove over to the Lutheran church and asked Virginia and Carl to come in with her. They went to the minister's office and everybody went in. The minister knew Carl and greeted him with a big strong handshake. Carl told Reverend Converse he wanted get married. He introduced him to Virginia and told him they had a schedule problem as they were both living out of town and were involved in the Army's efforts. The minister asked Virginia and Carl to come with him into his private study. He wanted to talk with them and he suggested that Barbara take a 20-minute walk.

The minister led them into his study and they discussed a lot of things about their love for each other. The minister asked them. "When they wanted to do the ceremony?" Carl started

Kenneth Orr

to speak up, but Virginia spoke and said, "Can we get married in the morning?" Carl just smiled. He was not unhappy with Virginia's request. Everyone agreed that they would meet in the church at 9:00 AM tomorrow and the service would be performed in the church sanctuary. Everyone went back to the office and Barbara was waiting.

They told Barbara what they had planned and Barbara was anxious to make sure that everything went as well as it could on such a short time schedule.

Barbara told Carl to go see what was happening at the local hardware store and she took Virginia to the best lady's store in town. Virginia picked out a new white dress and a matching pair of shoes. She also picked out a wedding veil and a pair of long white gloves. The lady who owned the store was an expert seamstress and she had Virginia try on the dress. It fit very well but the seamstress wanted to take up a section to make it fit a little better. After all, Virginia was not that big and the dress was just too loose. Virginia took off the dress and while she waited the adjustments were made. The seamstress had her put it back on and it was perfect.

Virginia had the lady put everything in a big box and asked what she owed her. The lady said, "Sweetheart, you don't owe me a cent. The dress and all of the other things you have, are my gift to you. Carl's dad gave my dad the best deal in buying his ranch, that anyone could ever get. I grew up there and I always wanted to do something to show how much we all appreciated Chalk Goodwin." Virginia was surprised, but she was learning what Carl's family and their reputation in Bandera, Texas was all about.

They walked back to the Packard where Carl was waiting. Virginia spoke up and said she wanted Barbara to be her bridesmaid at the wedding. Carl said, "I have been gone so long that I have lost touch with most of my childhood friends." Then he thought for a moment. He then said, "He would just not have a best man." Barbara looked at him and smiled and suggested that he call John Harmony.

The Cowboy's Kids

John was getting older but he had known Carl all of his life and he would be honored. Carl agreed. John was surprised to hear from Carl and even more surprised to be asked to stand up with him for his wedding. He agreed and got all of the schedule information worked out.

Barbara said they needed to celebrate and took everyone to a nice Mexican restaurant. The food was delicious and Virginia loved all of the spicy tastes in her food. She also had a glass of chilled wine. The meal was topped off with some chocolate cake and vanilla ice cream.

After lunch Carl drove all around Bandera and told Virginia all about everything that he could remember about his younger days. After the local tour he drove out to the cemetery and showed Virginia where he and Barbara had buried their parents and Barbara's deceased husband.

Barbara said she had found out something that Carl should know. Sarge had passed away about a year ago and the Army had buried him in the military cemetery in San Antonio. Carl was saddened but he knew that Sarge had always been one of his very best friends.

Barbara spoke up and suggested that they stop by a local jewelry store and get some wedding rings. Virginia agreed and asked Barbara where to go. Carl knew that the local hardware store had always sold jewelry. He knew they had the best selection in town. Carl drove to the store and Virginia and he made their selections. They then drove back to the ranch house and relaxed for a few minutes.

Barbara told Carl that she was going to spend tomorrow night with a friend who lived nearby. He and Virginia would have the whole house to themselves. Carl said he appreciated her thoughtfulness and he told Virginia about Barbara's plans.

Carl suggested that Virginia and he saddle up some horses and take a ride down to the river. Virginia had ridden a horse before but her response was not real quick. Carl saw

Kenneth Orr

the concern and said they would take the small horse drawn buggy instead. The horses were hooked to the wagon and the ride was underway. They were gone about two hours.

Barbara took the time to get the housekeeper to plan some special things for the home. The wedding was on Tuesday morning and they planned to be back home by noon. The housekeeper was going to have lunch and a small-precooked dinner placed in the icebox.

The master bedroom was to be decorated with flowers and a new set of white bed sheets. Barbara called the local flower shop and asked them to have some flowers at the church before the wedding. She also called a few close friends who knew Carl and told them about Carl's wedding.

Barbara was going to take a small suitcase with her to the wedding and after the wedding she was going to go home with her friend. Carl would have the Packard for his use. Then Barbara was planning to go home on Wednesday morning about 10:00 AM. Carl had to leave Bandera by 5:00 PM to go back to Randolph Field. Barbara and Virginia were planning to take him back in the Packard.

Virginia was going to stay with Barbara until Friday evening. Barbara was going to take Virginia back to San Antonio to catch her train at 9:30 PM. Friday night. Carl's schedule was tight but the military had rules and they had to be honored. This schedule would allow Virginia and Barbara some time together and they could get to know each other a lot better.

The buggy ride was over and when Carl stopped, he got out first and went around to the other side. Virginia was sitting in the right seat and Carl helped her down. She had never had such a long buggy ride and her body, especially her bottom parts, were a little sore. She took it all in stride and soon she was feeling fine. The evening came and passed with a lot of small talk and a long walk down by the river. Time was short for everyone so they were trying to enjoy every available moment that was available.

The Cowboy's Kids

Carl and Virginia both thanked Barbara for all she was doing to make them happy. The all knew that a war was probably inevitable and they all avoided any discussions about this topic. They did say that someday when life was a little less complicated, they wanted to all live near each other and become an even closer family. Virginia said that she was going to investigate being transferred to Texas so she could be near her husband. The military was never easy to move around within unless there were specific job openings for a skill someone had. The future was foggy but the fact that Virginia and Carl were now going to be man and wife might make some difference.

CHAPTER 3-5
A Wedding and Then Tears

Tuesday morning came early for everyone. The sun was brilliant in the east as there were no clouds in the sky. Barbara was up first and soon she had breakfast ready on the table. Virginia came in next and she was anxious and a little tense. She knew this was her wedding day but she also knew that the day could not last forever. Carl wandered in shortly and sat down. Virginia came over to him and gave him a kiss on the cheek. She knew he was still not fully awake but this was the real Carl. He liked to sleep late and to take his time to wake up. She had never seen this side of his daily life. He also needed to shave and his hair was a mess. Breakfast was great and the aftermath of activity was about to get intense.

Carl took a shower, shaved and combed his hair. He got his freshly cleaned Army uniform, brushed it up a little and shined his pilot's wings and put a clean cloth on his shoes. He dressed and got ready to go to town. Barbara gave him the keys to the Packard and told him to get out of the house and go find his best man at the church. Carl understood. He made sure he had the wedding ring for Virginia and an envelope with some money inside for the preacher. He went out and got in the Packard and drove to Bandera.

Virginia was just as eager to get ready. She bathed, got dressed and with Barbara helping her put the final touches on her wedding attire. Barbara put on a white dress and

The Cowboy's Kids

finished packing her overnight case. Both then got in the 1939 Ford that Barbara used as her everyday car. They drove to town and arrived at the Church at about 20 minutes before the scheduled wedding time. They went into the church and a local crowd of friends saw them enter. They came to Barbara's side, as they were all anxious to meet Virginia. The introductions were simple and everyone was impressed with Virginia's good looks and sincere words. The preacher came to Barbara and Virginia and asked them to come into his study. They were to stay there until it was time to go to the altar.

Carl was in a small room with John Harmony, his best man. There were a few friends also coming in and out of the room. The mood was light and festive. Promptly at 9:00 o'clock the piano began to play a wedding song. Carl and John heard the music and went to the front of the church and stood silently before the minister's altar.

There were about 50 people in the church. This turnout surprised Carl, but it also pleased him. Then, with a change in tempo the piano began playing the wedding song, "Here Comes the Bride." Virginia and Barbara came from the rear of the church behind led by the preacher. They were walking slow and finally reached the preacher's alter. The preacher went to a position in front of the alter. Virginia took her place next to Carl and Barbara went to a position next to John Harmony.

The ceremony took about five minutes and soon Virginia and Carl were Mr. and Mrs. Carl Goodwin. The preacher asked everyone to come to the small dining area where cookies, drinks and snacks were being served. Carl and Virginia went into a small room and spent a few minutes together, they then joined the folks that were gathered in the dining area. When they entered they were greeted warmly and soon everyone was involved with meeting the newest member of the Goodwin family. Virginia was already becoming a popular and well-accepted member of the local clan. There was no turning back now, Virginia was married to Carl.

Kenneth Orr

Barbara slipped away and soon Carl and Virginia were in the Packard driving out of the churchyard. They took a road to the south and drove out to Medina Lake. They found a spot on the side of the lake and parked. Carl and Virginia just sat and looked at each other and they talked about the life they wanted to build for themselves.

Virginia was not sure of a lot of her future plans as she was being inducted into the Army almost as soon as she returned to Ohio. Carl knew he was going to be in Midland for a while and when they could have a life together, was still not clear. All they knew was that they loved each other and they wanted to make the most of their lives as a family. After about an hour, they drove back to the Goodwin ranch and went inside.

The rest of the day was quiet and the evening went as planned. For a few hours the old home place was like it had been when Carl was growing up, peaceful, happy and completely honest. Carl and Virginia were a new family and the hopes for the future were alive.

Wednesday morning arrived much too quickly. The morning sky was full of sunshine but the clouds were gathering in the north. About noon Barbara came driving up the driveway.

The day was going to be both wonderful and sad. Wednesday was the first full day of married life for Virginia and Carl. It was also the day that Carl had to go back to his assigned military post.

Breakfast was simple; coffee and sweet rolls. Lunch was better; warmed food from the icebox. The pressures of getting married were past and the time to relax and enjoy a 12-hour honeymoon was all that remained. Barbara had come home and was glad to see Carl so happy. She saw him growing into the same stature, as their dad had been when he was alive.

This was the point in his life where she finally was feeling she had to release all holds she had ever had on helping him

The Cowboy's Kids

grow up. The future was going to be difficult for him and for Virginia and everyone knew that life in the near future was going to be unsettled.

At 3:30 PM Carl knew it was time to leave and he packed his suitcase and personal things into Barbara's Packard. He, Virginia and Barbara then drove to San Antonio and went to the front gate at Randolph Field. Everyone walked over to the gate. Carl reached over and gave Barbara a big hug and kiss. Then he hugged Virginia and told her he loved her. Everyone was in tears. The time to go inside was at hand and he had to turn and walk into the base.

Barbara and Virginia watched as he turned a corner behind a building and was instantly out of sight. They then went to the car and drove back to Bandera. The trip was quiet at first and the mood was very serious. About halfway home Virginia spoke up and started asking Barbara a lot of questions about Texas. Barbara was glad to see that Virginia was able to handle the situation and was able to smile. This was the starting point of learning how to live with the situation that was around them.

CHAPTER 3-5
Texas and Tough Times

Barbara had a lot of things to discuss with Virginia. They had all day Thursday most of Friday ahead of them. The time was not planned or restricted to any event, other than getting back to meet Virginia's train on Friday evening. Both women were glad for some free time and being together on the ranch was even better.

Barbara filled Virginia in on many of the events that she and Carl had experienced while they were growing up. Virginia was very interested and she listened intently as Barbara explained the past. Virginia had no idea as to what the Texas frontier had been like and was impressed and fascinated with all of the many tales she was hearing. The fact that Carl's dad had served in an Army frontier fort was a whole story unto itself.

Virginia had an equally interesting past. Her two brothers were older and she was always a tag along sister. Her dad had been a retail merchant in a small town just south of Nashville. He was also active in the cattle selling business. He owned a "sale barn" where livestock were bought and sold on a weekly basis. The deep south had little industry and the two brothers went to school and studied law. They knew that there were always going to be legal problems, and this field was never oversupplied with talent. The oldest brother, Amos, had married a girl from Pulaski, Tennessee. She was a "spoiled little spitfire," as Virginia described her,

374

The Cowboy's Kids

and her relationship with her was never close. The other brother, Robert was a much better lawyer she thought, as he was a lot smoother and more in-depth than his brother. He had married a local girl from his college class and they were very low key in almost everything they did. Virginia said she did not like any attention being given to her, as she was shy and preferred to be a sideline player. Barbara understood.

Virginia said she had studied mathematics and wanted to find a good job in a bank or some similar institution. When she graduated the country was in a deep depression and the south was as poor as ever. There was no work and to stay in Tennessee was a dead-end life. She traveled to Pittsburg, Pennsylvania and worked for a steel company for a year. This job was not what she wanted but it was an income.

Her job was to go out into the mill and gather reports from various departments and then make out reports reflecting the status of daily production. The heat and dirt were hard to take and after a year she gave it up. She then went to Columbus, Ohio where she went to work for a company that was making machined parts for airplanes. Her job was in the accounting office and the work was easy. She liked her job and she liked the people around her but the pay was very low. Men doing similar work were making much more money. They were also doing less work.

The military had started to build up the facility at Wright Field in Dayton and the word on the street was that they were looking for qualified people. Virginia heard a lot of these stories and saw a new opportunity to do better. She went to talk to a friend she knew who worked there. She suggested that Virginia apply. Her application was submitted and in about an hour she was called in and asked to talk with a Army Captain about a job. The Captain was involved with information gathering and if Virginia was to work for him she had to have security clearances. He explained that her past history and education in mathematics were ideal for his job. He told her he would hire her but she would work in non-classified assignments until the investigation people

Kenneth Orr

were able to do the security work. Virginia told Barbara that she jumped at this opportunity, as she wanted to be a part of this effort.

Virginia said she was handling both classified and non-classified materials when Carl came to work in Dayton. She had noticed him and was impressed with his looks and quiet, laid back attitude. He was obviously a smart young man and she noticed he did not have a ring on his finger. She had spoken to him several times and they had worked on projects together, but he was always reserve about developing a deeper relationship.

She had gone to lunch with Carl and a couple of other people several times. She had noticed he was not all that easy to get to know. He always kept a strict professional distance from co-workers. Then, out of the blue sky, he invited her out for dinner just as he was about to leave town. This was a major event for Virginia and she was more than willing to let her feeling show, now that she had the chance.

She told Barbara that Carl apparently had been following the same path on her. Virginia said Carl was always a perfect gentleman and his respect for me was never an issue.

Barbara just listened to Virginia talk and smiled. She was sure that this marriage was going to work well. Barbara suggested that they sleep late on Friday, as the train ride was not a good place to get sleep or rest comfortably. Virginia agreed. They got up a little past 8:00 AM and had a big breakfast.

Virginia had fallen in love with Mexican food and a traditional breakfast with eggs, beans, meat and hot spices was prepared. Barbara asked Virginia if she would like to see some of the sights in San Antonio. Virginia agreed and she was happy that Barbara was giving her such good treatment. It was suggested that they take a leisurely drive to San Antonio, have lunch, see the sights and have a good meal before Virginia got on the train. This became the plan for the day.

The Cowboy's Kids

The day was overcast and cool but the mood was very positive. Both ladies were happy just to be alive and involved with life. The trip went well and the local sights were soon seen. Virginia enjoyed the "Alamo" visit most of all. She had heard a lot about Texas history and her visit made her feel a lot more sensitive about what had happened on that site. Lunch was had on a small Mexican restaurant in the south side of town.

At 5:PM Barbara took Virginia to the Menger Hotel for dinner. She told her how this was a very old and historical place and that the restaurant was famous for many reasons. After dinner they went to the train station. Virginia's train was at the gate and was scheduled to board in about 20 minutes. The women talked and spent this time planning on how they would keep in touch. Finally that call came to board. Virginia went to the identified train car and Barbara walked with her. After Virginia boarded Barbara went back to her car and as she started the engine, the train whistle sounded the signal that it was leaving. The drive back to the Goodwin ranch was lonely and a little sad for Barbara. She was feeling like she had not only gained a sister-in-law but a friend who was almost like a sister.

CHAPTER 3-6
Military Schools and a World Crisis

Midland, Texas's airport was being turned into a major military base. The Army had built several new structures and a new fleet of twin-engine A-11 training planes was arriving daily. In 1941 the war in Europe was taking all of the headlines and the local residents were confused as to the reasons behind all of this activity. They knew the war was at the bottom of all of the activity and they were proud to be involved.

Carl was assigned to be an instructor, holding classes both in classrooms while flying. The first groups of trainees and class sizes were small and some instructors had to serve in both teaching locations. The first job was to select and train some qualified instructors. The Army needed to get enough people capable using the bombsight, then train these people to teach others. Selecting candidates was a difficult problem. Security was always a major concern. The ability of each candidate to teach also had to be determined. Carl was good at picking people, as he was quick to see what skills a new man might have.

One candidate was a big rough looking fellow from Idaho. He was brash and crude in his mannerisms, but he bragged that he was also a good elk hunter. The physical exam he had taken indicated his eyesight was as good as the examiner had ever seen. However, he had some problems. He had an offensive body odor and his personal language

The Cowboy's Kids

was full of cussing and dirty-sounding words. Carl just watched him do some simple hand and eye co-ordination tests and "Ole Pork," as he came to be known, was as good and better than most on test evaluations.

Carl called him aside and asked him if he was interested in becoming an instructor. "Pork" smiled and said, "Only if I can fly in an airplane every few days. I have never been in the air and I am anxious to fly in one of those damn airplanes." Carl made the deal and soon "Pork" was one of the best instructors in the school. Carl made sure he learned how to take a bath every day and to clean up his language. There were several other similar stories concerning other men, and soon the school was staffed and capable of accepting large classes of student cadets.

The Bombardier Training School staffing plan was finalized and training began in October 1941. Some of the ground school training was temporally being done at Randolph field and some in facilities on the Midland base. Students were bussed back and forth between the two bases until Midland was ready to take over all training duties.

105 new buildings had been completely or partially completed and work was frantically underway to complete the 99 additional buildings that were planned. Training classes for additional new instructors were started at once. Formal cadet training was scheduled to start in January of 1942.

Carl had been calling Virginia every chance he got. She was always glad to hear from Carl and her physical separation from him was painful. Carl had informed his superiors that he was now married. This was a new situation for him, but in the military, being separated from your family, was not considered that much of a concern. That was just part of being a soldier.

Barbara was equally concerned about both Carl and Virginia. She knew that any weekend liberty time for either of them, would be short. She took an attitude that she would travel to see them at every reasonable opportunity. Virginia had been

Kenneth Orr

sworn in the Army a week after returning to Dayton and was cleared to work a project that she could not discuss. Her college degree qualified her to become a First Lieutenant. There was a lot of pressure being put on her in her job. She handled it well and soon was recognized as one of the top people in her operation. Her brothers were keeping in touch and she was writing letters every day.

The air base in Dayton was being expanded at a rapid pace and the need for more people to do the construction, and then to support the Army's efforts in the new facilities was critical. The new addition was toward the north and was named Patterson Field. John Patterson had been a major industrialist with the National Cash Register Company and was a most respected person in the Dayton community. The new local name for the base became "Wright-Patterson" field.

Ohio was a very active industrial state. The center of the machine tool manufacturing industry in the United States was located within 100 miles of Dayton. Adequately skilled labor was currently available to support this industry but, semi-skilled labor was just not available.

The result was a rapid and massive influx of new people into the whole area. Most of these folks were from farms and other semi-skilled trades in the southern United States. They came in droves and soon Dayton, Ohio, like a lot of other Ohio cities, had a major shortage in living quarters.

Local schools were immediately over crowded. The local native Dayton population often took a defensive posture about all of the new problems that were being created. One of the quick term solutions for housing was a dynamic increase in the manufacture of house trailers. This solution filled some of the first housing needs and "trailer parks" were soon everywhere. Many of them were set up in former farm fields. The sewage and drinking water problem associated with many of these trailer communities were serious. Wells were often the only immediate source for drinking water. Public water systems were often not near

The Cowboy's Kids

these developments. Compounding the problem, there were few men available and the materials required to expand the existing facilities were not available. Septic tanks and shallow piping for discharging sewage into the system were all sources of problems.

Finding electricity was also a major problem. This housing expansion all around Dayton, especially in the areas closest to the Army base, was out of control. A lot of local enterprising people were raking in profits renting semi-shanty, low quality houses that were being built on any available land. Kerosene lamps and candles were being used until new power lines could be strung and the power turned on.

The housing need was still not being satisfied and a new concept in rapid built housing came along, the "Defense Cabin". Defense cabins were simple homes being built on a large flat wood substructure that resembled a giant shipping pallet. They were about 10 to 12 feet wide and came in lengths of 32, 36 and 40 feet long. The insides of these cabins had no insulation and no plumbing. The only interior improvements were two 100-watt light bulbs, 4 electrical wall sockets, a front door and a back door. Windows could be were added at a fee per window. The walls were made from 2 X 4 studs covered with a composition fiberboard exterior wall. Exterior paint colors were simple, White, tan and light blue. Delivery to a site within a local area was included in the purchase price.

People would buy these "homes" on a priority list and had to wait until it was built and delivered. The purchaser would need to find a place to park the home and have it ready when delivery was scheduled.

Delivery was normally planned for a small lot of land, approximately 100 feet wide by 300 feet long. Some of these land plots were rented and some were sold at very high prices. The manufacturer would deliver the home, set it on a few concrete blocks and collect his final money. From there on the new owner was on his own.

The owner would then need to drill a well, dig a hole for an out house, get an electrical connection to a power pole and then set up housekeeping. It was not much on comfort but for a great many, it was all that was available.

A lot of property was cut into "lots" and sold for about $500 each. The streets were made from crushed stone and the neighborhoods often turned into slum locations. Law enforcement was often left up to old men who were called "Constables". They had a badge but when they needed help they had to call on other local law officers.

A lot of people who purchased these homes came from Kentucky, Tennessee, Alabama, Georgia and other southern states. They were coming north to find work. There was no meaningful work in much of the south and the hope for the future, for a young family in a lot of southern communities, was bleak.

Virginia filled Carl in on the latest Dayton conditions and he was saddened to hear that the federal government had built a large public housing facility on the old McCook airfield sight. They called it "Parkside Homes". He had always considered this place as a sacred part of the history of aviation.

Virginia also had a lot of information concerning the current expansion many other Army bases. There were massive amounts of buildup in almost every current military base, both in the Navy and the Army. This information was public knowledge and there were few security restrictions in most instances.

The daily newspapers were full of the events going on in Europe and the growing strength of Germany's grip on all of the area. Hitler had proclaimed himself as the commander of all the military. He had also stepped up his purge of Jewish people and their ability to move freely in all of Germany.

The Cowboy's Kids

London had come under more severe war conditions and the German bombers had begun to pound the whole country. Germany had invaded North Africa and was expanding the war on every front. The League of Nations had already expelled Germany and Hitler made no pretense that he was out to become the world's leader. Italy had joined in with Hitler's war and they were quick to also put extreme pressures on Jewish people.

Japan was playing a coy game with the United States and negative diplomatic tensions were growing rapidly. The diplomatic efforts to resolve issues were going nowhere and the President was growing more concerned that the war in Europe was drawing in the United States. Roosevelt remained under strong political pressures to avoid any war involvement. The reminders from World War One were still strong issues within the American population.

The focus on war had taking over the theme of peaceful co-existence. The world was in a state that had never been witnessed in any prior recorded time. The new weapons of war were very sophisticated and the capability to deal havoc on any targets by this technology, were vastly more intense than ever before. The worst part of the current situation was that a mad man was waging war in any region he chose to occupy. He used fear and military devastation to his advantage and he was not being challenged by any capable military force.

Carl, Barbara and Virginia were all recognizing the same dismal vision for the future. How could The United States avoid becoming involved?

CHAPTER 3-7
The Challenge, The Confusions and the Pain

Carl was excited to finally get his first class of bombardier students. There were 126 cadets in the group. All 126 men had been screened for appropriate security clearances and had passed. By he time the school was over, 103 men were awarded bombardier's wings. They had mastered the Norden bombsite and were ready to move into their next section of training.

Prior to the first graduation, Captain Goodwin called a class meeting. He wanted to congratulate the men who had made bombardiers, but he also wanted to share his deepest feelings. The training room was in a secured room with an armed guard standing outside the classroom door. After everyone was inside the door was closed and Carl stood up in front of the group.

Carl called everyone to attention. He called the roll and then put everybody "at ease." Then he had the group recite the Lord's Prayer. When they were finished he asked them to sit down and in turn each man was to come to the podium and introduce himself. He wanted everyone to be casual and to tell everybody where they were from and a little personal history about what they had done prior to being in the Army. The men began standing up and the introductions began.

The Cowboy's Kids

There were a lot of men from farming background. There were two plumbers, an undertaker's helper and a lot of people who just said they worked in factories and were production people. Two men had college training and 38 men had finished high school. There were six young men who said they had attended school but dropped out.

The atmosphere was now more comfortable for everyone as the group had gotten to know a little bit about the other guys in the class. Up until that point in training, Carl kept his classes very formal and pointed toward the lessons at hand. Carl thanked them for their introductions and then told everybody to sit down and get comfortable.

Then Carl went to the blackboard and in big letters he wrote the word "WAR". He looked at the men then closely watched their reactions. Then he walked to the center of the front area and asked. "Has anybody ever heard of a **Good War**?" Everybody looked at him and just waited. Carl was also waiting.

Soon a young man from Arkansas spoke up and said, "I think the Mexican War was good as we made sure that we got the Rio Grande established as our country's southern border." Carl looked at the group and soon another man spoke up and said he had a good feeling about World War One. This war was good as it put the Germans in their place.

Then Carl said, "OK, some of you people are making me feel that war is a good thing." He waited a few moments and singled out the second man and asked him some questions.

"Sir, let me ask you a few questions, Did World War One start because some people like us got mad at each other and they started shooting at each other?" The man answered, "I don't think so." Carl then said, was the First World War started by a political or military motive?" The man answered, "The Kaiser of Germany was aggressive and wanted to expand his country." Carl then asked him, "Who was shooting the

Kenneth Orr

guns and doing the fighting and killing, the Kaiser or the soldiers?" The man answered, "The soldiers."

Carl then asked him if there was any suffering from the war. The man looked confused but soon answered back, "Sir, a lot of people got hurt and killed. Suffering was everywhere." Then Carl looked at him and said, "Do you know how many Americans were hurt or killed in this war?" The private looked at him and said he was not sure but it was in the thousands. Carl asked, "Did the Kaiser ever put a gun on his side and go to the battlefield?" The answer came back as probably not.

Carl let the class sit for a minute and then said, "If we go to war soon do any of you think you will suffer or be killed?" Then he waited a few moments and said, "Lets take a break. While you are on break I want each of to think about my questions. When we get back we will look at this a little more". The class took a 20-minute break and everyone was back on time.

When they got back Carl stood up and said, "Have you thought about my questions?" An older man in the back of the room stood up and said, "Sir, war is never a good thing. You can never regain what is lost in a war and the pain and suffering is not only on the battlefield. I lost my dad and an older brother in World War One and they will never be back home. They are in Flander's Field under a small white cross. My Mom never got over losing dad and we all had a much harder life growing up without them." Carl said. "Please accept my sympathy and respect. You, Sir, know the real price of war."

By now the class was wondering where Carl was taking them. Then Carl spoke up and said, " I want each one of you to know and respect the fact that this training you are just about to completed will enable you to drop bombs on targets that our Generals have directed us to take out."

"Our Generals and our Nation's leaders are counting on you to do your job with accuracy and with pride. We all can

The Cowboy's Kids

recognize that the United States is soon going to be under attack from an enemy that is determined to whip our tails and take over our country."

"We also know this as the political leaders have evaluated the intents of our enemies. Should our enemies somehow overcome our military we are all are going to be in harm's way. Does everybody understand what I have just said?"

"I also want to tell you that the odds for all of you to survive in a war are not good. You need to learn everything you can to do you assigned job to the best of your ability and to learn to protect yourselves. If war does come we need to get it done and over with just as soon as we can. The longer a war goes on, the more pain and death we will endure".

"Oh, by the way, your new assignment will require that you will kill people and inflict harm on the enemy in any way that you can. You need to recognize the power that you are being given. Has anybody in this room ever killed another human being?" Nobody answered. The atmosphere was now very sober.

Carl outlined the training program they had just completed and said, "I want each of you to realize that your ability to drop a sack of flour on a target accurately, is not a game. It may have seemed like one as you developed your skills. Each of you has spent 15-hour days going through instruction and when Sunday came around most of you still found the time to go to Church. I commend all of you. In the near future you will probably be in the sky headed for real targets and the enemy will do everything they can to stop you before you reach your destination. Some of you will take hits and you may not make it home, but hopefully most of you will be successful."

"The pride that comes from being in the Army and of flying in a bomber is going to be a part of your life and you will never forget what you are going to experience."

Kenneth Orr

Carl added, "If your airplane is shot out of the sky you will need to do whatever is required to survive. Your life will then be at an even higher risk. The Army will give you additional training in survival when you are assigned to a specific bomber squadron. You will spend more time in training to become a bomber crewmember and when you pass those basic requirements your airplane and crew be assigned to a bomber base. There you will be folded into an active bomber squadron."

Lunchtime was at hand and everyone was told to keep all of the information from the classroom confidential, no exceptions. The class went to the base chow hall and waited in line. They had all learned that waiting was a basic part of being in the Army.

After lunch, Carl presented a current review of the soon-to-be-available bomber aircraft in the Army Air Corp. The class was intently interested and there were a lot of good questions and answers.

The Base Commander, Lt. Colonel Davies came to the classroom and congratulated everyone. He shook everyone's hand and told them orders for their next assignment would be available in a couple of days. He suggested that they finish all of their school paperwork, relax, for a couple of days and get rested up for whatever was ahead.

The class was anxious to get involved with an airplane. On Monday of the next week orders came through and the men began to pack and move to their new assigned Army Bases.

The trainer AT-11 airplanes were being flown by a group of new but well-trained pilots. The bombing trainers were already familiar with historical bombing maneuvers and the next graduating classes of cadets were all well trained bombardiers.

The Army was moving quickly in every area. Getting ready to go to war was no longer a question of if; it was when.

The Cowboy's Kids

The training of personnel was going to be a major job, as so many of the new tools of war were completely new to everyone.

CHAPTER 3-8
The Coming of War

World tensions were escalating and it appeared that there would be no peaceful end to Hitler's aggressive and inhumane war.

On July 26th, 1941 President Roosevelt suspended all relationships with Japan and froze all Japanese assets in American control.

August 1st The United States announced an oil embargo against all aggressor states and made sure that all shipments were halted immediately. President Roosevelt and British Prime Minister Churchill shortly thereafter, announced that they had formed the Atlantic Charter, which bound both to mutual efforts to protect each other both at sea and on British and American soil.

On August 20th the German Army attacked Leningrad, Russia. On September 1st The Germans ordered all Jewish people to wear a yellow star on their person. On September 3rd the Germans tested their new gas chamber that was designed specifically to kill Jews. The facility was located at Auschwitz Prison camp. The world was not yet aware of what horrors Hitler had planned.

Then on September 19th, the German Army took the City of Kiev in Russia. On September 29th, the Germans massed

The Cowboy's Kids

and killed 33,771 Jewish people in the city of Kiev. Shortly thereafter the Germans started a campaign to takes several additional large cities as they marched toward Moscow.

Germans submarines torpedoed and sank the British aircraft carrier "Ark Royal," off the coast of Gibraltar on November 13th. It was now obvious to the world that the German Army is not going to stop until they take control of every country they wanted to invade.

In early December the German Army reached the perimeter of Moscow and begin a major offensive to take the city. The cold Russian winter and troops that were tired and running low on supplies were unable to conquer Moscow and had to begin a slow retreat. The Russian Army began a savage counter assault and soon re-took much of the territory that the Germans had occupied. Russia was the first country to mount a defense that worked on the German Army.

In the Pacific, on the clear Sunday morning of December 8th the Japanese, using an aircraft carrier based fleet of fighter-bombers attacked the United States Naval Base at Pearl Harbor, Hawaii.

Now there is no escape, The United States is at war. On December 9th both The United States and Great Britain declared war on the Japanese. Shortly thereafter Germany officially declared war against the United States.

President Roosevelt understand the situation better than most political leaders and immediately orders the War Department to mobilize and move into full readiness for a war as soon as possible. He also went on the radio and addressed the American people who are in shock. He tells them that "fear is not going to sway our efforts to protect ourselves." He also asks them to buckle up a little tighter and switch gears into an economy that supports the military. He says that all non-vital domestic issues must be halted at once.

Kenneth Orr

His most famous words turned out to be, "The only thing we have to fear, is fear itself." American was now moving to protect itself and to provide the tools of war that were so urgently required. The military draft was instituted and every branch of the military was looking for capable men and women to meet their challenges. Men were lining up in long lines to enlist and every Post Office in America was a focus on helping to win the war.

The countries larger universities and colleges were soon training officers and technical personnel how to lead men and keep the tools that were already available, running. People were eager to help and the nation came together as one force and began to demonstrate to the enemy that they were not about to surrender.

There were negative happenings that also were associated with the war build-up. The United States had grown in size and culture from the middle of the 1700's. The United States was a nation made up of large numbers of immigrants who had come from the European and Oriental countries.

Many families were now fourth and fifth generation Americans and were dedicated loyal American citizens. The majority of these original immigrants had settled in the eastern portions of the then small United States and became good, productive and loyal citizens. The west coast had large numbers of Oriental citizens and they had been in the United States for several generations.

After the First World War a large number of immigrants from European countries that had been ravaged by war also followed in the footsteps of the original immigrants. Time and American economics had attracted many of these people to migrate to the northwest and southwest parts of the country.

The west coast oriental immigrants had been in the west since the early days of building railroads and the original families had acquired land, built homes and businesses and gone on with life. The areas around every major west

The Cowboy's Kids

coast city had large populations of oriental families and they supported a large part of the local economies.

When war came, there was a major wave of distrust concerning many foreign cultured groups and the government was concerned that many of them were potential spies and supporters of the countries that were now our enemies.

It was apparent that these people were also targets for many unhappy American citizens who lived in the same area and the government quickly stepped in. On the west coast large numbers of oriental people were forced to leave their homes and go to internment camps. On the east coast the same fears were present. People's physical features were not good indications of a person's native nationality. The approach to evaluate a person's loyalty was largely left to people who were conducting security clearance work and their findings. Several large groups of suspect Germans and people from countries that the Nazi Army had taken over were also interned.

This problem was kept out of most of the public's sight and as the war effort was expanded, the loss of these people in a community was overshadowed by the more immediate efforts of war mobilization. These people were moved to camps at old military bases and to locations where the general public were not likely to visit.

One ironic story happened in California. A young oriental man, who was an accomplished artist was taken to an internment camp near San Francisco. He was not charged with any wrong doings but his features were definitely oriental. The Army discovered his artistic skills and assigned him the task of drawing Army Recruitment posters saying "Uncle Sam Wants You." His posters were fantastic and they were used all through the war as a tool to draw young men into the military. His name was William Fong.

Another major problem was the internal friction between Negro and White soldiers. Slavery had been outlawed for almost 100 years but the aftermath of racial segregation was never overcome. White soldiers did not want to serve next to Negro soldiers and they had every excuse to support their attitude that was imaginable. This was most obvious within military groups where the men were predominantly from the southern states. The military was aware of the problem, but fixing this problem in the middle of a war, was not going to happen.

Negro soldiers were volunteering and serving in every branch of the military. They were just as loyal as any other Americans. The Army was aware of the situation and in some cases they were pressured to support segregated activities. The Negro soldier was characterized by many, as an uneducated and unskilled individual. To resolve the internal friction they were often placed in "Negro Only" combat groups. A perfect example was the development of the "Tuskegee Airmen" fighter squadron.

The Generals, who were commanding the war effort, had little time to work with these issues and they were delegated to junior officers to handle. Some of these officers were skilled in leadership and recognized the value of the Negro soldier's contributions, some were not and they made their lives miserable.

Carl was stationed at Midland, Texas at Midland Army Air field. Virginia was married to Carl but she was stationed at Wright Field in Dayton, Ohio. Barbara was in the Army reserve and was living in Bandera, Texas. The events of going into war had an immediate and dynamic effect on all of them.

Carl was instructing young men to become skilled bombardiers. He had to condense his training efforts as much as possible and turn out as many graduates as possible in a short time. This program adjustment called for longer hours of work, no liberty or holiday time off and tighter security on everything involved with his program. Carl wanted to

The Cowboy's Kids

see Virginia but the only potential opportunity would be if he could get a trip to Wright Field in connection with his program.

Virginia was working with message coding that was involved with data transfers between military bases and the War Department in Washington, D.C. She had been given a lot of responsibility and the military had required her to give up her apartment in the community and move on base. She wanted to see Carl and her time was so restricted, that she had no idea as to how this could ever happen.

Barbara had been living a semi-comfortable life in the home on the old Goodwin ranch. Her contacts with friends and former Army personnel in San Antonio were still active but they were much less often, now that she was in Bandera. Barbara knew that the hospital at Fort Sam Houston would be deeply involved with caring for injured soldiers when the war got going, and she was fearful that a long war would over burden both the hospital and the medical staff.

The phone calls between Barbara, Virginia and Carl increased, both in length and in frequency. The concerns from everyone were understood and nobody was going to enjoy any time together in any of the foreseeable future.

CHAPTER 3-9
1942 and More Adjustments

Time and war both have serious and often similar means of measurement. The progress of military campaigns and battles won measures a war's progress. Time spent in battles and the number of resulting casualties, defines a war's impacts. The entire Goodwin Clan was going to be effected by both.

In the spring of 1942 the Bombardier training school at Midland, Texas reached an acceptable level of performance. The Base Commander was made aware of the increasing demand for even more bomber crews. The key individual in a bomber's crew is always the pilot. His directions and orders are always the "one and only rules" when the airplane is on a mission. He is the manager, the leader and if necessary, even the Chaplin during a mission.

Major Malone, back in San Antonio, had always recognized Carl's leadership abilities. He mentioned his name to a Colonel who was at the base looking for qualified flight crew personnel. Major Malone informed the Colonel that Captain Goodwin was in Midland instructing cadets on the use of the bombsight system. His contributions were an important part of helping the base come on line. He also complimented Carl on his flying skills and his training abilities. The Colonel, a man of about 50 years old, asked Major Malone if Captain Goodwin was available for reassignment. Major Malone said, "We all are available if we are needed and have the right

The Cowboy's Kids

skills and an urgent need arises". He Added, "You need to be aware, the management at Midland may not be willing to let him go." Colonel Yarbourgh understood the answer.

Major Malone called Captain Goodwin on the phone and told him about the conversation with the Colonel. He asked Carl if he was interested in being a pilot instructor for B-24 Liberator aircraft. Carl was silent for a moment and then he said, "Lets talk in an hour, there are people in the area that I do not think need to be a part of this." Major Malone said, "You call me when you are free," and he gave him his private telephone number.

Carl had never dreamed he would have a chance of becoming a bomber pilot instructor. The whole new situation was a shock to him. He went to a private phone and placed a call to Virginia and she was available.

This was a rare event. Most of the time she was unavailable. He told her about Major Malone's call and asked her if she had an opinion.

She was obviously concerned. Her voice was different and she quickly asked him if he was going to fly combat or be an instructor. Carl said he did know a little about the new airplane. The B-24 was one of the newer bombers that were being developed in San Diego. The first new airplanes were still in production and were being rushed through the factory.

The Army had a major shortage of pilots of all aircraft. Carl said he would find out more and get back to her as soon as he got some good answers. Carl told her he loved her and he would call her that night for sure.

Carl then called Major Malone and started asking him a lot of questions. Major Malone said he had very little to go on but he was sure that the Colonel was building a combat wing training group. He wanted to train pilots who were going to go into war zones and deliver bombs. The message was clear. He could likely become a combat bomber pilot. Carl

Kenneth Orr

asked Major Malone if he had any choice in the decision to go, or stay in Midland. Major Malone said, "You may have some but you may also get over-ruled." Carl thanked Major Malone for his support but he was not sure what to tell Virginia or Barbara.

That night he called Virginia and broke the latest news to her. She was not happy and she cried. He tried to comfort her, but a thousand miles away is a long way from providing a shoulder on which to cry. Then she called Barbara and told her his latest news. She had a similar concern and soon she was crying.

Carl went to his quarters and got out his Kentucky whiskey and finished off the half full bottle. His work at Midland was difficult and he enjoyed the training atmosphere. He thought for a minute and he said to himself that the men he had been training were all going into harm's way, why should he not go with them? He said he would just wait and see what happened and then go from there.

About a week later, Carl was called to come to the training office. He had an important visitor. Carl went as requested. He walked in and said, "Captain Goodwin, reporting as requested." A Lt. Colonel came out from a small office and introduced himself.

He said, "I am Lt. Colonel Ronalds. You have been recommended to me as an excellent pilot and a man with great leadership skills." Do you have a few minutes so we can talk? Carl already knew what was coming but he said, "Sir, I would enjoy talking with you."

They went into a small private room and spent almost an hour talking. Carl was right about the opportunity that was being extended. He was surprised to hear that he would be required to go to a training base in Montgomery, Alabama, Maxwell Field, and learn all of the requirements to fly a B-24. If he were selected as an instructor he would train new pilots. If he were selected to command a bomber he would be involved in picking his crew. He would also get

The Cowboy's Kids

an immediate promotion to Major. Carl asked if he had any choice as to acceptance and the return answer was, "Well....." Carl understood.

Carl asked when he should plan to make the change? The answer was quick and clear, "As soon as you can get released from here. The Army had told us to expect the arrival of the first B-24 airplanes early in January." Carl said he would start planning to relocate and hoped his fellow training people would be overburdened by his leaving.

Carl left the office and went back to his training area He told his superior about the conversation. His immediate superior said he was happy for his success, but he would be missed. Carl went to his quarters and called Virginia and filled her in on the latest news. He was going to be transferred to Montgomery, Alabama and had just learned he would be leaving next Tuesday.

Virginia said she would like to drive down to Alabama to see him as soon as she could get some time off. Her classified work area was very busy. Her boss understood that Virginia wanted to see her husband before he might be relocated overseas.

Virginia went to her boss and asked when she could have some time away from her job. He scratched his head a moment and said, "You find out when he has some free time and plan a couple of weeks away from work around that time." She called Carl and told him about the offer and asked him to let her know.

The report date at Montgomery was checked and the Lt. Colonel said, "When you get here we will have about two to three weeks before you will start training. The information was great. He called Virginia as soon as he could. She was happy and all of the travel plans were started.

Carl called Barbara and told her the news. He said he would fly back to San Antonio and come to Bandera on his way to

Kenneth Orr

Alabama. Carl checked all of the information he could find about Maxwell Field.

Barbara also had some news. The hospital director at Fort Sam Houston had called her and asked her to come in for a very important meeting. She was scheduled to be there on January 15th and told that she would be spending three days in San Antonio.

About two hours later Carl got an urgent phone call, "Come to the training office at once." The Lt. Colonel from Maxwell Field had called and cancelled Carl's planned reporting. He said there had been some major changes in plans and he would advise of future status when the new plans were finalized. The Commander at Midland was surprised but he was glad that Carl would be able to stay in Midland's training staff.

All of the military's plans were being developed in a world that was very uncertain. Everyone always hoped that there would not be any last minute change, which seldom was the case. Changes in plans were a common event in the Army.

The training commander, a newly promoted Lt. Colonel, asked Carl if this change would be any problem to his personal life? Carl replied, " I got married earlier this year and I was planning to make my trip to Maxwell include a stop in San Antonio. I really want to see my wife." The Colonel told Carl, "Take a 12-day liberty and go see your wife. It is almost Christmas and this may be the last Christmas any of us will have for a long time."

He told Carl, "Use an A-10 military aircraft to travel to Wright Field. I want you to check in with the base information officer before you leave to transport any mail they may have. Treat the airplane like it's yours and bring it back in one piece. After all, you are an Army pilot and you must keep up with your flying time requirement. Your carrying the military mail to Dayton will make this a legal trip." Carl thanked him and saluted.

The Cowboy's Kids

As he turned to leave he suddenly turned back and asked the Lt. Colonel if he had any information as to the reason his orders to report to Maxwell Field had been cancelled. The Lt.Colonel said, "Yes I do, the new B-24 airplanes are not on schedule and they will be late to deliver the first airplanes to Maxwell."

The British have convinced our Army to change the delivery schedule so they can have the first six airplanes. The whole B-24 production program is being replanned to involve a much broader manufacturing base. This has caused Maxwell to be late in receiving their first training aircraft. This will also effect the deployment of the B-24 until at least the middle of next year. Oh, by the way, that's classified information."

Carl thanked him for his answer. The Lt. Colonel told him that everyone knew the rules about deployment changes and security. Carl understood.

Carl went to a phone and called Virginia. She was glad to hear the new plan and was eager to see Carl.

CHAPTER 3-10
Barbara's Decision

Christmas was at hand and two birthday celebrations were also in order. Barbara had been informed about Carl's new travel plans and she wanted to be with him and Virginia to celebrate Christmas.

Barbara was concerned as to what the Army wanted from her as she was now 42 years old and the normal age cut-off for draft or re-call into active service was understood to be 40. She called an old friend at the hospital and inquired if she knew what was going on.

Barbara had called the right person. The latest information was that the hospital at Fort Sam Houston was going to be involved in the outfitting of an Army Hospital ship. The workload for this mission was going to be on top of an already overloaded staff. They needed additional qualified help at once.

Carl was never one to stop thinking. He called Major Malone and told him about his upcoming trip. The Major told him it would be nice if he could stop at Randolph Field and fill him in on the training at Midland Field. Carl knew this was an "excuse" to come to San Antonio but he loved it. Carl called Barbara and told her the news. She was pleased. Carl said, "Pack your suitcase, you are going to go with me to Dayton, Ohio to see Virginia." Everybody was happy. As

The Cowboy's Kids

Carl had learned, changes are not uncommon, they are a part of life in a wartime atmosphere.

The trip happened on schedule and Carl and Virginia had several days together. Barbara was alone much of the time, but the Van Cleve hotel in downtown Dayton soon became a happy and fun-filled oasis for everyone.

When the liberty time was up, Carl left Virginia in Dayton and went to the communications center and got the mail for the Midland Air Base. There were three large boxes. He stowed it in the airplane and he and Barbara flew to Randolph Field.

Barbara got out of the airplane quickly, the mail was removed and Carl refueled and flew on to Midland Field. The birthdays, Christmas and New Years celebrations were all over and it was time to go back to the work of fighting a war.

Barbara drove over to the hospital and went in the management office area. She was looking for a friend who she knew might have some more information about her invitation. The facility director, Jack Wirtz, spotted her and quickly went to say hello. She greeted him warmly as they had both known each other a long time. He invited Barbara to sit down in his office and have a cup of coffee. She gladly accepted.

The conversation was opened with a discussion of how Paul had served and how tragic it was that he had passed away at such an early age. Then Barbara spoke up and asked what was going on that the hospital wanted to talk with her. The reply was quick.

The director, a man of about 50 replied, "The Army knows that there are going to be a lot of battle field casualties in the very near future. They want to station hospital ships in strategic locations so our troops can receive good medical attention as soon as they can be evacuated from

Kenneth Orr

the battlefields. We have been given orders to support the planning, staffing and deployment of one of these ships."

Barbara was not surprised to hear his news but she still wondered why she was being called in for a three-day meeting? She looked Dr. Wirtz straight in the eye and said, "What are they calling me in for?"

Dr. Wirtz spoke up and said that anyone who had any Army medical experience and was potentially capable of helping with this effort was being contacted and requested to come in for this session. He said, "I am sure that your name is on that list." Barbara said she was still in the Army reserve. She was not sure of what that status was worth at this time. The director said he was not sure of anything concerning this issue, but he knew everyone at the hospital knew her and respected her as a well-qualified Army nurse.

Barbara thanked him for his information and then drove home to Bandera. The trip was cold as the winter winds were blowing down from the north. Barbara knew that Carl would be fighting a strong headwind all the way back to Midland Field.

Carl arrived back at Midland, delivered the mail to the proper people, parked the airplane on the apron and went to his quarters. There were three paper notes hanging on his door. All of them had the same message, contact Major Malone at Randolph Field as soon as you return. Carl knew something very important was up.

Carl went to his phone and had the operator place the call. It was after normal duty hours, but Carl knew that the war effort was keeping everybody in their office much longer every day. Major Malone came on the line and said he was glad to hear Carl's voice. He asked Carl if he was alone as he wanted to talk in privacy. Carl told him he was alone and the conversation began.

Major Malone told Carl, "The Army is beginning to deploy Air Corp troops and equipment to England. These first efforts

The Cowboy's Kids

were begun with very little planning or involvement other than political. The "Brits" as he called them, have some very good pilots. They are flying into Europe every day trying to take out targets that are deemed strategic. What's really happening is they are being shot down at rates so high, that they are going to run out of men and airplanes. If this continues on the current path, the Germans will be able to invade Britain and the war will take on a whole new negative situation."

"The Brits have spitfire fighters that provide token aerial cover for the bombers part way to the target, but their flying range is too short to allow them to go all the way to the target and still get home. Our bombers are joining in these operations and we are not doing much better."

Carl asked Major Malone about, the need for B-24 pilot training at Maxwell Field. Major Malone said, "The need to save the men who are fighting right now and supply additional equipment in England is an even greater problem. We are concerned that the current bomber loss rate must be reduced and more of the bombs reach the targets."

"We have a lot of training underway and in about five to six months we will be better prepared to become more aggressive but that too far away to do much good today. We had a top level meeting with key War Department people last week and they want us to send our best people over there right now and get them involved with the daily planning. That's where you come in."

"You are older than most of our new pilots and I know from experience that you have a lot of great experience in planning and organizing activities. You also are firm enough in your decisions that some mouthy officer with some crazy, not thought out idea will not sway your good judgment. The British have a lot of youth in the RAF but they don't have much experience."

"I have been wondering if you would take an assignment in England immediately and go there and be my helper."

Kenneth Orr

Carl was listening intently. Major Malone told Carl that the Germans were attacking the Russian cities and were heading toward Moscow for a second time. They also were using captured soldiers to build battlefield reinforcements along the French coast and many of the captured officers were being shot. Carl just listened some more.

When Major Malone was finished with his information dump he said, "Carl, I forgot to tell you that your promotion to Major went through the channels quickly and you now can get your uniform upgraded." Carl was pleased and he thanked the Major for any part that he may have played in this promotion.

Major Goodwin said, "Major, I just got in my quarters and have flown almost all day. Can I get some sleep and call you in the morning." Major Malone agreed but added, "Carl you are the right man to help our forces do a better job and I look forward to your call."

About nine o'clock Virginia called and Carl was all up tight when he answered the phone. She knew something was up and she had been watching the events in England as a part of her assigned work. Carl told her about Major Malone's call and said he was probably going to be going to England very soon. He almost forgot to tell her that he had been awarded a promotion. Virginia was proud for him. She also knew that Carl would now be directly in harm's way.

The next morning was cold and a light snow shower was falling on the Midland Airfield. The officer's mess hall was a short walk away and Carl was in line getting his favorite military breakfast, orange juice, a cup of hot black coffee and "S O S". The cook always made good S O S, as he knew how to add the right amount of salt, pepper and a mystery ingredient that Carl found out was "saltpeter." The saltpeter was supposed to reduce a man's hormone levels and keep him more focused on the Army's business, not on young ladies.

The Cowboy's Kids

After breakfast Carl called Major Malone and got some additional information about the immediate future. They wanted Carl to go to Washington and blend into a group of similar men who were being organized to go to England.

The Eighth Army Air Corp was already being alerted to travel in the near future and the planning group was being planned to deploy prior to any massive troop or aircraft relocation.

Major Malone added, "I am also going to be one of the group for this operation." He added, "Carl why don't you fly to Randolph Field tomorrow and we can go to Washington together?" Carl grunted out a clear and very respectful, "Yes Sir." Carl hung up the phone and immediately called Barbara. He told her he was going to fly to Randolph Field tomorrow and then fly his small personal airplane to Bandera and land on the pasture just west of the horse barn. The airplane was still hangered at Randolph field. He would put the airplane in the big barn as the doors were wide enough to pull it in and then Barbara would need to drive him to Randolph Field. Barbara agreed and the final plan was in place.

It was now January 13th. Carl, per his plan, flew his personal airplane to Bandera and circled over the ranch. Barbara heard the airplane and went outside and stood just a little outside the barn. The wind was cold and the barn was a great windbreak. Carl picked up on the wind direction from the smoke in a neighbor's chimney and got lined up to land. Before he was touched down he pulled up and took another circle over the old home place.

He knew he might not see it again for a long time. Then he landed. Barbara greeted him and together they tugged the tail of the plane until the entire airplane was inside. Then the door was closed. Carl took out his baggage and put it in Barbara's Ford. Barbara suggested that he get some fresh biscuits and coffee to eat while she drove. That was a good plan. There was no time to spend in other activities.

Kenneth Orr

They said goodbye to the housekeeper and started the drive toward San Antonio. It was cool outside but much warmer than it had been in Midland. The ride was comfortable and Carl opened the small wing window to let in some fresh air.

Barbara told Carl about her latest conversation with the hospital people. She said they had called her at home two additional times. The last call was almost pleading with her to come back into the Army full time and help with the medical workload that was certainly coming. Barbara was in agreement with the prediction of near term major medical overload, but she was not sure she wanted to jump in and get all involved so quickly.

They arrived at Randolph field and Carl asked Barbara to go see Major Malone with him. She was glad to be included in Carl's world.

Major Malone had met Barbara several times and they were already good friends. When they entered his office, he hugged her and made her feel welcome. Then he shook Carl's hand and said, "Major, we need to talk. Barbara is welcome to sit in on this and she can probably understand what's happening in our war, if she listens in."

Major Malone went to the wall and uncovered a map of southern England and all of France. He proceeded to point out cities and current Royal Air Force air base locations. Using a pointer he traced the paths that bombers from Germany were using to bomb London and other key cities. Then he pointed out the Allied Forces flying paths into the German held countries and how we had been losing airplanes over Germany, Holland and France. Barbara and Carl were all ears.

The map made it obvious that the Germans had little difficulty in shooting down Allied Forces Bombers going into German cities. It also was obvious that the grip on most of France and other nearby countries was a solid base for advancing land based German military operations into England.

The Cowboy's Kids

Major Malone had several additional comments about the current war status, all of which emphasized the weakness of any efforts from the countries Germany had already invaded, to combat the invasions or to protect their national interests.

One of the key comments involved the resistance movement in France that was being headed up by Charles DeGaulle and other responsible French civilian people. The French government that was in power when Hitler's forces entered France, the government offered no resistance and allowed the Germans to take over the entire country with little military resistance.

Then Major Malone put up a map of Germany. He pointed out the key industrial and seaport cities that the Germans were thought to be using to supply their war effort and said, "These operations must be shut down if we are ever to gain a foothold on winning this war. This mission is falling on the bombers of our Allied Forces."

The room was silent. Carl looked at Major Malone and said, "Are we going to mount an offensive in England or do something in another location?" Major Malone said, "The Germans have also invaded North Africa and we are still developing plans on where and how to make a meaningful assault."

"You are being drawn into this decision making process because of your experience and first hand knowledge of the new bombers and bombsight work that you have done. I have been requested to get involved with activities in North Africa and will probably be sent over there in some role very soon. In the mean time, I am going to go to England with you."

Barbara looked at Carl and cautioned him to be careful and take care of himself. She knew he was going to be in the center of the action in one way or another.

Kenneth Orr

Major Malone said, "Carl, we need to get our bags and get our airplane in the sky. The meetings are already underway in Washington and they need all of the players there as soon as possible."

Carl hugged Barbara and told her he loved her. He asked her to call Virginia as he was out of time. He said he would call her as soon as he could find the time and be near a phone. The room was silent. Major Malone said, "I will meet you on the flight-line," and walked out. Barbara saw the urgency and followed. Carl left last and held Barbara's hand until it was time to go separate paths.

Barbara went to her car and waited until she heard the sound of an airplane leaving the runway. She knew Carl and Major Malone were going off to war.

Barbara drove home and spent the next day sitting in the front of a warm fire. The fireplace was always a place where the family had enjoyed times together and she took pride in the fact the fire had not destroyed this part of the house. This was her centerpiece of activity when she was home.

The January 15th meeting was only a day away and Barbara was torn as what to do when she would be confronted to come back into the Army. She had lost a husband, a close friend and his brother and both parents, and all of them had suffered through the trials of being a military family. Carl was now headed for a certain war involvement in Europe and his wife was in Ohio serving in the Army. The next decision was strictly on her shoulders. Carl had told her to do what she wanted to do in her heart and the decision would be the right way to go. She was still not clear as to what to do.

The morning of the 15th came very early. Barbara was up, dressed and on her way to San Antonio before 6:00 AM. Her headlights were cutting through a thick layer of ground fog every time she went over a small hill and she had to slow down just to be safe. There were a lot of deer feeding next

The Cowboy's Kids

to the road and one could run out at he so quickly that it would be difficult to not hit it.

South Texas is never bitterly cold for long in January, but the weather is never very predictable. When she arrived at the front gate at "Fort Sam" she identified herself and the gate guard found her name on a list of approved to enter people. She went straight to the hospital. The meeting was about 20 minutes from starting so she got some coffee and a small snack.

Right on time, a small bell rang in the meeting hall, which was the signal for everyone to go to a seat and sit down. There were military doctors, military nurses, civilian nurses and a couple of people who had on dark blue business suits in attendance.

The hospital director went to the center of the room and asked everyone to identify themselves by name and occupation and if they were in the Army to give their rank. Everyone did as asked. The men in the blue suits said they were the Captain and first mate from the Ernest Hinds troop ship. Everyone was immediately all ears.

Public domain from the US Government

The officer leading the meeting said that the hospital had been given the responsibility to take currently operating

Kenneth Orr

Army personnel transportation ship and convert it into a medical or "floating hospital ship." The Ernest Hinds had been selected and was going to be docked in a seaport with a shipyard and undergo a rapid conversion.

He went on to describe several details about the ship's new mission. He said the Army would be completely responsible for the ship. The Captain and key ship personnel would be assigned to operate and maintain the physical control of the ship.

"There would be no arms or guns of any kind installed to make this an aggressive vessel, and all of the personnel on board would be considered as non-combat personnel. This was based on a treaty that was agreed to by all of the world's major nations after World War 1."

"The ship would have a new paint job, with everything above the waterline painted white. A prominent large red cross with a wide red stripe would be placed on each side that would identify this ship as a "Hospital Ship." This will be visible both in the day and the night. At night strong lights will shine on all of the ship's sides to make these markings visible."

"The ship will have all of the interior rooms and facilities that are not required to run and maintain the ship, converted to uses that support a complete capability medical facility. In addition, the lifeboats and other supporting small craft will have similar markings."

He added, "OK, now we have a ship to work with and the next requirement is selecting a first class medical staff, complete with specialized medical skills and all of the required support personnel to man this vessel. Each of you was invited to this meeting because we already know each of your skills and capabilities. Some of you are already in the Army and on active duty. Others are on military reserve status and are subject to recall if the Army deems you are needed. However, after you reach 40 years of age you can

The Cowboy's Kids

refuse a call-up if you choose. Then, others in this group are civilians."

"The executive staff for this ship has already been identified. The chart I am about to uncover will identify who those people are. Each of them needs qualified personnel to staff their duty sections. All of you are qualified to fill several of these openings and before you sign up make sure you have selected an area where you feel comfortable."

"Those of you on active and reserve status and are not exempt for age are required to sign up. You are to be assigned to the ship as soon as it is ready, to develop its medical capability. Until that time you will be assigned to duty that fits the current needs of this Army Hospital. Those of you who are not legally required are strongly requested to also sign up. If you have a good reason to decline I will personally meet with you and hear your individual situation. Are there any questions?"

The room went silent, then a young Captain, who was a doctor asked, "Sir, when is this ship going to sail and where will it be going?" The reply was quick, "We will sail as soon as the ship can be made ready and our destination will be somewhere in the Atlantic, Pacific or perhaps in the Mediterranean Sea; wherever we are needed. That's all I know so that's all I can tell you."

Barbara sat back and looked at the crowd flock to the newly uncovered chart and began to look at potential assignments. After about ten minutes an older doctor Barbara had known for a long time came over and sat down next to her. He saw she was crying. He gave her a handkerchief and told her he understood.

Barbara looked at him and said, "I just hate to think of what's ahead. Our boys are walking into a situation they did not cause, but they are going to be paying for Hitler's hell with their blood and lives. I am really upset and there is absolutely nothing that any of us can do to stop the upcoming slaughter."

Kenneth Orr

The Doctor, who's name was Major Eversole, looked at Barbara and asked her if she was going to sign up? Barbara just looked ahead and finally she turned her head and looked him in the eye and asked, "Are you going?" The Doctor said, "Yes." Barbara asked him, "Why are you going?" He said, "How can I sleep in a warm bed her in Texas and know my fellow Americans need my help on this ship? Yes, I cannot help if I do not to go."

Barbara asked him if he needed a nurse that was just about over the hill? He said, "If you are over the hill, I would hate to see you when you really get old, you are a fine nurse and yes, I do need a nurse that I can depend on. Are you ready to sign up?" Barbara went to the chart and wrote her name in a slot under Doctor Eversole's staff. Her decision had been made.

Barbara went to the operation's office and told them what she had signed up to do. They said to come back in two days and they would have all of the paperwork ready to process her back into active status.

Barbara then went home to Bandera and went out on the cold front porch and sat for a while. She knew why Carl had taken an extra loop around the old home place before he landed. This was home and would always be home to her and she was going to miss being in Texas.

CHAPTER 3 –11
Going To War

January was about over and both Carl and Barbara were now in the active Army. Carl was in Washington having meetings with key people on what to do in fighting an Army air based war and Barbara had closed up the ranch house, except for dismissing a Hispanic maintenance man. She took care of matters and moved to Fort Sam Houston. Virginia was in Dayton, Ohio and the phone lines between all of the locations were busy every day. Life was taking on a whole new direction for everyone.

Virginia was becoming involved with very sensitive cryptographic issues and was handling her assigned duties well. Coded messages had to be sent to military commanders in the field and they all had to be checked to assure they were in the proper secure configuration prior to being sent. There were also other messages that were coming from the same military commanders. The clock was never involved with when to send and receive messages. The needs in the battle zone were the driving force. Virginia was assigned to a key job in the military code team at Wright Field.

The government knew that the enemy military, both from Germany and from Japan, were intercepting many of these messages and the codes were changed on a regular basis. The United States was also intercepting coded messages from the enemy. The importance of many of these messages was broader than the scope of any one military installation.

Kenneth Orr

It was a common practice to send a dummy message to some outpost just to see what replies between the enemy code folks might say. They were doing the same thing to the Allied Forces and it was a game to keep the real information separated from the decoys. The War Department had been intercepting messages from both Japan and Germany for several years and had assembled a Central Intelligence Operation in countryside near the Washington D.C. military headquarters.

The coded message center at Wright Field was a major focal point for Army Air Corp. activities and Barbara was assigned to a key job in that organization. She was also awarded the rank of Captain. The responsibilities that went with the job were seemingly never ending and her days and nights all were running together.

Germany had expanded the war into North Africa and the Army Air Corp was working to locate a base somewhere in the area. Germany's General Rommel had assembled a large tank offensive force and was attempting to conquer all of the countries that bordered the Mediterranean Sea.

The purpose of the Army base would be to fight in North Africa and to attack German troops and targets. With forces in both Africa and England, the combat effectiveness of air attacks would be greatly enhanced. The War Department wanted to control much of the planning from Washington and Wright Field would become the second level of decision.

Virginia was called into a secret meeting and told about the program. She was also told she was being assigned to work in Washington and be a central point of information for Wright Field for all top secret message exchanges. She was restricted from telling anybody, including her husband, what her job included. She was ordered to leave Dayton in 24 hours and fly to Washington.

Virginia went to her quarters and packed. She processed her internal Army paperwork quickly to clear Wright Field activities and was ready to leave. A special airplane was

The Cowboy's Kids

scheduled to fly the next morning from Wright Field to Washington D.C. She and two one star Generals were going to be the only passengers.

Virginia drove to work and had a co-worker take her car home to where she lived in Dayton so it could be stored until she had an opportunity to come and get it. The next morning arrived and the flight to Washington left the runway on time.

Upon arrival at Langley Field in Washington, a special car came and picked her up at the airfield. There was a lady in the back seat dressed in civilian clothes. She identified herself but said she would not give out her name just yet and asked Virginia to just call her "Lady." Then, she provided Virginia with a new set of orders. The new orders were in a much different code that Virginia had ever seen. The Lady, who was also a Major in the Army, told her that she would be wearing civilian clothes and her duty station would be at a remote location about 25 miles away from Washington. She told her that her working location was at a "horse farm" that had a secret underground operation, devoted strictly to intelligence work. Virginia was surprised at all of the new conditions, but she took it all in very quickly.

The car drove to a location outside of the Air base and the lady, and Virginia got out. There was a new black Plymouth automobile sitting in the parking lot and the lady took Virginia over to it and told her to put her baggage in the trunk. Then she gave Virginia the keys and told her this car was hers to drive to and from work while in Washington. She told Virginia to go to a specific local hotel and change into some civilian clothes. She was going to follow her in her car. Then she would take her to see her new work site.

Virginia had few civilian clothes with her, but she had a pair of slacks and a blouse that were not too wrinkled and got dressed. The lady told Virginia to take her Army uniform to work and leave it there; that was part of the security required to do her job. Her appearance was to be as non-

Kenneth Orr

military as possible to avoid any interests from people who might be spies or have interests in military information.

Virginia and the lady drove south from Washington into a lush, well-maintained farming district in northern Virginia. The farm fields were all bordered with fancy white fences and the homes were very fancy and well landscaped. They pulled into a small driveway and drove about a mile back into a farm that had fancy horses in almost every field. They parked the car by a barn and went inside. Virginia was not sure as what to expect. When they entered an armed soldier who was wearing farmer's clothes greeted them. He looked at both of their military identification. The lady gave him her government identification to review and then Virginia gave him her military identification. He checked her name against a list he had and saw she was new to the area. He told Virginia to have a seat.

In a couple of minutes a man came to the area and asked her to come with him. He took her into a room and had her fill out some special security papers. Then he briefed her on her security requirements. She was then given a special pass and taken back to the reception area. The lady that had brought her there was gone. Virginia asked as to her presence and the guard said, "She did her job and got you here, then she left."

Then a small thin lady came and got Virginia and said, "Follow me." They went into a close-by room that had a locked door on one side. The lady said, "My name is Kate. I will be your supervisor while you work here and by the way I am a Major. I also want to tell you, in this facility rank has little or no meaning."

"We are all here under the tightest of security and we will not allow rank to ever sway our judgment on any issue. Welcome and I hope you can enjoy you new assignment."

Kate unlocked a second door in the back of the room and took Virginia down a long flight of stairs into an underground room that was far below the outside surface. Kate showed

The Cowboy's Kids

her an office and said this is where you will work and there are several more people here doing the same kind of work so get to know them quickly, they can help you get started much quicker and you can learn from them. Virginia walked around the area with Kate and got introduced to everyone. Everyone was on a first name only identification. Last names were never to be discussed.

Then Kate took her to a room where there were a lot of telephone lines, boxes full of electronics and a lot of large books. Kate said this is the code room. Every code we know about is in one of these books. We are good at cracking most new codes quickly and we know the enemy will use a code as long as they think we have not cracked it. Your job is to help us keep up with the increased traffic. You will see what I mean quickly.

About two minutes later a noisy machine started bringing in a new message. The message was in code and one of the people in the group said, "That's a Japanese message. This is a new code but it is similar to a code, number "j-673" they were using last week. Let me see what I can do with this one."

Before the first message was complete a second message started to come in on another machine. Another individual went to the machine and started to look at what was being received. The process repeated itself several times and soon Virginia saw that she was in the center of the most sensitive intelligence operation in Washington.

Kate told her to just watch and learn and she would soon be up to speed with what was happening and what to do when a message was being received. Kate said, "We also code a lot of outgoing messages but we do that in another room." Virginia was instructed as to where to park her car, her hours of planned work and where the government had already provided her with an apartment. The keys to the apartment were in Kate's possession and she gave them to Virginia with a map of how to get there.

Kenneth Orr

Virginia told Kate her husband was in the Army and was somewhere in Washington attending meetings with some high ranking officers. Kate knew she was married, but the news about her husband's location was not expected. Kate said, "You can contact him and spend time with him as you are able, but always remember, he cannot know what you are doing here in Washington. You cannot discuss anything about your work other than to say I am in a classified job assignment." Virginia agreed and understood the reasons for such tight security.

Virginia finished her day and got in her car and started out to find her apartment. Her drive was short and soon she was in a nice plush one-bedroom apartment in South Alexandria, Virginia.

She went into the room and there was a telephone already installed. She had a telephone number where Carl should be so she had the operator dial it. A voice came on the phone and she asked for Major Carl Goodwin. The male voice asked who she was and she identified herself. The man said, "Please hold on," and left the line open. In about two minutes a new voice came on the line. It was Carl. Virginia said "hello" and just waited. Carl said. "Virginia, is something wrong?" Virginia began to chuckle and Carl immediately knew she was not calling to tell him bad news. She told him she had just transferred to a new job and was now living in the Washington area. She told him she already had an apartment.

Carl was confused. He had talked to her three days ago and she was in Dayton and made no mention of moving. She said, "I cannot discuss it but I do want you to come over and we can go somewhere for dinner tonight." Carl said he had news for her and he would be over as soon as he could get away. He thought it was going to be soon. He got directions and told Virginia to watch for a jeep. He had been issued one to drive while he was at Langley Field. Virginia said she had landed at Langley Field earlier in the day and did not know he was there. He laughed and said "I love you, See you real soon".

The Cowboy's Kids

Carl got away as soon as he could and drove to the apartment complex. It was only three miles from the air base and the instructions were easy to follow. When he arrived Virginia was still wearing her slacks and blouse and Carl was in his uniform. Virginia was glad to see him and the reunion was special. They went to dinner and ate some great steak. Virginia said she had to go shopping and buy some new clothes.

Carl was confused, but when she told him she was wearing civilian clothes to work now he knew she was in a special security assignment. He never asked more. Virginia went to a small ladies store and bought several dresses, new shoes and a warm coat. Washington winters are cold and harsh. She wanted to keep warm and was enjoying a ladies favorite hobby, buying new clothes.

Carl said he would spend the night with Virginia and plan to leave early enough the next morning to be in a meeting at 8 AM. Virginia said, "What's your news?" Carl said he was going to ship out to England in three days and be involved in some flying activity with the RAF. Virginia was sad, but she knew how the events within the war were changing so quickly and understood.

The next three days were special for both Virginia and Carl. He was spending his days in meetings and his nights at Virginia's apartment. They both had never had any type of honeymoon time together and this was as close to such an experience as they had been. Parting was going to be a painful and tear filled experience for both of them.

The pressure on both Carl and Virginia was heavy and they both were looking to the evenings they had together. Carl called Barbara and told her of the current situation. Barbara then told him about her new status as a full time Army nurse destined to someday serve on a hospital ship. Everybody was surprised at her decision but there was little to be happy about. War was never a planned or enjoyable event. Being in the middle of all of the activity was going to

Kenneth Orr

test everybody's character and mental health, and everyone knew it.

CHAPTER 3 – 12
Duty Stations

It was now mid February and the worst days of winter were here. Virginia was going to work every day and her working hours were never predictable. The short days of winter were depressing as the sun was down when she went to work and it was already dark when she went home. Ice and snow on the roads did little to improve the situation.

Barbara was in meetings every day and her quarters at the Fort Sam hospital quarters were not warm as the furnace in the building had major problems. The plans for setting up the hospital ship were moving ahead, but the Navy was currently using the ship. The Army conversion was slipping behind schedule.

Carl had relocated to England and he was getting involved with the daily bombing activities against the Germans. His daily duties were focused on helping the RAF bomber pilots and crews learn how to use the new bombsight. He also became involved with training young British men to learn to fly the B-17. Carl was an expert instructor and was skilled in the way he taught inexperienced youngsters to fly.

The air war over England was intense, as the Germans had been bombing London and other major manufacturing centers for over a year. The German's Stutka dive-bombers were accurate in locating targets and the resulting

Kenneth Orr

destruction was awesome. The English civilian population was undergoing horrible bomb raids and when the night air raids would begin they went to shelters hoping to stay safe and away from the bombs and resulting fires.

Several RAF airfields had been set up in rural areas where open fields were easily converted into runways and aircraft service areas. The military had developed a new type of structure called a "quonset hut" which was made from many pieces of similar shaped sheet metal fastened together in the shape of a half-moon. There were no center supports required and the ends could be closed to keep out foul weather. These structures, along with simple wooden buildings were enough to support a bomber operation, but they were minimally capable.

The RAF had been sending bombers into German held territories on a regular basis and they had only been marginally successful. A squadron of British bombers was usually made up of some British Lancaster's and a few early model B-17s. The bombers all had machine guns and cannons for defense but they were a poor defense for fending off the German fighter planes. British Spitfire fighters would fly as protectors, much of the distance, to a target site with the bombers for protection. However, they lacked the fuel capacity to go all of the way to the bomb targets and still have enough fuel to return to the base in England. The German fighters would wait until the British fighters turned back and then attack.

The Germans would load the sky near a bombing target with "flack" and cannon fire and the unescorted bombers were easy targets for the fast and well armed German fighters.

British losses remained high. Losses of both life and equipment were continuing to hurt the Allied Forces efforts. The bombers that did return to their base were often too damaged to fly again and several of the flight crewmembers were either dead or severely injured.

The Cowboy's Kids

Carl saw many problems and most of them were so serious that they were not going to be repairable until there were more airplanes and the crews were better trained. Carl recognized that the situation was so out of control; the current effort was never going to be effective without additional help. A major problem with the skill of bombardiers was surfaced and Carl was assigned to work to improve this situation.

The Intelligence from war status bulletins told everyone that Hitler was still taking territories and he was expanding his efforts to take Egypt. The United States was busy building more bombers and training large numbers of new flight crews, but it was still something that would help in the future. On May 30th, the British mounted a massive 1000 bomber attack on Cologne, Germany where many of the German defense product factories were located. The casualty's British losses were extremely high.

Intelligence informational revealed that in June, Hitler had begun gassing large numbers of Jewish citizens. He had built large rooms where people would be stripped naked, marched in, the doors locked and then large diesel engines would be started to gas them. Hitler hated Jewish people and was out to exterminate as many as he could find.

This news finally was discovered and it shocked the entire world. Winston Churchill was continuing his efforts to keep the British people safe, but the Germans were obviously building additional strength to potentially mount an invasion.

Carl saw the situation with a new set of eyes and his assessment was that things had to change dramatically before the German efforts could be stopped. He privately feared that all of Great Britain might be invaded and overtaken by the Germans.

America's General Eisenhower was developing several new war plans and on June 25th, he arrived in England. His arrival marked a turning point in the war, as there was additional

Kenneth Orr

military leadership in the battlefield to wage new offensives and plan better, stronger and more effective attacks on the German's strongholds.

The war in the Pacific was having an equally hard time in getting started. The Japanese were fierce fighters and the war was largely a war for islands. Islands could be used to set up American military installations and advance toward the Japanese homeland. The largest United States possession to fall was the Philippines. The Navy battleships, invading Marines and Navy aircraft carriers were becoming the front line for American Pacific War operations.

When an island could be taken the Army and Marines would set up a base that was situated to focus on taking the next island. The war in Europe was equally as frustrating. Neither war could be diminished to assist the other and both must be won.

President Roosevelt had issued mandatory orders to control the use of all war use raw materials and rationing was begun to control fuel, certain commodities and all products that used any of sensitive-use materials. Rationing coupon books were issued to every household and every purchase that involved products that were deemed critical to the war effort. Any purchase of the effected items had to be supported with a coupon. The local economies in every American town and city were all altered. The manufacturing strengths of America's factories were redirected to produce war goods and no non-essential new consumer products were to be manufactured.

One of the first household products that became scarce was soap. The ingredients use to make soap could also be used to make explosives. A box of commercial soap became a rare sight at the grocery store.

The fight was being carried to every segment of the society. Working weeks were adjusted to include seven days and the hours were expanded to whatever a person was capable and willing to work. Women were introduced into every

The Cowboy's Kids

segment of the workforce. Women were now doing jobs that had never been done by female labor, and they proved to be more than capable.

The children were also involved. School children in areas where they had "milkweed vines" growing on fences would be excused from school to go gather the mature seedpods. The white fluffy seeds inside the pods, known as "Kapoc," were usable as a filling for life vests. There were monthly "paper drives" to collect old newspaper and cardboard. Local Boy Scout movements often headed up these efforts.

Toothpaste was in short supply. If any was available, the buyer had to turn in an old used metal tube to get a new one. The news that some store had just received a case of toothpaste would always spread quickly. Long lines would form almost instantly and last until the last tube was sold.

Tin cans that were used to contain food products were to have both ends cut out, flattened and thrown into collection boxes for reuse of the metal. Every family was encouraged to plant a "Victory Garden" and grow part of their food requirements. Many people made "lye soap" by boiling grease drippings and lye together. The soap that resulted was then poured into cookie pans or bread pans to solidify. The soap cakes were either used to wash your body or shaved into a finer flake to wash clothes. The results were never hard to see. The soap was strong. One's skin would get red and their clothes would lose some color from the strong chemicals present in the soap.

Packaged cigarettes were almost never available as they were being sent to the soldiers. Men started to "roll your own". The new way to smoke became "Bugler" tobacco, "Bull Durham" in a small cloth sack and "Prince Albert" pipe tobacco, which came in a small flat tin can. Pipe smoking became more popular as raw tobacco was a little more available and the smoker could puff a few times and put his pipe out until he wanted to smoke a little more.

Kenneth Orr

The chewing gum business went to a new formula and "Fan Tan Gum" was about all that was available. The availability of real butter was low. The replacement became oleomargarine.

The first margarine was a white paste that was shaped like butter but the women were slow to use it. Then the manufacturers started adding a light yellow color to make it look more like butter and it became better accepted.

The transportation industry underwent major changes. All civilian vehicle production was halted in mid 1942. The factories were converted to make tanks, airplane parts, military trucks, jeeps and other vehicles that were going to be used to wage war. The clothing industry also switched to making military clothing, parachutes and tents. The heavy equipment business increased capacity to build more bulldozers and more earth moving machinery and all of it was painted olive drab.

The American public was just as much at war as were the troops in the battle zones. The only differences were they were not under the enemy's direct fire and they were not wearing uniforms. The political climate changed dramatically.

Prior to the war it was always a common event in America's Congress to debate the problems associated with military cost. After the war started, the debates were shifted to focus on how to get something built quickly at any cost. The role of the politician changed, they became cheerleaders for winning the war.

The American civilian population's duty station became the factories and the farmlands of the country. The war was a must-win situation and every person who was capable of making any contribution was a member of the team. We had to win!

CHAPTER 3-13
Actions and Reactions

The RAF was getting shot to pieces every time they went on a bombing mission. The standard practice at the airfield was to send out a bomber mission and then wait to see how many would return. Carl was considered a part of the ground supporting team as he was an instructor and trainer on bombsights and he was a strong leader in helping the bomber pilots understand their airplanes. On several occasions Carl would be asked to fill in for a co-pilot or bombardier on an airplane crew that was short handed. Carl flew seven missions in these roles but was never assigned as a full time crewmember to any one bomber. Luck was with him. He was able to survive all of these missions and came back to England, unharmed.

In early 1943 there were several bombing missions where the losses were extremely high. The operations commanders would try to reorganize flight crews from airplanes that were too damaged to fly again into new airplanes. The improving supply of new equipment from the United States factories made this possible. Every new airplane needed to have a full crew of qualified personnel. Major Goodwin was deeply involved with the crew development process. Major Malone had been a senior pilot for a long time. He had helped Carl develop his skills in bomber crew selection and it was vital that the new team of men would bond together and instantly become an effective fighting team.

Kenneth Orr

There were always shortages of qualified gunners, radio operators and bombardiers. On a late Sunday evening in May the operations commander was planning a new crew for a B-17 nicknamed "Chief Firewater". The airplane had been given this name because several of the crewmembers were from Native American decent.

The airplane was a veteran of six successful missions and the Pilot, Captain "Frances Trick", was a skilled pilot and recognized leader. The current crew had been together for all six missions. On the last mission the bombardier had been hit by a bullet from a German fighter and killed. They had already dropped their bomb load, and even with the damages, they were able to fly back to the English airfield. The airplane had been repaired to an acceptable flying condition and was scheduled to become a part of the next day's air raid over Germany.

The Operations Commander had been promised four additional bombardiers but they had not yet arrived. Major Malone's assistant planner called Carl and asked him if he would fill that flight crew position for a mission or until some additional qualified personnel became available. This would be his eighth bomber flight and he gladly said, "yes".

Carl was eager to fly on this mission as he had enjoyed the experiences he had on previous bombing raids. The time for the preflight crew briefing arrived and Carl was identified as the fill in replacement for the missing man. Everyone knew Carl and he was immediately accepted. Prior to flying the Aircraft Captain went over his standard instructions.

1. There will be absolute radio silence until I give the OK to use the onboard system.

2. German fighter aircraft are anticipated to attack as we cross the border between France and Germany and our fighter support today will be Spitfires and P-47's. They will stay with us as long as we need them or until we are about 75 miles from our target. Then they must turn back or run out of fuel.

The Cowboy's Kids

3. Our target today is Munich, Germany. Several major factories on the north side of town are known to be vital to Germany's defense efforts. We are specifically going to target the factories in this aerial photograph. Then he put a picture of the facility on an easel and explained the details.

4. Our bomb load will be un-armed as it is loaded. The arming operation will occur about five minutes prior to our arrival over the target. If we take a hit and are unable to make it to our target we will drop the bombs somewhere on our way back, hopefully on a secondary target or some non-developed site.

5. Your skills and your buddy's help are just as important to making this mission successful as are mine in flying the airplane. Our Second Officer, Lt. Harry Crow, is equally skilled at flying, and if I become disabled he can do a good job of getting us home. Major Goodwin is also a skilled pilot and when his job of dropping the bombs is over he will be available if needed.

Then he asked for questions and there were none. Then all of the men bowed their heads and the captain led them in a prayer. The were all aware that their lives were in danger and wanted to spend a moment in quiet prayer before they got onboard the airplane.

The ground crew had the airplane fully loaded with bombs and the fuel tanks were topped off. The crew did a small walk around and then climbed into the airplane. Everyone took his or her assigned position. The Captain had assigned everyone a short one-syllable name that he would use to talk to them. He wanted any communication in the air to be quick, clear and properly directed. Carl's nickname was simply "Carl."

The four engines were started and the airplane pulled into a line of other airplanes getting ready to take. Today's mission would have flight formations of seven bombers flying in a V-pattern and seven V-patterns in the entire flight formation.

Public domain from the US Government
B-17 In Flight

The bomber formation had planned a route to take them south over most of France and then turn to the east and approach the German border. The escort fighters were going to follow them into this area and depending on the situation stay with them as long as their fuel would allow. The take off went as planned and soon all of the bombers were in their assigned places flying across the English Channel. The men knew that they must put on their oxygen masks as the airplane gained altitude. The thin air at higher altitudes was not adequate to keep them alive and thinking sharply and an oxygen mask was always a high altitude flying requirement.

The sky was full of low altitude clouds and there were no ground features available to assist in navigation. The compass and lead from the command bomber were the only navigation tools. A squadron of Spitfires joined the bombers as they reached the French shore. Then, like a blanket was removed, the clouds disappeared.

The ground below was clear and green and from 35,000 feet it looked like a flat and spacious plane. The mission proceeded as planned and with a planned turn they headed

The Cowboy's Kids

straight for the target. Shortly afterwards, the fighter escort turned and headed back to England.

Carl was sitting next to the nose gunner and they struck up a conversation. They had seen each other on the airfield but had never been in any real conversations. The gunner said he was from Muskogee, Oklahoma and he was part Cherokee. Carl immediately told him his grandmother was a full-blooded Cherokee from somewhere in Carolina.

The men bonded with this information. They struck up a different conversation discussing this relationship. The gunner's name was Charlie White. He also had an Indian name, which only he could pronounce. He said it was "Running Buffalo" in the English language.

Then, with an urgency that was obvious, the pilot shouted to everyone, target zone in ten minutes. Just then two German fighter planes came zooming overhead. The fighter escort had been gone for about five minutes and the bombers had to depend on their own firepower. The gunners all took their positions and made their cannons ready to fire. In a minute, or less a pack of German fighters came in behind the bomber squadron and began firing.

Two airplanes were hit, one was a British Lancaster and the other was an American B-17. Both were still flying but the Lancaster was smoking in the right wing engine area. All of the aircraft continued on toward the target zone. Everyone knew that to break away from the formation would probably mean being shot down. This area was definitely not somewhere you wanted to go down. The Lancaster had apparently had an engine fire but the on board extinguisher had stopped the fire for now.

Munich, Germany was dead ahead and the bomb bay doors were opened. The bombsight flight system was initiated. The airplane was being guided by the bombsight targeting system working with the pilot. Large black smoke billows were appearing all around the squadron and everybody knew this was "flack." The airplane directly to the left was

Kenneth Orr

hit by one of these explosions and a piece of the tail flew away. Another Lancaster was hit by fighter bullets and immediately went into a steep and obvious crashing dive.

White parachutes began to come out of the escape door and the plane continued to fall. Carl counted three parachutes and the Lancaster went out of sight. One of the gunners went to the bomb racks and armed all of the bombs. The operation was simple, remove a pin so the detonation system can function.

The target was now right ahead and the bombsight showed that the bombs were about ready to be dropped. Carl had his eyes glued to the eyepiece on the bombsite and as the crosshairs lined up he pushed the button to drop the bombs.

When the right moment arrived, Carl released the bombs at the same time he yelled, "Bombs Away." The bombs leaving the airplane was more than just dumping a payload on the enemy. It was also a major flying adjustment. The weight of the bombs leaving made the airplane instantly lighter and an immediate small gain in altitude took place.

All of the airplanes were experiencing the same situation and luckily there were no mid air collisions. The bomb doors were closed immediately as they were a big source of drag. The Pilot took command of the airplane flight from the bombsight and the entire squadron turned left and began to circle to go home.

Carl had not paid any attention to the nearby machine-gunner, as his bomb drop duties were his first priority. He had heard the gun firing almost continuously and knew that the fighters were trying to inflict as much damage as they could to the bomber.

Now that the bombs were gone, Carl went to see what was happening to the gunner. He was fully occupied with his gun. When he saw Carl was available, he asked him to hand him a box of ammunition that was stowed in a space

The Cowboy's Kids

near his gun. Carl got the ammunition box and opened the top. The shells were on a tape and when loaded, the cannon would advance them from the box into the gun.

The flack continued and Carl saw five more airplanes go down. Two were British Lancaster's and there were no parachutes. Carl looked to the rear of their airplane and saw a large hole just in front of the top turret gunner's position. The top turret gun was silent and it looked like the gunner was bleeding. Carl went to see and it was quickly obvious that he had been hit by something and was dead. The flack finally quit. When the squadron reached the French border the German fighters retreated. The return trip to England was sad. The pilot told the crew that by the count of the squadron lead airplane, they had lost 16 airplanes.

He added, there were three additional planes with damage so bad they may not make it home. They are trying to maintain enough altitude to ditch in the English Channel so friendly forces can pick them up. Carl said a prayer and thanked the man upstairs that his airplane was still able to go home.

One of the Lancaster bombers was flying just ahead of Carl's B-17 and it had a large hunk out of the right wing. The Lancaster was a durable airplane and could still fly with a lot of damage. Carl was impressed.

The English Channel was coming into view and the clouds they had flown through when they left the airbase were still hanging over the water. All of the German fighters were now gone and the flight back home from here should be routine. The Pilot came on the radio and said a B-17 just ahead had lost all engine power and was going to try to ditch in the area next to the French coast. Carl looked out the front enclosure and the airplane was descending quickly. Seven parachutes came out of the airplane. Carl knew there were at least two or three more men still in the airplane. The plane continued to go down and disappeared behind the squadron.

Kenneth Orr

The pilot said one of the airplanes on the rear of the formation was going to circle and see if the plane landed somewhere in a safe spot or crashed. The rest of the formation continued, on toward England.

The English Channel was now under the wings and the Pilot was descending to get into an approach pattern to get ready to land. The airfield was about 60 miles away and the formation had to land in a planned sequence to avoid ground confusion or accidents in the air. The Squadron Commander had called out that five airplanes were to land first as they had serious problems and needed to get down as quickly as possible. The others would follow in the planned sequence. The Pilot said they were about 15 minutes from touchdown and they were low enough that they could stow their oxygen masks. Everyone was pleased to hear this. It was cold inside the airplane and the oxygen mask seemed to make it feel even colder.

The bomber approached the airfield and the wheels were lowered. Soon the tires were skidding on the ground and the B-17 was home. Carl was relieved. He had flown another bombing mission and survived.

These bombing run experiences were ones he would never forget. His appreciation for aerial combat had taken on a much more realistic and serious understanding. He knew that there were a lot of good men dying in this war and he was realistically upset.

The B-17 parked on the apron in its assigned space and the engines were stopped. The Pilot said a quick prayer and then told everyone to get the hatch open so the medics could get to the gunner in the turret. The medics came aboard and the first man to reach the gunner saw that he was dead. He asked everyone to exit the airplane so they could remove the body. The rest of the crew went outside and an Army truck was waiting to take them to a building for a mission debriefing. Carl jumped on the truck and sat on the back seat. He needed to go to the bathroom and

The Cowboy's Kids

wanted to get off as quickly as he could when they got to the command building.

The briefing went per the standard Army reporting procedure, and soon the crew was about ready to go get some food and liquid refreshment. The Pilot asked all of them to come with him to the Chapel and say a few words for Sgt. McLemore, the dead gunner. Everyone went with him.

After the service, the Pilot called everyone into a small meeting and told them he had been told their airplane was grounded for repairs and the crewmembers were going to be put on temporary reassignment to other flight crews, until the repairs were made.

One gunner wanted to know how long the repairs would take. The Pilot said he did not know for sure but it could be a week or more. He said they might get a new airplane from the USA if enough new ones arrived. The new equipment arrival schedule was never completely predictable. This crew was a well-bonded group of men and all of them were not anxious to be split up.

Carl went to his quarters and mail call had run while he was on his mission. There was a letter on his bunk. He picked it up and quickly saw it was from Virginia. It had been mailed over six weeks ago and had obviously been delivered by the slowest Army delivery service that was available. He opened it and began to read. The first paragraph was mostly "I love You" stuff and Carl was pleased just to see her writing.

The second paragraph was something different. Virginia had been to see a Doctor and he had told her she was going to be a mother.

She told him what the Doctor had said the arrival date might be. Carl was shocked, but overjoyed at the same time. She went on to say that she had talked to her senior officer, Kate, and she had told her that she would be discharged from the Army and allowed to go home to have her baby.

Kenneth Orr

Carl looked at the calendar in his footlocker and the timing of the birth was exactly nine months from the weekend he and Virginia had spent together in Washington.

Carl wanted to tell somebody but the only person at the airfield that Carl knew really well was Major Malone. Carl went to Major Malone's office and he was in. Carl forgot all military protocol and said, "Malone, I am going to be a daddy!" Major Malone yelled out "Congratulations, sounds like you just landed a big one this time and I am happy for you."

Major Malone got up from his chair and said, "The day is almost over so lets go celebrate." They went to the little Officers lounge where a cold beer and a shot of whiskey could usually be found. Carl ordered a round. Carl was too happy to eat and too excited to sleep so he had a few more shots of whiskey, and about 11:00 PM Major Malone helped him back to his quarters and poured him in the bed.

Two days later Major Malone received orders to transfer to North Africa and head up a B-24 bomber operation. He had known a long time this assignment was going to happen, he just did not know when.

Carl hated to see him go, as he had been his closest friend and confidant when he needed to talk to somebody. Carl knew Major Malone was walking into a very dangerous situation.

CHAPTER 3 – 14
Activity Back at Home

Barbara had almost completely shut down the old home in Bandera and was living on base at Fort Sam Houston. The plans for setting up the hospital ship were behind the original schedule, as the ship was still being used to perform other war-related duties. The available time in between was more than fully occupied with work at the base hospital.

This war was much different from other wars that had been fought in several ways. World War One was a mixture of horse drawn cannons and primitive tanks. Airplanes in World War One were very simple and flight crews of one or two people were all that were involved. The injuries were largely from bullets, exploding shells and gas attacks. This war was more mechanical and the machines and weapons of war were much more aggressive and were almost always associated with fire and burned flesh. The needs for a new patient care plan at the hospital were soon apparent.

A special ward, dedicated just to treat burns, was quickly established and the best Doctors in this field were recruited. The soldiers who had suffered burns were quick to die if a good medical treatment and proper facility to use the procedure were not available. The Army began to develop field hospital techniques that would provide some level of burn treatment. The intent was to apply treatment as soon as the injured soldier could be brought to the treatment

Kenneth Orr

area. Even with all of the best efforts a lot of soldiers were dying from burns.

The field-trained medics also needed to have new emergency treatment instructions. Burn victims are subject to much different levels of trauma and shock. Barbara became involved with the effort and soon she was spending most of her day treating new patients and working to plan for a special field hospital dedicated to burns. All new medic trainees were given a crash course in burned victim treatment and Barbara was instructing many of the classes. She was very matter-of-fact and often her classes were held with actual patients in attendance.

Barbara had received a call from Virginia and the impending news of another "Goodwin" family member was beginning to spread. Barbara was as excited as Virginia. It was now early July and the new baby was scheduled to be here sometime in late October.

Virginia was going to continue to work in the Army code office until the first of August and then be discharged. She had said that she would go to a proper home somewhere, and wait for the baby to arrive.

She told Barbara of her plan and Barbara immediately said, "Your home is now in Texas and the ranch house is setting out here in Bandera just waiting for you to get here." Virginia said, "Would Carl want me to go there?" Barbara laughed and told her what Carl wanted right now did not matter a hill of beans. He was over in England fighting a war and he didn't have time to worry about this. This was a matter for the women to take care of." Virginia agreed and said she would let Barbara know when she was getting out of the Army and what her travel plans might be.

Barbara had always wanted children and having a baby in the house, no matter who the mom and dad were, was a great objective for her to hold on to. She told herself that this child was going to somehow something wonderful to look forward to in the midst of such an ugly and savaged world

The Cowboy's Kids

situation. She knew that Carl would want to have Virginia go to Bandera and Barbara helping with the situation was her job as a member of the family while Carl was away.

In late July Virginia called Barbara and said she was mustering out of the Army on August 12th. She had checked on train tickets to San Antonio and there was a passenger car seat open that she could still get. The departure date was going to be August 13th. Travel on any public transportation was so overcrowded that train and bus line tickets had to be planned to assure seating. She would arrive in San Antonio on the 15th a little before midnight. Barbara told her to go ahead with the plan and she would meet her at the train station.

Carl had written both Barbara and Virginia when he got his last letter and let them know how excited he was. He was in a situation where he could not make phone calls and the only access he had to the outside world, was by mail. In an emergency situation the American Red Cross was there to help. He asked Virginia a lot of questions and was not sure what the Army job she was doing would mean to her having a baby.

Carl asked Barbara to get in touch with Virginia and do whatever she could to make her comfortable until he could get home. Carl was more eager than ever to get this war over and to go home to his family.

Barbara had some time off on the upcoming weekend and drove to Bandera to see how the old home was holding up. The grass needed cutting and the weeds around the old barns were getting tall. The part-time housekeeper was at the house when Barbara arrived and she said the inside was in good shape. All it needed was some dusting and somebody to live there. Barbara told her about Virginia and the upcoming need to have the house ready to have her and a new baby live there.

The housekeeper, Claria, was excited to hear the news. Barbara asked her if she could go to work full time and get

Kenneth Orr

everything ready. The answer was a quick, "yes." Barbara knew she might need to leave San Antonio and go serve on a Hospital Ship and she asked Claria if she would get the doctor lined up and stock the kitchen with all kinds of good food and baby clothes, when the time came. An agreement was reached on getting the house ready.

Barbara asked Claria if she knew a good man to cut the grass and cut the weeds. Claria said her younger brother, Felix was still home and he would surely want to make some extra money. She said he was too young for the draft and he had a health problem that would probably keep him home. Barbara told Claria to have Felix get started with the clean-up work and keep track of his time. Barbara gave Claria a sum of money large enough to cover the immediate food and other bills and put some money in her pocket. Everybody was happy. Barbara spent the night in her old bedroom and had a good night's sleep. The next morning she drove back to San Antonio.

Barbara's job was very stressful. A large number of the soldiers she was attending were obviously going to die. Barbara became a hero in their eyes and some wanted her to write letters to the people back home. Several of these letters were written just a day or two before the soldier would die. The loss of a soldier's life was always hard on Barbara. When they would say what they wanted her to write they would cry and their voices, which were already weak, would quiver and the words often were not clear.

Barbara would do the best that she could, to make the letter accurate and then she would sign the soldiers name and put, "written by an Army Nurse" at the bottom of the letter. The Chaplains were usually nearby as death was becoming a common event and it seemed like it was never going to stop.

Some of the hospital staff were growing cold and were withdrawn from all of the stress and loss of life that was all around. Barbara saw several of the better nurses go into this state and asked the head Doctor to give them some time off. They were just human like her and she knew it. She also saw what was happening to her and the stress of so much pain and death had made her a lot less comfortable with the way she was conducting her own life.

She also remembered losing her own husband to a sickness and understood the pain that one suffers when death is so near. Barbara saw herself as someone who had been near death's door and she survived. She wanted to become somebody who could help others who were going through the same experiences.

Public domain from the US Government

August came and Barbara had saved her gasoline coupons so she would make sure she would have enough gasoline to make the trip to Bandera. On the morning of August 13th she went to a local gas station and got one stamp's value of gas and paid for it. Then she went to another gas station and bought another stamp's worth. Gas stations were limited as to the amount of gasoline they could sell one customer. That would get her to Bandera and allow for a couple of trips into town with Virginia to see the Doctor and buy supplies.

Kenneth Orr

She planned on filling up the gas tank as much as she could before leaving Bandera so she could get back to San Antonio. She wanted to make sure that Virginia had a stress-free trip when she arrived. The car and gasoline to operate it should not be an issue. Barbara had no idea as to what Virginia might bring with her, but she went into a store in San Antonio and bought some baby diapers, some blankets and a little baby sized dress. Down deep she wanted Virginia to have a girl and if it were a boy the dress would still fit for a while. Barbara also bought a new Maytag washing machine that she found in a store in San Marcos, Texas. The store had ordered it before the war started and the buyer had been transferred away and never came to pick it up. Barbara knew that diapers had to be washed and a new machine would be a great assist to Virginia.

Barbara had written Carl a long letter telling him about her and Virginia's plans and she knew that Virginia had done the same. They both wanted Carl to feel good about what was happening back home and not worry about his family. He had a war to fight. They also knew that mail was slow to arrive and Carl was probably going to be moving around a lot and mail may have a hard time of catching up to him.

On the morning of August 15th, Barbara put her uniform on and went to work. Her day was full of the normal stress and changes in plans that are common in the medical field.

At 3:00 PM she went to see her supervisor and informed her that she could be off the next day, as she wanted to take Virginia to Bandera. She would need the day to get Virginia settled in and feeling comfortable in the house. The Supervisor understood and said, "Take two or three days off, you need some time away from all of this stress and this sounds like the right way to spend it." Barbara agreed and went to her quarters.

At 7:00 PM she drove downtown to the railroad station and parked her car in a lot near the unloading platform. A troop train was loading soldiers. All of them looked happy to be going somewhere else. The word on the street was that the

The Cowboy's Kids

basic training at "Lackland" Army Base was difficult and you never left there looking to return. She saw the proof written on the soldier's faces.

Barbara checked on Virginia's train. The station agent told her it was running about 15 minutes late. He added, "This troop train needs to get out of here soon so the train you are meeting can have a place to unload."

Barbara saw the urgency in his eyes and said, "These guys are happy now but when they get where they are headed those smiles will go away quick. Let'em have a little fun while they can."

The steam engine finally sounded the whistle and an "All Aboard" was heard clearly from the conductor. The train pulled out and the tracks were open.

In about five minutes a black smoke puffing engine rounded the curve and headed to the loading platform. It stopped right in front of Barbara, and Virginia saw her through the train's window. Barbara was looking into the cars and she soon spotted Virginia.

When Virginia got off, it was a reunion like neither had ever known. Virginia had her arms around Barbara and they were more like sisters than anything else. There were three trains in the station at the same time and the noise from all of the engines letting off excess steam was ear shattering.

Barbara helped Virginia get her baggage and they loaded it into her Ford. Barbara never asked Virginia any questions. She drove straight to a Mexican restaurant and Virginia was pleasantly surprised. They went in and the place was crawling with soldiers. Two unescorted women in the restaurant quickly got the guys attentions. The catcalls and whistles lasted about 30 seconds and when they got no response, they stopped.

Kenneth Orr

Virginia wanted some cold water and a large glass of iced tea. Barbara had the same. Then they ordered dinner, ate quickly and went to the car. The trip to Bandera was full of conversation and seemed like it was over almost before it started.

The housekeeper was planning to stay over for the night to help Virginia when she arrived. Her luggage was carried into the house and Barbara took it into the bedroom that would have been her mother and dad's. Virginia asked why not one of the smaller rooms. Barbara said, "This is now your home and you are going to be the mother of the next Goodwin, so you get the best room. Its that simple."

The night was spent talking and finally the plan for the next day was finalized. The women just about went to sleep in their chairs but they had so much to discuss. Barbara and Virginia went to their rooms and went to sleep. The housekeeper slept in the last vacant room.

Barbara asked Claria if she could be there more while Virginia was waiting to have the baby, and make sure everything was planned far enough in advance. Clara agreed.

Barbara had noticed that the refrigerator and food cupboard were all well stocked and told Claria she had done a good job. The new washing machine was in a small hallway and next to an outside door. Virginia saw it and said, "You sure have thought of everything Barbara."

The next morning was a typical Texas August day, hot, dry and a mild wind from the west. Barbara and Virginia went to Bandera and met with the local female focused Doctor.

Virginia had her medical records from the Army and he reviewed them in close detail. He said, "You look as healthy as a horse and that baby looks like it's doing fine." They went to a local shoe store and Virginia got a pair of new black boots. She said, "Now I feel like a real Texan." Barbara just laughed and told her to keep them shiny so they would look good when Carl got to come home.

The Cowboy's Kids

The second day was a lot less structured. Barbara had a lot to talk about and as a nurse she had a lot of health advise for Virginia. Everybody had a good day and about five PM Barbara started her drive back to San Antonio. When she got about half way, she saw a gas station and went in. She spent her last gas-rationing coupons on five gallons of gasoline. Twenty-one cents a gallon was a high price as compared to the normal nineteen cents she had always been paying in San Antonio.

CHAPTER 2-15
Bombing The Germans

Carl was continuing to serve as a bombsight and bomber pilot instructor. His work was seemingly never done. The repair rate on bombsights and related battle damages were always a major problem after every bomb raid. He was a good friend to many of the pilots, as they trusted his work and his quick work made him a valuable part of their ground support team.

Two weeks after Major Malone was gone the new operations officer ran into another problem with manpower. He was still short on qualified bombardiers. He knew that Carl had been used to fill out flight crews in the past, so he went to Carl and told him he was going to fly on a B-17 bombing raid the next morning.

Carl was always willing, but he knew his luck was running thin. He could easily fill these vacancies, and so far had always been able to come home with a good bomb drop and a relatively safe airplane. The bomb crews were all made up of great young men, but nobody ever took another man's place as well as Carl.

Carl asked which pilot was going to be flying and the officer said it was a new Pilot named Captain Calvin Quinn. Carl did not know him so he went to find him and discuss the role he was going to serve in the mission. The Captain was

The Cowboy's Kids

a smart, but short-tempered young man. He was rather cocky and short with Carl. Carl could tell he was nervous and had a lot of fears about the bomb raid. This was going to be his second mission and he was not comfortable with the target they were going to bomb. His first mission was shortened when he had to turn back because of an engine problem. He had never seen actual combat and his nerves were getting to him. Carl tried to talk to him but he was not willing to listen.

The next morning came early and the pre-flight briefing was routine as compared to the others Carl had attended. The mission was going to bomb a series of factories located in the area north of Cologne, Germany. This area was well protected from both the ground and from the air. There were two German fighter bases in the area and the cannons on the ground and ack-ack guns were well positioned to block most approaches to the area. Carl told Captain Quinn he had been over this target before and wanted to expand his pilot's knowledge of what to expect.

He soon found out that the Captain's fear of getting hit was a much greater issue than he had expected. The Pilot's obvious level of concern kept Carl on edge. The bombing force took off and Captain Quinn's airplane took their place in the middle of the massive formation.

The trip to the target was especially dangerous as the German fighters planes were everywhere. There were 48 bombers in the original formation and German fighters destroyed seven of them before they reached the target zone. The balance of the formation re-grouped into a close formation and continued to fly toward the target zone.

About 15 miles away from the target the ack-ack guns began pumping shrapnel shells all around the formation. Several planes took serious damage. The B-17 Carl was in, got a hit on the left wing and another hit in the number three engine. One piece of shrapnel came into the nose of the plane and struck Carl's right leg. The impact was hard and Carl saw the blood start to flow. There was a lot of pain

Kenneth Orr

but he was right in the middle of a bombing run and could not stop his work to try and stop the bleeding. In about three minutes the bomber was right over the target and the bomb load was dropped. Carl watched the bombs fall and they hit right on the target.

Carl made sure that the pilot was now flying the airplane and the bombsite's interface was terminated. He took out his handkerchief and wrapped it around his leg, trying to stop the flow of blood. The nose gunner was fully occupied shooting at German fighter planes and did not notice that Carl had been hit. In about five minutes Carl got the bleeding stopped and he knew he had probable suffered a broken leg. He was in a lot of pain. He looked up at the gunner and saw he was also injured. Blood was coming from his right arm.

The formation turned and headed back toward the French border and as they crossed the first turning area the number three engine quit. The right wing had taken a second major hit from a cannon. The Pilot had major concerns and told everybody to be ready to jump if the order was given. He was concerned that the plane was not going to make it to the home airfield. About six minutes later the number four engine quit. The right wing had a lot of damage and there was oil streaming over the top of the wing. Carl and the gunner were both injured. They moved to an area in the airplane next to the escape hatch, just in case they were ordered to jump.

The airplane was rapidly loosing altitude and it was now obvious that they were going down. The airfield in England was almost an hour of flying time away. It was now obvious the B-17 flight crew needed to jump. The altitude was still sufficient to use parachutes. The area below the airplane had developed a thick cloud cover and the airplane was coming down fast.

The pilot came on the radio and told everyone they were 5,000 feet above ground and they needed to start bailing out.

The Cowboy's Kids

The two flank gunners came and helped Carl to the escape door. They made sure he was strapped into his parachute correctly. They told him what to do to open his chute. He had never jumped before and the whole thing was going to be a new and somewhat concerning experience, especially with an injured leg.

The escape hatch was opened and Carl stepped out into the opening and immediately was falling toward the earth. It was almost noon and the upper sky was bright. The thick, gray cloud cover directly below was hiding the ground and Carl was going to land somewhere below these clouds. Carl saw the smoke coming from the right side of the falling B-17 and he knew it was going down very soon. More parachutes were now coming out of the escape hatch. The B-17 was soon out of sight.

Carl quickly fell into the clouds and started to do as he had been instructed, to open his parachute. The pilot chute came out and then the main chute deployed. When it opened it stopped his free-fall with a sudden snap and suddenly he was hanging and swaying back and forth under the canopy. He was still in the clouds with no idea as to what was below. He descended for almost a minute and then he broke through the bottom of the clouds and about 500 feet below him was a farm field that looked like a lot like one from back in Texas. He was approaching the ground rapidly and he pulled on the parachute shroud line like he had been told to do, and the parachute seemed to tip. The wind was calm and he landed in a rolling touchdown and it seemed like he would never stop.

He had landed safely on the ground and his leg was starting to bother him. When he put his weight on it, the pain was obvious. Carl knew he was behind German lines and needed to take cover as soon as he could. Survival school had taught him that the first thing he needed to do was to hide his parachute. The Germans would know he was in the area if they found it.

Kenneth Orr

Carl unbuckled his chute harness and rolled it up into a small ball. He carried it to a hedgerow that was about 30 feet from where he had landed. He put it under a small thick green bush and it was practically hidden from view when he left it. He then walked as best he could, down the hedgerow and found a small grove of trees. He had been told that the Germans used dogs to track downed fliers. He thought to go too far would leave a better trail for them to find. He was also concerned about his leg. He found a tall bushy tree with thick foliage and decided to climb it, if he could.

After a lot of effort and pain he reached a branch that was about 12 feet above the ground. He made himself as comfortable as he could. He decided he needed to take a short rest and look over the nearby landscape to see what the situation around him might be.

There was a farmhouse about 600 to 700 yards away from the tree grove. There were two people out in the yard. He wondered if they had seen him come down. If they had spotted him, he hoped they were friendly.

The afternoon went without any event and Carl used the time to check on his leg and to check out his sidearm and make sure it was loaded and ready to use, if needed.

About an hour before sunset, the people in the farmhouse went out to their barn and opened the doors. In about ten minutes they came riding out in a wagon pulled by two horses and with a pile of hay in the back. They drove out to where Carl had landed and somehow were able to come directly toward him. As they approached he saw that one of the people was a man and the other was a woman. They came to within 20 feet of the tree and in an accented French voice said in English, "We are friends. We are in the French resistance and want to help you." Carl just listened and they repeated the same message again. Carl wanted to make sure this was not a trick just to get him to surrender.

The man was looking all around and somehow he spotted Carl. He got down from the wagon and came to the base of

The Cowboy's Kids

the tree. He spoke English and said, "Come quickly, there are Germans in the area and we will protect you." Carl had no better option so he came down the tree as best as he could. He knew he had been discovered and the only hope he had of staying free from the Germans was that the man was telling the truth.

When he got on the ground the bloody right leg was obvious. The man said, "Come quick, in the back of the wagon under the hay." Carl went in and under the hay like a snake and he wondered what was ahead. In about five minutes the man drove the wagon to where Carl had hid his parachute and retrieved it. He put it under the hay to hide it and than drove back into the barn. The barn doors were closed and the man and a woman came to talk with Carl.

They gave their names as Pierre and Marsella and said that was all he needs to know. He had his name on his uniform and they said, "Carl, are you a German?" Carl smiled and said he was an American. They asked him about how he had hurt his leg. Carl told them, "Shrapnel, in an aerial attack," and stopped there.

Pierre said they had watched him come down in his parachute and had to wait to see what happened before they did anything. They were concerned that the Germans might have also seen him.

The lady said she had some skills in medicine as a home nurse and said she would look at his injured leg. They hobbled Carl into a small back room in the barn and told him this was a safe place and he could spend the night here. They then brought him some fresh water, some wine and a sandwich.

Carl thanked them and the lady said, "Take off your pants." At first, Carl thought the lady was forward, and then he realized she wanted to see his wounded leg.

Carl allowed Marsella to look at his injured leg. Marsella found a small hunk of sharp metal still imbedded in Carl's

Kenneth Orr

leg. She said it had to be removed and it would hurt a little. Carl said, "I guess I have no choice. He took a drink of wine, laid back and said, "Go get it." The hunk was bigger than it looked and the pulling out process was extremely painful. Carl just bit down on his teeth and suffered. Soon it was out. Marsella poured some alcohol on the wound and then she covered the wound with some red medicine she said would kill germs. Carl let her finish the dressing and put on a clean pair of civilian pants the man had brought from somewhere. Pierre then gave Carl a shirt and told him to dress like a French farmer and his identity would be easier to hide.

Carl put his military clothes in a small sack and put it under a board. . Carl hid his sidearm under his shirt.

Carl knew he was in safe hands for now, but he had no idea as to what to expect in the next few days. The thoughts of visiting with Virginia back in Washington and Barbara living in Texas started to cross his mind and he was worried. He thought a lot about his training in survival and started wondering how many of the men, on the B-17 had jumped from, had made it to the ground safely. He knew that the airplane was going down fast.

The next morning came slowly. Carl had not been able to get any real sleep or rest. His leg was sore and standing was almost too painful to think about. Pierre came out to the barn just before sunrise and went to Carl's small hiding room. He told him that the resistance movement had an underground system set up to help downed airmen who were in shot down in France behind the German's lines.

Pierre said he had been on his radio during the night checking on several options that might be available for him. Carl said he wanted to get back to England somehow and he would appreciate any help that Pierre would give him. As they were concluding the discussion Marcella came out to the barn with some warm food and fresh bandage material for Carl's leg. Carl was hungry and he ate everything she brought. She then said, "Pants down again!" Carl understood and did

The Cowboy's Kids

the whole process to let her check and redo the dressing. The leg was swollen but the wound did not appear to be getting any worse.

Pierre said Carl should stay there for a few days until a man with a motorcar was scheduled to come by. He would take Carl to a small town about five kilometers from the ocean and from there another planned move would be attempted. Carl agreed and settled back into his room knowing that all was not lost.

The days were long and the nights were longer. There were German troops in the area and their fighter planes were common sounds as they passed overhead. Carl also could hear what sounded like a giant swarm of Texas honeybees approaching when the Allied Army bombers were flying bombing raids into Germany. The farm was almost directly in the normal flight path for several German targets.

The day's passed slowly and soon it had been two full weeks since Carl had arrived. The transportation Carl was awaiting had not arrived and the waiting was getting to him.

Carl asked Pierre what might have happened and the answer came back with some concern. "The driver has not been seen for a few days and we fear he may have been caught by the Germans."

Pierre said we have another plan but I need to know something about you. Carl said, "What do you need to know?" Pierre asked Carl if he could fly an airplane. Carl asked him, "Why he wanted to know?" Pierre said he knew where there was an old French airplane called a "Spad" that is probably in good flying condition. Carl said, "Where is it located?"

Pierre said that an old man who was a fighter pilot in World War One had owned a late model Spad and had stored it in a barn about three kilometers from the farm. He flew it about every month and was a meticulous maintenance person. There was an old airfield there in the first war and

Kenneth Orr

the old man who owned it had flown the plane regularly until he died about four years ago. The local people never did anything with the airplane and it was still there from his latest report.

Carl was getting anxious. A Spad was not much different from his old Jenny and he knew if the engine would run and the airframe was in reasonable condition, he could fly it.

The next plan would be to go see the airplane and get some feel for its condition. Carl's leg was feeling better but it had taken a crooked twist as it was healing. He knew he would need to work the foot pedals in the old airplane to fly it properly but he was looking at this as a small but manageable problem. He wanted to get out of France alive and this might be his only opportunity.

CHAPTER 3 – 16
Planning For An Escape

The next two days were spent on developing a plan to go see the old airplane. The weather was wet and the opportunity to go out too far from the farm could draw unwanted German soldiers attention. Carl knew that his protectors would be shot on the spot if they were caught hiding an American. He also knew that the Germans were well entrenched in local people's homes, enjoying their food, wine and available young female pleasures. This situation was well known in the community but there was little that the local people could do to halt the German's unbridled behavior.

The French resistance movement was active in many areas, and drawing attention away from downed airmen was always a high priority. They would create incidents in the small towns to occupy the German troops while they moved airmen to new destinations. All of these activities were well planned and were focused on areas where the Germans were known to have significant troop levels. Carl was aware of this activity and was glad he had been lucky enough to get help from this underground effort.

Carl got to know Pierre well enough to discuss some of his Texas home life. He told him he was married and he had grown up on a ranch in south Texas. He also told him that he had just learned his wife was going to have a baby and he was very concerned that he was not with her.

Kenneth Orr

Pierre told Carl that his family had been farming the same ground they were living on, for several generations. They had endured several wars and all sorts of political changes. The worst experiences were probably the killing of so many men in World War One. He pointed to the horses in the barn and said that they were descended from horses that the American soldiers had left after the first war was over. Pierre was bragging on the horses and said they were good workhorses and could be used as riding horses.

Pierre also bragged on the Americans as they had used his barn as a blacksmith shop to keep the World War One Army horses and fighting equipment, in good working order. When they left France they left all of their blacksmith tools. Pierre said he was still using them.

Pierre told Carl that his dad had built the small room he was using to hide the children while the war was at their doorstep. The room was well hidden in the rear of the barn and the only people that knew about it were his family and a few trusted members of the French Resistance movement. Carl told Pierre that his father had raised horses and that the Army used some of the horses in France. The two men bonded a little closer when they discovered a possible link that war had put into their lives.

On the next day, the sky had a very low ceiling and the road was so thick with fog that the fences just ahead were barely visible. Marsella changed the dressing on Carl's injured leg and Carl put on clean French farm style clothing. Pierre asked Carl if he was well enough to ride a horse. Carl looked at him and said, "I am from Texas and horses are my favorite form of transportation." Pierre said, "Let's saddle up and go see the old airplane, the fog will help us keep hidden." Two saddles were put on the farm horses and soon they were riding in the back woods and cutting across short sections of open farm fields.

Pierre pulled his horse up in front of an old building that looked a lot more like a hay barn than a hangar. He helped

The Cowboy's Kids

Carl get down so he did not hurt his leg. They went inside using a small side door.

There it was. The old Spad was in immaculate condition and the bright paint on the wings was almost as shiny as the day it was made. Carl went to the front and pulled the propeller a few times and said, "This airplane is in great shape. The engine has great compression and turns freely." Carl asked, "Is there any gasoline anywhere so we can make sure it has enough fuel to get to England?" Pierre said he knew where he could get some fresh gas. He said he would go and get the gas and Carl could put it in the airplane's fuel tank. Then he could see if the plane's engine would start.

Pierre said, "Wait here". He went to a building close by and brought back a five-gallon American "jerry can" that was full of gasoline. He said the resistance movement had stolen several cans of gas from the Germans who had previously captured it from the Americans. He added, "We have a lot more." Carl poured the gas into the tank and waited while Pierre went for more. Soon the tank was full. Carl took a small rag and put some gas on it and squeezed it over the engine's air intake and made sure the engine had some level of prime.

Carl looked inside the cockpit and found the magneto switch. He placed it in the "on" position. He set the throttle to a low speed and went back to the front of the airplane. His leg was hurting but he had no concern about the pain at that point. He just wanted to see if the airplane engine would start.

After about six good spins, he heard the engine catch and soon the engine was running smoothly at idle speed. The noise was very loud as the big doors on the front of the building were shut. Carl looked at Pierre said, "Pierre, you just found me my ride home. I will remember you all of my life." Carl then shut the engine down, as he did not want the loud sound of the running engine to be heard.

Pierre asked him when he wanted to leave. Carl looked at him and said, "lets go outside a minute". The area in front

Kenneth Orr

of the building was flat and the field that was just ahead was level as far as Carl could see. The fog was lifting a little and Carl stood there a moment and said, "Pierre, I am ready to go right now. Tell me which way the coast is located and about how far I will need to go to get out over the English Channel. I will get this airplane in the air and headed that way as soon as we a can pull it out." Pierre pointed toward the right and said, "The coast is about 20 kilometers in that direction. The channel is about 60 kilometers wide at that point and the English coast is always foggy this time of the year". Carl understood and nodded his head.

Pierre opened the building's double doors and both men pulled the airplane out into the early morning fog. The nose was pointed toward the open field and Carl found a small log to put under the left front wheel.

He asked Pierre to help him get going by pulling the wood away when he signaled. Pierre agreed. Carl went to Pierre and gave him a strong hug and told him how much he appreciated what he and Marcella had done for him. Carl said a final goodbye, gave Pierre a big hug and shook his hand for one last time.

Carl restarted the engine and let it warm up for a couple of minutes. Then, with some unbridled and painful effort he climbed himself into the cockpit. Carl checked over the instruments to get some idea as to what was there and how they were working. There was an old pilot's cap hanging on the instrument panel and Carl put it on his head. It was not much protection from the weather, but it would help keep him warm while in the air.

The engine had warmed a little more and Carl signaled to Pierre to pull the wood wheel chock. Pierre did his job and Carl gave the airplane more throttle. The engine responded flawlessly and the sound was music to Carl's ears.

The Spad rolled quickly onto the grassy field and Carl instantly gave it full throttle. In less than 200 feet the airplane was in the air and Carl was on his way back toward England.

Public domain from the US Government

CHAPTER 3 – 16
A Flight to Remember

The Spad was lifting above the ground quickly. Carl looked on the instrument panel to find what the altimeter was doing. He found a simple altimeter and the readings said that the airplane was about 1,000 kilometers above the ground. Carl could see to the north for about a mile. The heavy fog and low thick clouds were blocking any further vision. Carl remembered his basic combat flight instruction back at San Antonio and how he had learned that thick clouds were a good place to hide. He climbed to about 1,800 kilometers and was completely engulfed in a dark and well formed cloud formation.

Carl knew from information he had seen in planning bombing missions that was high enough to clear any hills or towers that were known to be in the area. The moisture in the clouds made the inside of the cockpit damp, cold and slick but these issues were of little concern at this point.

The next concern was to head the airplane for the English Channel. Carl knew he needed to fly accurately to reach the coast and then go straight to England. Fuel was still a concern. Carl had no idea as to how long the tank of fuel he had started with would last. He found the compass and swung the nose of the airplane to the right until he was pointed on a course of 345 degrees. He remembered the compass setting on the bomb run as they headed home. He knew that this heading would lead to the coastline and then

The Cowboy's Kids

across the channel. This setting also was in agreement with the direction that Pierre had pointed.

The Spad was a spunky little airplane. The old Jenny he had owned had similar handling characteristics but the Spad was faster and more responsive to all of the controls. The Jenny was a two-passenger airplane and had a longer fuselage and the wings were longer. The Spad was a smaller and more compact airplane with a much stronger engine. The foot pedals were easy to operate and his injured leg was not causing him any additional pain from flying.

This airplane had one cannon mounted on the nose. Some of the later model airplanes had been converted into sporting airplanes much like the old barnstorming planes back in the states. It was really fun to fly.

The airplane continued to travel toward the north and the time was passing like a slow running river. Carl desperately wanted to get out over the English Channel and get into air space where he felt safe.

As long as he was over France he knew he was over German occupied territory and any kind of airplane related problem would mean more danger. He did not want to go down and be a German prisoner. His leg was also a concern, as he knew he could not run if he had a chance.

Virginia was on his mind and he was wondering where she was living right now and how she was doing with a baby on the way. He started to think that he might never make it back to see her, and the baby would never see him.

He also wondered what would happen to Barbara if he were to be lost in the war. He and Barbara had always shared life's experiences and after she had lost her husband, this bond between her and Carl had became much more important to both of them.

All of these thoughts were swirling around in his head and he kept his eye trained on the compass. He was continually

Kenneth Orr

correcting the flight path to stay on course. The wind was coming from the east. He knew that wind was compromising the exact direction of flight.

An hour passed and Carl estimated he should be well past the French coastline. He wanted to go to a lower altitude to see what was down below. He considered this would be a safe move, but still was not completely convinced that he was out of the danger zone. Finally, he got up his nerve and decided to go down a little and take a good look.

Carl reset the throttle set back to about 60% power and the cruise speed started to slow. The airspeed indicator was not calibrated in miles per hour like American airplanes. It was in kilometers. He slowly guided the airplane to a lower altitude and an air speed of about 100 kilometers. Below where he had been flying, he came into a thinner layer of clouds. He looked down and there was open water everywhere.

He was over the English Channel. If his calculations were correct he should be seeing the western shoreline of England very soon. The east wind was blowing whitecaps on the ocean and the sea looked rough and dangerous.

The overhead clouds were still thick and the morning light was gradually growing stronger. He knew that the cloud cover was thinner up ahead as daylight's glow on the horizon was stronger. There was a consistent stiff wind from the east and Carl had to turn the airplane toward the east to keep from being pushed back toward the French coastline.

The water had small whitecaps everywhere and they were present as far as Carl could see. Then as quickly as a light bulb could be turned on, there was a coastline off to the left almost parallel to his flight path. There was a point of land jetting out into the ocean dead ahead. This had to be England and Carl was starting to feel some level of relief. He was out of German occupied France and back over a friendly country.

The Cowboy's Kids

The airplane crossed into the English countryside and there were no familiar landmarks or indicators that could help Carl determine where he had arrived. He started looking for a highway or some other ground features to help him find a friendly place to land. Then he started to thinking about what was going to happen when he landed.

He said to himself, "What would a man dressed as a French farmer be doing flying a World War One airplane into England? His landing would certainly be at some unknown place and the reception he received could be dangerous. Would he be considered as an unusual Frenchman or a German spy? He did have his American Identification in his billfold and his Army dog tags hanging around his neck. He thought that some quick talk about his identity he might be able to get to the right people before he was shot.

Then he started to think about the way he had left Pierre. He was wondering what might have happened to him and did he get home without any problems? He never knew Pierre's last name for sure but he saw some papers in the barn that were addressed to a man named "LeMonde". That must have been his last name.

He told himself that there are good people everywhere in the world and it is such a shame that war has to make life so difficult for everyone. He was convinced that the Allied Forces were going to win the war. There was no good reason for a mad man like Hitler to ever expand his grip on good people. Carl always believed that good will win over evil in the long run. The war would pass and peace, in some form will be restored.

Carl looked at the fuel gauge and if the gauge was working correctly, he still had almost a half of the fuel left. He decided to continue to fly north and hopefully he would find an airfield or some reasonable and civilized location to put down. The clouds were lifting and suddenly he saw a small airplane flying just ahead and to the right of his Spad. The plane came closer and he saw it was a British Spitfire.

Kenneth Orr

The pilot saw him and they waived at each other. The Spad was obviously not being considered an enemy fighter and the Spitfire pilot was not going to shoot him down.

Carl was in an open cockpit, had on an old style flight cap and was obviously cold. The Spitfire pilot was inside a closed cockpit but the smiles between the two were obviously not signs of fear. Carl put his hand outside of the cockpit and pointed "down". The other pilot saw his gesture and answered with a similar signal. Carl flew in behind the Spitfire and followed him. In about ten minutes the Spitfire cut power and began to land. Carl followed and soon a runway was in clear sight.

There were lots of American bombers setting on the side of the field and a lot of Spitfires and British Lancaster's lined up on the other side. The view was a major relief for Carl and he knew he was about to land in a friendly place. Carl also saw both British and American flags flying over a small building. He let the Spitfire land first and then followed him down. He knew he was landing at another RAF airfield that was about 50 kilometers south of the airfield where he was assigned.

When he touched down he taxied over to a big building that looked like a command center. He positioned the plane to be out of the main traffic pattern and killed his engine. Two military police came out to greet him and they were Americans.

The first MP to reach the Spad said, "Sir, what's your business flying into here?" Carl said, "I am an American and I just escaped from France. I have identification and I really need somebody to help me get out of this damn airplane, my leg is injured."

The second MP went to the building in a fast dash and soon an ambulance pulled up next to the Spad. Two corpsmen jumped out and went to the cockpit and began to talk to Carl. They had him out and sitting on a small stool in a very quick time. Carl reached into his shirt and pulled out his dog

The Cowboy's Kids

tags. The identification process went quickly and Carl knew he was with friends. One of the medics looked at Carl's leg and said, "Let's get this man to the hospital so his leg can be looked at." Carl was loaded into the ambulance and soon he was being looked at by a military Doctor.

The Doctor asked Carl how he was hurt and Carl told him his story. The entire ordeal had been spread over a month and a half and Carl was tired, mentally worn out and suffering from an infection that had started in his leg. The bandages and medical patch job that Marsella had done was outstanding considering the circumstances but there had been little she could do to fight an internal infection.

The Doctor said his leg had also been broken and the bone was mending but it was going to cause his leg to be crooked. He told Carl that his leg needed to be repaired surgically and the infection was also a real medical concern.

The Base Operations commander came over to see Carl. Carl told him about all of the things he had experienced and praised the help he had received from the French farmer and his wife. The commander, a Lt. Colonel, took down all of Carl's personal information and went to the personnel officer with the data.

They looked up the information on a data sheet that had been issued about a month ago and found his name listed as "Missing In Action." They knew that this information had been issued back to Washington D.C. Army headquarters and his nearest of kin had probably already been notified of his status.

The base personnel Officer sent a message to the Army's Washington headquarters using the quickest method to inform them that Major Carl Goodwin had been found and was alive. This information needed to be sent to the same family member who would have received the first message.

CHAPTER 3 – 17
News and More News

San Antonio's civilian population had become extremely involved with the war effort in both the European and Pacific war theaters. The Army Hospital at Fort Sam Houston was training combat medics as fast as the men could learn basic medical procedures. Large numbers of civil service employees were working at all of the local military bases adding support to the war support efforts.

Barbara had been told she would not be sent to serve on a hospital ship and was needed to be a burns care trainer and to help with the patient load at the hospital. She was happy to hear the news, as she wanted to be in Texas when Virginia delivered her baby.

In early September, at about 3 PM in the afternoon, Barbara got a call to come to the main hospital office. She was never surprised to get a message like this as many of the daily hospital issues were causing overloads and Barbara was an excellent helper in many areas. Barbara went to the office and a Captain she had never met asked her if she was the contact person for Mrs. Virginia Goodwin? Barbara said, "Yes, what do you want to know?" The Captain said a message had come from Washington that her husband, Major Carl Goodwin was "Missing in Action". Barbara looked at the Captain and turned pale, The Captain asked her what was wrong? Barbara replied, "He is my only brother."

The Cowboy's Kids

Barbara went to a small private room and sat down and began crying. She knew she needed to talk to Virginia in person. She also needed to call her and let her know she was coming to Bandera. But first, she had to get her own emotions under control. News concerning missing soldiers was not an uncommon event in the hospital.

Many of the young men going into battle zones as medics were also showing up on the list. The "Missing In Action" list did not mean that someone had been killed. It indicated that they had disappeared from their assigned post in a battle zone and were currently unaccounted for.

Barbara found some strength in this knowledge and decided that she would was ready to call Virginia. She told her supervisor she had to leave immediately and go to Bandera. Then, she told her the reason. The supervisor told her to take what time she needed and come back to work when she was ready.

The report from Washington said he had not returned from a bombing mission and his airplane was lost in combat. Barbara knew that Carl would do everything he could to survive and that was her only hope. She drove to Bandera and went straight to the ranch house. Virginia was sleeping on her bed and had been feeling bad for a couple of days.

The housekeeper told Barbara about her not feeling good and Barbara said she had to wake her up as she had some news that she had to know about. The stoic look on Barbara's face was a dead giveaway, it was really bad news. Barbara went into the bedroom and Virginia heard her and sat up in bed.

Barbara went to her and put her arms around her and in half tears and half talking voice told her, "Carl is missing in action somewhere over the German occupied territory." Both of the women broke down into tears and they were both unable to talk. The emotions were just too much for either of them to handle. In a few minutes Virginia swung her legs off the bed and said, "Barbara, I am not going

Kenneth Orr

to allow myself to think the worst. I know that Carl will somehow find a way to survive."

Barbara said she would do the same and she knew that he might still be alive. Whatever the situation, he will do his best to find a way to survive. They both agreed to keep up a strong hope level and the moment started to calm down.

Barbara had not seen Virginia for about two weeks and they talked about the latest Doctor's health report to Virginia. He said the baby and new mommy were both doing fine but for some reason he thought the baby might come early. Virginia said that her stress level was high pretty and that was probably why the Doctor said what he did. Barbara agreed.

Barbara and Virginia spent the rest of that day together and about noon the next day, Barbara had to leave and go back to her job. Virginia walked out on the front porch and hugged her and they said goodbye.

Barbara went back to the hospital and stopped by the front office to let them know she would be back on duty on her next scheduled shift. A Major in the hospital's staff saw her and went to her and said he had heard the news about Carl and he was sorry about his situation.

Then he said, "There are a lot of men who fly and a lot of airplanes being shot down. A lot of the crewmembers are able to get out of a damaged airplane safely and parachute to the ground. Our medics see this all of the time." He added, "The way the Germans operate is well known. They capture a soldier and put them in a prison camp and they are held there in some form of a shelter. When we take over France our Army expects to find a lot of these men and free them. Keep your hopes alive and don't allow yourself to think the worst."

He turned and started to walk away and then he turned and said,

The Cowboy's Kids

"The French Resistance Movement had found many of our downed fliers and helped them return back to England. Perhaps you brother is in their hands, prey for this to be the case." Then he walked away.

The next month was a nightmare for both Barbara and Virginia. The new baby was due in late October and both women were at a loss as to how to look at the possibility that the father may never come home. The pressure was building with every passing day. Two letters had come from Carl after he had been announced as missing. They had been written before Carl was declared as missing.

He told Virginia that he was substituting for missing crewmembers as a bombardier on occasion, and he was no better and no worse than anyone else to be put into harms way. He was a good soldier and his commitment to doing his job well was obvious, no matter how much danger it involved.

On October 4th Barbara got another urgent call to come to the office. The same Captain who had given her the first message looked at her as she entered and when she saw him he had a huge smile on his face. He said, "Let me read a message I just received to you. Major Carl Goodwin has been found and he is in England undergoing medical treatment. He is not in a life threatening condition and should be in contact with you in the near future."

Barbara looked at him and ran over and hugged him. She said this was the best news she could ever remember getting. The Captain and her were both crying tears of joy. The occasion had just brought too much joy for either of them to hold back.

Barbara went straight to a telephone and called Virginia. She told her the good news and soon they were both crying. Finally they were both able to talk and Virginia had more questions than Barbara could ever answer. Barbara told her exactly what the message had said and said as soon as any word from Carl came in she would let her know.

Kenneth Orr

Virginia said she was going to have a small glass of wine to celebrate and then lay down for a while, she was tired. Barbara asked to talk to the housekeeper. She told her what had just happened. She asked her to make sure that Virginia was not overdoing anything and made sure she had the Doctor's phone number if he was going to be needed. The latest news had somehow made everything better and was wonderful news in the middle of a bloody and horrible war.

CHAPTER 3 – 18
Back in England

The United States Army along with the British and other allied countries were continuing to build up their strength to mount an offensive on the ground in German occupied France. General Eisenhower was leading this effort. Winston Churchill was keeping the civilian population aware of every move and the efforts from everyone were heroic. British General Montgomery had been assigned to lead the war efforts in North Africa. His efforts were proving to be successful. Carl knew that Malone was in the thick of the efforts.

Admiral Nimitz and General McArthur were running the war against the Japanese in the Pacific. They had suffered severely, both on the sea and on island warfare. The Japanese soldiers were unwilling to surrender, even when it was obvious they had lost the battle.

In 1944 the United States had begun to supply larger B-24 bombers to both the European and Pacific war zones. The impact was starting to show. B-24 Liberator airplanes were able to fly longer missions and carry a heavier bomb load than either the B-17s or the Lancaster's. Their arrival on the scene did little to relieve either of the smaller bombers from wartime service. They just added more bomb carrying capacity.

Public domain from the US Government

The Russian Army had been holding the Germans away from capturing Moscow and in the spring of 1944 the Germans were running out of materials and men. The war in Italy was also swinging in the favor of the Allied forces and General Patton was moving north in Italy into the stronghold of German troops.

Carl had been put into a hospital in England and they had done repair surgery on his right leg. The injury was about eight inches below his hip and the bone had been broken, but not separated.

The Doctor in England saw that the healing process was started but the bone below the break was slightly twisted. This would cause Carl to walk with a limp and the injury had become infected. The field hospital repair was adequate to control the infection and allow Carl to walk but the twist was not fixed due to a limited hospital capability.

The only right way to repair his leg was to open the wound, re-break the bone and align it properly with a pin. Carl had no immediate prediction as to when the right repair could be made and he was glad to just be able to walk and not have excessive pain.

The first thing he wanted to do was call home. The Red Cross tried to get him a long distance line to Virginia's number and finally after three days and many tries the effort succeeded. Virginia answered the phone and was surprised to hear Carl talking to her from England.

The Cowboy's Kids

He told her his leg had been injured but the Doctors had operated on it and it should be fine in a few weeks. He said his status in the bomb group was yet to be determined and that his assigned commander had come to see him just a day before. He wanted to see how he was doing and cheer him up a little. He asked Virginia to let Barbara know what was happening. Phone calls to the states were very hard to get.

Virginia told him she was about a month away from having their baby and said she was doing fine. Carl said he had picked out a name if the baby was a boy. Virginia asked him what he had selected? Carl said, "Pierre." Virginia asked why this name and Carl said he would explain it in a letter and that his time allotted for the phone call, was up.

Carl would soon be able to walk around with a crutch. His leg was in a plaster cast and the size of the thing would not allow him to wear his normal uniform. Instead he was wearing either a hospital gown or a pair of farmer's bib overalls. Both would cover his body and allow him to move around. He had a nurse sew Major's insignias on the overall straps and his pilot's wings were pinned to the front of his bib.

The 8th Army Air Group was massing a large number of airplanes in England and the need to keep the bombsights working was an obvious problem. Carl's training and skill were needed more than ever. As soon as he was able to walk away from his bed, the Commander asked him if he would come and work in the bombsight repair station. Carl was not ready to quit and it was his duty, as he saw it, to help where he could.

On the 31st of October he put on his fancy overall uniform, went to the base phone station and called the Commander. He told him that he would come work in the repair station as soon as he could get somebody to drive him. The Commander was pleased.

Kenneth Orr

Then the Commander asked him what he wanted to do with his personal airplane? Carl was confused. He asked, "What airplane." The Commander said, "Your Spad, the people at the airstrip where you landed have put it in a spot inside a remote hanger and said it's yours, They don't want it." Carl chuckled and said, "Tell them to give it to some museum when the war is over, I don't have any way to take it to Texas."

The same day, Virginia gave birth to an eight-pound boy in her home at Bandera, Texas. Barbara had been alerted and she was with Virginia and all went well for both the mother and baby "Pierre."

CHAPTER 3 – 17
The Next Part of Life

Barbara tried to call Carl on the phone several times, but all the lines to international calls were always tied up. There was no way to contact Carl directly. Virginia had a friend in Washington who had special access to military transmissions and she asked Barbara to call her. Kate was a real asset. Barbara told her about the arrival of Pierre and Kate said she would send a coded message to the air base where Carl was stationed and let him know. The baby information was supplied to Kate and the message was on the way in rapid time.

Barbara was taking off a couple of days to be with Virginia and to help her get started into motherhood. The cool days of the Texas fall were pleasant and the time at the ranch was a double treat. A new baby and nice weather all were part of Barbara's most enjoyable events.

The Army had been notified that the hospital ship was finally being fitted out in San Francisco and would be routed through the Panama Canal to New Orleans. Upon arrival it would take on a crew and medical staff to be deployed to a war zone. Barbara's supervisor knew that Barbara had been very involved with the planned nurse staff and he asked her to look over the current plans. She also wanted to know if the people who were scheduled to go on the ship were still available.

Kenneth Orr

Barbara was glad to do this review and in a couple of days she reported that the staff was short three nurses and seven nurses assistants. The medical staff was also reviewed and the report was similar. They had lost a couple of people for various reasons.

Barbara's supervisor asked Barbara if she would pick out enough nurses to fill the ranks from the current hospital staff and select some qualified nurse's aids to fill the shortages. Barbara agreed. Barbara began to interview nurses and soon had more than enough volunteers to fill the opening and even had some extras. The same process was successful for nurse's aides.

Barbara gave the list to the supervisor and the base personnel office began to cut orders for the transfer of all involved personnel. The ship's operational staff was to be manned by civilians and the Army was conducting interviews to fill these positions.

The available labor pool was slim as most of the men were already in the Army and the applicants were predominantly women. The staff was almost complete when the ship finally docked in New Orleans.

Barbara's supervisor asked Barbara to go to New Orleans and oversee the first couple of days on the ship and make sure the duty responsibilities were understood and covered adequately. Barbara was not given any choice, but to go and do this task.

Barbara looked at the calendar and she saw that the build-up of troops, ships and aircraft in the European war was becoming focused toward some sort of a major planned operation. The Army wanted this ship and several others, to be deployed and available in the area just away from the French coast when this operation began. She kept this classified information to herself, as she knew that security around this information was very important.

The Cowboy's Kids

The assigned personnel and medical supplies arrived and the ship was quickly made ready to sail. There were enough beds to take care of about 300 soldiers, and the ship was well stocked to cover this level of battlefield support.

The plan was to deploy, be in the right area when needed, take on injured soldiers, and provide care to the best possible level and transport them back to some port in the United States for transfer to a shore based hospital. Then the ship would restock medical and operating supplies and return to the war zone to aid more injured soldiers.

The Army had already set up several battlefield based medical facilities but they had limited capabilities. They were also subject to an enemy attack should Hitler decide to attack medical facilities. His intentions were never clear and he recognized no limits when it came to inflicting pain and suffering on his enemies.

The ship was loaded and all of the non-designated to serve on board were requested to leave. Barbara walked down the gangplank and stopped at the bottom. She looked back and half heartily said to herself, she was sorry she was not going.

The ready-to-serve hospital ship sailed to the east and Barbara and others who were on similar assignments went back to San Antonio. They had done their assigned mission.

Over in England the special message to Carl had arrived and he was excited to learn he was a father. His current duty assignment was more than a full time job. The new B-24s were not exactly what they had been when he looked at the prototype airplane. The military designers had modified the gun ports and mounted the bombsights in a little different position. Carl adjusted his thinking to match what was presented to him and went forward. They were in a war and change was always a part of making progress.

Kenneth Orr

The newest models of the B-24 had several improvements over the B-17. The new wing design would fly slightly faster and lift more weight than the wing design used on the B-17. The B-24 was designed to sit on a nose wheel rather than a tail wheel. This allowed the airplane to take off on a shorter runway. It also made ground operations easier and made it easier for the pilot when he taxied the aircraft. The bomb bay doors were designed to slide up and down the side of the fuselage. This design eliminated the disturbance of air in the open position that was associated with a hinged door. The engines were more powerful. In total, the B-24 was a better bomber and it was quickly becoming the new standard for a modern bomber.

German bombs and aircraft guns continued to pound Great Britain daily. Every major city had evacuated most of the civilian population. The cities set up regiments of block wardens to monitor and assist the citizens with problems caused by the attacks. They would assist getting everyone into a bomb shelters and having sufficient food.

The British government built four "fake factories" in remote locations to divert the German bombers. The theory was that the Germans would use their time and weapons on these targets and avoid attacks on the real factories. They would also build fires at night to confuse the incoming planes and to cause additional dilution of the German's attack damages.

The Germans were busy developing new weapons and in 1944 "buzz bombs" started coming from German outposts in France. They were aimed toward London and other key British cities. Buzz bombs were small-unmanned aircraft with a big bomb and a simple jet engine that would run until the fuel was gone. The bomb would then crash into the ground below. Aiming them was crude but the magnitude of the effort was large enough to cause substantial damages.

In 1944 the Germans surprised the Allies with the world's first jet-engine-powered fighter aircraft. The ME-262 was faster than any other fighter in the air and had good

The Cowboy's Kids

firepower. The effectiveness of the new fighter was limited as it was introduced when Germany was in the losing stages of the war and the impact to the war was limited.

The United States was also busy developing new weapon systems and exploring new approaches to fight battles. There was a major concern among the Allied Army forces that the Germans might overtake Great Britain.

Every bomber in the Allied Forces inventory in 1944 lacked the capability to fly from the United States to Germany, drop bombs and return to the United States non-stop. This problem was both a political and military concern. Should Britain fall under German control, the political stability of every nation in the world would become unsettled.

This fear was more important than most people realized. The war in the Pacific was requiring that vast resources be supplied from The United States. Should he Allied Forces be required to fighting a European war from the United States resources that were already stretched to the limit would be even further stressed. Political leaders from every Allied Forces Country were very concerned.

The military and United States government initiated a program to design and build a long-range bomber that could operate from the United States and return after the bombs were dropped. The giant B-36 was the result of this effort.

The original design used six piston engines installed to push the airplane rather than pull it, like all other bombers. Two jet engine pods with two jet engines each were later installed under the wings to increase air speed and reliability. This airplane was never placed in a war zone environment.

Other new weapon designs were common. Steel had always been a critical war material and the supply was running low. Old cars, unused railroad rails, scrap tin cans and any other steel items were being melted down and made into bombs. There was approach helped but steel was still a critical and short in supply material. One new approach was a project to use reinforced concrete to make bomb casings.

Technology was being used to develop a completely new bomb design. A Professor in Chicago had been working to develop a bomb using a nuclear reaction as the source of energy.

A prototype weapon was developed and built. A prototype was tested on a remote New Mexico desert. The results were very impressive. The resulting effort led to a massive new effort in Oak Ridge, Tennessee to refine a special material from the element "uranium."

The development team was located in a remote mountain ringed location in northern New Mexico and the work was expedited. Los Alamos, New Mexico instantly became a high security facility and all access was by special passes and secret passwords.

Carl was working at several airbases in England servicing bombing systems and working to help new bomb crews understand how to use the equipment. He was on limited duty as his leg was still in a cast and was not healing as fast as he had hoped. He was aggravating the situation by being as active as he wanted to remain.

On March 18th, 1944, the British dropped 3,000 tons of bombs on Hamburg, Germany. The German Army was also being driven back in Italy and in a portion of France. General Eisenhower and his staff began planning an assault on the French coast. The Allied Army would land and begin to drive the German Army back toward the east. Carl was made aware of the master plan and directed to have every possible bomb crew's equipment ready to go at a moments notice.

The Cowboy's Kids

In mid-May a massive bombing effort was launched to soften up German forces along the French coast. Most known enemy locations were pounded daily and the only restraint became the weather and a few German fighter planes. The Americans now had the P-51 Mustangs and the Lockheed P-38 fighters. Both airplanes were superior in many ways to earlier fighter aircraft. These efforts continued until early June. Intelligence being gathered by French Resistance forces was extremely valuable in the planning the upcoming attack.

The major assault was planned to start around June 1st but has to be delayed by a severe north Atlantic storm. All of the men and equipment were ready and waiting but weather forced the attack to be put on hold. On June 5th General Eisenhower ordered the attack to begin the next morning.

On June 6th, the invasion of Normandy beach began. The allied forces were able to make a successful landing, but the toll in lost soldiers was staggering.

Army Hospital ships had been stationed in key positions waiting to help care for the injured and dying troops. The numbers and severity of injured soldiers quickly overburdened Army medics on the battlefields. In spite of heavy enemy fire, the medics continued to do as well as they could to save lives.

A few days after the initial landing, the Army was able to start transporting the injured out to the Hospital Ships. There, they were given the care they needed. Many troops were already injured so severely that they could not be given much meaningful help.

Back in San Antonio the hospital was full of injured and dieing soldiers. There are several funerals daily and the military cemetery located on the base receives record numbers of new burials. Barbara was working long days and often into the night just to try to keep up with the worst of the demands. She recognized that this pace was taking

Kenneth Orr

too much out of her health but also wants to help save the lives of as many soldiers as she could.

Virginia was living in the ranch house in Bandera and she and young Pierre were hoping that the war would soon be over. The whole nation was anxious to see the troops begin to come home. There were a lot of new friends living in the Bandera neighborhood and they visited with Virginia often. Life in Texas was stressful for everyone as the war effort has touched every community in the country is some way. Most of the young men were gone to war and the women were holding life together on the home front.

CHAPTER 3-19
Success and Pride

The Allied offensive in France was underway and slow, but steady, bloody progress was being made. The Allied air efforts were deeply involved with daily tactical battles and with supplying the troops on the ground with the materials support they needed. C-47 cargo planes were carrying paratroopers over drop zones and adding more manpower to the ground efforts. They were also towing glider aircraft to areas where they were cut loose and allowed to land on open fields. The fighters and bombers were attacking enemy troop convoys and imbedded enemy positions. The invasion and subsequent march toward Berlin was a combined effort of ground and air operations and it was working.

One of the unique approaches used to fool the Germans, was to drop small dummy dolls dressed like soldiers on small parachutes. The Germans would see the drop and rush to attack the parachute soldiers. The dolls would hit the ground and instantly explode hopefully taking out the German soldiers. This trick worked several times and became a huge embarrassment for the Germans.

The Germans were never to be counted out, even when it was becoming clear that they were not winning. In June of 1944, they began firing V-2 rockets toward England. Rockets capable of traveling this far were a whole new way to wage war. The launching sites were believed to be in France and an air effort was quickly undertaken to locate

Kenneth Orr

and destroy these new targets. The effort was working but some of the launchers were portable. This situation made the elimination of this threat almost impossible.

All was not well with the German citizens. In July, an assignation attempt was made on Hitler. The German people and many of the officers in the German military recognized that Hitler had led them down a path that was resulting in the complete destruction their major cities and wanted him out of power. Hitler continued to survive. He became even more dedicated to follow his current path and had many people who he believed were involved with the suicide plot killed.

In mid August the French Resistance movement staged an uprising and came out into the open. The French citizens were fighting alongside the Allied troops. By late August, Paris had been liberated and the Germans were finally on the run.

German troops were never considered cowards. They retreated toward the German border, and as they came closer to their homeland they fought harder than ever. The ground war was bloody for both sides and the air war continued, as the allied forces kept up the intensity of bombing major German targets. Carl was busier than ever keeping bombsights repaired and offering leadership to young fliers. The battle casualties continued to be high on both sides and the brutality on the battlefield was horrible.

In early February Churchill, Roosevelt and Stalin gathered in Yalta to discuss new ways to bring down the German Army and stop the war. They spent three days on political plans and exploring new military strategies. Agreements reached at this meeting were converted into military plans on the battlefield. It was clear to the three leaders that they were going to ultimately win the war but the end was still not in sight.

The Cowboy's Kids

On April 12, 1945, back in the United States, President Roosevelt died. He had been in ill health for several years but had never let it interfere with his resolve to win the war. Harry Truman, his Vice-President from Kansas City, Missouri took over. President Truman had been in close contact with the war, but he did not have a military background. He had been a haberdasher back in Kansas City and had been placed on the election ticket to assure that the mid-west votes in the election would go to Roosevelt.

The Allied Forces war in Europe was moving forward rapidly and the Germans were continuing to loose ground. The Allied Forces had entered Germany and actually were drawing close to Berlin. On April 18th, the German forces on the Ruhr River surrendered to the Allies and shortly afterwards the Russian Army entered Berlin. Hitler realized that he has lost the war and in an act of desperation on April 30th he killed himself.

Soon after his death was known the remaining German Army forces recognized there is nothing left to fight for and surrendered. On May 7th, the German High Command Generals surrender on unconditional terms. The Day after the United States celebrates V-E [Victory in Europe Day]. The war in Europe had finally come to and end.

A few days after the surrender the Allied forces held a meeting to divide the German territory and to divide the city of Berlin. The city of Berlin was within the section of German territory that was to be occupied by the Russians. Berlin was divided into similar occupying zones and almost immediately the Russians started to restrict all travel through their identified territory to reach Berlin. The seeds for another conflict were already taking root.

The war in the Pacific was still as active as ever, and the Japanese soldiers were determined to fight until the death. Japanese Pilots have begun attacking United States Navy

Kenneth Orr

vessels by crashing their airplanes into American ships. The airplanes were loaded with bombs and their attempts were often successful in causing major damages.

The island wars had taken hundreds of thousands of lives and the entire south Pacific and southwest Asian areas have taken a pounding from the military forces on both sides.

President Truman developed a belief that to invade Japan and take over their country would require many more American soldiers to die. The key military leaders in the area agreed with him. President Truman was at a crossroad that he never wanted to see. He had been waiting for the new bomb out in New Mexico to be tested, as he had not convinced himself that it was really going to work.

On July 16th the bomb was tested, and as the developers had predicted, the results were much more destructive than any weapon ever put into the battlefield. President Truman now had another option to use in fighting Japan.

On July 16th, Winston Churchill stepped down as the British Prime Minister and a new leader assumed the leadership of the British Government. The new Prime Minister was of the same attitudes as Churchill and the transition came without any real political changes.

President Truman personally directed that the new atomic bomb be used to destroy two Japanese cities. He and the Pacific war military leaders had calculated that the impact would make the war shorter and save thousands of additional soldier's lives. The first atomic bomb was dropped on Hiroshima, Japan on August 6th. The airplane delivering the bomb was a B-29 named the "Anola Gay". The airplane was named after the pilot's mother.

The results were devastating and the Japanese government and civilian population were in shock. On August 9th, a second atomic bomb was dropped on Nagasaki, Japan. This bomb was also delivered by a B-29. The airplane was named "Bocks Car." The pilot's last name was Bock.

The Cowboy's Kids

On August 14th, the Japanese political leaders came aboard the USS Missouri and with General Douglas McArthur representing the United States, signed an unconditional surrender. The war in the Pacific was over and peace was restored.

Back home V-J [Victory in Japan Day] was celebrated everywhere in all of the countries that had been involved in the war. It was over and the killing had stopped. The horrible situation left behind for everyone to live with was a major problem. Europe was in a state of ruin in most major cities and the population was torn as to what future they might have.

The United States was structured to operate in a state of war and the switch back to living and functioning like they had before the war would be slow and painful. The detained prisoners of war, from both Germany and Japan needed to be sent home and the old fears from internal spies were lessened.

The factories that were now set up to build tanks, airplanes and guns had to be restored to their original products. The most serious problem of all was, the mental stress that needed to be relieved. The American troops that had fought the war would be coming home and the women who had run the factories and farms were waiting with open arms. There were also thousands of soldiers who had been killed and their families were in mourning. These families had many problems to face as they looked to their future.

CHAPTER 3 – 20
Homecoming

Texas and the Goodwin family were starting to slow down its war related activities. The old ranch house in Bandera was all dressed up in anticipation of Carl's planned return. The homecoming was never set for any specific day as the actual return of every soldier depended on many things.

The B-17s in Europe, that had flown a great many missions, were full of patches and mechanical damage. Many were mechanically not capable of flying all the way back to the United States. Some were still airworthy. The normal aircrews on these airplanes were told to plan to return to American east coast airfields. Some of the others were repairable and they were serviced, as required, to make them airworthy. Still others were junk and they were turned over to the British to be used as they saw best. The same was true for the B-24s and several fighter plane squadrons.

Carl had been performing ground support functions on bombing equipment. He did this work until the end of the war. This equipment was still considered as "classified" and had to be collected from every airplane and shipped back to the repair and inventory center in the United States. Carl's last official job was to collect this equipment and package it for transportation to American air bases. The last shipment was being sent home on a DC-8 freight plane and Carl was told he could come home on that airplane. He arrived back at Langley Field on September 29th, 1945.

The Cowboy's Kids

When he got off the airplane, he signed off his cargo slip for the classified materials and went straight to a telephone. He called Virginia. He had not talked directly with her since he had gone to Europe. Letters had been their only means of keeping in touch. The sound of her voice made him shudder with joy.

He told her he was at Langley airfield and would see when he would be released to come home. He knew that almost everyone who had been in a combat operation would be coming home soon and their Army career would potentially be over. Virginia was happy. She told him about Pierre's baby habits and Carl was anxious to see him. He had to hang up as the line to call home was full of soldiers waiting their turns and Carl understood the impact of these moments.

Virginia called Barbara and let her know that Carl was back on American soil. She was glad and happy for Virginia. The Army hospital was full of injured soldiers and the funeral processions were still a common, seemingly unending, daily pattern.

Barbara had made friends with a Doctor who had been injured in France and he was lonely for a lady to accompany him in his idle hours. Barbara and he had somehow bonded as close friends. They were good for each other. His name was Joe Winslow. Joe had been married and had two grown children. His wife had died in 1937 in an automobile accident. His children were both married and studying in Los Angeles to become Doctors. He and Barbara had a lot in common.

The Army was moving soldiers back to their home as soon as they could discharge them and provide transportation. Carl found out about a DC-3 cargo flight going to Kelly Field in San Antonio. He went to see if he could get a "hop" as a passenger. Luck was with him. They needed a co-pilot and Carl got the job. The radioman, Arnold Ortega, on the flight had served in North Africa and was on his way home. He lived in Santa Fe, New Mexico.

Kenneth Orr

Carl asked him if he had known Major Malone?" He said he had known him well. Then he looked at Carl and said, "Major Malone was killed about nine months ago on a bomb raid. He was leading a bomb raid and his plane was shot down. Everyone was killed." Carl just sat back in shock. He knew "Malone" was doing what he believed in but he also knew he was going to miss him.

The DC-3 landed in Tennessee and refueled and then flew on to San Antonio. When the airplane landed at Kelly field and Carl was back in Texas. The easiest way to get anywhere from the base was to take an olive drab military shuttle bus to town and then get on a "Greyhound Bus" going to where you wanted to go. Carl went to the bus station and saw that a bus to Bandera was leaving in five minutes. He wanted to call both Virginia and Barbara but there was not enough time. He went to the ticket counter and got one of the last seats that were available. His duffle bag was put in the luggage compartment and Carl got on. He was limping as he had been doing, since his leg operation, but his step was quick and determined. He was going home.

The bus went north to get out of town and made a stop in Boerne, Texas. A lot of people got off. Nobody got on. It was late in the afternoon when the bus arrived in Bandera. The ole town really looked good to him.

Carl got off, got his duffle bag and found a taxi that would take him to the ranch. He knew the driver very well. His dad had been a cowboy for a nearby ranch and his son was too young to go into the Army.

He was too young to fight in a war and had stayed in Bandera and helped with keeping the local economy going. The cab was an old 1934 Ford that had been patched together over the war years just to keep it running.

The taxi pulled into the driveway and Virginia saw it. It was almost too dark to see more than the headlights, but she knew it had to be Carl. She ran out the door and as the taxi came to a stop, she saw it was Carl riding in the back.

The Cowboy's Kids

She grabbed the door handle and opened it as quick as she could. Carl hopped out and put his arms around her. The cab driver got out and closed the door. He got Carl's duffle bag out and put it on the porch. Carl was so busy holding Virginia that he never saw the taxi driver pull away. He had not paid him....

They went into the house and Carl wanted to see baby Pierre. He was sleeping in a small bed and had a white blanket over his body. Carl picked him up and wanted to hold him next to him. Pierre woke up and soon was making baby noises for his dad. Carl was home.

About 30 minutes after Carl got home he was setting in his favorite chair, enjoying a glass of "Kentucky's Finest Whiskey" and the telephone rang. Virginia answered it and it was Barbara. She told her that Carl had just come home and Barbara wanted to say hello to him. They talked for about 15 minutes and Barbara said she would come see him tomorrow. She had the day off and her supervisor had told her to take some time off, she was worn out from working so many hours. Carl was looking forward to seeing her and told her he loved her.

Carl was limping and Virginia saw his limping problem. She asked him, "What was his problem?" He told he had been injured in his leg but the doctors had saved his leg by doing a field hospital bone reconstruction. This had made him limp but he was not unhappy. He said a lot of men had suffered a lot more serious injuries. Virginia understood. Carl did not want to talk about it and the conversation was quickly changed.

About 10:00 PM they went to bed and the night passed quickly. Carl put baby Pierre in between them and they went to sleep as a family.

Barbara came the next day. She arrived early and said she would be glad to watch Pierre if Carl and Virginia wanted to go somewhere. She also noticed Carl's limp and asked him to let her see the wounded area. Carl was not anxious

Kenneth Orr

to show off a wound but he allowed her to see what was there. Barbara took one look and said, "Carl, Your leg is still infected and you need to see a doctor right now. That could turn into something more serious if you do not get some help." Carl looked at her and said, "It has been sore for several days but I have been too busy to worry with it, I was coming home."

Barbara said she would take him back to San Antonio with her and have a Doctor look at it that evening. He reluctantly agreed. Barbara asked Virginia if she wanted to go stay in quarters on the Army Base that evening and told her baby Pierre would be most welcome. Virginia agreed. They all got in Barbara's Ford and Barbara drove straight to the admitting entrance of the hospital. She knew everyone and they all knew her. Carl was rushed into see a doctor immediately.

The diagnosis was that there was a lot of infection and the doctor thought the bone repair was causing the problem. He told Carl that he needed to have an operation to go inside his leg and find the problem and then have it fixed right. He said, "Battlefield hospitals do a magnificent job, but sometimes they are just not good enough to fix the problem the right way. We can still fix this one if we do it now and someday soon you may be walking just like you did before you got hurt."

Carl agreed to have surgery the next morning and was admitted to the hospital. Virginia and Barbara went to the visiting officers quarters and got a place to stay for a few days. The next morning Carl had the operation and then went to the recovery ward. The surgeon saw Barbara and Virginia waiting for some report and he said the bone repair had become infected. He said he had rebuilt everything at the original break and the results looked good. Carl would be on crutches for a few weeks but then should fully recover and walk without a noticeable limp.

Time proved the Doctor's words to be true and soon everybody was back on the ranch celebrating Christmas.

The Cowboy's Kids

In the next spring Carl and Virginia selected a spot near the banks of the Medina River and had a new home built. Barbara and her Doctor friend had become more than friends and decided to get married.

The ceremony was simple and they were both much happier, as they had somebody with which to share life. They all lived on the ranch and found new avenues to fill their life's direction.

Barbara left the Army for good in 1946 and became a fulltime housewife. Her new husband set up a local medical practice and worked out of Bandera and Kerrville. Virginia had a second baby and then she became a fulltime housewife.

Carl never knew what to call his new job. He was skilled in flying and servicing airplanes and he started a small aircraft maintenance service on a small airstrip he built near his home.

Carl would frequently go to San Antonio and do similar jobs for pilots who had small airplanes at local, non-military airfields. He used this occupation to keep in touch with his old buddies from the Army. He never worked for any company, but he always had more to do than he could get done. He enjoyed his lifestyle. He was enjoying life and having his own family. He and Virginia were both happy and they had everything they wanted.

The division of Germany had caused major political problems. The Russians refused to allow open travel between Berlin and the American sector, which was east of their occupied territory. The result was isolation for the people living in the American sector of Berlin. The airport in Berlin was located in the American sector and it became obvious that all supplies to keep the city going in the American occupied sector would need to come in by air. The Army Air Corp dedicated a fleet of DC-6 freight planes to make hundreds of flights weekly to keep Berlin supplied, and to demonstrate to the Russian government that America would not accept this situation.

Kenneth Orr

The engines for the DC-6 airplanes were seeing extended service and had to be rebuilt much more often. The overhaul work was done at Kelly Air Base in San Antonio. Carl would go over to the base when he was in San Antonio and keep in touch with a lot of his old friends. The comradeship between fliers seemed to never end, and Carl was one of the most outspoken spokesmen supporting the Air Corps peacetime missions.

In 1947, the United States Government recognized many of the problems that had been discovered during the Second World War. President Truman dissolved the War Department as a cabinet position and replaced it with a much broader department called The Department of Defense. The President retained his position as the Commander in Chief of all military forces and had a new office building built in Washington called the Pentagon. He recognized the Air Force as a separate branch of the military and removed them from the traditional Army command. Each major military branch, The Army, The Navy, The Marines, The Air Force and The Coast Guard were each assigned a portion of the Pentagon and a Joint Chief of Staff for all of the Military branches was created.

Life in The United States was also adjusting to the calm that had become present after the war. Many of the technical discoveries that had helped to win the war were put into commercial products and into making the life of the average American more comfortable. The advent of commercial television, diesel powered trucks and trains and a small, but working commercial airline industry, were all part of the fallout from the war. In Texas life was good and the rest of the nation went to work to make the United States the leader of a free world.

Carl, Virginia and Barbara would go to visit the family gravesite every Christmas and put fresh fall flowers on all of the family members graves. Christmas was always more involved at the Goodwin gatherings as the two birthdays of Barbara and Carl were also celebrated the day before. In the spring, the whole Goodwin family began an annual event

The Cowboy's Kids

of going to California and spending a week on the beach. The del Coronado Hotel was their favorite destination. Carl loved to fly and he always made sure that they flew on Trans World Airlines, TWA, for both ends of this trip. He claimed, "They had the best airplanes and the service was always great."

The Goodwin's was proud of their roots and their ability to tell everyone, "We are all proud to be Texans and Americans. We believe in saying. "God Bless America," every time we have the opportunity. We have done or part in keeping America free and we would do it again if it is ever necessary."

Public domain from the US Government

ABOUT THE AUTHOR

The Cowboy's Kid's is my second book. The story is a follow-up to my original book "Chalk". This whole effort started about three years ago when I was told I had to have surgery. The thoughts of just sitting for a long time and doing nothing were more of a threat to me than the actual operation. The cure was to write "Chalk".

Chalk was a collection of family experiences and stories from friends and key people in my younger life and I wrapped it into a fictional story that ended up in Texas. The hero from this first book and his wife had two children. I purposely left out a lot of the original story as it concerned the "Kids" as the first book would have been too long. I saw a lot of ways to write a second story, mostly structured on the history of the early 1900's and forward, which would relate a lot of information I personally had gathered in my youth.

My family was originally from Alabama. Dad and Mom moved to Dayton, Ohio in 1932 and I came along in 1936. Most of my youth was spent living near Wright Patterson Air Field on in government homes that had been built on the old McCook flying Field. During the Second World War my Dad worked two jobs. His day job was at the Frigidaire plant, which was building machine guns. His second job was at a plant that was building oil coolers for B-17s. My mom worked at a company that was making precision glass lens. We did not know it at the time but they were going into classified bombsights that were also being built in Dayton.

Our neighborhood was full of hard working people who were all involved with support of the war effort. My Boy Scout Leader, a fine man named Francis Trick, came home after the war and helped me a lot as my Dad died when I was early the ninth grade. Francis had been a B-24 Pilot and there were several old B-24 airplanes at the Dayton airport. He had to fly every month until he was discharged and he would sometimes sneak me on for a local flight.

My first Cousin, Randy Willingham, was a P-47 fighter pilot and was an Army Ace. He came to Dayton several times and his vivid war stories never were forgotten.

Late in the war steel was a precious resource and the Army was using every possible source to find more. My Dad came up with an idea to make bombs out of concrete and he took his idea to some key people at the airbase. His involvement lasted for a few weeks but I know his concepts and suggestions were a major part of the program that followed.

In the late 1940's the Army was re-organized to make the Air Force a separate branch of our military. We all thought their new blue uniforms looked a lot like Greyhound Bus Drivers outfits. In 1954 I graduated from High School and almost immediately got a draft notice. I went to see an Air Force Recruiter and signed up. This brought me to Texas for the first time. I knew right then, that someday Texas was going to be my home. I fell in love with the life style, the people and the pioneering spirit from the past that was still alive. After the military I attended The Ohio State University and after school, I went to work making Automobiles. Jobs came and went as companies moved work out of the country. In the 1970's I went to work for McDonald Douglas and worked on airplane modification projects. Airplanes were always special to me.

In 1981 I was lucky and got a great job with Lockheed Missiles and Space Company. I had reached my ultimate goal in employment and the next 14 years were spent on all kinds of projects. I even got to work on the solid-state boosters for the shuttle program. Throughout my life I have seen the world of aviation grow and somehow the thrill has never diminished. I have also met some wonderful people who have served our country as both military and supplier contributors.

I am now in my 70's and my wife, Jewell, tells me I am retired. Not so fast.... My mind is still alive and active. Writing has become a great outlet for my energies and a path to record some of the things that I feel are worth remembering.

Everyone needs to know about what has happened in the past to really appreciate the present. The next time you climb on a commercial airplane and go somewhere please remember this. Pioneering people who were probably supporting some Government program, or trying to build an airplane to go fight a war developed the airplane. Their efforts did most of the development work for your modern day air transportation.

I hope you enjoy reading my book and that you leave it with a better appreciation of what has happened in our Nation's continuing effort to keep the peace and still keep our homes and families safe.

Oh yes, I met my wife in the parking lot at the Officer's Club at Wright Patterson Air Force Base in 1971. She was a "keeper." She is still cooking my dinner and keeping me honest after raising two daughters and putting up with a crazy life style that we enjoyed for all of those following years.

LaVergne, TN USA
31 August 2010
195358LV00003B/1/P